TWICE UPON A TIME

ANJALI BHATIA

FINGERPRINT!

Published by
FiNGERPRINT!
An imprint of Prakash Books India Pvt. Ltd.

113/A, Darya Ganj, New Delhi-110 002,
Tel: (011) 2324 7062 – 65, Fax: (011) 2324 6975
Email: info@prakashbooks.com/sales@prakashbooks.com

facebook www.facebook.com/fingerprintpublishing
twitter www.twitter.com/FingerprintP, www.fingerprintpublishing.com
For manuscript submissions, e-mail: fingerprintsubmissions@gmail.com

ISBN: 978 81 7234 509 9

Processed & printed in India

To

My Nani, who would have been so proud
And to my parents, who showed me where to look for truth . . .

PROLOGUE

In the stillness of the afternoon, you can hear their voices coming from the clearing by the river—a soft indistinct murmur, in the lilting tones that are peculiar to the language of the hills. If you step closer to the edge of the clearing, close enough for you to observe them better, but not for them to catch sight of you, you will see that they are young and pretty, the two of them. Their hair is thick and long and wavy, falling in loose braids from under the bright red scarves they have wrapped around their heads. Their woollen tunics are an appealing, endearing flash of colour in a landscape that is predominantly blue and green and grey. Their faces, hidden in the shadows of the conifer they are sitting under, are a weather-beaten fair with just the faintest touch of pink on their cheeks . . . and their eyes are big and dark and deep. Like pools filled with secret dreams and desires, you think. But they are sitting with their back towards you and you can only imagine all of this.

They are talking disconsolately and wistfully about the river . . . it is really just a torpid stream now, murky with clay and refuse, its current sluggish and weak. They are talking of a time, much before they were born, when this river was gay and alive and breathed magic spells of prosperity and fertility into the ears of the believers. It used to have a song then, an alluring song which called out to women even half a mile away, to come and dip their buckets into it and carry home its sweet water. But the song is gone now and the river is silent . . . dying.

They wonder why the rain has been so headstrong and angry this year. It refuses to come for days together, and then when it does come, it descends upon them with a pent-up fury which sweeps away swathes of land and splits tree trunks into half. Even now, some of the men in the village are busy repairing the roofs of their houses—the shingles had come undone during the storm last night.

There is enough rain, but it's an angry, vengeful rain that will not revive the river. They don't know why the Gods are angry with them, or why the natural springs which once danced around the hillside are disappearing . . . but they know that it all started on that accursed day twenty-six years ago, before they had even been born. A day when the elders of Gumgyaat village took a decision which ran through their lives like poison poured down a hillside.

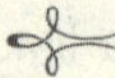

The bed grows hard under him like a huge slab of rock. He turns on his side, the roughness of the rock cutting right through his clothes and grazing his skin. He tries to cry out in pain, but water rushes into his mouth before any sound can escape his lips.

And then he starts sinking. Fast.

The rumble of water rushing into him and pulling him down fills his ears and drowns out all other sensations except for the cold. He feels long, icy fingers begin to curl around his lungs in a vice-like grip, drawing the breath out of him.

Suddenly his feet touch sand . . . or is it quicksand? Will he get sucked to his death? Has he reached the bottom already?

Drowned already?! He panics now; he doesn't want to die, not yet, not like this. He starts flailing around desperately. Isn't there anything he can hold on to? He is sinking at an alarming rate. Down, down, down . . . down to where the sand is treacherously and seductively soft. And warm. If only he could lie there for a moment or two. He could gather his strength and try swimming back to the surface.

Something tickles his nostrils. Weeds. They smell of rotting vegetables, stagnant water, and vomit. The smell makes him dizzy and nauseated, but before he can throw up, something, or someone turns him over on his stomach and pushes his face into the sand. The sand enters through his parted lips and fills his mouth. There's sand in his ears. In his eyes. In his nose. He opens his mouth to scream, but finds himself flipped over again.

The water is not pressing down on him anymore. It feels warm, strangely comfortable. Everything is quiet now, like sound has been cut off in entirety. It's a hollow, eerie silence. He feels himself rising up now, floating towards the surface, and then, just as suddenly as he had felt the water rush in and drag him down, he tastes the dry dust of land.

He opens his eyes. He's been set down in a dusty street that looks familiar. He's spent innumerable summer afternoons here as a child. He gets up and starts walking. He doesn't have any shoes on and the scorching sun has heated up the tarmac, but he continues to walk on, ignoring the hot flashes of pain emanating from his feet. He knows they'll be tender and sore later, but he does not care.

He knows exactly where he is. He can almost sense when the lanes will start closing in on him. He starts running now, faster and faster. And just as the weather-beaten buildings of the ghost town start leaning over, seemingly intent on trapping him there forever, he escapes from their dark, dangerous shadows and bursts out into wheat fields. Wheat fields?!

He slows down now. The wheat stalks, golden and heavy, bend protestingly under his fingers as he caresses them. A light breeze ruffles his hair and cools the sweat on his face. A little ahead in the distance, he sees a mimosa tree. There's a swing hanging from its thick branches, still swaying, as if someone had just gotten off it.

He hurries forward. The fields now give way to the courtyard of a big, unpretentious-looking house. He's been here before as well. He knows that for sure. There's a huge mango tree in the courtyard and he remembers scampering up its trunk as a child. There used to be a dog here, old and lazy, always sleeping under the tree, not bothered with the comings and goings of the household as long as he got his meals on time. He remembers how he would try to annoy the dog by poking it with a stick while it slept in the hot summer afternoons.

The house appears deserted now. It is so quiet that he can hear the bees buzzing over the *bhor* of the mango tree. Where are all the people? He approaches the house cautiously. He knows he has to reach it before . . . before what?!

As he walks in through the gate, he sees a hand pump to his left. He turns and walks towards it. It is hot and all the running has made him thirsty. But as he puts all his weight on the handle and thrusts it downward, a dry malicious gurgle tells him that there is no water. He tries again, pushing with all his might, but not even a drop trickles out.

When he turns back, there is an old man standing at the door of the house, leaning heavily against a walking stick, and dressed all in white, with a long white beard flowing down from his chin. He walks closer towards the house; the old man says nothing, but his stance is unwelcoming. As he climbs the steps to the house, the old man turns his face away and stands with his back towards him. He knows that he should beg for forgiveness from this shrivelled old man, but he doesn't know what he should beg forgiveness for. He throws himself at the old man's feet.

"Go away, Baldev! Just go away!" the old man speaks slowly, hurt and dejection underlining his words.

"No, no! Please, you have to let me in. You have to give me a chance!" he begs now, a terrible sense of foreboding gripping him. But the old man stays silent. "Look at me! Look at me once at least! Please!" he screams now, scared and desperate. He gets up and grips the old man's shoulders in an attempt to turn him around. But in the next instant, the old man whirls around and without saying a word, pushes him away. He falls down the stairs and lands in the dry, dusty courtyard of his childhood. He's cut his lips and he can taste blood. He looks up at the old man in horror, in recognition, in anguish. But before he can say anything at all, something heavy and unforgiving hits his head. He feels his skull crack open.

The last thing he sees before the cold darkness descends is the face of the old man—deeply wrinkled and cracked like dry earth, disintegrating into dust and eroding away . . .

CHAPTER 1

Nobody noticed him at first. With his unkempt hair, his crumpled clothes, and the premature wrinkles that had begun to appear at the corners of his mouth, he looked totally out of place in the middle of the manicured and perfumed set there.

He watched them from a distance, half-hidden behind the tall French doors of the exhibition hall, hands thrust in his pockets, shoulders slightly hunched, and his face haggard. He stared at the people in front of him—chattering and twittering on and on in circles of meaningless, mindless words, with accents acquired through expensive private tutorials in the plush secrecy of their homes. The women sashayed through the room, resplendent, glittering, and glowing, and the men sauntered around, trying to look powerful, like animals on the prowl. For all he noticed, though, they could all have broken into some primal jungle dance with the men yodelling and beating their puffed-out chests and the women fluttering delicately and throwing open their plumage.

Someone tapped him on his arm, breaking his reverie, and a deliberately-husky female voice exclaimed, "Arpit Singh! What are *you* doing here?!"

He turned around and flashed a practiced smile at the woman in front of him. She was dressed in a burgundy silk something.

For the life of him, he could not recall who she was. "I do have occasional aesthetic urges, you know. Had you written me off as a butter chicken-Patiala peg businessman?"

"No, no! As if I *could* have . . ." The fake huskiness disappeared in a high-pitched laugh.

Now Arpit remembered. Soundarya Sidhwani: socialite with intellectual pretensions, patron saint of a hundred-odd charities, and passionate lover of gossip.

"I haven't seen you around in ages! Hadn't you left for New York again? You can't stay away from that place for very long, can you? Not that I blame you . . ." Her voice had the edge of envy.

"I haven't been to New York in months, and I have no intention of going there anytime soon," he replied.

Oblivious to the bitterness in his voice, Soundarya lightly took his arm and said, "Come, I will show you the exhibit I like best." Without letting him say anything, she led him towards a little alcove right at the end of the hall and pointed towards a small, unframed charcoal sketch of a man and a woman falling off an enormous wheel whose spokes were entwined with serpents. Grey flames awaited the unlucky pair at the bottom. "Such pathos," she sighed, "such uncompromising tragedy. To tell you the truth" —she lowered her voice, not that there was anyone around— "I don't think this is Sandeep's work at all. He always harps about fine balance and poignancy, but this work? It has the absolution of doom. The inevitable fate of . . ." And she launched into a long monologue, critically analysing the sketch.

She had probably memorised it from some review magazine, Arpit thought as he stared at the sketch, unimpressed. It was amateurish, really. But as he stared longer at it, something in the scene struck him a blow. Abruptly, he turned to Soundarya and said, "I must leave."

"What? Aren't you staying for the book launch at three o'clock?"

"No. I must go."

She looked disappointed. Arpit had been the only person so far who had let her ramble freely like this for the last five minutes. She had no intention of letting him go so easily. "Wait! You've heard of Dr Hari Mishra?"

"Not really."

"Oh!" Her moue of disappointment was perfect. "I thought you would have, considering you are better schooled than most people here. You won't believe how illiterate some of them are!"

"He's launching his book at three? What is it about anyway?" he asked tersely, irritated with her persistence.

"Oh no, not him! Vindhya Desai has written it. He is one of her special guests. Apparently, he supervised her doctoral thesis. I can't help wondering why she writes such kitschy chick-lit when she is so educated. And why on earth did she drop her academic career in theoretical physics to pursue fiction that doesn't even sell?! Anyway, he is here and I am dying to meet him. He has specialised in astrophysics, or umm, quantum physics, or nuclear . . . well, anyway, he is the best in his field. I thought you might be interested in his theory of time travel. I definitely am. I hope he will share the secret of going back to one's youth and preserving it forever!" She giggled. "You should stay. You might end up offering time travel packages to your guests!"

Soundarya's shrill, silly laughter bounced off him, but her words resounded inside his head. The haunted look in his eyes assumed the steadiness of expectancy for a moment. It didn't seem possible, but maybe it was finally happening. He had been wandering around the city in vain, looking for ways to relieve his morbidity and get back what he had lost. He felt scared to trust his luck now. But perhaps his hopes were really being answered at last. Perhaps, Dr Hari Mishra was going to save him.

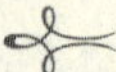

The function started late—the chief guest, a minister in the Delhi state government, typically arrived fifteen minutes behind schedule. After the lamp-lighting and the mandatory round of speeches, the author invited "my most esteemed and enlightened guide, Dr Hari Mishra" to the stage. But he, having already shunned the dais to sit in the front row, signalled his refusal.

Soundarya nudged Arpit in malicious delight. "I love him already. What a snub! I bet he regrets coming here! It's such a pathetic title! And her style is so flippant! And look at her sari . . . ugh man, she is such a wannabe!"

But Arpit was deaf to everything. Would Dr Mishra not speak at all? Would he even get a chance to talk to him?

Fortunately, Dr Mishra seemed to be in no hurry to leave after the book launch. While the author busied herself in pandering to the wishes of her buzzing crowd of fans, he serenely sipped his coffee and allowed his small set of admirers to besiege him with questions.

Arpit hung around the fringes of the little group. He had finally escaped Soundarya who had slipped away to pay her compliments to "dear stupid Vindhya." He noticed how the distinguished Dr Mishra stared with finely-disguised contempt at those whose questions he considered stupid. He had just managed to muster enough courage to approach the scientist when someone asked his question for him, "Sir, can a time machine really exist?"

The professor took a delicate bite of his marinated tofu before answering, "Theoretically, yes. Einstein's Theory of General Relativity predicts the existence of wormholes in space-time, only hypothetical so far, but maybe sometime in the future it won't be just a hypothesis . . ."

"So when will it be possible to actually travel in time?" someone questioned him.

The physicist narrowed his eyes and quipped, "If I could travel to the future, I would find out when and tell you." There was polite laughter.

Then a voice, taut with desperation, cut through this gentle atmosphere of inquiry and asked, "How much money would you need to fund your research?"

People turned around to see who had asked the question. When they saw Arpit, with his crumpled clothes and longish hair, they glared at him. Who was this scruffy-looking young man who looked like he had been adding something to his coffee?

Arpit stared defiantly at the scientist until he shot back coldly, "Probably more than what many governments are already willing to pay."

"Dr Mishra, I do understand that you would have more than many generous sponsors backing up your research. But not many people would be willing to offer themselves as human guinea pigs for your experiments, would they? What if *I* offer to be a subject for your research, even at the risk of my life? Could you take me back a few years then?"

"Young man, I appreciate your enthusiasm, but I'm afraid I don't have the fantasy-fulfilling apparatus that you are looking for. Perhaps you should search for a spirit healer or a mystic?" The sarcasm in the scientist's last words was unmistakable.

Arpit shuffled away, disappointed. All eyes turned back to the professor, except one pair which continued to follow the dejected young man as he walked down the corridor.

He straggled outside, fumbling in his pockets for his car keys. It took him a while to find them. Once inside, he hastily snatched out a cigarette from the glove compartment—it had been lying there, torn and twisted, a singular reminder from a pack finished long ago. Lighting it up, he took deep, long drags and stared hollowly at the building in front of him. He should have never gone in. He had hoped for too much and too soon.

He felt a hot sour wave rise up from the pit of his stomach and burn its way to his throat. Quickly getting out of the car, he ran back to exhibition hall and threw up in its elegantly styled black-and-chrome washroom, inviting disgusted glares from the others there.

Soundarya caught him the moment he came out. "Left me in the lurch! And I thought you were the one gentleman here!"

Wiping his mouth with his sleeve, he ignored her thinly-disguised demand for an apology.

"It takes wit to understand sarcasm, I always say," Soundarya continued, ignoring Arpit's silence, "and Vindhya Desai has neither wit nor talent. No wonder she couldn't understand that I was laughing at her the whole time. I bet she thought I was one of her biggest admirers! Some people are just so delusional! Anyway, so did Dr Mishra reveal the secret of eternal youth to you?" She giggled.

Not wanting to have anything to do with her anymore, Arpit replied tersely, "I've stayed much longer than I thought. Catch you later." Escape, however, wasn't going to be so easy as Soundarya put an insistent hand on his arm.

"Arpit, how long are you in Delhi?"

"I don't know, probably till tomorrow . . ." he muttered, trying to free himself as gently as possible.

"What happened to your new hotel? Still firm on building it in Patiala? Don't you think Manali would be a better bet?"

"We had trouble getting environmental clearances . . ."

"Oh, come now! Surely *you* know how to get around these stupid governmental regulations?" she winked conspiratorially and continued, "Then again, I am just an ignorant woman helplessly fascinated with this whole business. But you can bet I will be one of your first guests when your hotel is up and running! Arpit," Soundarya abruptly adopted an uncharacteristically concerned tone, "you look so lonely. A charming young man like you should be taking better care of himself. Why don't you have dinner with me . . . ummm, with us tonight? A little conversation will perk you up."

"Mrs Sidhwani . . ."

"Soundarya. You must call me Soundarya like all my close friends do."

"Erm . . . yes, but I am extremely tired today, and tomorrow I have a fully packed day. Perhaps you and your husband can visit me in Chandigarh sometime?"

Soundarya's 'hmm' had the hiss of resentment. But the next moment she brightened up again. "Your business should be over by tomorrow night, surely? Then you can come over and join us at our very select get-together . . . none of your loud-mouthed politicians or celebrities, just nice, cultured people like us—painters, playwrights, academicians, activists—the kind of people who are searching for the essence of ecstasy. A couple of hours with them will lift you from your melancholy and put you right into higher realms."

He didn't know whether she was being comforting or covertly seductive. A party at the Sidhwanis', he had heard, was definitely prone to 'lift' one into the rainbow clouds of psychedelic drugs if one stayed long enough into the night. He had had enough of that already. But the prospect of spending an evening with people who would be even more bent on self-destruction than he had ever been held a morbid fascination. He agreed to come.

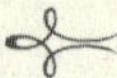

When Arpit opened the door of his hotel room a little while later, the lingering traces of a once-familiar, sickly sweet smell greeted his nostrils. He froze in the doorway. The room was shrouded in darkness, but he knew she was there. It had to be her.

"SURPRISE!"

She jumped on him the minute he stepped in and switched on the lights. It wasn't completely unexpected. Andreja, his Russian girlfriend, was unpredictable, if nothing else. It was probably one of the things that had attracted him to her initially. But was 'attracted' the right word for the reckless self-abhorrence which had made him deliberately and heedlessly fall into a relationship with someone as diametrically opposite as Andreja? Was 'attracted' the right word to explain the quicksand of suffering and despair that he fell into time and again? Probably not . . .

Tall and lanky, Andreja could have been straight out of a high-end fashion magazine, if only she cared. Her fiery red hair hung perpetually in limp disarray around her face, and her face itself was full of freckles. Her eyes, an attractive, alluring green otherwise, were always blank and vacant. She was the only child of one of the new Russian capitalists and had nothing to do except tramp across the world getting bored. She had been on her own from a very young age. He did not know when and where she had picked it up, but her pipe—filled with mysterious substances which she had been only too willing to share with him—was her closest confidante and sole companion now.

It had been easy to let such a creature attach herself to him.

She stayed, conveniently so, on the fringes of his life, forbidden to access that black hole—no, *wormhole*, like that scientist had said—at whose edges he stood, waiting to be shredded apart.

She threw her arms around him now, the fruity smell of her perfume clashing with the sickly sweet odour of her pipe. He pushed her away from his face and asked, "When on earth did you arrive? And how did you get in?"

"Around twenty-four years ago," she giggled, "but I don't think that's what you meant by 'on earth.' Delhi, I reached around noon. As for getting in, it's nothing a little smile and a few Euros cannot do. Anyway, since then, I have been soaking in all the crafts and colours at Dilli Haat. So exotic, all these lovely handicrafts and . . . you know, the local . . . oh, everything. I think I really encouraged Indian culture today. Just look at all my shopping bags!"

She reminded him of Soundarya right then. He smiled wryly, wondering how they would get along if they ever met. Wait, why not? Since Andreja was here, he might as well take her to the Sidhwanis' party. Soundarya would probably resent it—she would not take kindly to his asking if he could bring his girlfriend along, but he didn't want to let go of the invitation either. At least the prospect of the party was better than staying at the hotel or getting dragged out for a ridiculously expensive dinner somewhere. No, he better pass Andreja off as a friend. For the moment though, she was too busy recounting the retail conquests of the day to bother with anything else, so he allowed his thoughts to wander until she was just a sound in the background.

It was the smell of the crack pipe being lit up that snapped his thoughts back to the present. "Don't!" Arpit crinkled up his nose in disgust. "If you light up that thing here, the smoke alarm will go off."

"Fine, I'll step outside then," she snarled. Something about broken cowrie shells and her new *bandhani dupatta* had set her off.

Arpit, however, was thankful for this small respite from her. The present state of affairs with Andreja was strenuous. There was no love lost between them anymore and they both knew it. He couldn't understand why they still hung on to each other. She probably stayed because he didn't ask her any questions about the kind of life she led. And he, he stayed because he had no one else.

Long hours later, just as he was turning in for the day, Andreja asked him about his day. He mumbled a monosyllabic answer, devoid of any details. His disappointment was too raw for the cloying balm of her sympathy.

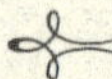

"Whad sdupid work do ya have doday?" Andreja croaked, stretching her bare, shapely legs out of the blanket.

"Wake up enough to speak coherently first. And I have a meeting," Arpit reprimanded her mildly. He had woken up a little irritated. The smell of Andreja's crack pipe had permeated his sleep and he had spent a restless night dreaming psychedelic dreams.

"You have a *meeting*? Aren't you going to take me around Delhi?" Andreja demanded.

"I came here on business, Andreja. You are the one who's dropped in out of nowhere, and *minus* a plan."

"Planning! Ugh! Nothing I like worse! Let's ditch your crappy meeting and go to Neemrana. I wanna stay at the fort."

"Not possible. By the time I am done with my 'crappy' meetings, it will be too late to drive down to Neemrana. Besides, we are going to the Sidhwanis' party tonight."

"Sidh, who?"

"You'll find out for yourself at night," he replied. "Why don't you shop for a new dress to wear tonight while I attend to my work?"

"Too lazy to stir out," she retorted and leaned back into the pillows, a note of interest creeping into her voice. "Are you building a heritage hotel in Patiala?"

"Not a hotel, a homestead. There is this building which was first a school and then a community recreational hall, but for some strange reason, it didn't do well in either avatar. I bought it last month. All I want now is a restoration architect who can transform it into a base camp for our day tours into the neighbouring villages. We will keep it as simple as possible—sparse furnishings, no air-conditioning, food by local cooks, and bathrooms minus showers." He could not suppress a twinge of perverse pleasure over the disgust which clouded Andreja's face as he described his plan.

The next moment, though, she turned suddenly quiet and pensive. "Why don't you forget everything else and spend the day with me instead, Arpit?" Clumsily wrapping the bed sheet around herself, she slid towards him on the bed. Staring with unmistakable meaning, she whispered huskily, "We could, you know . . . stay in bed all day . . . we haven't, umm . . . stay with me Arpit. Just stay with me."

But he backed away from her and stalked into the bathroom to get ready for the gruelling day ahead.

CHAPTER 2

In a shady lane off one of the seedy neighbourhoods of New York City, a well-dressed man, using his designer suit to disguise the paunch whose existence he could no longer swagger away, sat inside a makeshift office. His eyes gleamed with greed as he watched the man sitting opposite him stuff a bunch of papers into a cheap plastic folder. He could not help but marvel at how big a potential goldmine this bunch of fake identity papers was going to be.

Baldev Singh, Dave for his American colleagues, was not relishing this downmarket experience. But there was hardly anything he could do about it. Sunburst Inc.—one of the biggest global food corporations with which he was waiting to crack a distribution deal—wanted to add a little something to their hugely-popular burger-and-fries menu: Mexican food. Enchiladas, tacos, and tortillas were guaranteed to be a hit not only with the American palate, but also with the Asian-American immigrant's aspiring palate which sought a more global culinary experience. The only minor impediment to the execution of this diversification plan—and Sunburst Inc. was in a tearing hurry to launch the plan—was that they needed a huge workforce. And they needed it within two weeks.

There were, of course, any number of Mexicans in New York City willing to work in their kitchens. But when other food chains offered better pay and cleaner working conditions, it was not so easy to get so many cooks who could be hired, and later fired without notice should the need arise, *legally*. The ones who could be got easily did not have their papers in order. And this was where Baldev Singh stepped in. He badly wanted to liaison with this corporation for their expansion plans in India. The opportunity to dominate the Indian fast-food industry was too good to pass up, after all. He was willing to do anything to tip the scales in his favour, and right now, that meant 'helping' the company acquire their workforce. If work permits for willing immigrants could not be acquired quickly enough by legal means, there was always Arvind he could rely on. Sitting in front of him and busily stuffing the fake papers into the plastic folder, Arvind, or Addy as he preferred to be called, specialised in forging documents for immigrants dying to get into the USA at any cost. If the fraud was discovered after the deal got finalised, Baldev could always claim ignorance of the forgery. And he knew Addy well enough to know that he would be far away from the reaches of law by then. It was a calculated risk, but there was nothing that he liked better, especially if the loss was likely to crash on others and not him.

It was another hour before Baldev was able to escape from the stifling atmosphere of Addy's office and walk into the plush interiors of his own Manhattan office. He strode briskly up to his cabin, nodding curtly to the 'good mornings' of his employees.

The first thing he did after settling down at his desk was to log into his computer to check his emails. And for the next couple of minutes, all he did was mutter angrily to himself and stare in utter disbelief at the screen. Then he burst into a long string of expletives. But once he had marginally cooled down, he didn't waste a moment in placing an international call.

Arpit's cell phone rang just as he was stepping out of his bath and reaching for the one expensive cologne he had brought along on this trip. Besides making himself presentable for the Sidhwanis' party, it would also help to cover up the traces of Andreja's smoke pipe.

"What the hell are you up to?" the voice at the other end stormed, "What is the meaning of all these photographs in my email?!"

"Dad, it's an alternative tourism project, heritage tours into the villages of Punjab. For that I need to offer an authentic homestead experience to my clients. I just wanted you to take a look at the property . . ." Arpit quickly rallied his thoughts and snapped out of the familiar sensation of helplessness that seemed to grip him every time his father spoke to him. Every time, but not this time.

"Cut out the crap, Arpit. I can tell you right away that it's not going to be viable. Your bird-watchers and nature-lovers may take a fancy to it, but they will not help you recover your costs. Patiala? Hah! How are you going to get the money, huh, Arpit? If you think you can waste *my* hard-earned money on *your* hare-brained schemes, you can think again!"

Arpit's voice was smooth as he answered, "Dad, I have some good news for you. You don't have to worry about financing this project. The profits I made from my last tour have not only recovered my start-up investment, but they will also be sufficient enough to fund at least the restoration part of this new plan. As for marketing, between me and my loyal employees, we will work out the cheapest option."

"*Cost-effective*," sneered Baldev. "If you want to run a business, you should get into the habit of using professional terms which won't embarrass you when you talk to real clients . . . that is, if your sweet little venture lasts that long. Till then of course, you can carry on being entertaining in your amateurish way. And son, there are such things as 'operating costs' too. When you have figured out how to squeeze *those* out from your paltry profits, you can email me again. Of course, if ever you are badly in need of financial help, one phone call will be enough."

Arpit hung up on his father before he could have the satisfaction of one last sneer before disconnecting the call. He had to admit, however, that his father was right. It wouldn't be easy to finance this operation. He could have easily gotten a loan if he was willing to use his father's name, but that was out of the question.

When he had first started this business of alternative domestic tourism, his primary motivation had been to step out of his father's looming, ominous shadow. This venture was his conscious and deliberate opposition to all that his father stood for—big business, metropolises, and ruthless competition. It was his way of repenting the passivity and the inertia which had torn him away from all that he had ever loved. It was akin to planting a single tree in one's backyard after having silently stood by and watched an entire forest being chopped down. The rage that had been festering inside him for years—a malevolent growth that had ruthlessly and rapidly eaten into him like a cancer—was the very force which was now pushing him into trying to change things . . . into trying to make amends . . . into trying to get back what he had lost.

CHAPTER 3

"Arpit! I'm so glad you condescended to come!" Soundarya shrieked from across the room, rushing towards Arpit with her arms outstretched, and before he could splutter out a flattering, banal nothing, he found himself enveloped in a heady cloud of expensive perfume—what was it that all these women wore? Chanel N°5? Whatever.

The embrace ended just as quickly and suddenly as it had begun.

"Oh! Umm . . . is she with you?" Soundarya had seen Andreja standing behind him.

"Oh yes! Andreja . . . is a friend," he smiled and continued apologetically, "I am sorry for bringing a guest along without asking you first, but Andreja was very keen to see your house. I thought I would infringe on your hospitality for once."

"Oh no, it's not an infringement at all! I keep telling Gautam that our house is like my Facebook profile, open to all friends and all friends of friends. She is . . . ahem . . . most welcome." The temperature of her greetings, however, had dropped a few degrees.

Arpit surveyed the room dispassionately. There was a smattering of people—the typically pretentious lot that Soundarya moved around with—dissipated businessmen, a few small-time models, a couple of cricketers, a few Bollywood wannabes who had flown down to Delhi to inaugurate boutiques and spas, and some of the young breed of politicians who dressed stylishly and applied management principles to their professed development agendas. He thought he spotted Vindhya Desai too, not that he was surprised to see her there, but he wasn't very sure it was her. Did that mean Dr Hari Mishra was there too? He just wasn't keen on running into him. He hoped Soundarya hadn't invited him too.

Gautam Sidhwani strolled forward, clutching his drink for dear life, his eyes glued to the dizzyingly high hemline of Andreja's floral, black silk dress. "It's great to see you after such a long time, Amrit," he said, addressing Andreja's hemline.

"Arpit," supplied Soundarya hastily.

"Oops! It seems I am drunk already. But you know what, pal, this is my first glass! Yes, the first one of the evening! Unbelievable, no? I have been a teetotaller for . . . umm . . . now, how long has it been? Eighteen days! Yes, eighteen! Amazing, if I may say so myself. But, but . . . when you are pouring out the finest poisons from the best-stocked bar amongst all the farmhouses this side of Delhi, you deserve to indulge yourself a bit, what say?" He laughed loudly, spluttering a few drops of alcohol on Andreja who, however, did not notice. Her eyes were glazing over already; Arpit wondered if she had taken a few secret puffs, unnoticed by him, before leaving their room.

"I think this intoxication has something to do with all the lovely ladies here. Do you agree, ma'am?" By now his gaze had slid up from hemline to neckline, which revealed even more.

"Honey," fluttered an extremely embarrassed Soundarya, "Mr Chadha has been asking for you for the last half an hour. Why don't you go see him?"

"Bloody Chadha! Always pestering me about that bloody swimming pool! How does he expect me to fill the goddamn pool when those bloody slum-dwellers siphon off all our water from the pipes and when that bloody Pathak says the whole matter is out of his jurisdiction? Huh?!" He tottered away, muttering angrily, his anxious wife in tow.

Andreja's eyes were wandering towards an inconspicuous little door that stood a little apart from the buzz and banality of the party. A few people were discreetly moving in and out through it and Arpit had a pretty good idea about what was going on inside the room which attracted his girlfriend so much. But he laid a warning hand on her arm. "Look, your favourite cricketer is here!"

"Dravid?!" Her expressionless features brightened for a moment.

"What? I thought you were 'in love with' Harsh Patil! And there he is, a few metres away from you. This is your chance!"

"Oh, I've lost interest in him. If he remained unsold in that Premier League auction, then he isn't good enough for *me*."

"Nonsense! You know you will regret not meeting him once we are back in the hotel. I don't want my sleep to be disturbed by your whining. Now go before someone else hijacks him. Go!"

Having safely distracted Andreja from trying to explore the Sidhwanis' den of 'ecstasy'—the room where a small-time drug supplier was doling out exorbitantly expensive doses of his magic powders—Arpit made his way to the bar, and a well-stocked bar it truly was. He got himself a Scotch and stood at the bar, leaning against it and contemplating the scene in front of him. He would need a drink to fortify himself if he really intended to immerse himself in this shallow pool of humanity. Everyone appeared to be just as purposeless as he was. Perhaps worse, for he, at least, was propped up by his irrational obsession with going backwards. An amorphous lump, that's what they all looked like—mindless, thoughtless, senseless. And that was all they would ever be through the rest of their—

"All you absolutely wonderful, wonderful people," trilled Soundarya.

How did this woman ALWAYS manage to hack right through his reveries? And that too with maniacal accuracy! Arpit glanced in exasperation at Soundarya who stood across the room, beaming happily at her guests. He sighed and set his glass down in a corner. It would be of no more use tonight.

"All of you are in for a treat," Soundarya continued. "Allow me to introduce my dear friend, Sapna Kochchar, who has just flown in from Mumbai." The predictable whispering started. "Now who is Sapna Kochchar?" "Sapna Kochchar?" "Kochchar? Who?" But Soundarya was not going to indulge in guessing games any longer than was necessary to build up the correct level of curiosity. "Now, Sapna, as most of you probably know, is one of the best Tarot card readers in the country. Normally, you must understand, she only does readings by appointment, but for the sake of our old friendship, she has agreed to demonstrate her talents here. Only three lucky people will get a chance, though. Can we draw lots?"

Arpit heard sneers and murmurs of scepticism greet Soundarya's announcement. Sapna Kochchar wasn't a name he had heard before. Her round, vacant, and heavily-kohled eyes didn't hold much promise of clairvoyance either. But, either way, it might just prove to be an interesting distraction. Besides, appearances could be deceptive. For all he knew, this woman might really know her job. And if he was one of the 'lucky' people whose name came up for a reading, he wondered if Sapna would then be able to see the searching emptiness in his life. But what if she did? Didn't all his solutions rest in the past and not in the future?

Harsh Patil had been a dead bore and not half as handsome as he looked on TV. Andreja had, therefore, returned listlessly to Arpit's side just when the first requests started drifting towards Sapna. The moment she heard what was going on, her face lit up. Andreja was always game for anything 'exotic, erotic or esoteric,' as she never failed to remind Arpit. He had often suggested that she add 'erratic' to the list.

Not one to leave anything to chance, she frantically waved two hundred Euro notes before Sapna. "Hey there! I dunno what the others are paying, but you can bet your last spell that I want this for myself! I will go first, okay?"

By now, almost all the guests had become interested. They stood in a speculative circle around Sapna and watched as she spread her three decks of Tarot cards on a stylishly-carved, low wooden table and let Andreja draw her cards.

"The Tower . . . hmm . . . it means that you are set to scale the heights of success very soon. Your ruling suit in this reading is Wands, which means that things will materialise out of thin air, almost as if by magic. Now, if you would draw a single card from the Soulmates deck which I have designed myself—"

"What nonsense!" An indignant voice arrested Andreja's hand in mid-air.

"Excuse me? Does anyone have a problem?" Sapna asked, trying rather unsuccessfully to raise a single, scornful eyebrow.

A petite woman—dressed in a deep blue silk sari with a pink paisley pattern along its border, a string of rice pearls around her neck, and a small red bindi on her forehead—stepped through the crowd. There was an alluring radiance about her and Arpit found himself inching closer to the front of the group to get a better look at her. She had clear, pale skin and long, black hair that flowed down her back. She could have been in her thirties or forties, it was hard to tell from her absurdly-young eyes.

Suddenly, she turned around, and looking straight through the crowd at Arpit, she smiled in recognition. He found himself smiling back. But when she turned back to face Sapna again, Arpit remembered that he had never met this woman before.

"Wait, wait, wait! What's going on?!" Soundarya was frantically making her way through the crowd. "Oh! Umm . . . Nishi! Welcome. A bit late though, aren't you?" Soundarya spluttered, a why-did-I-invite-her-here look on her face when she finally found the reason for this disruption in her party.

"I have been here for well over an hour now, my dear," the woman replied, a soft smile tugging at the corner of her lips. "It was a tad too cosy inside, so I went to take a walk in the fresh air and lingered back. Lovely rose garden you have."

"Thanks. Nishi, ugh, Sapna here, umm . . . she has been doing this for years. She has a number of celebrities among her clientele. Sometimes her interpretations are a bit . . . ahem, unexpected, but then isn't that the whole point of clairvoyance? I mean, why would you want to be told something you already know?" Soundarya smiled nervously and finished her weak defence, acutely conscious of Nishi's utter lack of amusement.

Nishi was already attacking Sapna. "Sorry, but I can't sugar-coat this. You are ruining the reputation of my clan. Your interpretations are ridiculous!"

"And you are . . .?" Sapna enquired icily. "I don't seem to have heard of you. Ever . . ."

"No, you probably haven't," Nishi replied calmly. "I don't do celebrity amusements. Anyway, I am not here to show anyone up. I just wanted to warn this gullible girl here, that her future isn't going to be what you have predicted."

Andreja had been staring at the two women all this while, her mouth open, half in surprise and half in resentment. Now, however, she spoke up, her voice edged with challenge, "How about *you*, then, lady? Will you tell me my future?"

"Hmm . . . no, I shouldn't. You might be disappointed. It's nothing as exciting as my friend here is predicting."

"A little knowledge is a dangerous thing, and a total lack of it is very convenient for heckling," Sapna remarked loudly to no one in particular.

To her irritation however, Nishi burst into laughter. "I am not rising to the bait. I will do a reading only when, and for whom, I feel like it."

And though she was not looking at him, Arpit got the uncanny feeling that this statement was meant specifically for him.

Andreja, however, wasn't one to rest easy till she got her way. In less than five minutes—even as Soundarya soothed Sapna's ruffled feathers and tried talking to Gautam about how to get rid of their unwanted guest discreetly—she and a crowd of other hopefuls like her had descended on Nishi and convinced her to do a few readings. Giving in to their persistent requests, she began calling them out, one by one, to Soundarya's garden, "since I don't want to inconvenience our host," she explained, as a sparkle of mirth flashed in her eyes.

"Who is this Nishi?" Arpit asked when he finally managed to corner a much-hassled Soundarya.

"Nishimaya is an old acquaintance from the days when we lived . . . umm . . . outside Delhi. Our fathers were great friends. I thought it would be, err, polite to invite her. We always do, of course," she hastily added, "but she never comes. I was surprised to see her today." She sounded more dismayed than surprised, however.

"Is she an astrologer?"

"I have no idea if she is! I know her father was into all this, but it was a hobby. She however, is an architect by profession, does restoration work on heritage buildings. God only knows when *she* turned into a prophetess!" Soundarya left in a bewildered huff, leaving Arpit standing alone in the middle of the room, looking for the drink which he had abandoned half an hour ago.

When Andreja slipped back in after her reading, she did it so silently that only Arpit noticed her. She seemed quieter than he had ever seen her before. Standing by his side, she absent-mindedly played with the sleeve of his shirt, crumpling it between her fingers.

"What happened? Does she seem genuine?"

It took Andreja a moment to register that he was asking her something. Her reply was uncharacteristically guarded, "I think she is."

"You *think*?"

"Hmm . . . she told me details about my family that no one could possibly know. There were other things as well . . . but they were about the future."

"And of course, you can't tell if they are right or not."

"I believe her." She lapsed into sullen silence.

"Andreja, you must be tired. Let's go back to the hotel."

"I am going in there," she pointed defiantly towards the room Arpit had earlier prevented her from going to, and he knew that nothing could dissuade her this time. He might as well be prepared to carry her back to the hotel.

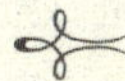

The hosts were extremely relieved when the party broke up a couple of hours earlier than expected. In spite of her vehement protests, the group around Nishi had swelled to more than twenty-odd guests. Most of them, however, returned to the house disappointed and a trifle abashed. Nishi had refused their pleas with such unbending humility that there was little else they could do. Still, by the time she had finished with the few requests she had agreed to entertain, there was an excited buzz in the house.

"She is so *freaking* accurate! She told me where I have studied and how I met my husband!"

"She knew my boss is an asshole."

"It doesn't take psychic powers to know *that*. Everyone's boss is an asshole."

"Not mine. Nishi said I am up for a promotion."

"And I will be travelling overseas very soon."

"I am scared, guys. She told me I will suffer a big loss very soon."

Arpit was ready to call it a night and was looking for some way of calling Andreja out when Soundarya caught him, "Arpit! Leaving? Do come over the next time you are here. Sapna is here for a while. You will definitely be impressed by her powers."

"Thank you. Can you have Andreja called? She went in there." He pointed awkwardly towards the closed room. He didn't want to go inside. He didn't want to breathe in an atmosphere that reeked of everything that he had given up in disgust many months back. Everything about those days repulsed him now.

"But there is no one in that room now. She must be somewhere else."

"But . . . but she told me she was going inside! Are you sure?"

"I am positive. I had it locked half an hour ago. I think she wanted an excuse to get away from you. She must have returned to the hotel," giggled Soundarya, her coquettishness returning.

He nodded, perplexed, and walked out.

When he was a few feet away from his car, he stopped and

turned towards the rose garden, gazing at it for a long moment before walking towards it. That woman had said it was quite something, but he saw no special aura around it. It was easy to convince a bunch of drunken fools, after all. But he knew better. He would not let this get his hopes up. He didn't know anything about this Nishi. Another disappointment would simply destroy him.

"I am sorry to see you go home without your girlfriend. But you must be prepared to have her leave you very soon." A woman's voice seemed to loom up from the shadows behind him.

Arpit whirled around in surprise, peering into the darkness. He'd thought he was alone. "Sorry? Who's—"

"It's Nishi," the woman cut him short, pre-empting his question. "I told her something about you."

"What?" His heart seemed to be thumping down his left arm.

"That you have never loved her."

"Oh, that," he sighed, repressing his astonishment at her acuity. After all, it would be obvious to anyone with even the most marginal powers of observation. There was nothing really magical about this. "She doesn't love me, either. Why should this upset her?"

"Does it surprise you? Several people take love for granted, even when they are unwilling, or unable, to return any. *You* would know . . ."

Arpit knew then that she was not talking about Andreja alone. And that she was exactly what she claimed to be.

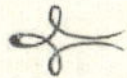

Andreja wasn't in the hotel when he got back, not that he

bothered to look for her. He just crashed into his bed and drifted off into the soundest sleep he had had in months.

He had a strange dream that night. He saw himself walking through a city that was excruciatingly familiar, but he just could not remember its name. He was looking for someone—who? The lanes of the city were narrow and stifling and as he walked through them, they just got narrower and narrower. They began closing in on him. He ran, but he was trapped . . . in an instant he would be crushed. And then, just as suddenly, the walls started crumbling and he found himself in a vast golden field. He started running through it, trampling the ripe wheat. He still hadn't found the person he was looking for, but he knew, intuitively, that the person was somewhere nearby. He saw an old ruined building ahead of him and he knew he would find some answers there. But when he reached the building and stepped eagerly through the faded doorway, the entire building crashed upon him.

Arpit woke up shivering. Andreja was back in the room and was listlessly pushing her things into her bag.

"Are you going somewhere?" he asked, his voice hoarse and unsteady from the effects of the dream.

"Yup. Dunno exactly where, but Goa sounds good." She didn't turn back to look at him.

"Well, this is unexpected." He knew he was lying even as he said it. Hadn't Nishi predicted this?

"I am bored here. Bored to death. Delhi stinks. I need a break from all this."

"I wish I could come with you" —another lie— "but there is so much work right now . . ."

"Oh, you need not bother. I'll be fine." She finally looked at him and smiled tightly.

"Mind you, don't get involved with those junkies in Goa, then."

"I have hitchhiked across the world alone. Don't worry." She gave him a hug and a kiss and was gone before he could think of something better to say.

He knew that she would not return. The thought, however, did not upset him too much.

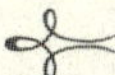

"I knew you would want to talk," Nishi said with a slow smile.

It had taken Arpit a little persistence and a lot of flattery to get Nishimaya's address from Soundarya. She had been unwilling to give him this information even when he told her that he desperately needed a restoration architect. He didn't have much hope of being able to afford Nishi's fees; still, it was worth a try, and it would give him an excuse to get acquainted with her. When he reached Nishi's flat in Vasant Kunj and rang the doorbell, she greeted him with an almost maternal warmth. Dressed in a simple cotton kurta and *churidar*, she exuded such a casual sense of elegance that Arpit wondered if she was the same woman he had met at Soundarya's party.

"I just didn't trust Soundarya enough to actually give you my address. Well, she rose to the occasion, for once," Nishi was saying.

"Isn't she your friend?" he put in lamely. This wasn't what he had prepared himself for. He'd been racking his brains for a proper way to start the conversation and explain what he really wanted, but Nishi had somehow bypassed everything and landed them straight in the middle of things.

"We have known each other a long time . . . but that does not always amount to friendship . . ." Nishi replied, her face scrunching slightly.

"But I believe old bonds are the strongest."

She stared intently at his face for a long moment. When she spoke, her voice was soft and quiet. "You appear to have dwelt upon old bonds lately, haven't you?"

Arpit drew a sharp breath, startled by her perceptiveness. Still standing awkwardly in her doorway, he couldn't think of a quick and effective escape from her scrutiny.

"Come in, Arpit. Have a seat. Would you like something? Tea? Coffee? Something cold? I am afraid I don't stock cigarettes."

He started. "How do you know I smoke?"

"Nothing mystical about it," she smiled. "Your clothes are reeking of it."

"I'm sorry, ma'am, I . . ."

"Nishi. You can call me Nishi." Abruptly she added, "Arpit, I never attend parties at the Sidhwanis'. Yet, I made it a point to be at this one. Do you want to know why?"

"Why?"

"Don't you feel you have seen me somewhere before . . . before the party, I mean?"

"I-I don't know. For a moment I suspected, but . . ."

"Ah, for a moment at least! That's not bad. But Arpit, you have to stop drugging yourself. You can't afford to cloud your cognition. I was present at the book launch where you met Dr Hari Mishra. I was part of the group which was buzzing around him."

"But . . . but Soundarya would have . . ."

"Soundarya was too busy buttering up Vindhya Desai to take notice of me. Besides, I wasn't in the usual finery I don while meeting her. She is one of those people who are swept away by appearances. Anyway, your question to Dr Mishra had intrigued me. I had seen you with Soundarya and I sort of guessed that she would invite you to her party . . . and her party was my only chance to find out whether your question was anything more than a boyish fascination with science fiction or not."

Arpit shifted uneasily under her penetrating gaze. "Can you get me a glass of water, please?"

"Oh! How rude of me! I didn't even offer you a glass of water! Give me a minute. I'll make you a cup of tea, all right?"

Arpit just nodded. The minute Nishi left the room he took a deep steadying breath and rubbed his forehead distractedly. To calm himself he started looking around the room. The paintings on the wall in front of him were attractive. There was nothing unusual about them though, nothing to apprise a visitor of the fact that this was the house of a woman with strange powers. They were all quaint village scenes—a nice, soothing subject. He could have stared at the snow-capped mountains and the lush, green terraced fields for hours.

"You seem to be enjoying the scenery," Nishi remarked, returning with two cups of steaming tea and a tray of salted biscuits.

"Oh! Umm . . ." Arpit fumbled a little; he hadn't heard her return. "They are fantastic . . . really. The painter has shown wonderful imagination."

"Look closely, Arpit. These are not paintings."

Intrigued, he took a second look. Nishi was right. They were photographs, but of such an impressionistic quality that from a distance they appeared to be paintings. "You know, there is a surreal feel to this place, almost as if it's too beautiful to be true. If you hadn't told me, I could have sworn that this place never existed."

Nishi seemed to struggle with an answer for a few minutes. Finally, in a voice laden with longing and regret, she said, "You are not far off the mark. This village existed at one time. But not any longer. Now . . . now it's alive only in the memories of some."

"You have lived here?"

"This was my native village."

He could almost hear the mountain breeze whistle wistfully through her words. "So, what happened to it?"

"We can talk about that later. How much sugar do you take with your tea?"

"Are you trying to change the subject?"

"No. I am trying not to tell you too much too soon."

"Why?"

She stirred the sugar in his cup and handed it to him. "My work is to help other people with their secrets, not reveal mine to them . . ."

"Your work? You are an architect."

"Yes. My job is to rebuild and restore . . . but in more ways than one." She smiled slightly. "You got a glimpse of it at the Sidhwanis' that day. Has Andreja left already?"

He nodded.

"And you are quite happy about it."

"Hey, no!" he protested, only to stop sheepishly. It was no use pretending before Nishi. "You are a lady of many talents, I must say. Architecture, clairvoyance, and photography . . . is there more?"

"Photography? These modern cameras put me out of my depth. I have to use them, of course, for my work, but it's definitely not something I will take up as a hobby."

"Then who clicked these stunning pictures on your wall?"

"They are not photographs, Arpit, but projections. And they were created long after the actual scenes had been destroyed."

He stared at her in sheer disbelief. *Projections*?

"It's simple, really, but then most people run away from simplicity, so I don't know if you will believe me. Anyway, tell me this, how often do you dream?"

His mind flickered to the dream he had seen after coming back from the Sidhwanis' party two days ago. It had been so vivid—the starkness of the city, the panic rising in his stomach as the lanes had closed upon him, the dampness of the earth as he had trampled through the field, blindly trying to outrun the city collapsing on him, and the blows of the ruined house falling upon him in cruel retribution.

Nishi saw his discomfort at once. "Sip your tea slowly," she commanded, "and breathe deeply. Did you just recall a dream?"

"A mishmash of a dream and a memory, rather." He shuddered.

"Hmm . . . It's so difficult to sift dreams from memories, isn't it? Memories are dreams of what once was, and dreams are but memories of what is to be."

"*Memories of what is to be*?" Arpit repeated distrustfully. "Are you talking about prophetic dreams?"

"Not altogether. Ordinarily, people do not experience the dreams I mentioned just now. Their dreams are nothing but crude reconstructions of everyday experiences. They are mundane in their content, a place for subconscious desires and regrets to express themselves. Now, though I used the word 'place', we don't really go anywhere, do we?"

"Not unless we sleepwalk . . ."

"Ha ha, but that's not what I meant. Have you ever thought of it this way: a dream is a *memory* you carry back from a place you visited during your sleep, when your spirit journeys into realms just as real, or perhaps more real, than your waking world?"

A tingle of excitement prickled at the base of his spine. Arpit shivered.

Nishi continued explaining. "Most people are so tightly bound to their accustomed world that even in the freedom of dreaming, they don't journey very far. Sometimes, though, you may travel to a place beyond the bounds of your usual dream-wanderings, and then you may witness scenes that never were. You must have had at least one dream in which you were whisked through strange and beautiful lands, or where you performed feats physically impossible in the real world, haven't you? All of this happened in the Land Which Never Existed, at least not for your conscious mind. Yet, you remembered it in the morning when you said you had had a dream. Now, this is what really happens: When you wake up, irrespective of how far you journeyed, your mind plays a movie of your travels. You call that movie a dream. But for a movie to play, it should have been recorded in the first place."

"I don't quite follow you."

"When you watch a movie in the theatre, what you are watching is not the actual scene which was enacted; that scene was in the past, after all. What you are watching is the *memory* of that scene stamped forever as an impression onto the roll of the film, or onto a digital medium."

"So the film *remembers* the scene, as you put it."

"Precisely. The better the quality of the film and the better the technique of shooting, the closer the recorded memory is to the actual scene. Similarly, what and how much you remember of your dream-wanderings will depend upon how far you have evolved or, ummm, let's say 'upgraded' your mental software."

"And how do I upgrade it?"

"Ah, that takes years of self-discipline and concentration."

"*Your* mind is powerful for sure, then."

Nishi's voice became wistful for a moment. "My father taught me everything. He was a deeply spiritual man with uncanny abilities which he didn't ever reveal fully, even to me. I am just trying to arrive as close as possible to where he had reached a long time ago." Briskly shrugging off her momentary despondency like a wet shawl, she resumed, "Now, if a dream-journey can be resurrected in your waking consciousness, why can't the powers of the mind be extended a little further?" Noting the swirl of confusion in Arpit's eyes, she continued explaining, "Your state of consciousness has switched over from sleep to wakefulness. Yet your memory of the dream world is still 'compatible' with the very differently-programmed 'software' of your waking mind. You can *consciously* 'play' the dream over and over again. This shows that the human mind is equipped with the capability to convert experiences from one form to another. In a similar manner, the thoughts and images created by the waking mind can also be converted to another form. A consciously-summoned image can be projected onto gross matter, in this case a blank sheet of paper."

Arpit's mouth dropped open with incredulity. "You . . . you mean you just *burned* your memories of your village into these pictures?"

"Yes. I thought about these scenes with love and longing and concentrated on them with reverence till they materialised."

"Ridiculous." Scepticism, systematically bred and nurtured in the elite boarding school he had studied in, was kicking in. Arpit put down his cup on the low table next to his chair with a loud clank. "I'm sure you have great powers, Nishi, but what you are telling me is impossible. Simply impossible."

"Years ago, people must have said the same thing when experiences captured on film were developed into photographs. Think about it, Arpit, my mind just did what a camera usually does, but you are not prepared to accept it, not even as an idea. Why this blind belief in the tangible, as opposed to the 'psychic'? Is it because your school taught you about the conversion of energy to matter and vice-versa, but never gave you a glimpse into the transformation of dream-elements to consciousness and of consciousness to matter?"

"Nishi! The two things are not the same. Dreams and

memories are mental mechanisms. They cannot, just cannot, be converted into physical reality!"

"In your dreams you often see glimpses of scenes from the day that has gone by, don't you? If the physical world can become a dream-image in sleep, then why can't mental images take on a tangible form?" Seeing him mulling silently over her words, she pushed on, "Arpit, haven't you ever had a single dream come true in the 'real' world? And if you have, is that not proof enough of your mind's potential to materialise your heartfelt longings?"

"Those dreams of mine which came true? I regret having dreamed them in the first place," Arpit shot back bitterly. A little tired of this conversation, he half-rose, as if to go, but he suddenly remembered the original reason for his visit. "Nishi, I actually came here on business. I have started a company called Silver Cloud which offers sustainable heritage tours. I want someone who can restore an old school building in Patiala and make it worth a decent night's stay. But I . . . ahem . . . I don't know how much . . ."

"I will help you," Nishi answered his question without even waiting for him to complete what he was saying. Her words were soft, belying the intensity behind them. "But . . . is that the only reason you came?"

As her guileless eyes searched his tortured ones, trying to plumb his sincerity, he gave up the last fragment of stoic pretence that had held him back so far. Nishi knew what he had really come for, of that he was sure. But he also knew that she was waiting for him to put it out in the open in so many words. His words, therefore, when unleashed, were pulsating with years of longing, "No, Nishi. You are the only one who can pull me out of my agony. I want you to take me back to that place where I can unlose her."

CHAPTER 4

Arpit and Nishimaya were heading towards Patiala in his car. He kept stealing glances at her from time to time. While she had agreed to work as a restoration architect for his upcoming tours—this trip would be her first site visit to the old school building Arpit wanted to restore—there had not been a single word from her about his other request. Had she been pitifully amused with his desperation? Or was she just taking her time, testing him to see just how intense his agony was?

"Was there any particular reason for choosing Patiala as your base camp?" Nishi broke the silence.

"Hmmm . . . I love the architecture of the town. It has an old-world charm which is quite missing in our bright and efficient Chandigarh," he smiled slightly. "Moti Bagh, Sheesh Mahal, the Baradari Gardens . . . there's quite a lot to admire. Besides, it's close to all the places we plan to include in the itinerary, like Anandpur Sahib and Ropar which is a famous Harappan site. Personally, I would have preferred a village house as base camp, but I can't afford to plunge completely into eco-tourism yet. My guests would be aghast at the absence of basic urban amenities." Arpit laughed a little ruefully at the idea.

"Don't worry, your enlightened minority will find you unfailingly. Anyhow, I was wondering, how many people are working for your company?"

"Around twenty, including you and me," Arpit answered, his eyes twinkling. "Scared that it's too small to pay you?"

"Not at all," she returned calmly.

"I have been lucky in my business so far. I got this house in Patiala at a throwaway price. The previous owners believe it is jinxed. First, the school failed, then the recreational centre couldn't draw enough people to sustain itself, and then finally, during some election, when the house was being used as a polling station, two rival political groups got into a huge fight and a man got killed. They were glad to get rid of it now."

"Didn't the jinx scare you?"

"I've suffered so many jinxes that they don't bother me anymore."

"Hmm . . . I have a suggestion. I think you should have a second base camp in one of the villages on your itinerary. That way, your guests can have a place to stay overnight if they wish to go on further excursions without having to bother about coming back all the way to Patiala."

"I have been thinking of that, but all in due course. One day I would love to take my guests into the *Majha* of Punjab, into my own land."

"Come again?"

"*Majha* . . . ummm, it means in the middle or in the centre. Majha Punjab is the heart of what the ancient Punjab region was. Amritsar, Gurdaspur, Tarn Taran, they're in the Majha. A bit of Pakistan is also included . . . Lahore and Narowal, though I don't know if you've heard of Narowal."

"The border areas, you mean? That explains why history hangs so heavily on you."

"Well, that is just one reason."

Nishi lapsed into a thoughtful silence for a few minutes. When she spoke again, her voice was soft and tender, "Arpit, do you know what my father used to say? He used to say that by trying to cling on to what has happened, we are preventing *what is meant to happen*. I admit, though, that I haven't followed his advice too well . . . those pictures on my wall are a proof of that."

"And what if the future is so bleak that the most humane thing to do would be to prevent it?" Arpit retorted with bitterness.

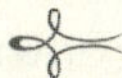

"Umm . . . d-e-l-i-c-i-o-u-s! Better than those dainty-looking canapés at the Sidhwanis' that day! And what else did she have? Oh oh, yes! Crispy potato skins with a creamy chives dip and avocado tarts! There's just one word for all of this—Food Pretentiousness. Whatever happened to real food?!" They had stopped at a roadside *dhaba* for lunch, and Nishi, clearly enjoying her food, smiled a trifle wickedly as Arpit launched into a tirade against the Sidhwanis, only to pause a moment later to enquire, ". . . which reminds me, Nishi, Soundarya told me that your father was an astrologer? Is it true?"

"He *is* a lot more than that," Nishi shot back.

"Sorry. I thought he was . . ."

"Dead? To the world, yes. But I know he is somewhere in the Himalayas now, roaming around with a band of ascetics as free-spirited as him. I don't use his surname anymore. It confines his identity and his freedom to his caste and his village, and I don't want that."

"Nishi-Maya," Arpit spoke slowly, understanding dawning upon him. "I get it now, this unusual choice of name. 'Maya' can double as a surname!"

"Exactly! But my real name is Himani. Himani Gaur. My native village is in the mountains of Garhwal."

Arpit peered intently at her. "But why this concealment of your identity? Are you not proud of where you come from?"

"Nothing could be further from the truth. I love my village passionately, even though it no longer exists. What I am ashamed of is what its inhabitants did to it. I think it's time I told you my story . . .

"It was the river which gave the village its name: Gumgyaat. It means 'the gush of swift water', and the river did full justice to it, running swift and strong down the mountain, breathing life as it flowed.

"Gumgyaat was a small village with about thirty to forty-odd households scattered along terraced slopes. It lay nestled between thick forested mountains and the river, with the farms huddled together on one side. My house was closer to the forest than to the river, but you could hear the river sing its way down the slopes from anywhere in the village. During the rains, the sound it made was deafening, but we were never scared of it. It didn't threaten us . . . Mornings used to have a woody, smoky smell to them and on my way to school, I would often stop and look down at the village and see thin wisps of smoke come curling up from the houses below for the hearths would have been fired up by then and the women would have started cooking. The farms in the village were small but prosperous, and wealth was counted not in land or money, but in having enough for one's needs, and, more importantly, in being respected in the community. In that sense, my father, Devishankar Gaur, was one of the wealthiest men in the village. People used to call him Panditji because of his penetrating spirituality. When he was not poring over ancient Hindu texts or practising mysterious rituals in secluded groves, he was taking me out to the forest to teach me the language of the spirits. We would go around hunting for different kinds of tree barks, seeds, and leaves. People often found the two of us in the forest, bent over a patch of grass and scrutinising it for some particular herb or the other and I would be so lost in my pursuit that I would never know that they had been watching us, until they would meet us later and say so. At home, we would experiment with the herbs and make different concoctions. And when the concoctions were successful in warding off physical and mental ailments, no one was happier than us.

"But even Baba had no cure for the contagion that was lurking around the corner. There had been rumbles of discontent, most of them justified, about the absence of modern medical facilities and electricity, about the scarcity of jobs and the lack of education. My father and the village elders had approached the district authorities time and again about these problems, but without much success. The officers and clerks of the administration were a disgruntled lot, unhappy with being posted to our godforsaken hills, and their annoyance coagulated into a languid indifference towards our plight.

"Forced to fall back on their own resources, my father and his confederates started coming up with home-grown alternatives. They pooled their resources to start a village school with the cooperation of some of the educated youth of Gumgyaat who had chosen to stay back in the village rather than escape to the marginally better life in the valley. Later, they came up with a 'pony procession' which carried some of the brighter children of the village to a government school some thirty kilometres away where the teachers had agreed to give up their weekly day-off to tutor these students from Gumgyaat once every week.

"My father also came up with the idea of a watermill to generate electricity from the generous flow of the river. Apart from a few glitches now and then, it worked reasonably well. He also delved deeper and deeper into his indigenous healing methods to compensate for the absence of doctors and hospitals. Thanks to him and an enlightened handful, things were manageable.

"The deprivation, however, stung some more than others. And Soundarya's father, Rajendra Bisht, was one of them. She used to be Sunita in those days, but the demands of her Delhi circles necessitated a transition from Sunita to Soundarya.

"Anyhow, the spartan, austere life and the resilience of Gumgyaat did not go down very well with Rajendra Bisht and his family. And to cap it all, surrounded by villages where alcohol consumption was the bane of every second household, Gumgyaat, thanks again to my father, was one place where total abstinence was more the norm than an exception. Rajendra Bisht, however resented all of this. He wanted to get out of the village. Getting a secure and comfortable government job was the pinnacle of his aspirations. But he knew it wasn't easy. Gumgyaat was not alone in facing administrative indifference and apathy. The district in which it fell was one of the most neglected districts in Uttar Pradesh. There was talk of demanding a separate state so that the people of the hills could have their own representation, but the realisation of that political dream would take years. The only other way to live a decent life was to sell your land and move to the plains where you might just find good employment. But the opinion in the village was not in favour of such a move. Besides, there were no buyers either.

"One day, however, a group of men arrived and drew aside the elders of Gumgyaat. For some strange reason, my father was excluded from this conversation. When the elders returned, change had already started streaking their faces. My father saw it. He came home and said to me, 'Himani, I'm glad you are old enough to manage on your own . . . who knows what the future might bring?' But I knew for sure that my father already knew what the future would bring for Gumgyaat. That day, however,

I could only nod my head silently to mask the fear rising in my chest.

"As it turned out, those men had come with a proposal. They wanted to build a dam on the river. They assured us that it would bring electricity not only to our village, but to at least ten others lower down on the slopes. They pointed out how many of our youngsters could be employed at the construction site. They also said that the company which had been given the contract of the project would soon build a hospital and a degree college in Gumgyaat. It sounded too good to be true. And it was.

"My father smelled it right away. He warned the panchayat members that those men would take our river, our land, and our peace. They would chop down our forests to clear land for their project and they wouldn't even spare the sacred groves where our gods resided. Animals would be rendered homeless and would attack our village in bewilderment. The dust and concrete from the construction site would choke our natural wells and springs and whatever little of the river they would leave for us. He told them that he had read about such things happening in other parts of the world. But, for the first time in his life, he was questioned and his advice ridiculed. How did he know all this, they asked, a man who had stepped out of his village only twice in his entire life and then too had never ventured further than Varanasi? How would *he* know what happened in other parts of the world?

"I have often tried to figure out how the contractors managed to persuade the villagers. Was it with alcohol? Or was it with money? It must have been money . . . that and the assurance of jobs. They didn't even bother to take the consent of the neighbouring villages. The whole thing was a clear violation of our rights. The government is supposed to conduct a public hearing before taking such a major decision. They did conduct a public hearing, but only Rajendra Bisht and his coterie of friends were informed about the date and place of the hearing. And their word, very conveniently, was taken as collective consent. Even then, there were a few people who listened to my father as he raised questions—Why was the government thinking about us after all these years? Would the electricity light our homes or would it help run the manufacturing units of industries down in the plains? Would we have enough of a river left to run our own watermills?

"When the officials were questioned, they said that yes, the river would be diverted, but to an easily accessible distance. They also said that they would channelise a pipeline to send water to our homes. In the end though, the river's course was diverted by seventy-six kilometres. All that remained for us was a minor rivulet. Those beautiful landscapes on my wall? They were the first to go when they started blasting the mountain.

"My father tried . . . he tried with every pore of his being, to stop all this. But Soundarya's father successfully rallied the majority behind him. The company's representatives and the local officials had appointed him as the mediator. People also said that he had been paid a huge amount for it. I believe that. After the construction of the dam started, Rajendra Bisht was the first to move his family to Delhi and buy a house there.

"Today, Gumgyaat is a ghost village. It was not able to survive the drying-up of the river and the mass migration that started once the project was underway. But my father did not stay to see all this. The day the panchayat decided to give its sanction to the scheme, he decided to leave. He made arrangements for me and my mother to stay with my relatives in Varanasi, and then, he just left . . ."

They sat quietly for the next couple of minutes. Nishi had lapsed into a brooding silence—remembering everything had been exhausting, the memories were sharper than she had thought. Arpit meanwhile, was staring into his cup of tea as if he were in a trance. Nishi's story had hit him hard. Inside his head, he could imagine the scene—the villagers standing in a circle, glassy-eyed but talking animatedly, lured in by false promises of money and jobs, their heads filled with visions of a better life, their excited chattering drowning out Nishi's father's voice even as it grew increasingly dismayed with their stubborn self-destructiveness. He spotted a face in the crowd shining out with a terrifying vividness—his own! What was he doing there?! And next to him, smugly authoritative, was Rajendra Bisht who, despite being garbed in the typical dress of the hills, had the unmistakable face of his own father!

Arpit snapped out of his reverie with a jolt. "But how can the loss of a river overturn the lives of so many people?" he blurted.

"The same way the loss of a sacred lake can . . ." Nishimaya murmured tiredly, convincing him that she had divined his story already.

CHAPTER 5

Manjot Shergill—Mandy for all her acquaintances in Leeds, England—shrugged her shoulders with borderline politeness and shook her head in refusal when Jay asked her if she had watched him play at the last county cricket match. Her husband, Simarjeet Shergill, called Sunny by all, looked anxiously at her from across the room. If only she would look a little more alive and interested. If only she would make a pretence, if nothing else, of entertaining their friends. They had all been such good neighbours, dropping in every day with books and flowers and home-cooked food, filling the house with love and warmth so that Mandy could heal. Of course he understood that she was traumatised by what had happened, any woman would be, but six whole months were more than enough for a woman to recover from a miscarriage and at least resume some semblance of normalcy. Gazing across uneasily at her, he wondered if Mandy was slipping into depression. She was sitting by the patio door, holding a glass of wine in her hand and listlessly staring at their small kitchen garden outside even as Jay, having tried without any success to get her interested in a conversation, walked away. Dressed in the pale blue dress he'd gotten for her last week, she looked even more frail and fragile. She had lost some weight after the miscarriage. Her hair was lacklustre and her complexion was pallid. Perhaps he should take her to see somebody . . . Shaina would be able to recommend a therapist, someone not known to the Indian community in Leeds; he did not want news of Mandy's despondency and slower-than-normal recovery reaching their families back home.

Sonia and Vik had sauntered over to where Mandy was sitting. They were talking about the latest Bollywood blockbuster. Sunny hoped she would say something *now* at least. Hadn't she told him on the day of their engagement that she loved dancing to Bollywood songs? She had asked him, a little shyly, if he listened only to 'English music'? He had laughed then and assured her, "My friends and neighbours in UK are all addicted to Hindi and Punjabi music. If you experienced my house aurally, you might end up thinking you are in Ludhiana, not Leeds!" She had looked up at him then, eyes big and round, like she didn't really believe him but was ready to play along.

But come to think of it, her laughter had been a bit restrained even back then. He had attributed it to the shyness typical of an Indian girl from a small village. And he'd been right. After their wedding, it had taken her a few days to open up, to shed her inhibitions and be comfortable around him. Things had rolled along so smoothly in that initial year. He was happy with her and he had thought she was happy with him too. She had taken to her new life quickly, allowing Sunny to take on the role of guide and interpreter on her journey into this new world of clipped accents and uncertain weather. He had expected the pregnancy to bring them closer than ever. If only he had not made that colossal mistake of visiting India to celebrate the news. Everything had fallen apart after that.

He walked over to her; she was still playing with her glass of wine. "Don't you like it?" he leaned over and demanded in an impatient whisper. "Danny brought it especially to perk you up. She made it at home. At least sip it to show your appreciation."

She turned around to look at her husband. He was staring at her pointedly, exasperation threatening to rip through the polite host demeanour he was dutifully sporting. He was asking her why she wasn't drinking. She looked down at the glass in her hand and obediently took a sip of the mulled wine. In the next instant, she felt a strong suction drag her to the bottom of a lake. Water gushed in everywhere, drumming loud and hard against her. But before she could struggle and scream for help, she felt someone grip her shoulder hard and shake her. She blinked. Sunny was saying something to her and looking at her as if he wanted to shake some sense into her, but was restrained by his customary gentleness. His gaze travelled to her hand; she followed it. The wine glass, nearly full until just a few seconds ago, was now empty.

The mulled wine had reminded her of the flavour of a sticky-sweet lollipop, melting and sticking to its plastic wrapper . . . a lollipop thrust hurriedly and secretly into her hand right before her cousins came running to say that it was time to go home.

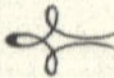

Perhaps Arpit had begun to count too much on Nishi's clairvoyance. So, when she demanded, "Well, I've told you my story. Now you tell me yours," he was properly taken aback.

"I thought you already knew everything!"

"I have only gleaned wisps of your story. I know there is a lake whose loss gushes underneath the surface of your life just as the loss of Gumgyaat surges underneath mine. I know you have lost the one whose love you understood a little too late . . . but I don't know her name."

Arpit raised his face to the sky. The shadows of the

afternoon had lengthened and the sun, mellow in its warmth now, was trickling through the trees in a farewell caress. "Mannat . . ." Arpit paused, as if the name was a delicate bubble of glass that he was afraid of breaking. "But her real name was Manjot Kaur Meharsar. Veerji, her grandfather, had looked up the alphabet 'M' in the Guru Granth Sahib. He had also insisted that everyone in the family attach the village's name to their own names. Meharsar was the name of our village, therefore . . ." He trailed off before adding the next sentence quickly, "My mother knew how desperately Veerji had longed for a girl in his family. When Mannat was born, Ma said that she was the answer to Veerji's prayers. Therefore, Mannat. But the family preferred Manjot. Ma, however, continued to call her Mannat."

"And so did you."

"It suited her." To change the subject, he quickly added, "Well, I am a little relieved you haven't managed to read my mind as clearly as you did with all those people at the Sidhwanis' that night."

"Shallow waters are easy to plumb. Their lives revolve around a few banal themes—money, marriage, mobility, morbidity. But your story, though it seems akin to my own, is not so simple, is it?"

Arpit sighed. "You be the judge of that. Sometimes I feel it's just a case of gross stupidity; at other times it seems like a conspiracy of the gods. It's impossible for me to relate my own story with detachment. I hate myself too much for that." Arpit stared disconsolately at his hands for a few minutes, as if trying to decipher the quirks and vagaries of the lines that criss-crossed his palms. Nishi's silence weighed heavily on him. He looked at her, half-expecting her to say something, but when she didn't, he took a deep breath and decided to plunge directly into his story.

"Mannat was born a month after Operation Blue Star. Veerji

considered her to be a sign of the Lord forgiving man's follies in what was going to be a year of violence and bloodshed. The first girl in the family, after three generations of boys, Mannat immediately became the apple of her grandfather's eyes. And it was not just him, she was such a sweet-tempered, affectionate, chubby baby, that everyone doted on her.

"When the riots started, I was a little over a year old. My father, Baldev Singh, thought it safer to move us back from Amritsar to Meharsar. We had relatives there—Beeji, my uncles, aunts, and cousins. And we had long-time friends in Veerji and his family. Veerji and my grandfather had been firm friends. Meharsar was a safe place to escape to. Dad didn't think that the mindless violence would reach the village. And he was quite right. However, just to be on the safer side, he cut off his hair and trimmed his beard. He also shaved off my hair. My mother was quite distraught over that. Apparently, she used to love my black curls.

"Anyhow, by the time he decided to move back to Amritsar, I was about four-years-old. It was quite difficult for my mother and me to settle down in Amritsar again. It was not easy leaving Beeji and everyone else behind; both of us had lost our hearts to Meharsar. My mother had grown attached to the Meharsar Lake, which, it was popularly believed, had powers to destroy ancestral sins. My grandfather had been an officer in the Indian Army, and during the 1971 war, he had been driven to kill many enemy soldiers. Ma worried that he, a diabetic with high cholesterol, would suffer from the consequences of what he had done in the line of his duty. So every year, when she visited her parents' home, she took along a bottle of water from the lake and carefully sprinkled it in Nanaji's room. Perhaps it was the miraculous water or the sheer force of Ma's faith, but my Nanaji is still hale and hearty, even though . . ." He stopped for a moment, stirring in more sugar than he needed in his tea, before continuing, ". . . from then on, every Sunday, my mother would bundle me into the bus which would take us to Meharsar and climb in after me. We never really bothered about my father, he was unwilling to accompany us most of the time.

"My earliest memory of Mannat is from one of my Sunday visits to the village, possibly the third or the fourth one after we moved back to Amritsar. It's strange how I don't remember anything about her from before . . . but I think even if I knew about her, on this particular visit, she was the last thing on my mind. For a small boy, the thought of his Beeji's *aloo* parathas waiting for him was more appealing than the thought of a little girl who was much tinier than him and who would've hardly made him a worthy playmate. When we arrived at Beeji's house on that cold winter morning, I was unaware of a pair of bright eyes following me from the rooftop of the adjoining house. I didn't know that a little girl, a mere toddler, squirming with excitement, was calling out my name in her soft, broken baby voice, and I didn't realise that she was getting increasingly exasperated with my persistent failure to notice her, given that I was busy being hugged and cosseted by Beeji. I did not know any of this until that little girl, making sure that her *bua*—who was on the terrace with her, spreading out the day's washing to dry—didn't catch her, started pelting me with pebbles she had earlier picked up because they were fascinatingly warm. The first pebble missed its mark, but not the second. The second one hit me right on my head.

"Naturally, I yelled out in pain and then burst into tears. Everyone looked at me, alarmed and surprised. They were wondering why, in the middle of so much love and affection being showered on me, I had started crying so hysterically. No one had seen Mannat throw the pebbles. Only when they looked up and saw her watching the whole scene from her perch at the edge of the terrace railing with a rather scared and guilty look on her cherubic face, did they put two and two together. But who could really stay angry with Mannat? Bua's attempts at admonishing her were brushed aside and shushed. Veerji rubbed my head where the pebble had hit me and said that a man, big or small, takes such things without flinching. I could hardly have taken any offence at being attacked thus, at least not with everyone fussing around me! And during the much-anticipated breakfast, as I sat gobbling one paratha after the other, when Mannat offered her share of the home-made butter as a peace offering, my heart melted faster than the butter . . ." Arpit looked at Nishi with a crooked smile on his face.

Signalling for two more cups of tea, he continued, "After that day, Meharsar was not just about Beeji and her *aloo* parathas anymore. It was about Mannat. I would rush through the week impatiently, waiting for Sunday to arrive. Come Sunday, we'd reach the village early in the morning as usual. I would stuff myself hurriedly with Beeji's parathas and then accompany Ma, Beeji, and Veerji's family to the tiny village gurdwara, chafing at all the time the elders were taking to pay their obeisance there because it was only after this that I would be allowed to do as I pleased for the rest of the day. And it was with Mannat that I would spend the rest of the day. After a couple of months, Veerji decided that it was safe to resume their visits to Harmandir Sahib in Amritsar—they had stopped because of the riots. And so, the pattern of our Sundays changed. Now, every alternate Sunday, everyone from Meharsar would pile into a tractor and reach Amritsar in time for the noon *langar* at Harmandir Sahib. After that, because I knew the temple complex and the surrounding neighbourhood like the back of my hand and because I was the eldest of the lot, I would take Mannat, her brothers, and her cousins around. We'd go running all over the place, watching people, pointing things out, marvelling at new toys in the shops. We'd pool our pocket money for chaat and lassi. I was always richer, in terms of pocket money. I guess my father wanted me to know that he was doing well in life. Sometimes we would buy lollipops if there was money left over from stuffing ourselves. Since I was the eldest, I would take it upon myself to divide the lollipops with exact justice. I would almost always buy five lollipops since there were five of us, but, if I somehow managed to buy six, I would stow away the extra one as a secret gift for Mannat, and I would slip it, furtively and self-consciously, into her hands when she would be leaving for home.

"When she was six-years-old, Mannat's father, Harpal Singh, succeeded in landing a government job in Amritsar. And though his wife and younger children stayed back in the village, he thought that it would be an ideal opportunity for him to provide a worthier education to his daughter. Oh, yes, she *was* a bright little girl! She used to have a ready stock of questions, probably the week's savings, for me when we would meet on Sundays. Perhaps she thought that being one year older made me more intelligent! I struggled to answer them for most were quite beyond me. And even now, there are some questions I wish I had answered at the right time . . . Anyway, Mannat now became the first child in her family to be enrolled in a co-educational school—Little Blossoms Primary School, Amritsar. And my world could not have been better and brighter, for it was the same school which I attended.

"She was in the first standard and I was in the second, but that hardly kept us away from each other. We were together, perpetually—in the same school, sharing our tiffins, playing together during the recess, riding home in the same bus after school, having lunch at my house, having Ma herd us off together for the mandatory afternoon nap, playing and doing homework together in the evening till Mannat's father returned from his office and took her home for the night.

"But in less than a year, my world changed.

"We were going to Kapurthala the next morning; it was a school trip. Dad was away on one of his business trips. Mannat and I were bubbling with excitement, thinking about the boat rides and the picnic lunch which Ma had promised to pack for us. By the time she managed to bundle us off to bed and finish all the house work, it must have been past midnight. She must have been tired beyond belief that night as she lay down in bed . . . she would have sighed with satisfaction and smiled as she drifted off to sleep. But I don't know any of this, Nishi. It is only my imagination I can rely on now. Ma never woke up in the morning. She died that night in her sleep."

Nishi had guessed from the shadow passing over Arpit's eyes that something like this was coming. She reached reflexively for his hand, but Arpit forestalled her and rubbed away at the moisture lurking at the corner of his eyelids. "No one knew she had a heart defect. She probably did not know it herself. As unscientific as this sounds, Nishi, I will forever believe that her heart just burst because of all the love she held inside it."

CHAPTER 6

Though it was only eight in the morning, he had been up for well over four hours now. Waking up before dawn was a habit, one that stubbornly persisted as the years crept up upon him.

"Veerji? Chai . . ."

"Hmm . . . *rakh de puttar* . . ."

He sat here every day, without fail, in an old rattan chair on the terrace of his house with his breakfast laid out on a small table next to him. The only concession to change that he made in his routine was to move his chair under the awning when it rained. But the day was warm and pleasant today. The blistering sun had not scorched the landscape yet. So he sat near the edge of the terrace, looking at the fields stretching out in front of him, reminiscing. As always, he was dressed in a crisp white kurta-pyjama with a white *pagg* tied around his head. Though nearing eighty, he was tall and heavily built, with a thick white beard flowing down his chest, and bushy eyebrows dominating a strong face. He was not bent or gaunt with age, but stood strong and firm, the proud farmer with an unflinching will. There was something to be said about the figure that Joginder Singh Meharsar cut as he sat on his terrace, deep in thought with a worried frown on his face.

He took a deep breath—the delightful, wet smell of uncut

wheat filling up his nostrils—and ran his gaze over his land. No matter how dispirited or disillusioned he felt, the sight of his fields glowing proudly with the fruits of his family's labour never failed to comfort him. But reality was corroding this last comfort too. Every year, the wheat harvest grew smaller. Once known for its sugarcane, the village was now on the verge of abandoning its cultivation altogether. And so many farmers had already left for the city . . .

He knew the reasons, of course. He knew when and how all of this had started. But harbouring regrets and dwelling upon them was not his way of dealing with problems. He could not let himself brood over how Baldev had let him down. Not with there being so many problems still to solve, not with the villagers still clamouring for his advice as they would with an elder brother—which was what 'Veerji', the title the entire village used to refer to him, meant—even though his influence had waned in the last few years. As long as he was alive, he would do his duty and fight with all his might for what he believed in. But just for this one morning, just for today, he would indulge himself by remembering the past . . .

Till as far back as he could remember, the villagers used to come to his father for advice, a mantle Veerji had taken on after him. It seemed almost as if life in Meharsar revolved around their house. But he never allowed this presumptuous belief to linger. It was the lake, the Pool of Blessings, which was the real centre of their lives.

Legend had it that during the bloody days of Partition, Meharsar had remained untouched by all the communal violence. The reason for this was a fakir who had come to the village during those troubled days and set up camp there. The lake had been just a pond then, an ideal afternoon bathing spot for the village buffaloes. The water was slightly brackish and not fit for drinking. But after the arrival of the fakir, the rains fell with such gusto in the region that the water inundated the entire infertile stretch of land to the north of the pond. Within a few days, the lake swelled up, as if by magic, and its water after that was clear, sweet, and pure.

It was said that on that fateful day of Independence when the inhabitants of the village did not know whether to rejoice or weep, they looked at the lake and found seven rainbows dancing off its surface. They considered that an auspicious sign. When they went to look for the fakir, he was nowhere to be found. No one knew who he was or where he had come from. He had maintained a vow of silence from the day of his arrival until his abrupt departure. Finding no clue about the holy man, the villagers named him Bhagat Mehar Baba and the lake, Meharsar—the Pool of Blessings.

Meharsar was saved from the butchery of Partition because of the holy vibrations of Bhagat Mehar Baba. But human aggression does not always manifest itself crudely in violence. It has other insidious ways of destroying people. Instead of cutting off the heads and limbs of human beings, it cuts off their roots, condemning them and their spirit to a slow but sure death . . .

But now his musings were getting morbid. Veerji shook them off to pick up another thread of nostalgia.

They had been the best of friends, Baldev's father and him—living like brothers, their lives intimately interwoven. Their houses stood next to each other, with no wall separating one from the other. They worked together, took decisions together, and the seams separating their families were indistinguishable, nearly non-existent. His son, Harpal, had grown up with Baldev and everyone had fondly expected the two boys to be bosom buddies like their fathers before them. But it was never to be so.

In 1962, when the war with China started, Veerji could not help getting swept away in the patriotic fervour that gripped the nation. He had wanted to fight, but was unable to get a medical clearance and transferred his ambitions onto his young son. Harpal was but six or seven at that time. But as fate would have it, polio struck the child before anything else could. It took him a while to accept the bitter truth about his son. Harpal would not only never join the army, but his studies would also be continuously disrupted from then on and he would never be able to become a farmer like him.

He had shifted his attention towards Baldev then, hoping that his friend's son would fulfil his dream. But the unexpected death of Baldev's father threw all his hopes and dreams awry. Baldev's mother, a simple, uneducated woman, had been struck hard by the untimely death of her husband. There was no way she would ever allow her only son to risk his life on the battlefield. Veerji had smiled stoically and let it be. He vowed, instead, to do all he could for the lad who showed a drive and promise unusual for his age. But a contrary streak in Baldev never quite let him pierce the invisible wall between them.

Baldev was a bright lad. Veerji had realised early on that the village school would not be enough for him. He was probably the first to sense the boy's ambition, for his own relatives were bringing him up in the same complacent manner in which they had brought up their own children—giving them a little bit of education, marrying them at a young age, encouraging them to have children quickly, and tying their lives to the land. One could not really blame them; they knew no other way of life and their children had never resisted their impositions. But in Baldev there was a restless eagerness which bordered on arrogant impatience, and Veerji's watchful eyes had spotted it.

Undoubtedly, Baldev had used his opportunities well. He did brilliantly in school, never fell into any kind of addiction, and won scholarships which made it easier for him to put the boy through college. When Baldev's *tayaji* admitted that he would be unable to finance the boy's education, he had taken up the responsibility without so much as batting an eyelid. Baldev was sent to Chandigarh to do his graduation. After topping his batch, Baldev decided to study agriculture in the university at Ludhiana. Though he himself knew enough only to sign his name and check the farm accounts, that too only with Harpal's assistance, and though he had no idea what Baldev's specialisation in agriculture really meant, a dream was already forming in Veerji's mind.

Meharsar had been fairly self-sufficient in its production of wheat, sugarcane, and maize, but the farmers never seemed to get the best price for their produce. Small cultivators found fertilisers expensive. He hadn't been convinced himself about how these chemicals could permanently sustain productivity. As far as he was concerned, it was like being chronically dependent on medicinal drugs to keep one's body healthy when a good diet and regular exercise would have done the needful. His common sense told him that if they optimised their traditional methods of farming, they would all need to invest less. His own experiments with organic techniques had been successful. But though his neighbours respected him tremendously, they weren't following his example. Only an expert could have convinced them of the stupidity of dependence on chemicals. And who would have been better for this job than their very own Baldev?

After completing his MSc, however, Baldev rejected a fellowship to pursue a Doctorate in the same university and, instead, joined a company based in Mandi, Himachal Pradesh which specialised in extracting and preserving jams and juices from the hill state's abundant fruit orchards. His job was to establish the brand at retail outlets all over Punjab. He married Loveleen, a girl he had met earlier in Chandigarh, and settled down to an ambitious life in the city.

And from his house in Meharsar, Joginder Singh Meharsar had watched it all, a twinge of disappointment clouding his days as Baldev distanced himself from all of them. But he still had full faith in the old ties of friendship and family and he was convinced that they would coax Baldev's wandering feet back to his birthplace.

But Loveleen's death changed everything.

Strangely, it was not the motherless Arpit, but the hitherto rather detached husband who was shattered by Loveleen's unexpected death. He coped with his grief in the only way he knew: by plunging ferociously into work. Luckily for him, the Indian economy had kick-started the process of liberalization. Baldev left his old job to join one of the multinational soft drink corporations setting up their plant in Punjab. Though he stayed on in Amritsar, he clearly wasn't interested in returning to his native village.

The winds of change sweeping the country had stirred up a draught in their lives too. It was only a matter of time before Baldev would shift base to one of the bigger cities. And then what would happen to Beeji, his siblings . . . and to Arpit?

Harpal ruminated, "He blames the lack of medical facilities . . . he thinks that if they had been living in a better city, Loveleen's condition would have been diagnosed early on. But I don't understand, Amritsar is as good as any other city in India when it comes to hospitals. The manner in which it happened was so sudden, no one could have done anything, anyway!"

"*Puttar*, grief does not understand reason," Veerji had replied. "Give him time. He is running away from his own emptiness. He will come back . . ."

But it was another three years before Baldev returned. He came back only to inform his family that he had enrolled Arpit in a boarding school in Shimla, and that he was shifting permanently to Delhi. He asked his mother to move with him to Delhi, but she was far too attached to her sprawling family in Meharsar to think of leaving. Baldev did not insist. Nor did he return to the village.

If this was bad enough, the worst blow was yet to fall.

Two years went by before Baldev unexpectedly returned to Meharsar. He had sent no word prior to coming. So his arrival at his mother's doorstep was not only unexpected, but also a bit of a shock for the poor, frail woman. When the news reached Veerji's house, they had all been ecstatic. Hope had flickered in his heart again. But it all came to nought. Baldev had not come for them.

Verva Cola, the company he had been working for, wanted to establish a new bottling plant in Meharsar. And Baldev had come to make sure that it happened.

Verva Cola had been shrouded in controversy ever since it had set up operations in India, thanks to the dubious credentials of its Indian collaborators. But even back in the USA, where its headquarters were located, the multinational had been under fire for an unhealthy concentration of sugar and caffeine in its drinks. It had also been facing allegations of traces of alcohol being present in its products. The Meharsar plant would have been their first one in Punjab, and even though the government was on their side, the *swadeshi* lobbies had proven to be quite a handful. Local protests and resistance were the last thing the company needed. And this was where Baldev had stepped in. Loveleen's death had accelerated the process of Baldev's detachment from Meharsar. The village was no longer his home, it was a commercial resource and he had to facilitate its exploitation.

Veerji wondered, in retrospect, how he had failed to see that the Baldev who had come to meet him five years after Loveleen's death had changed beyond recognition. The boy had played brilliantly on old loyalties to get what he had come for: his sanction—Joginder Singh Mehsar's sanction . . . Veerji's sanction—for without it, the plant would never function smoothly. He had to give but one call and all of Meharsar would rally around him, ready to oppose the plant. Baldev had known all this and had played the game accordingly.

With smooth, polished charm and a practised deference, he had presented his arguments in favour of setting up the plant: the village youth, especially those whose families owned small agricultural plots, would get employment; with all the additional income that would come pouring into the village, there would be no need for this desperation of branding the land livid with chemicals to extract the maximum possible yield; investors would flock to build up infrastructure not just for the village, but for the entire block. The mathematical list of reasons had gone on . . . one imagined benefit spiralling into another. But Baldev had saved his winning card for the end, and with a sweeping, triumphant flourish he had laid it out on the table. "Veerji," Baldev had said, looking at him with what he had imagined was excitement and a rekindled love for Meharsar, but what must have been a realisation that he had won the game, "my company will set up an agricultural research centre for Meharsar and the neighbouring villages. It will sponsor research that will ultimately help you all add science to the love you already have for your land . . ."

He had suppressed the warnings of his inner voice and given his approval for the project. It was a decision he would regret for the rest of his life.

There did not seem to be anything wrong at first. The plant had been built and made operational much faster than any rural development scheme of the government had ever materialised. The foundation stone of the agricultural research centre had also been laid with much fanfare.

But after two years, he slowly began to perceive that the gilded-and-tinselled promises of Verva Cola had been mere lip service. He had wanted to speak to Baldev about it, but where was he? The day the plant started operations, Baldev had sped back to Delhi and not bothered to return.

It was after this that he had started noticing that there were fewer and fewer people who were actually tilling the land. With their financial anxieties taken care of, he had expected the people to return to the restful wonder of coaxing harvests naturally from the soil. But that had not happened. The wages from the factory, actually a fraction of what Verva would have been compelled to pay as the basic wage in most other countries, had not remained a buffering supplement to his people's primary income. They had come to rely wholly on those wages because they came quicker and easier. The company had also offered overtime benefits and free samples to them, and many had been promised transfers to the company's city offices in due course. Legally or ethically, he could not blame Verva for this. But neither had he been able to shake off that niggling feeling that all along, Baldev had known exactly what would happen.

The final jolt came one morning when he was dipping his hands into the waters of the holy lake; it was a part of his daily rituals. He felt blessed to cup the clear water in his hands and watch the sun sparkling in it, before feeling its comforting coolness trickle down his throat. But that morning, something had not quite been the same. There had been a queer malevolent glint in the water. It had stung his palm. Perplexed, he had held it close to his nose. The chemical smell was unmistakable. The water was no longer pure.

How could this happen? He had immediately summoned Harpal, who shook his head sadly, as if he had been expecting it for some time. "It's from that factory."

"But . . . but how?!" he had cried out, aghast.

He remembered now how shaken Harpal had looked, never having seen his father so upset. His voice had trembled just a bit as he ventured an explanation, "They are probably not disposing off their waste properly. If it's piling up on the surrounding land, a lot of it must be mixing with the rainwater and flowing off into the fields, contaminating the ground water. And from there, it's slowly seeping into the lake. All the poison from the factory is destroying our lake, Veerji."

"But the factory is miles away from our lake!"

But it was feigned ignorance . . . his last, futile attempt at shying away from the dreadful truth which he had so long avoided acknowledging. The unthinkable was happening, and he could no longer sit quietly and watch his Pool of Blessings be poisoned before his eyes.

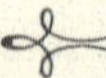

It didn't take him long to gather a band of loyal villagers around him. Some of them, admittedly, did not share his view that the factory had turned out to be the biggest threat to Meharsar's dignity and integrity. But when it came to the lake, they all unanimously agreed—no one could be allowed to pollute it.

First, they had sent a delegation to the District Collector. He had been sympathetic, but claimed that the matter was not in his hands. "The factory does not pose any threat to the law and order of this district, nor have there been any disputes between the workers and management. As for the pollution of the lake, you can't say with absolute certainty that it's happening because of the factory. Maybe the chemicals you are spraying in your own fields are draining into the lake?"

"But our village uses the smallest amount of fertilisers and pesticides in this district!" Veerji had protested, "And lately, we have been trying to get rid of those, too. Besides, it can't be mere coincidence that all this started after the factory was set up."

"Listen, I don't make this country's laws," the Collector had snapped. "Do you have any idea how many higher-ups gave their approval for the Verva Cola project? If you have a problem with the plant, go talk to the Chief Minister about it. There's nothing I can do."

He had been inclined to take the Collector's sarcastic suggestion literally, but Harpal had intervened, "It's no use. All of them stand to profit from this factory in some way or the other, Veerji. Even our youngsters, our own people . . . I am not so sure they will support us if we take this matter any further."

It was the day after they had met the Collector. Both of them were standing on the terrace, looking wistfully at the land stretching out in front of them. He had thought that the land looked tired, as if the desire to fight and live had somehow gone out of it, as if it was sagging under the weight of disappointments.

No, he had argued with Harpal, no matter how tempting life at the factory was, the people of Meharsar would never embrace it at the cost of their village. It simply wasn't possible. He would call them and ask them to resign en masse from the plant. He had vehemently brushed aside all of his son's arguments. It was simply not in the weave of his nature to give up so easily.

He knew that though legal action against the company was the only course open to them, it would take several years and a lot of money before they could hope for a judgment, a favourable one at that, and by then there would be nothing left of the lake to save. He decided therefore, to first go and confront the man responsible for all this, the man who had betrayed the trust of his native village—Baldev.

But Baldev's mother begged him to not go. "There must be some misunderstanding! My boy would sooner die than let any blight come upon the Holy Lake. When Arpit comes here during his vacation, Baldev will surely accompany him. Talk to him then."

He had given in to her, telling himself that he was only honouring her maternal instinct to protect her son from his wrath for the sake of his dead friend. But he knew better now. It hadn't really been Baldev whom she had tried to protect. She had been trying to protect *him* from her own son, for she did not know how Baldev would react when confronted on his own territory.

He had busied himself in trying to mobilise the panchayat towards his cause. The panchayat agreed with him in principle, but they were very pessimistic about their chances. There was no doubt that many local officials were hand in glove with the company's agencies, otherwise, how could they have missed the hillocks of waste that had been piling up right next to the highway all these months? Moreover, these multinational companies could easily tilt public opinion in their favour with well-designed media campaigns. And for people who were enamoured with the idea of holding an internationally popular drink in their hands, the contamination of one small lake in a nondescript village in India was of no consequence.

Nevertheless, inspired by his conviction, they had all agreed to make a concerted effort to save the lake. They would write to several ministries and departments of the Central Government, calling their attention to the many-pronged threats this issue posed. If not the ethics, then at least the economics of the damage might appeal to them.

And if nothing worked, he had his Plan B all ready—shut the factory by force, or die fighting.

CHAPTER 7

The lunch break in the dhaba, meant to last half an hour, had stretched on for much longer than that. When they had finished the meal, Arpit and Nishi ordered two rounds of tea to draw out their conversation, but the proprietor had started hovering impatiently around their table. At first, Arpit had shot him resentful glances. "What's the meaning of hanging around us like this? Can't we have a decent conversation in this place? We have paid for our meal! We have a right to sit here for as long as we want."

"Arpit, this is not a coffee shop. Look around, there are only eight tables here. We are holding up other customers."

He looked abashed at that, nodding silently at the proprietor as he pushed back his chair to indicate that they were done. Nishi echoed his silence as he cleared the bill and they got into the car, and for the rest of the journey, the conversation was rather stilted.

It was around six in the evening when Arpit spoke, "Nishi, I don't think we are going to reach Patiala before nightfall. It won't be possible for you to start your work today. Would you mind if we stopped at Chandigarh for the night? My house is not a bad place to stay; that is, if you trust me enough to stay with me . . ."

"I think life has taught me well about whom to trust and whom not to, Arpit," Nishi smiled. "I would love to stay there."

"Do you like the house? This was where my mother was born and brought up," Arpit asked Nishi as he reverently touched a framed photograph hanging on the dining room wall. "This is her. Isn't she beautiful?"

"Lovely Loveleen," murmured Nishi. "And where are your grandparents now?"

"*Nana Nani*? In Australia, with my *mamaji*. They migrated four years ago. My maasi is in Shimla though. Poor lady, she tries to keep an eye on me, but I am too elusive. For weeks together I don't tell her my whereabouts."

"And has all this running led you anywhere?"

"I am too hungry for your metaphysical inquiries, Nishi. Let me go to the kitchen to see what I can whip up."

Half an hour later, he re-entered the living room with a thick volume in his hands. "Just look at what I have here!"

Nishi looked up from the old magazine she had been riffling through and exclaimed in delight. "An old photo album!"

"Yes! With black and white photographs to boot. This belonged to my mother. It has all my childhood pictures."

They pored over pictures of him as an infant and a toddler, chubby, curly-haired, eyes sparkling with mischief. He pointed out the people in the photographs to her—his parents, Beeji, Veerji, Harpal, and the rest of his extended family in Meharsar—before stopping at a page towards the end of the album and saying, "And this . . . this is Mannat."

It was a small photograph of a pre-teen girl, clad in a knee-length checked frock which had clearly been let out many times. Her hair was neatly tied back in two tight plaits with red ribbons. Even in the photograph, her eyes were alive and her smile had the sweetness of half-a-dozen candies devoured on a lazy afternoon. She was not pretty, not how one would imagine a pretty young girl to be, and definitely not with her bushy eyebrows and plump figure. But there was a languidness and warmth radiating from her that was hard to resist.

"What a darling!" Nishi crooned. "But don't you have any recent pictures of her?"

"No. I don't have a single one."

"Why not?"

"Looking at them would have been too painful. She grew up to be such a beauty!"

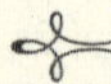

"Are you sleepy?"

"No . . . not really. Why?"

"Well, you could continue with your story, if you feel up to it, that is . . ."

Having finished their slapdash dinner a little while ago, Nishi and Arpit were still sitting at the dining table and dawdling. They were tired, but not sleepy. And though Arpit had mostly been reticent, Nishi decided there was nothing to lose if she asked him at least once about continuing with his story.

"You want to kill time before sleep descends, huh?" Arpit asked, a reluctant smile tugging at the corners of his mouth. When she smiled and didn't say anything, he chuckled. "Well, to pick up from where I had left off, things changed after Ma died. After her death, Beeji, Veerji, Mannat, and everyone else from Meharsar were constantly around us, trying to push us into a protective orbit of love and sympathy. And while I was able to accept all of it, my father was not. He spurned all their overtures and plunged himself ferociously into work. He had never been one for any display of affection. But after Ma's death, he seemed to be in a perpetual hurry to reach somewhere . . .

"He quit his job with the company he had been working for and joined a multinational corporation that made soft drinks. His work now required him to travel for long hours, but he made sure he was home every night to supervise my education with mechanical precision. He engaged an ayah to look after me in the afternoons after I came back from school. He had also toyed with the idea of hiring a private tutor for me, but he was unable to find one in Amritsar who matched his exacting standards. I think that strengthened his resolve to pack me off to that boarding school in Shimla. That, and his growing concern about my increasing attachment to Mannat and her family. He had big plans for me, and it was easy to sense that he wanted me to rise above the supposedly disdainful and abhorrent environment I had been born and brought up in. He even made me call him 'Dad' instead of *baoji* . . ."

Arpit fell silent abruptly and Nishi instinctively understood that here was one more task before her—helping him solve the puzzle of how his feelings of disappointed awe towards a man who had seen him only as an investment could have proved to be a stronger influence on him than the deepest, purest, and most fervent attachment of his life.

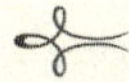

To Arpit's disappointment, no one in Meharsar, not even Beeji, supported his desire to stay back. Even if they felt a stab of apprehension, they refused to listen to his pleas. Baldev's decision was for the good of the boy's future, after all, they consoled themselves.

"You will start liking it, *puttar*," Harpal spoke soothingly one evening when Arpit had been particularly upset, "Especially when they teach you English. I know you are learning it here too, but these *firangi* schools give you an accent like you were born in England."

"But they will starve him, I am sure," put in Sukhmani in a voice loud enough for only Harpal to hear as she set a cup of tea for him down on the table. "He has so little flesh on his bones as it is."

"Oh no, no," Harpal waved his hand dismissively. "They have a doctor who comes to check every boy every single week; they serve eggs and milk at breakfast, and milk again at night without fail. Besides, he will play so many sports there. They will build up his body."

For a moment, Arpit saw himself as a strapping young man with rippling muscles. The image was too captivating to shake off. The next minute, his father strode into the room with a stack of glossy papers in his hand. It was the school prospectus. Handing it to him, his father exclaimed, "Just look at this, son! Have you ever seen such a beautiful school building anywhere? And such grounds! Playing fields, the auditorium! And look, this is the computer lab! They have the very latest of computers, and one for each boy."

Arpit's school in Amritsar had a makeshift computer lab with outdated machines which took excruciatingly long to start up, and there were never enough systems for the entire class, so they had to sit two, sometimes three boys to a desktop. His father's words made him feel, for the first time, that going to this school might be worthwhile. Of course he would miss Beeji and Veerji and Mannat very much . . . but wait, what was Harpal Chayaji saying to his father?

"Baldev, I am so happy that Arpit is going to this school! Mark my words, one day he will make us all proud," effused Harpal.

Baldev smiled, facetiously gracious.

"I was thinking . . ." Harpal began, only to stop awkwardly and flounder as Baldev raised an eyebrow questioningly.

"When you told me about Arpit's school, I started thinking . . . it's decent enough here in Amritsar, but children today need to be really up-to-date with their English and computer skills. It's not like the old days anymore when we could tutor them. I haven't even heard of half their subjects!" he chuckled.

Arpit could sense his father's contemptuous patience. It made him uncomfortable. He wanted Harpal Chayaji to stop before he got hurt. Then he wondered why he was feeling so nervous. Chayaji and Dad were old friends, after all.

". . . and so, I thought, Manjot is so intelligent. This year she has got a double promotion. Now she will be in the same class as Arpit . . . I should send her to a better place, too. I have collected the details of a girls' school in Shimla. It's like the *angrezi* school you are sending Arpit to. I would never have thought about all this on my own. You know Manjot's mother and Veerji would never let her go alone to a new place. But if Arpit is there, and you are keeping an eye on them—"

"Harpal," Baldev interrupted with smooth condescension, "it's not as simple as you think. The fee of such schools alone is much higher than what you are paying here. And with your income . . ."

"I know, I know," admitted Harpal, a trifle embarrassed, "it's going to be a strain on our resources, but I will manage somehow. The crop has been good this year. We will be able to save a good sum. And a little sacrifice will be worth our Manjot's bright future."

"When an older child gets a privilege, the younger ones expect it too. How will you explain this to Manjot's brothers? Or are you planning to send them to boarding school as well?" Only

Arpit detected the faint sneer in his father's voice. "That's why we had only one child. I can invest everything in him without worrying about how I will manage for the others."

"Oh, Gurpal and Harjeet are very happy looking after the fields!" laughed Harpal. "But Manjot is very bright; you know that, Baldev. She comes first in her class. I owe it to her. You don't worry about the finances. Just do me one favour: please talk to *bharjaiji*'s sister in Shimla and ask her if she can be Manjot's local guardian. The rest I will manage."

Arpit's *maasi*—Loveleen's sister—had a summer home in Shimla. She would be his local guardian.

At Harpal's words, Arpit's face started tingling with expectation. He knew his maasi would be only too happy to look after Mannat as well. It was too good to be true! Mannat in Shimla, with him! This changed everything. Now he was dying to go.

But Baldev's words cut sharply and cleanly through his reverie.

"I don't think it is a practical idea, Harpal. Arpit's maasi is busy enough as it is. She has only agreed to be his local guardian out of family loyalty."

"But . . . if you requested . . ."

"It's no use. She is very clear about what she must do for her family, but I'm afraid she won't show the same generosity for anyone else."

Arpit was close enough to see that first crack of disillusionment in Harpal's eyes. In that instant, the relationship between the two men changed forever, and a bewildered teenager was the only witness to it. He felt a wave of cold, helpless rage towards his father. It was a feeling that would return many times in the succeeding years, but at that moment, it was alien to him. He knew he should run to Beeji and tell her what had just happened. Despite her waning influence over her son, she did have the power to force him to humour Harpal's request. Or should he tell Veerji? Or better still, why not sneak off to the nearest public telephone booth and ask his maasi straightaway whether she could take in Mannat or not? Once she gave her consent, which he was sure she would, he could simply come back and announce it before everyone as a fait accompli. His dad wouldn't be able to refuse *then.*

But he would be offended. Very, very offended. He might even cancel his plan to send him to Shimla. Well, that was what Arpit wanted, didn't he?

Then his eyes fell on the glossy pictures on the school prospectus—the majestic school building, the green playing fields, and the magic world of the computer lab. And that smart dark green and grey uniform with an actual school blazer and black shoes gleaming to perfection, so unlike the scruffy navy blue sweater and unpolished shoes which no one bothered to check at his day school. Not going would mean losing all these.

Arpit decided to stay silent.

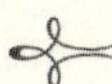

In the beginning, Arpit hated boarding school. It didn't take him long to perceive that his day school in Amritsar had not prepared him for the subtle class politics of these boys. There were snickering jokes about 'armpits' and imitations of his provincial accent. Though being labelled a country bumpkin had been Baldev's lifelong phobia, it was his son who experienced the materialisation of these fears.

No wonder, then, that when vacations came, Arpit rushed to Meharsar—to his grandmother, uncles and aunts and cousins, and to Mannat and Veerji—despite his father's all-too-obvious disapproval. He wanted the boy to spend his holidays with him in Delhi, not so much out of paternal affection as out of a desire to introduce Arpit to his smart new friends and their children who spoke English as if it was the only language they had ever known. Never mind, he consoled himself, the next vacations were not too far away. Baldev trusted that by then, Arpit would be sufficiently 'schooled', in more ways than one, to be struck by the difference between his classmates and his childhood companions. A few years at the school would be enough to make Arpit forget that doddering Veerji and his entire self-satisfied clan.

It took Arpit nearly three years to be able to spend another vacation in Meharsar. By this time, he was quite reconciled to going to Delhi and had started enjoying the gentry which his dad introduced him to, so like his friends in school. He still thought of Veerji and Harpal and Sukhmani and his relatives with affection, but he had to admit that life in Meharsar was rather dull compared to Delhi. Still, he had been getting worrying news about his grandmother—she was getting old and weak, pining away for her son and grandson. This one time he must go and meet her.

As soon as he made up his mind, the spicy fragrance of the fields in the morning drifted up to him as if he was already back in his village. With that scent floated an image before his mind's eye—a plump, sparkling, laughing face with naïvely inquiring eyes. Even as he had been conscientiously planning to see his grandmother, there surely had been another incentive to visit Meharsar . . .

Arpit had recently 'acquired' his first girlfriend. At the age of sixteen, being without one would have made him the laughing stock of his house. And the girl was pretty enough to make his friends wildly jealous of his luck, so he was very well satisfied with himself.

Then the holidays came. And Arpit was seized with curiosity about how Mannat would take this news. He meant to embellish the little details of his relationship, of course, and watch her reaction. It would be so much fun to shock her traditional sensibilities. Yes, that was all he wanted—a little fun at his playmate's expense. Nothing else.

Nostalgia engulfed him as he reached Meharsar. The distinctive odour of mustard oil coming from the kitchen reminded him of innumerable childhood snacks. The clothes drying on the roof seemed to be flapping a welcome just the way they used to during his visits with Loveleen from Amritsar, though their patterns had changed with fashion. School, friends, even girlfriend, all seemed to have faded into crumbling paper mansions. "How did I manage to stay away so long?" he found himself asking.

Though Arpit could no longer carry on a coherent conversation with his nearly-deaf grandmother, she did not need to hear his words of greeting. The moment she saw him, she pulled him into her embrace and wept. Perhaps Arpit put on temporary deafness too, for when she asked, squinting eagerly into the twilight, "Where is Baldev?" Arpit pretended not to hear her. She did not ask a second time.

He was disappointed to know that Mannat was not in the village. Their holidays did not coincide. Never mind, Amritsar was barely an hour away. He would catch the first bus tomorrow and surprise her before she left for school. But he overslept and reached Amritsar half an hour after Mannat had left for school. Sukhmani tried to make up for her absence by pampering Arpit with steaming hot parathas and flavoured tea, exactly as he used to devour on his weekend trips to Meharsar in childhood.

Harpal greeted him with customary warmth, but Arpit's eyes did not miss the slight reserve that had seeped into his manner.

After Arpit finished breakfast, Harpal asked gravely, "Did you meet Veerji before coming here?"

"No," he flushed guiltily. "I thought I would meet you all first. I am going back to Meharsar, anyway, for the rest of my vacation. Is Veerji's health okay?"

"Fit as ever. But he wanted to discuss something with your father. I was expecting Baldev to accompany you this time."

"He is . . . a bit busy with . . ."

Harpal cut him off, sparing him the necessity of making up a lame excuse. "Never mind, you don't need to bother about it. How are your studies going?"

While Arpit gave Harpal and Sukhmani a glowing picture of his academic achievements, his mind was grappling with the uneasy conviction that something was bothering Veerji in Meharsar. He resolved to ask Mannat about it the moment she came home.

But he did not have to ask Mannat about it. She told him everything before they had spent ten minutes together.

"Have you been to the lake?" she demanded.

"The lake? No, not yet," he replied, confused. His mind was preoccupied with looking for an opportunity to tell her about his girlfriend. "What happened to it?"

"It's dying."

"Dying? How can a lake *die*?"

"The waste from the cola plant is polluting the water. Veerji is terribly upset. No one is ready to listen either, not even the local leaders. Arpit," she gazed earnestly into his eyes, "you will speak to Baldev Chayaji about it, won't you? He was the one who brought the proposal here; if he comes to know what they are doing, he will surely make it stop."

"But Mannat, how can I . . ."

"You are his son. He will listen to you."

Though Arpit knew better, he nodded. There were tears standing in her eyes, clear and beautiful like a miniature lake. He stared at them in fascination. His fingers tingled with a strange desire to plunge into that sea, to caress the wetness of her cheeks. Then he remembered his girlfriend. "Mannat," he exclaimed gleefully, "guess what!"

"What?"

"I have a girlfriend!"

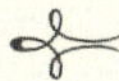

"Girlfriend?! How did she take it?" Even Nishi appeared a trifle excited at this point.

Arpit shook his head wryly. "Very casually. I think she wasn't even paying attention, she was so preoccupied with the lake. It annoyed me, I tell you!"

"So did you speak to your father?"

"No. I knew it wasn't any use talking to him directly. The only thing I could do was to call him to Meharsar somehow, so that Veerji and Beeji could talk to him. In Meharsar, there would have been enough pressure on him to force him into looking at the issue, and he wouldn't have ever snubbed Veerji so openly in Meharsar."

". . . but he didn't come and Veerji went to Delhi after him, and was humiliated?" Nishi asked, guessing the rest of the story.

Arpit pulled out a paper napkin from its holder and crumpled it up miserably. "I don't know exactly what happened. I had returned to school. But from what Mannat told me later, Veerji came back extremely dejected. The panchayat members, meanwhile, had appealed to a couple of ministers who had agreed to 'look into the matter'. They realised the need to do something drastic. So, they passed an order banning the village youth from working in the factory till the toxic waste problem was properly handled."

"And did the youngsters agree?"

"They were reluctant, but they respected their elders too much to protest openly. The panchayat's act shook up the factory managers. They were almost completely dependent on our village for workforce. There wasn't much they could do, except agree to our demands. They promised to clean up the pollution, and for a while they did honour their promise."

"For a while?"

"This is India, Nishi. We have been brought up on legacy of broken promises. You have enough experience."

"And do you have enough experience . . . in breaking promises?"

"Yes!" Arpit snarled. "I did not do as Mannat had asked me to. I didn't speak to my Dad about the factory issue. She forgave me for it because she thought I had tried and failed, but that was far from the truth. I had one trump card which I could have used to pull Dad to Meharsar. I could have refused to go back to school unless he came down to Meharsar and picked me up. And he would have come because he couldn't have afforded my missing all the extra classes and the coaching sessions that were to start in the school right after the vacations for all those aspiring to study in Delhi after the class XII boards. But I didn't do anything of the sort."

"Why not, Arpit?"

"Because I was too afraid of his anger. Because I didn't want to jeopardise my chances of getting into a famous college. And because I wanted to get back at Mannat for not being interested in the fact that I was dating someone."

"Oh, Arpit!" Nishi shook her head disappointedly. "And what happened to your girlfriend?"

"We broke off the day after I went back to school."

"You broke off?"

"She had given me a long shopping list for Delhi. Since I spent my entire vacation in Meharsar, I couldn't get her a thing. That led to a fight which broke us up. I didn't regret it, Nishi. What was the use of having a girlfriend if she didn't succeed in making Mannat jealous?"

Nishi shook her head ruefully.

"Anyway, do you want some coffee? I saw a couple of sachets in the kitchen earlier . . ." Arpit asked, changing the topic. It was easier said than done, this 'telling' of his story. He had given his past a shape and form and brought it alive between him and Nishi. And now it stood glowering disapprovingly at him.

"All right. I guess I could use a cup."

"I'll be right back then."

She let him escape, knowing that he would then claim to be too sleepy to continue. Perhaps it was just as well.

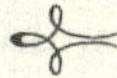

Arpit and Mannat did brilliantly in their school-leaving exams. Mannat had already decided what she wanted to do next. She wanted to become a nutritionist and had therefore filled up forms for colleges in Chandigarh offering Home Science Honours. No one in her family, however, knew exactly what that meant. She confided in Arpit when he came home that summer, gung-ho because the announcement of the cut-off list was days away and he was confident of getting into the college of his choice.

"Fantastic!" he laughed out aloud when she told him about her plan. "So you will be advising fat people about how to lose weight without exercising, and telling busy mothers how to feed their brats who don't finish their vegetables? Hmm, come to think of it" —sobering down— "it pays really well in Delhi and the big cities. You will have it made!"

"I don't intend to counsel city people. I will come back to Meharsar after completing my studies and do research on the best diet for expectant mothers. Even in our state, village women are often malnourished. I want to change that."

"You are idealistic, Mannat," he muttered, staring at her with a mixture of admiration and bemusement. "But well, good for you! As for me, I am all set to study Information Technology in one of the best colleges of Delhi, of the country, in fact."

"Good for you," she echoed his words, "You have been fascinated with computers ever since Chayaji brought you that prospectus showing the computer lab, haven't you?"

If Arpit had been honest with himself, he would have admitted that he had opted for this course because most of his classmates were moving heaven and earth to enroll in it and because Baldev felt it was the in thing and the new breed of emerging techies would be the nawabs of the new millennium. But he did not admit any of this before Mannat. She had the discomfiting habit of stripping his mind down to its bare bones.

Mannat, however, was preoccupied with something else. "Arpit," she began awkwardly, "there was something I wanted to ask you, request you for, in fact."

"*Request?* Turning formal, are we?"

"You might think I am asking for too much."

He leaned towards her, hopeful mischief in his eyes. "What on earth are you after, Mannat?"

"I don't want you to go to Delhi. Take admission in Chandigarh and stay close to us," she blurted.

Arpit spluttered with indignation, "I am not crazy enough to give up my seat in . . ." before stopping suddenly. "Do you really want me to?"

Perhaps he had been hoping for her gaze to falter as it met his. Perhaps he wanted her to blush and play with the lone silver ring on her hand. But when she did not do either of the things, his throat tightened. "You were right. I think you are asking for too much, and that too without any logic. I have my whole future in front of me. And I can't chuck it all aside for anyone's whim."

"It's not that . . ." But she wavered irresolutely. How could she tell him about what she had overheard her parents discussing in muted tones in their bedroom?

"Beeji is getting worse. She can't last much longer," Harpal had murmured despairingly.

"Don't say that!" Sukhmani stifled a sob. "She isn't old enough to go yet. And she was fine till . . . till Loveleen . . ."

"Everything started going wrong since then, didn't it?" Harpal sighed heavily. "Beeji has been losing little pieces of her heart. First bharjaiji, but that was the decree of Fate and no one could prevent it . . . But when your own son and grandson—"

"It's not Arpit's fault. Baldev Praaji should be more thoughtful about what Beeji needs at this age. True, all her other children are here, but . . ."

"You know the real reason. Beeji can't get over the shock of her son being responsible for this state of the lake. I am a bit afraid of how this might influence Beeji if anything happens," Sukhmani whispered.

"Exactly. The best of families can crumble over property disputes."

"Do you really think so?"

"If Beeji takes an unexpected decision, Baldev will not understand the whys and hows. He might do something rash. And no one will be able to handle the consequences." Harpal could not mask his bitterness any longer.

"I don't think Praaji can be expected to return, but Arpit can, and should. Only the grandson can soften the disappointed mother's heart."

Mannat could not deny the truth of what she had overheard. The Beeji who used to sing to herself as she plaited her hair and who waddled amiably around the house for the sheer delight of admonishing her grandchildren and chasing after them, was now shrivelled like a dried mango kernel. Her abilities were also waning. If her son's detachment engulfed Arpit too, then there would be no hope of a reconciliation. Arpit, therefore, must remain near Beeji. Chandigarh was close enough to Meharsar for him to drive down every weekend. She would make sure he did. Being in the same city would give her the advantage of keeping an eye on him.

She also realised that the farther Arpit stayed from Baldev, the better. The rush of delight as she played with this idea wasn't altogether related to Beeji, however.

As he stared at her irresolute face, Arpit experienced a sudden urge to forsake all the glorious plans that had been laid out for him, and plant himself somewhere near her. It would be just like the old days. But before he could make up his mind, he was shaking his head as if on auto-pilot and saying, "Not possible, Mannat. People are bribing left, right, and centre to get the seat I am aiming for. But I stand a real chance of getting it on merit! It is just too valuable to give up!"

Something snapped inside Mannat then, and she knew that she would never forgive Arpit easily for this.

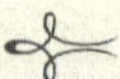

"Oh . . ." Nishi looked at Arpit listlessly drumming his fingers on the table. Perhaps it was enough for one day. He could finish the rest of his story later. "So, umm . . . what time do we start tomorrow morning?" she enquired with deliberate casualness.

"There is no hurry. You can get up at leisure; we've been up till late tonight. And Patiala is just about an hour and a half away."

"But I want to reach as early as possible. It's important for me to see the house in natural light."

"Come, then, I'll show you to your room." Arpit led Nishi upstairs to a cosy bedroom, slightly dusty but otherwise neat and daintily furnished. "Sorry, it's probably not as tidy as you might like. I do have a caretaker who dusts the house every two or three days, but I never allow him to enter this room."

"Why? Is it because Mannat used to stay in this room when she visited your relatives?"

He started. "That's true, though she didn't come here too often. She preferred to spend her weekends either in the hostel with her friends or with her parents if she had a long weekend. But how did you know?" He looked at Nishi accusingly, as if she had stepped on a secret before it got a chance to play hide-and-seek.

"I am Nishimaya the Prophetess, isn't it?" she asked with mock gravity.

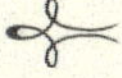

It happened exactly as Nishi had expected. As soon as sleep pulled its silvery mantle over her, scenes from the past rose up like obedient ghosts.

She was sitting on the bed—the girl from the photograph. The lines of her face had grown softer, shaped by the delicate sparring of girlhood and womanhood. Her hair was long and lustrous, no longer confined in two tight plaits held back by red ribbons, and her eyes, alive and sparkling, glinted not with mischief but with a dark, secretive longing. The languidness and the warmth had remained, as had the waiting dazzle of her smile. It was a captivating face now, but if she hadn't paid such close attention to the photograph earlier, Nishi would never have recognised Mannat now. It was as if she was looking at the girl through the lens of a camera. The whole room appeared just a bit distant, just a bit removed from her. There was a strange grey light enveloping the room and casting a long, wistful shadow over everything in it. And as she ran her eyes around the room, taking in the details and the changes in the scene, Nishi felt her own consciousness begin to seep into Mannat's. In the next instant, she felt in her own chest the impatient tapping of Mannat's heart as she tried to absorb herself in the book in front of her while a hundred distracting thoughts went marauding inside her head.

Someone knocked on the door just then, and before Mannat could ask who it was, the door flew open as if the person behind it could not bother to wait.

Arpit sauntered in. Tall and lanky, with his hair falling over his forehead, he looked like a typical college graduate. Flopping down next to her on the bed, he demanded, "Why didn't you come downstairs to meet me? I drove all the way from Delhi just to—"

"To show off your new bike?"

"Oh-ho! That means you saw it from the window!" Arpit grinned roguishly. "Were you watching me when I arrived?"

She felt the heat rising to her cheeks. "I just *happened* to be looking out of the window while trying to recall my list of kitchen dyes! Unlike you, I still have to give my final practical exams. Everyone except us is done with their courses, but the University is still dilly-dallying with our dates. It's so frustrating!

I can't go back home and I can't stay in the hostel beyond the end of this month unless I want to pay the rent for the whole of June."

"So who is telling you to stay in that stupid hostel? Shift here till your exams are finished. And stop poring over these files for now!"

"Arpit—"

"Shh!" Ignoring her protest, Arpit pulled the book from her hands and tossed it aside. "Mannat, I am leaving for Sydney next week. Dad has been promising me this holiday for a year now. But once I come back, it will be admission time again and I don't think studying for an MBA will leave me much time for fun. We only have this weekend, so let's make the most of it. Tomorrow, we go to Kasauli!"

Nishi could feel Mannat's heartbeat quickening painfully. "No. What will your nana nani say? You have one weekend with them and you want to use up one entire day from that to take me out? Besides, it doesn't look good."

"What doesn't look good?" he scowled endearingly.

"My going alone with you."

"Oh, stop being so coy, Mannat. They will have no problem at all. And do you really think anyone else in this city will give a damn if they see us together?"

"Well, I . . . I don't care much for Kasauli. I've been there too many times with my friends. It's inevitable after living here for three years. But of course, coming from Delhi, you must be excited to see it."

"I get it. You still haven't forgiven me for not staying here with you, have you? Mannat, that was THREE years ago, dammit! We have met a hundred times since then. Don't tell me you are still holding on to that!"

"I shouldn't, should I? You are right, it's been three years.

Three years that you have taken away from the time I wanted to spend with . . ."

He stared at her, first in confusion, then in wonder, and then in understanding. She could feel his ardent gaze on her skin. Her heart seemed to be riding a great crimson wave of disbelieving ecstasy. And then she heard herself murmur, "I will come with you."

He smiled crookedly then and squeezed her shoulder lightly before whispering, "Good night, Mannat. And sweet dreams."

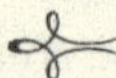

The route to Kasauli turned out to be hot and dusty and Mannat had to wrap her scarf over her face and arms. They stopped once for an apple juice break by the roadside, where Mannat shrugged off her scarf, exclaiming, "Ugh, how hot it is getting!"

Four young men in an open jeep whizzed stridently past them just then, yelling something at her in robust Punjabi.

Arpit bristled. "What were they saying?" he growled.

"You should know! Have you forgotten your Punjabi in three years?"

"Hell-oo! My ears can still tell Abohar from Amritsar! Those chaps were from Jalandhar."

"You saw the registration number on the jeep."

"Well, I still deserve some credit for recognising that. But what were they saying?"

"That I have hair like a snake charmer's rope." She blushed involuntarily.

His eyes automatically strayed to her long hair. She had not braided them today, a concession to the outing, perhaps. Cascading over her shoulders and reaching down to her waist, her hair was like a snake charmer's rope indeed—thick, wavy, and alluring. He had never noticed it before and it angered him now that those boys had noticed it before he did.

Mannt saw his eyes smoulder with resentment. "What's bothering you, Arpit? The fact that they complimented me?" She stared at him perplexedly. He was sucking the last of his apple juice loudly and was pointedly ignoring her question. "Forget it, Arpit. I'm just thankful they didn't return and create a ruckus. Let's just be on our way now…"

Arpit was silent till they reached the Lower Mall which was much more crowded than he had expected. "Shit, I didn't realise that half of Chandigarh would be here today!"

"It's almost always like this on weekends."

"You should have told me. After all your claims to have been here a dozen times…"

"What's wrong with you today? You are picking fights for no reason at all!"

Arpit stopped the bike. "Get down," he said gruffly. "We have reached the Church."

"You can go alone. My being with you will only make you feel crowded."

Without saying a word, Arpit stalked through the gate of the majestic Christ Church with feigned indignation. His annoyance was inexplicable even to him. The day had started so pleasantly. He was sure that Mannat wanted this trip as much as he did, then why was this happening to them? Those boys had spoiled everything. He wished he had chased after them. He should have grabbed the guy's collar and told him to bugger off!

He wanted to turn around and see if Mannat was following, but that would mean having to confront her reproachful face. Instead, he continued staring at the sundial which stood in front of the church, straining his ears for the soft sound of her approaching footsteps. Ten more minutes passed before he realised that she was not going to come. He turned around and dejectedly shuffled outside, only to find her missing. Concern stabbed him. Had she wandered away to the line of shops a few metres ahead? Or had another rowdy band tried to harass her, driving her to seek refuge elsewhere? But where?

Someone tapped him on the shoulder. He whirled around. Mannat was looking at him with a nonplussed expression. "Where on earth were you?" he yelled.

"Shh," she tried to quiet him, looking warily over her shoulder at the other visitors who were looking curiously at them. "I was inside the building, of course, waiting for you."

"But how come I didn't see you enter?"

"You were lost in your thoughts, or in the sundial. I agree it is beautiful, but—"

"Why can't you keep a mobile phone? I have told you a thousand times to get one. I had no clue where to look for you!"

"And I have told you a thousand times that it's no use having one since they are banned in our hostel!"

"I'm sorry," Arpit sighed, suddenly tired of the useless bickering. "Forget all this. Let's drive further up. I want some peace."

They breathed a sigh of relief on escaping to the quieter part of the Mall Road. Arpit parked his bike and they started walking. It was serene and peaceful—green sunshine filtering in through the conifers lining one side of the road, and the shadows cast by dignified colonial houses along the other. Arpit dug into his pocket and offered Mannat a chocolate, a rather sticky and fast-melting bit of chocolate, but she grabbed it readily.

"Mannat…"

"Yes, Arpit? What do you want to fight about this time?"

"Shut up. Don't embarrass me now. I just wanted to tell you that…that those guys were right."

"Which guys?"

"Those guys in the jeep. I hated how they said it, but it's true. Your hair…" he hesitated for a second before reaching out to stroke a lock that had escaped from her scarf to flirt with her cheek, "is beautiful."

Embarrassed, she unconsciously took a step back. To bridge the dangerous silence which had suddenly crept up between them, she blurted, "Arpit, did you…"

"Did I what?"

"Well, I was wondering if you had a girlfriend in college. Delhi is such a fast place, I'm sure you couldn't have avoided having one."

"Chandigarh isn't lagging too far behind in that department either!" he shot back. "You . . . never mind. Why should I tell you?" He was secretly delighted with her question, especially when he thought back about her apparent indifference to his telling her about his first girlfriend while still in school. But his delight was mixed with anxiety: Did she have a boyfriend? No, no, how could she? She studied in an all-girls' college and lived in a strictly-watched hostel. Besides, she was a simple girl from Meharsar. She wouldn't do such a thing!

"That means yes," she pronounced with provocative calmness.

"Okay, fine! I had one, sort of! But we have broken up now."

"Ohhhh. Why? Tell me about her. Was she very pretty?"

He found himself chuckling. "Hardly! She was this intensely academic type, with those big, round, owlish glasses that she didn't really need but wore to look intellectual. She was doing History Honours and aimed to become the next William Dalrymple!"

"Who?"

He sighed at her ignorance. "Never mind. You wanted to

know about my girlfriend, right? Her name was Binita Baruah, and she used to study in the college close to mine. We met in the University campus." And he recounted gleefully before Mannat how acrid, argumentative, and humourless Binita had been; how half her time out of classes was spent in the library and the other half in the cafeteria picking fights over obscure political controversies; how, from what he had heard, even some of the professors used to raise their eyebrows and glare at her if she threatened to ask a pompously intricate question; how she had no friends and didn't seem to miss them either; and how he was drawn to her precisely because of these reasons.

"Really?" Mannat grimaced. "She doesn't sound very pleasant!"

"She wasn't!" he grinned. "And that was the challenge. Not one of my friends could stand her for more than thirty seconds. So I decided to prove I could be her 'boyfriend' and show them that I was tougher than them. The first time I spoke to her was in the library. We started talking about a book which we both wanted to get issued—of course, I only pretended I wanted it— but the library had just one copy. Well, one thing led to another, and though it was extremely boring at first, I actually started enjoying it eventually. At least she was different. It was fun to annoy her."

"Then why did you break up?"

"Over the silliest of reasons. Someone forwarded an email to me which said that the Taj Mahal was not built by Shah Jahan at all. It was an interesting piece, so I took a printout to Binita and bang bang!! She just spluttered incoherently and said I was promoting a 'right-wing conspiracy of rewriting history', whatever that meant. It was amusing to see her so livid, so I kept quiet. But when she accused me of being a Hindu hardliner, I lost it. I told her to shut up because I was not even a Hindu! She was quite taken aback. The funny thing was that all this while she had not even known that I am a Sikh!"

Throwing back her head, Mannat burst out laughing. The clip which had been lightly holding back her hair opened and fell on the ground. Arpit bent automatically to pick it up. He looked up suddenly, and saw her bending over him with eyes sparkling mirthfully. Rising up, he handed her the hairclip. The next moment, his lips were on hers. She tasted like an oddly-exhilarating mixture of home-made butter and the chocolate he had given her . . . and then, to his astonishment, of all the candies he had smuggled into her hands in the bygone days. His senses reeled. For a moment, just one moment, the cool breeze ruffling his hair was replaced by the dry heat of Amritsar.

Mannat's first instinctive reaction was to draw back, but when Arpit gently placed his hands on her shoulders, she relaxed and kissed him back passionately. Her fingers wandered through his hair. He didn't want them to stop, ever. As they struggled to catch their breath again, he caught her gazing at him with a shy, but enquiring expression.

"What am I to you, Arpit?" Mannat asked softly, so softly that he almost missed the words. But instead of answering her, he drew her into his arms and kissed her again.

Nishi woke up weeping in the darkness . . . weeping for the two lovers whose lives had been unhooked from each other's by disturbingly familiar hands. Was she powerful enough to turn the cup back up and fill it again?

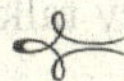

"What did you do after that?" Nishi asked soberly. Her eyes were heavy-lidded from the restless night she had experienced. She had caught Arpit looking at her a couple of times, but thankfully, he had not asked her anything about her tired and withdrawn face. She could not have told him about her dream. But while driving to Patiala, when he started talking about his trip to Kasauli with Mannat, she had been more than a little taken aback. Everything that he related concurred exactly with her dream from the previous night.

"Nothing. We came back by late evening. I spent the entire night tiptoeing to the door of her room and back, wanting to wake her up and talk about goodness knows what, but not daring to. The next day was spent at home with everyone else and I didn't get a chance to talk to her alone. I went back to Delhi after that, and a few days later, to Australia for that holiday."

"Did you call her after that?"

"No," he returned dully. "I had so much fun in Australia that I forgot about everything else for a while. When I came back, we got the news that Beeji was critically ill. Dad and I rushed to Meharsar. She died half an hour after we arrived."

"And you didn't get a chance to talk to Mannat then?"

"We just talked about Beeji. What else could we have talked about at that time?"

"Hmm . . . didn't you think of promising her anything?"

"I was a cocksure, arrogant fool who took her for granted. And in case you haven't noticed it already, I was also a terrible coward when it came to expressing my attachment to the Meharsar people in front of my father."

Nishi was silent after this. She stayed silent till they reached their destination, and then they talked only about work.

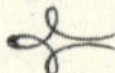

Beeji's death snapped Baldev's last emotional tie with Meharsar. What was left was a rather distant interest in his share of the ancestral property which, thanks to his high-flying career, he was in no hurry to stake a claim to.

He had been appointed the Regional Director, Sales and Marketing, of his company for the entire Indian sub-continent, but Baldev's ambitions extended beyond his multinational employer's reward packages. He had gathered enough experience and forged enough political ties to want to set up a business of his own. In fact, he was already working on a business plan, and it only helped to have a lawyer keep a discreet eye on things in Meharsar.

When this lawyer informed him that Beeji had actually made a will, Baldev was completely taken aback. The practice was not common in Meharsar. Even his father had not made a will before his death. But then again, he had never gotten the time to prepare for it. He could understand his siblings being more worldly-wise, but Beeji? Never! It had to be Veerji, with all his righteous presumptuousness, who must have advised her to make one. Oh well, it was a formality anyway; a legal proof of her division of the property in equal shares amongst him and his siblings would only work out well for all of them.

But a rude shock awaited him when the will was actually read. Beeji had, indeed, divided her wealth equally amongst her children, save for the largest swathe of land, a hundred metres from the lake and the most fertile land in the whole of Meharsar. *That* land she had made over to "my Guru-sent brother, Sardar Joginder Singh Meharsar, for investing in the education of my children, especially my eldest son, Baldev Singh."

Baldev was stunned—it was as if Beeji, always docile and seemingly timid and never having dared to admonish him during her lifetime, had been given enough courage in death to deal him a stinging slap. Even as he stared at Veerji and his family with contempt that was quickly hardening into empathic vindictiveness, Baldev resolved to teach them all a lesson. He would destroy this blasted village!

Arpit went to Bangalore soon afterwards to pursue an MBA from IIM. Mannat was still in Chandigarh. Post her graduation, she had decided to stay on in the same college to pursue a Master's in Home Science. Her plan, as she wrote to Arpit in a letter he was embarrassed to receive in the hostel where everyone else communicated through emails and cell phones, was to complete her PhD and then go back to Meharsar.

Of the village, she had a few terse sentences to say: Veerji was continuing his fight against the bottling plant, but the road was growing tougher and tougher. A number of youngsters had defied the panchayat's diktat to resume work at the factory, and more were expected to follow suit. It was apparent that Veerji would soon need all the support possible. He could count on her, she wrote. One call from him, and she would drop everything and rush to be by his side.

Somehow, the letter disturbed Arpit. It seemed to have been written by a Mannat different from the placid child he had grown up with; different too from the blushing girl-woman he had exultantly kissed in Kasauli. Her words seemed to quiver with a defiance he hadn't expected. And as he stood inside his recently-whitewashed hostel room where his roommate had plastered posters of a Spanish-American pop star, and where his own notes and case study reports lay strewn untidily over the bed, he wondered how he could stay in touch with this Mannat. Should he write back? But that would mean another letter in return which would only invite yet more sniggers and astonished glances from the other young men in his hostel. He had asked for her email address before leaving Chandigarh, but she had given it rather reluctantly, insisting that she rarely went online since she had no computer of her own and the cyber café in her college was always full. And Madam Mannat, of course, would not agree to buy a cell phone. Maybe she could not afford it? She had argued when he had started haranguing her about a cell phone. What if he arranged to have one sent to her? No, she would never accept it, and there would be the monthly bills anyway . . . Oh why did she have to make it so difficult for him?

Mannat's first letter went unanswered. So did the next one. None came after that.

Arpit completed his MBA and immediately got placed in one of the big software companies in Bangalore itself. It was not a job he loved, but in the initial days at least, it was exciting.

His father, however, had other plans for him. His own company was growing by leaps and bounds. He had just established offices in the Asia-Pacific and Middle East as well. It was only a matter of time now before he reached the big players, he thought triumphantly. In anticipation of this, he had already bought an astronomically expensive apartment in New York and he planned to gift it to Arpit on his twenty-third birthday along with the offer to fund yet another super-specialised MBA from either Stanford or MIT.

Blissfully unaware of the ambitious career package being handpicked for him, Arpit continued to enjoy his plentiful salary and his affable new friends at work. Meharsar and Kasauli seemed like episodes from a different life altogether, and Mannat became a beautiful phantom meant to be resurrected only in dreams. There was no time to visit any of them now. It was all he could do to fly over to Delhi on weekends. And when his father shifted base to New York, Arpit started saving up his leave allowances to meet him at least once in six months.

But when his *mama* and *mami* decided to relocate to Australia along with his grandparents, he decided to spend a weekend with them before they left. It was only when he landed in Chandigarh that Arpit wondered if Mannat was still in town. His heart thumped a little quicker at the possibility.

On reaching the house, he discovered that Mannat was not only in town, but she was right there in the house. His grandparents had invited her as well after he'd called them to inform them of his plan. Clearly, his family wanted everything to be exactly like it used to be in the old times. He could not determine whether that would be a good thing or a bad thing for him now. Mannat stood for everything that he was expected to rise above, and in the few seconds that passed between his nani telling him that she was in the house and his seeing her, he made up his mind to treat her as a childhood friend and nothing more.

The next moment, however, Mannat walked into the room and all of Arpit's resolutions flew right out of the window.

It was late by the time Nishi had finished her survey of the house. "I guess we will have to stay the night in Chandigarh again," remarked Arpit. "We can reach there in an hour. Or would you prefer to stay in a hotel here? I can search online for—"

But Nishi interrupted him. "Since we are converting this into a homestead, why not do a 'test stay' here?"

"But at this stage, this place is not fit to spend the night in. So much dust, and there isn't any furniture around either!"

"I have stayed in weirder places. Did I ever tell you of the Witches' Lake not too far from my village? I once spent an entire night on its shores."

"Did the witches come?" Arpit immediately asked, in spite of himself.

“I will tell you some other time,” she replied in a tone which, by now, he knew he must not challenge. “So it is decided—we inhabit the two first-floor rooms facing the balcony. They are in the best condition compared to the rest of the house.”

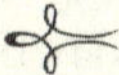

“Do you know my motorbike is still here?” Arpit whispered conspiratorially to Mannat. “I had it sent here four years ago when I went to Bangalore. Can we go out for a drive tonight?”

She was as lovely as he remembered her. Four years of progressively demanding studies had not taken away her radiance. He had been imagining a dour-faced activist based on the letters she had sent to him in his early days in Bangalore. Would she reproach him for not replying to them? But no, she didn’t. She was acting like they had never lost touch in the first place! Did that mean she had stopped caring? She couldn’t have, could she? If she had, he would change things a bit. The nocturnal bike ride would be a good way to probe whether she still remembered that authoritatively-seized kiss in the hills or not.

They drove to the University where a bored guard made no attempt to stop them from entering. It was only 9:45 p.m., anyway. Arpit turned his bike from the dying chatter of the main buildings to the tree-canopied lane that led to the Botanical Gardens. The whole place was deserted. The street lights were on, but ghostly green shadows lent an eerie air to the place. Mannat shivered slightly. She did not ask him why they had stopped here. Neither did she protest when he cupped her face with his hands and pulled her towards him. They kissed as if they were simply resuming what they had left off in Kasauli. She was pliant when he nestled his hand in the small of her back, caressing it gently, but when he tried to move his fingers under her shirt to touch her skin, she drew back.

"Arpit . . ." she whispered breathlessly, "will you take me to Amritsar?"

"What? Now?"

Bursting into irrepressible giggles, Mannat exclaimed, "No, stupid! In the daytime, some day before you return . . ."

He thought for a moment of his already-booked return ticket and then he saw her looking at him as if her very existence depended on his answer. He nodded vigorously. "I will!"

So the day after his relatives left for Australia, they started off for Amritsar early in the morning on his bike. Mannat was dressed in a green and yellow salwar kameez, redolent of the mustard crop which would have lit the roadsides had they been making this journey a few months later. When Arpit managed to tear his eyes off her, he was assailed by apprehension: What if they ran into Harpal and Sukhmani in Amritsar? The thought no longer filled him with delight. Quite the contrary. But Mannat informed him that her parents were in Meharsar now. Relief was quickly followed by guilt. He did not pause to probe his feelings.

They wandered through the lanes of the city, sampling kulfi and bargaining for knick-knacks, just as in the days of yore.

At the Harmandir Sahib, after they had knelt in the sanctum sanctorum and received the *prasad*, they wandered around the holy precincts till they reached the exit where Mannat stopped to check out the shops selling glass bangles and trinkets.

"You still fancy such things?" he teased, just to provoke her.

"Of course. Bangles are bangles, except that their size has changed." She smiled up at him.

"And what about hair clips? Does their size change too?" He deliberately reached over to touch her hair. She blushed and looked around warily to see if anyone had noticed. Paying for her purchases, she signalled to him to follow her out. When they were standing outside the majestic main entrance, she turned back towards the beautiful structure with a faraway look in her eyes. The steady stream of devotees continuously moved around them, at times jostling them. Mannat turned to him. Taking his right hand in both of hers, she raised it to the level of her heart.

"What can you read in my eyes, Arpit?" she whispered.

But instead of saying anything, Arpit adjusted her *chunni* which had slipped off her head.

"There couldn't be a better place than this for me to tell you what I have to . . ."

"Mannat . . . you . . ."

"Arpit . . . I love you. I loved you as a child and I love you now."

CHAPTER 8

It was the same village, the same panchayat, and the same people. But this time, there was something different. At first she couldn't put her finger on it, but when she looked at the faces closely, she saw what it was. The smooth, salamander-like face of Rajendra Bisht had morphed into the face of Baldev Singh. Facing him was her father, Devishankar Gaur, dressed in a pristine white kurta pyjama, with a turban tied around his head and a long, flowing beard—just like Veerji. She looked at . . . wait, who was *she*? Looking down, she saw herself dressed in a yellow-green salwar kameez. She was not surprised anymore.

But who was that hovering uncertainly on the sidelines, looking first at one, then at another as if unsure with whom to align himself? Rajendra Bisht beckoned to him—come to the front, dear lad. Now look at him, brothers and sisters, this is one of the brightest sons of our village, but see his plight—no jobs, no degree college. Let the dam be built, and there will be jobs galore.

As the faint threads of recognition began to weave themselves into a trap around her, she gasped, for though he had the figure and air of Arpit, the boy's face was that of the young man who had travelled miles of mountain terrain with her to attend the ragtag school in the next village. It was the face of the boy who had sat beside her as they grappled together with complex maths problems which there weren't enough teachers to solve. It was the boy with whom she had exchanged shy, secret smiles . . . and Rajendra Bisht was taking him away. She stirred and turned restlessly on her side. The scene swirled and shifted around her. She saw the young man's body lying on the ground, bloodied and waiting to be wept upon. He had taken up a junior supervisory role at the dam site. When the landslide happened, he was the only one there, having stayed back to drink in the last of the hillside's pure beauty before it was changed forever. *He had loved the hills so much that they took him with them . . .*

No one had told his parents yet. No one dared to. Had her father been still in the village . . . had *she* been still in the village, they would have done it. But she was nothing more than a phantom, unable to roll up the road back to the point where it should have stopped altogether.

In the next instant, she felt Mannat's disappointment course through her veins. In response to her confession of love, Arpit had made a feeble joke and changed the topic. But she knew, without a doubt, that he belonged to her . . . ever since the day she had hit him with a pebble, Arpit had belonged to her. For the third time, Mannat asked Arpit if they should drive on to Meharsar and give everyone a surprise. He shook his head.

"Veerji would be so pleased to meet you," she persisted. "He misses you more and more every day. Do you know that we are facing a new problem in the village now? That accursed factory has been pumping up so much groundwater that our wells are running dry. The water table has dipped. Veerji keeps running from pillar to post, but it's a bitter battle. I help him out when I come home, but I wish I could be with him the whole time," she sighed.

"Hmm." He looked bored that she was still hung up on that stupid factory. "Mannat, there was something I wanted to tell you."

She grew taut, scanning his face with a guileless expectant gaze. But he could not put off telling her any longer. "Mannat . . . I am going to the United States for further studies."

She was silent for so long that he rushed in to bridge the precipice. "It's going to be a joint MBA-MS from Stanford. Imagine what it will do for my career! I might get a job thereabouts!"

"You plan to settle down there," she uttered with a quiet conviction which made his feeble, insincere protests redundant. "And when you come back, if you come back, you won't get any time to visit Meharsar."

"Well, if you can come to Chandi—"

"I will be completing my thesis in another two years at the most. After that, it's going to be Meharsar for the rest of my life. If you want to meet me, you will have to come there." She raised her face, blushing no longer, to his. A sliver of hope still glinted in her eyes. But he could not bring himself to reinforce it.

Nishi woke up, shivering. This time however, she did not weep. Instead, she tiptoed to Arpit's room and quietly opened the door a little. In the moonlight streaming in through the glassless windows, she saw that he was sprawled peacefully on his makeshift bed. Nishi heaved a great shuddering sigh of relief. She was aghast with all that was happening, and her inability to explain it was beginning to scare her a little. She had used her powers to help many people, but never before had she broken the cardinal rule of emotional detachment from her subjects. How could she have slipped into Mannat's consciousness like this? What was Meharsar to her? Why was she becoming an actor in the scenes being recreated before her instead of staying an observer?

If she didn't do something about it, she might be unable to

help Arpit at all. And she would never forgive herself for that.

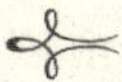

"You did not come back from the USA to visit Mannat, did you?" accused Nishi.

"I didn't! I didn't!" Arpit rubbed his palm miserably over his face. "In fact, jerk that I was, I lost touch again. No phone calls, no letters, no emails, nothing. The minute I got my degree from Stanford, I joined my Dad's company; he wanted me to. And after that, there was simply no time for me to go back to Meharsar. At the back of my mind I wondered if Mannat had been really serious about living in Meharsar for the rest of her life. How could she be fine with being stuck in such a tiny place? I resolved to go back sometime soon and convince her to come to Delhi for a few days. I would take her around and show her what city life was, and then she would start seeing things from my point of view. But I kept putting off that trip."

". . . and when you went back, it was only after she had pleaded with you to come. How did she find you, though?"

"She called my mamaji in Australia for my New York number. She called me, Nishi. She called me and told me to come quickly to Meharsar. And I told her I would try."

"You would try?" Nishi's voice was like volcanic ash.

"I love the indignation in your voice. It shows that you have come to love Mannat as much as I do. I was in the office with Dad when Mannat's call came. Her voice had the edge of desperation in it. I can remember the whole conversation even today . . . She asked me to come to Meharsar immediately, not dreaming that I would take her demand as an intrusion into my life. She had come all the way to a public telephone booth to make that international call; she didn't want anyone to find her there. Despite the huge risk she had taken, she refused to explain any further over the phone. When the line went dead, I turned around to find Dad staring at me."

"What did he tell you? That you needed to move on? That life demands new priorities and that you had to be realistic and not hang on to childhood attachments?" ventured Nishi, unable to keep sarcasm from bleeding into her words.

"Yeah, pretty much something on those lines. You have managed to read him well. He played on my ego, reminding me of how much *he* had achieved when he had been my age. I fell right for his logical blackmail. But," he paused, "to this day, Nishi, I am unsure whether I had imagined the undertone of menace in my father's voice or not . . . The phone continued to ring again and again for many days after that. But recognising the number, I didn't pick it up. It must be about the factory again, I told myself. Why couldn't Mannat understand that I couldn't come running to India to soothe Veerji's anxieties?

"A fortnight later, the possibility of a distribution deal in India gave me the opportunity I wanted. I flew to Mumbai, wrapped up my business, and then I informed Dad that I was going to take a break in the hills. Catching the next flight to Chandigarh, I arrived in Meharsar just in time to witness Mannat's engagement to Simarjeet Shergill."

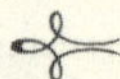

"Did you, by any chance . . . gatecrash her engagement?" Nishi's voice was almost hopeful.

"I didn't have to gatecrash it. They invited me, lovingly, and as one of their own. But Harpal Chayaji had guessed what was happening to me at that moment. He said, 'What a pity Baldev isn't here! He would have loved to see this, no? If only we had your address, we would have sent you an invitation. But what a stroke of luck that you happened to be here!'"

"So he wanted to wrench it into you, did he? What made him so hostile?"

"My absence, of course. I had snubbed them enough by staying away . . . What?" He was startled to see Nishi peering intently at him.

"Could that really have been reason enough?"

"What do you mean?"

"Did it ever occur to you that your Dad might have used the very excuse that you did? Perhaps his India trips weren't confined to business, either."

"What?! Are you saying that Dad had been to Meharsar while I was in New York?" he gasped.

"Quite likely. And I wouldn't be surprised if the outcome of that visit had a lot to do with why Mannat's father was so hostile."

"But how will I ever know what happened?"

"Simple. Just ask your father."

Arpit laughed bitterly. "And you think he will tell me the truth . . . or tell me anything at all?"

"In that case, there is only one other way. But we will have to wait for that. Anyway, it's going to be morning in a few hours. Let's go get some sleep."

"No, no, Nishi, hear the rest. Who knows if I will be able to screw up enough courage later? Mannat was to be married in a month's time. And instead of confronting her family, I met her in private and asked her to run away with me."

"You what?"

"I asked her to run away with me. I was just too damn scared. Had I done anything openly, the news would have reached Dad in a twinkling. I thought I would take her away with me to Delhi and we could get married there. Then we would come back to Meharsar and seek everyone's blessings."

"She didn't agree, of course."

"Hah! You know her better than I did at the time. She didn't just refuse. She was furious! Her reaction was understandable. It's only now that I realise what a child I must have seemed, pleading for a thing I had cast away and not bothered about till it was about to be given to someone else. Moreover, our elopement would bring disgrace not just to her family, but to the entire village. Me being me, I hadn't thought about these things. After that I went back to Delhi and began drinking myself half-insane. Sometime in those days that I spent in Delhi, wallowing in misplaced grief and alcohol, I found a bunch of hippies who were planning to trek through Himachal and tagged along. Oh, that was a glorious time! I moved from alcohol to drugs and tried everything—acid, grass, dust, smack. You just name it. And that's where I met Andreja, up in the hills somewhere, away from all noise and chaos, and high on a continuous dose of drugs. I drew to her like a moth to a flame. She was different, so very different from everything and everyone I had known until then. She whipped up a frenzy of abandonment around herself, and I fell into it. There was nothing I wanted more than to give up on the world. And Andreja was an old hand in saying "Boo!" to this world. She lived only for the moment, which suited me just fine. I didn't want to think about the past or the future, especially *my* past with Mannat and *her* future with Simarjeet. Andreja and I had some wild nights up there, sorry, Nishi," he checked himself. "You will find it bizarre, but thinking of how I almost destroyed myself gives me some consolation—*I had proved her wrong*. Mannat had said I didn't care enough, but I did. I was suffering like she would never have imagined.

"I threw my cell phone into the campfire one night so that

Dad couldn't get through to me. After we came back from the hills, I travelled and travelled. The need to keep moving would just not let me go. Wherever I went, I always found people to keep me company in my downward spiral. I don't quite know where all of that would have stopped had my father not found me after months of looking around. He had come to India to look for me after I had disappeared without a trace. One look at my condition and he knew that I would never be of any use to him anymore. I had destroyed all his grandiose plans. But he did put me in rehab. I managed to kick the drug habit, but I could not help getting sozzled every time Mannat rushed into my thoughts . . . and that was always. Always. I did come to my senses enough to understand that I could not work or live with my father anymore. My travels had given me an idea about starting my own company. That's how I came up with Silver Cloud. It was the best decision I had taken in my life."

"So the engagement was the last time you saw her? Who told you when she got married?"

"My nani. She also told me that Mannat had shifted to Leeds after her marriage. I was tempted a thousand times to fly to Leeds and sneak a glimpse of her, but only her family knew her full address, and they would never have told me had I even dared to ask. And no, it wasn't the last time I met her. I have saved the worst for the last."

⁂

Arpit and Andreja were celebrating the success of his first tour. Though it was supposed to be one of the quieter beaches of Goa, there was a large family party staying at the same resort as them, a family by the name of Shergill.

Even before he saw her, he knew that she was there.

Having attended the engagement, he recognised her husband straightaway—tall, pale-skinned, clean-shaven, and handsomely rich too, from what a thrilled Harpal had lost no opportunity in telling him. And he had earned every penny of his wealth. A self-made man, in other words. No wonder Mannat had chosen him over poor-little-daddy's-boy Arpit. He had no right to blame her, but he still did. After all, being self-made was no guarantee of goodness. His father had also hacked his own way through the world.

Ah, Arpit, so you finally understand how your Dad screwed everything up! If it took two bottles of alcohol to make you admit it, why not drink some more and confront a few other bitter truths this ruthless night?

He listened too well to his dazed brain, so while Andreja turned to her stock of hallucinogens to blur reality, he chose alcohol. With a bottle in his hand, he stood next to the window in his hotel room and looked straight down at the artfully-designed outdoor roofless dining area of the resort. Lowered inhibitions made him inquisitive and he leaned out, looking for Mannat. And there she was, sitting at a long table with the entire Shergill clan around her, an atmosphere of culture, gentility, and love surrounding the table. Arpit was driven to look around his room—rumpled bedsheets, clothes strewn everywhere, used tissues and half-empty packets of chips and soda cans littering the floor because Andreja couldn't be expected to look for the dustbin at all times, the cloying smell of drugs and sweat . . . he had crossed over irrevocably to the other side. And Mannat had been left behind forever.

No, no, that could not happen! Arpit stared desperately out of his window again. Sunny had his arm around Mannat's shoulders and was whispering something into her ear. Even with all the people around them, they appeared to be caught up in a world of their own. Why did they have their backs to him? He wanted to see her face. Just once.

Sunny eased his hand from her shoulders and Mannat got up. She turned towards the resort building. Arpit couldn't help but draw in a sharp breath. He could see her face clearly now. There was a strange serenity on her face, much against his expectations. Or was it much against his hopes? Was she also glowing, or was it the effect of the wretched full moon? Then she stiffened. He fancied he saw her expression flicker. Had she seen him at the window? It wasn't likely, not from where she stood. But maybe she had sensed him like he had sensed her presence in the resort even before seeing her. He did not attempt to move away. As he continued to watch her, she motioned to Sunny that she was leaving. Sunny smiled back in acknowledgement. It was a smile of security and contentment. A red-hot knife twisted itself into Arpit's ribs and he almost doubled over. Stepping away from the window, he quickly slugged down the last of what was in the bottle, the alcohol burning its way down his throat, and staggered out of his room.

He had to see her. He just had to see her.

By the time he reached the main lobby, he saw that the dining area was mostly empty. The Shergills seemed to have all dispersed. Mannat and Sunny were nowhere to be seen. He looked around wildly for a moment, attracting dubious stares. Then he relaxed. He had just glimpsed Sunny talking to some people who were still finishing dinner. Mannat would be alone then, he realised. He inched close to the dining area, hoping to catch some revealing snatches of conversation. A waiter came up behind him and pointedly cleared his throat, forcing him to turn back, and asked if he was okay, if he wanted anything. It was easy to detect the unease and the wariness in his voice behind the faint mask of politeness. He knew what the man really wanted to say, "Will you please leave? You make an ugly sight."

For a moment he wondered whether or not to knock the waiter over, but then he heard Sunny's voice saying, ". . . should be back in a while, she's just taking a walk by the sea."

So that's where she was! Somewhere on the beach, and alone. Without so much as a glance at the wary waiter who was still waiting for a reply, he sped towards the beach on feet of fire.

Nishi held up her hand pleadingly. "No more, please." Her voice came out in an agonised whisper. In the darkness of the passing night, her face, drawn tight around the corners of her mouth, shone out bleakly. If Arpit went on any longer, Nishi knew she wouldn't be able to avoid telling him about her dreams and a fact that her intuition had started screaming at her halfway through his narration. Arpit wasn't ready to hear anything like that just yet.

"Don't stop me now, Nishi. I want to get over with all of this now!" Arpit implored.

Nishi swallowed hard and gathered the tattered shreds of her customary coolness around her. "It's best that you go sleep now, Arpit. You have a lot of driving to do in the morning and it will be dangerous for both of us if you fall asleep at the wheel. So, please."

Arpit stared miserably at her for a few moments before getting up slowly and leaving the room. After he left, Nishi did not go back to bed. She knew sleep would elude her for whatever was left of the night. She stared instead at the heavy darkness outside which forebode a cloudy morning. And when a colourless dawn streaked valiantly across the sky, she got up and went to wash her face in the cracked and chipped washbasin. Gathering her crumpled dupatta like a shawl around herself and pulling her hair back into a knot, she shuffled downstairs to the unkempt courtyard.

It was barely five. She decided she would let Arpit sleep for another hour at least. How quiet it was at this time in the morning! Arpit had indeed chosen the right location. In Delhi, there would be residual shrieks of traffic and in the hills, the birds would be singing to an increasingly indifferent humanity. She tried to shake off such cynical, brooding thoughts and recall the pleasanter scenes of her childhood—her father teaching her the songs of wind and water, the secret perfumes of the earth and the legends of Nature's spirit guardians. She could imagine him sitting on the little patch of ground deep in the forest where the grass had grown flat with his sitting on it and meditating for hours. She was allowed to sit with him provided she did not talk or move while he communed with the Beyond. Sometimes, when she was particularly restless, he would draw a queer symbol on the ground—a star with its rays resembling the petals of a lotus enclosed within a circle—and tell her to concentrate on it. Whether the magic lay in its shape or in the skill of her father's hand she couldn't quite figure, but it always succeeded in quieting her. She had tried to draw it herself a number of times, but she had never been able to replicate the precision and the perfect symmetry of her father's drawing. Ever since she had left her village and her childhood behind, however, she had never attempted to draw it again.

But something compelled her now to kneel slowly to the ground, uncaring of the dirt, and retrace the remembered shape in the thick dust. The result was amateurish at best. She tried again and again, but with little success. Finally, when she gave up with a broken sigh, the disquiet in her heart had not lessened.

CHAPTER 9

Sunny helped her to the bed once she had finished throwing up the last of the wine. All the guests had left by then, clucking sympathetically and murmuring words of comfort. So kind of them, she thought vaguely, and so kind of Sunny to put up with all this . . . to put up with *her* after all her exasperating indifference. As he tucked the covers around her, she gripped Sunny's hand.

"Don't!" His tone was sharp. "I have not washed after wiping up the mess."

"Doesn't matter . . ." She took his other hand too and held them both to her heart. "I am sorry." He turned away from her and sat on the edge of the bed, facing the bathroom. "Sunny," she persisted, "I am sorry. I know you think I am not, but I am. Right now I am nothing but a liability to you—"

"You aren't . . ." he interrupted, with some gentleness creeping back into his voice.

But she went on, "I never wanted to put you through this. This phase shall pass. I promise you that everything will be all right once they save the lake. I promise!"

"The lake?"

"Meharsar, Sunny . . . the Meharsar lake!"

"Are you in your senses, Manjot? What in the world does that lake have to do with *us*?!"

"Everything. Sunny, everything! It was where it all started, and it is where it will all end."

Sunny stared at his wife in perplexity as she smiled wanly and drifted off to sleep, once again entering the world which did not welcome him into its secrets. What was she hiding? Things had never been the same after that accursed day in Goa. When he had carried her back to the resort, she had seemed normal enough, albeit a bit limp and listless. He had attributed it to the change of climate, thinking wryly that just one year of English weather had lowered Mandy's immunity to Indian conditions. He put her to bed with strict instructions to just rest and sleep.

Somewhere around daybreak, however, the trouble had started—first the frequent trips to the bathroom, then the nausea and the vomiting, and then the traces of blood which threw him into panic. He rushed her to the nearest hospital, but it was already too late. They had lost their baby.

Mandy had gone so quiet and rigid after hearing the news that he had been terrified about her sanity. For days she didn't utter a word, wrapping herself up in silent grief. Then, much to his relief, she had suddenly started talking and moving about. But he had never been completely at ease after that. The doctors said that the mishap might have been triggered by stress. But, what stress? He had kept her as comfortable as possible, pampering her ever since she told him about the pregnancy, bringing her small gifts and flowers almost every other day, personally monitoring her diet and daily schedule, taking her out to meet their friends sometimes, and just generally trying to keep her happy. She had seemed so calm, so *intently* content. Had some trouble been lurking beneath the still waters all this while?

Eventually however, he had put it down to the long flight to India and the unhygienic air of the place. And to that lout who had scared her in Goa. Though she kept insisting that he hadn't dared to do more than follow her from a distance and that he had run away after she made that phone call, perhaps the anxiety caused by that incident had triggered the miscarriage. Sunny wished he could come face-to-face with that creep just once. He would make him pay for what he had done to their blossoming marriage.

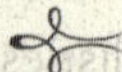

He staunchly refused Sukhmani's offer of a walking stick. "There is still enough strength in these old bones to climb a mountain. In fact," he looked past her into Harpal's anxious face right behind her, "I will need to climb one soon."

"What is it you want to do, Veerji?" Harpal asked, his voice trembling just the slightest bit.

Veerji did not answer immediately. Instead, he let his gaze travel over the rain-washed landscape, as if locking it in in his memory forever. In the distance, a dim, smoky cloud hung like an evil spirit's cloak over the green fields. It was a sinister reminder of what the Verva factory had done to them in the last sixteen years.

There was precious little they had been able to do. They had met government officials and legal experts. They had even tried to organise a press conference once, inviting media persons who seemed sensitive to their cause. Representatives from a total of three newspapers and one TV channel had turned up. The resultant coverage moved the local MLA to create an expert panel to conduct a preliminary Environmental Impact Assessment. The report had been duly submitted to the State Legislature, along with a request for sanctioning more funds for a large-scale study, but with other political debates rising in ferocity at the same time, the issue of Meharsar got sidelined again.

A few years ago, an environment-protection NGO had discovered Meharsar. Their research, with inputs from Veerji and other villagers, led to a well-publicised media report titled, *The Slow Poisoning of Rural Punjab*. The NGO had also filed a Public Interest Litigation in the Punjab and Haryana High Court demanding that Verva Cola clean up the toxic waste being generated by its plant. The Court had finally directed the company to clear the waste, a small victory for Meharsar, but Veerji knew that trouble would never be too far away now. If it wasn't the waste, it was the amount of groundwater Verva Cola had been pumping up, leaving far too little for agriculture. How many PILs could they file after all?

Mannat had wanted to continue the fight, but Harpal put his foot down. Enough was enough, he said. If they were all destined to fall into ruin, they would accept their fate with resignation, but he would not give anyone the malicious satisfaction of seeing his daughter's accomplishments poured down the dying lake. It was time to get Mannat married, time to send her away from the dark shadows of Meharsar. And as much as he loved his father, Harpal vowed that he would not let Mannat immolate herself in the flames of his lost cause anymore.

When the matrimonial proposal for Mannat came from the Shergill family, therefore, he lost no time in saying yes. But when Mannat begged him to give her some more time to think about the proposal before consenting to it, he reluctantly agreed. Veerji had not contested Harpal's decision. His hope of seeing Mannat united with Arpit had fallen apart anyway. True, he felt a little weakened in Mannat's absence, but he had other things to worry about now. Nothing mattered to him now, except what he knew was fair and right. And nothing would stop him from fighting for it. Even Harpal's fluttering disapproval would not sway him anymore. Therefore, there was not a flicker of doubt in his voice as he tore his gaze away from the fields and declared to his son and daughter-in-law, "I mean to start a fast-unto-death within six months if the Verva Cola people don't agree to shift the factory away from here."

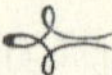

"Septuagenarian vows fast-unto-death against cola plant!" screamed the headline of the innocuous-looking local newspaper a couple of days later. Harpal was aghast. "Does he really mean to go through with this then?" he asked Sukhmani in bewilderment.

"Knowing Veerji, he probably does," she replied grimly. Her immediate concern, however, was that this news should not reach Mannat. Thank God she was far away in England. She had already suffered so much. The last thing the poor child needed was this. However, she did wish sometimes that Mannat was still unmarried and living with them during this challenging hour. She had always been so idealistic and such a pillar of strength, especially for Veerji. But ever since the miscarriage, there had been malicious whispers about women marrying foreigners to settle abroad and then growing indifferent to their husbands and letting their married life fall to fragments.

Sukhmani tried to shield Harpal from all this. She knew how it would enrage him. But for her the gossip had poisonous dregs of truth. Mannat should not have been married off like that, and she, her mother, should not have been so quick to interpret the resignation in her daughter's eyes as acceptance of what was being decided for her.

Involuntarily, her thoughts wandered to Baldev and Arpit. Like everyone else, she had been disappointed when Arpit and Mannat did not end up together. But her disappointment could not quell her sympathy for the rootless, motherless lad. And even though she knew it was dangerous to entertain such thoughts, she wondered again if Arpit knew of Mannat's condition.

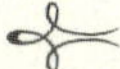

Mannat's face was clouded. She had just finished reading the weekly updates on the website of *Earth First*, a magazine which reported, with stinging bluntness, on the environmental outrages in the Third World. For the last five days she had been in bed with an erratic temperature which had Sunny worried yet again. Realizing guiltily that she had caused him too much heartache already, she chided him and told him to go on with his work and not worry about her—all she needed was a little rest, not another course of antibiotics. This time he agreed without putting up any fight. Maybe he was also getting tired of it all . . . or of her.

It was when she got bored of watching the endless soaps on the Indian channels—Sunny had subscribed to them after the miscarriage, thinking that homesickness might be one of the reasons for her slow recovery—that she switched on the laptop and started browsing through the Internet.

The *Earth First* report that she was reading, highlighted the mockery that was being routinely made in India of the environmental clearance process required for major mining and dam-building projects. With chilling commonality, the Chattisgarh, Uttarakhand, Orissa, and Karnataka governments participated in the staging of fake public hearings to get clearances for these 'developmental' projects. There were no questions raised over the fact that these projects endangered the quality of life of hundreds of villages. Obviously, the bureaucrat-big business-land mafia nexus couldn't care less.

Mannat fought down a rising tide of alarm. Though there had been no mention of Punjab in the report, let alone Meharsar, it was a loud enough hint about the shape of things to come. A couple of days back, she had read that Sunburst Inc., one of the biggest conglomerates in the American market, was planning a major expansion into the Indian market. Delhi, Punjab, Haryana, and Maharashtra were the states they would target first for setting up their exclusive snack joints. Their reach would be intensive—one snack bar every fifty square kilometres. And they were going to collaborate with Verva Cola for packaging their preserved foods. Their Indian franchisee was a name scaldingly familiar to her: India Mantra Limited, Baldev Singh's company.

She fought to calm her brain, to prevent it from putting the implications of the two news items together, but it continued to flagrantly disobey her, exactly like it had done on that night in Goa when Arpit had risen up before her as if from the sea waves.

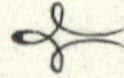

Navneet Sodhi, Member of the Legislative Assembly from the constituency in which Meharsar fell, had a sneaking sympathy for Veerji. The stubborn old farmer had persistently refused to pay the price for development which ninety percent of the developing world's population would have paid without a murmur. Somehow, Veerji was immune to temptations of money and threats of coercion alike.

In the last couple of years, there had been isolated attempts by the representatives of Verva Cola to come to a compromise with Veerji. They had thrown hints of a secure financial future in case he agreed to drop his agitation. When he smoothly pretended, or so they thought, not to understand what they meant, there came rather direct warnings that his 'anti-development stance' was going to create problems for him. In complicated legal terms, they told Veerji that he was misusing his democratic right to protest, and that he might end up getting himself arrested for disrupting the peace of the land if he continued with his demonstrations. They had hoped this might cow him down. Instead, Veerji simply stopped replying in Hindi and slipped into his customary Punjabi with such a thick accent that even the company's interpreter seemed confused.

Nothing had come out of these meetings and attempted negotiations, and Sodhi was getting worried. He knew the system and the stakes. He himself had often accepted 'gifts' from those seeking his help in setting up their business enterprises. Sometimes he obliged them, and sometimes he didn't. His decisions were based on a careful cost-benefit analysis. But Veerji was a different deal altogether. This man naïvely believed that the universe would align itself with his cause if only he pursued it doggedly enough.

"At his age it's rather difficult to teach him the ways of the world," Sodhi thought wryly. Being a first-generation politician who came from a family of proud farmers, he could identify with Veerji's devotion to his land. But the man was being impractical. He would try his best to convince him to call off the fight. And if he couldn't convince Veerji, well, he had no choice but to help him out a bit. Damn, he was all set to get into trouble with his party's leadership. All because of his grudging respect for this old man who did not know the meaning of the word *convenience.*

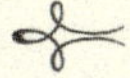

Baldev was all set. The first four Sunburst restaurants in Punjab would open in Chandigarh, Ludhiana, Jalandhar, and Amritsar. Within four months, ten more would follow. He knew all too well the name he wanted heading the list for Phase Two.

He was painstakingly involved in research which would show the amounts of wealth flowing into the areas adjoining Meharsar, thanks to the Verva Cola plant, and the resultant political interest in the place. A strong road network was already being constructed, and mass transport—though almost exclusively controlled by influential private operators—was easily available to and from every single village in the vicinity of the factory. Land prices were soaring, and many landowners were rapidly converting their agricultural land into commercial holdings. Some of them even sought the help of his agents to find good buyers. True, schooling was still the same and the sanitation system was still in shambles, but why should this matter to the Sunburst people? They had no idea what a teeming market lay waiting for them in this nondescript land . . . and what a sweet revenge lay waiting for his hungry eyes.

CHAPTER 10

"Seven," Nishi mumbled to herself. The star her father used to draw had seven rays.

Arpit looked quizzically at her.

"I am trying to map your history in my mind," she explained. "The way I see it, there have been seven major instances in your life when you could have, rather *should have*, chosen to flow the river down a different course. You can say, in other words, that there were seven switches which you turned the wrong way."

"Only *seven*?"

"Yes. Think hard. On seven different occasions in your life, you took a decision, or avoided taking one, that radically altered the course of your life. If you want to go back, you must turn back each of these seven switches."

Arpit shook his head in confusion. "The way I see it, my life has been one long, endless litany of errors and misjudgments. Looking for seven mistakes is like searching for grass in a one-hectare plot of weeds." He smiled ruefully at the agrarian simile he had just used. Even today . . .

"Maybe I can help you get started?" Nishi offered. "The first switch was when you did not intervene to help Harpalji send Mannat to the boarding school in Shimla. The second, as I can discern it, was when you refused to use your power over your Dad to call him to Meharsar to discuss the lake issue with Veerji."

"The third, when I did not stay on in Chandigarh for my studies, and lost three years that I could have spent with Mannat."

"The next time was when you took her to Kasauli and kissed her and then went away without a promise . . ."

Arpit nodded. "Switch number five, when, being the blockhead that I was, I did not tell her in Amritsar that I loved her too."

"And the sixth, not coming back to Meharsar when she called you in New York, before she could be married to Simarjeet."

"The last," Arpit's voice quavered, ". . . but you did not let me complete my story the other day. In Goa I—"

"Don't, Arpit. You need to save your strength for the re-streaming process . . . or re-dreaming, if you wish to call it that. Believe me, it's going to be more painful than anything you have experienced till now."

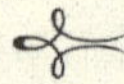

It wasn't easy explaining the process to Arpit.

"You must understand," Nishi said earnestly, "that it is impossible to actually change the past. Your karma has already been mapped out on the basis of your actions till now. And each action hacks the path for the next. So what I will do is, I will put you into a state of trance in which you will re-live—"

"What!" Arpit exploded. "Is this some sort of an exercise in catharsis? '*Poor boy, he must be allowed to let go of all the emotional pain . . .*' I did not come to you looking for therapy, Nishi! I thought you had powers to solve my problem!"

"Arpit, I am an *intuitive mortal.* Neither I nor any mortal can violate the laws of the Universe. Listen to me for a moment. Do you remember the conversation we had about dreams being *memories of places* our mind travels to? As mortals, we cannot access that pool of Time where the past, present, and future converge. We can do so only in sleep, when the subconscious opens the gateway to that realm. Even then, ordinary dream-journeys do not carry a person very far. Most people are so tightly bound to their daily world that they only touch this pool briefly before being pulled back into waking consciousness. So, I will be the Pathfinder in your dream—guiding you, one-by-one, to each of the seven switches. In that borrowed Time, you will confront the complacency and perversity which had prevented you from doing what was right, and change your decision."

"Only a dream-change," Arpit put in bitterly. "It does not help at all."

"It does. The past sows the intentions for the future. I also told you that *dreams are memories of what is to come.* A powerfully summoned and deeply desired dream is strong enough to be carried back into your real state and significantly change the course of your present life. And the present will ultimately influence the future."

"It's not the future I am seeking to change. It is the past."

"You are wrong, Arpit. What you really want in the end is to get back all you have lost. What was lost backwards can only return forwards. There is no other way."

"So if I do what you tell me to, I can hope to have Mannat back in my life tomorrow?" He became the eager schoolboy again.

Nishi shook her head with a faint smile. "I can't guarantee that, Arpit. But one thing is certain. If you truly manage to confront your fear and loss and if you take the right decisions this time around, you will get what was meant for you from the start. Man's folly can put off divine will for only so long. Remember, for every switch that you turn the other way, there will be a corresponding change in your life here and now. Those changes might be extremely disturbing, tumultuous, even destructive. But you have to accept them and continue till the very last switch. Once you have turned all the seven switches, you will find that the map of your life has been redrawn."

Arpit sat in a thoughtful silence for many minutes. Then he raised his head and asked, "Nishi, if this works, why didn't you use it to reverse the destruction wreaked on your village?"

Her face became streaked with pain. "Because redreaming can be used only to amend one's own follies. What happened to Gumgyaat was not my doing, nor my father's. In that sense you are luckier than me. You still have a chance to undo things."

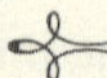

"We need to find the right place to carry out the redreaming. It should be a place that evokes nostalgia, a place you feel secure in, a place with strong emotional associations," Nishi mused. "Ideally, it should be Meharsar."

"No, no!" Arpit shook his head agitatedly. "I just don't have the courage to go there. It's impossible for me to face them."

"Well, you must think of some other place then," Nishi said. *But for how long could he avoid facing them once they started with the redreaming?* she thought.

"What about my house in Chandigarh? Mannat and I spent a lot of time there . . . we were under the same roof there for many weekends."

"Hmmm . . . I wanted a more outdoor-ish surrounding. The Meharsar lake would have been ideal, but you say you can't stand it. Well then, Chandigarh it is."

"How long will it take?" Arpit's voice came out in a strangled whisper.

"One session could last anywhere between one hour, which

is not likely, to one day. And we won't do more than one session a month, so, seven months. By that time the restoration of the house should also be completed. It will be symbolic," she smiled.

"Seven months!" Arpit gasped in dismay.

"It's not too long, not when you compare it to twenty-nine years of blighted existence. Arpit, one month is the minimum time we need for the karmic effects of your redreamed decisions to start emerging. You will go back one switch at a time, from the last to the earliest. Every change will make the next one easier," *and more difficult*, she thought, keeping this last bit to herself.

They chose the room where Mannat used to spend her weekends. "I haven't dared to sleep here in years, though I was strongly tempted to. It would have brought her accusingly close." Arpit touched the bed with mingled reverence and regret. "Such hopes I harboured during those days! Some of them were borrowed, some my own. What do I need to do with this?" he raised an eyebrow as Nishi held out a bottle of mustard oil.

"Rub it on your nostrils. It might just take you back to Meharsar . . ."

"Throw a couple of pebbles at me, then," Arpit retorted and laughed, his eyes suspiciously damp as he stared out of the window at the dim twilight. A scraggly mango tree had sprung up in the empty backyard, and it seemed to be struggling against the desolation of the place. But the mango tree back in Meharsar had been thick and tall and full of childhood secrets. Was it still there?

Nishi seemed to hesitate for a second. Then she leaned over and drew something in chalk at the foot of the bed. Arpit peered at it in curiosity. It was a star enclosed within a circle, its rays resembling lotus petals. He scanned Nishi's face for an explanation, but her expression was inscrutable.

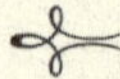

The bed grows hard under him like a huge slab of rock. He turns on his side, the roughness of the rock cutting right through his clothes and grazing his skin. He tries to cry out in pain, but water rushes into his mouth before any sound can escape his lips. And he starts sinking. Fast.

The deafening rumble of water rushing into him and pulling him down fills his ears and drowns out all other sensations, except for the cold. The water is freezing and he feels long, icy fingers begin to curl around his lungs in a vice-like grip, drawing the breath out of him.

Suddenly his feet touch sand . . . or is it quicksand? Will he get sucked to his death? Has he reached the bottom already? Drowned already?! He panics now; he doesn't want to die, not yet, not like this. He starts flailing around desperately. Isn't there anything he can hold on to? He is sinking at an alarming rate. Down, down, down . . . down to where the sand is treacherously and seductively soft. And warm. If only he could lie there for a moment or two. He would gather his strength and try swimming back to the surface.

Something tickles his nostrils. Weeds. They smell of rotting vegetables, stagnant water, and vomit. The smell makes him dizzy and nauseated. Suddenly something, or someone, turns him over on his stomach and pushes his face into the sand. He wants to throw up now, but his face is in the sand. The sand enters through his parted lips and fills his mouth. There's sand in his ears. In his eyes. In his nose. He opens his mouth to scream, but finds himself flipped over again.

The water is not pressing down on him anymore. It feels warm, strangely comfortable. Everything is quiet now, like sound has been cut off in entirety. It's a hollow, eerie silence. Sinister, empty. He feels himself rising now, floating towards the surface, and then, just as suddenly as he had felt the water rush in and drag him down, he tastes the dry dust of land.

He opens his eyes. He's been set down in a dusty street. The street looks familiar. He's spent innumerable summer afternoons here as a child. He remembers it now—Amritsar. He gets up and starts walking. He doesn't have any shoes on and the scorching sun has heated up the tarmac, but he continues to walk on, ignoring the hot flashes of pain emanating from his feet. He knows they'll be tender and sore later. He does not care.

He knows exactly where he is. He can almost sense when the lanes will start closing in on him. He starts running now, faster and faster. And just as the weather-beaten buildings of this ghost town start leaning over, seemingly intent on trapping him there forever, he escapes from their dark, dangerous shadows and bursts out into wheat fields. Wheat fields?!

He slows down now. The wheat stalks, golden and heavy, bend protestingly under his fingers as he caresses them. A light breeze ruffles his hair and cools the sweat on his face. A little ahead in the distance, he sees a mimosa tree. There's a swing hanging from its thick branches, still swaying, as if someone had just gotten off it. Everything looks strangely familiar. But he can't stop here any longer to figure out the why of it. He has to find her . . .

He hurries forward. The fields now give way to the courtyard of a big, unpretentious-looking house. He's been here before as well. He knows that for sure. There's a huge mango tree in the courtyard and he remembers scampering up its trunk as a child. There used to be a dog here, old and lazy, always sleeping under the tree, not bothered with the comings and goings of the household as long as he got his meals on time. He remembers how he would try to annoy the dog by poking it with a stick while it slept in the hot summer afternoons. Suddenly, he realises that he is in Meharsar and that the house in front of him is Veerji's house. But the house appears deserted now. It is so quiet that he can hear the bees buzzing over the bhor of the mango tree. Where are all the people? He approaches the house cautiously. He knows he has to reach it before . . . before what?!

As he walks in through the gate, he sees a hand pump to his left. He turns and walks towards it. It is hot and all the running has made him thirsty. He pumps again and again. A mocking gurgle tells him that there is no water here.

When he turns back, there is an old man standing at the door of the house, leaning heavily against a walking stick, and dressed all in white with a long, white beard flowing down from his chin. He walks closer towards the house; the old man says nothing, but his stance is unwelcoming. As he climbs the steps to the house, the old man turns his face away and stands with his back towards him. He knows that he should beg for forgiveness from this shrivelled old man, but he doesn't know what he should beg forgiveness for. He throws himself at the old man's feet.

"Go away, Baldev! Just go away!" the old man speaks slowly, hurt and dejection underlining his words.

"No, no! Please, you have to let me in. You have to give me a chance!" he begs now, a terrible sense of foreboding gripping him. But the old man stays silent, his face turned away from him. "Look at me! Look at me once at least! Please!" he screams now, scared and desperate.

He gets up and grips the old man's shoulders in an attempt to turn him around. But in the next instant, the old man whirls around and without saying a word, pushes him away. He falls down the stairs and lands in the dry, dusty courtyard of his childhood. He's cut his lips and he can taste blood. He looks up at the old man in horror, in recognition, in anguish. Veerji!

Before he can say anything at all, something heavy and unforgiving hits his head. He feels his skull crack open.

"Go away, Baldev! And don't ever come back." He hears Veerji say.

The last thing he sees before the cold darkness descends is Veerji's face—deeply wrinkled and cracked like dry earth, disintegrating into dust and eroding away . . .

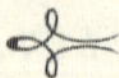

"What happened?" demanded Arpit, bewildered and scared. "Why could I not reach the switch?"

"It is inevitable that you will dredge up some sediment while mining the river-bed of memory," Nishi replied cryptically.

He glared at her with such indignation that she was driven to laugh. "You're such a child, Arpit! These are not instant noodles. This was only the first attempt. We'll try again, it will happen. Don't worry."

"Were you, umm, able to see what I saw?"

"I was. It was fearful, wasn't it?"

"Horrible," Arpit shuddered. "Nishi, do you think Veerji . . ."

She guessed what he wanted to ask, but she deliberately stayed silent.

"After all I did *not* do for him, and for the village, is it possible that he has come to hate me?" It had never struck him before. Whatever might happen, it had seemed impossible that Veerji could harbour even the smallest of a grudge against him. But after the dream, he was not so sure anymore.

Nishi's voice was firm. "No, Arpit. I am sure he does not hate you."

"How can you be so confident? Did he not strike me in my dream?"

"That was only an embodiment of your own guilt. Now that you have lived its horror, it will not trouble you again and it will be a little easier to proceed with the redreaming now. To be on the safe side, however, I think we should do the next redreaming session at daybreak. You will be less susceptible to morbid vibrations then. And this time, I will put a basin of water next to your bed. You must imagine that you are lying on the shores of a lake."

"What on earth for?"

"Don't you understand? Meharsar is the *sutradhar*, the unifying thread in your entire tale. You need to keep it in your consciousness whenever you try to go back. Since you did not take the lake with you, the lake nearly took you with it. You can say that it made full use of its one chance at retribution. Usually, Nature is not so vindictive, which is not to say that she is not ruthlessly exacting. But it was partly my fault. When you refused to do this redreaming in Meharsar, I should have looked for another way to have you near water, even if it was symbolic. Thank God I had drawn that symbol by your bed. Otherwise, you might have lost your mind even before waking up."

Arpit sat silent with shock. Though he had not really had a clear idea of exactly what the redreaming would entail, he had definitely not expected this. His mind scrambled now to make some sense of the implications of the dream he had just had. Suddenly, he sat up. What about his father . . . if Meharsar was so angry with him, then . . . Arpit shuddered. "Nishi," he turned frantically towards Nishi, "if what I did could make Meharsar so angry, what punishment awaits my father?"

It was Nishi's turn to shudder. "Don't even ask that, Arpit. Don't even ask."

This time it works. Almost as soon as he starts imagining the sacred waters of the Meharsar lake lapping at his sides, he finds himself being gently pulled inside that cushioned coolness. This time there is no revulsion, no terror, no water rushing into his body and filling up his ears and pulling him down. The lake draws him softly into its lap. And then, in the next instant, he finds himself deposited, just as gently, on a beach.

Ah, he knows where and when this is. Mannat would be here any moment now. He gets up and tries to flatten his unruly hair with his hands.

It seems like he has waited an eternity before he sees her appear. Against the smudged ink of the night, her long yellow skirt gleams like a leftover sunset. She has grown slender since he saw her last and her face has lost its sunrise glow. Have those people been starving her? Arpit bristles. She is staring towards the sea as she walks towards it, oblivious to everything else. He hides behind a coconut palm to watch her.

She stops where the waves curl around her feet and run back. For a moment and more, she stays still, and then she starts walking further and further into the sea. He panics. The tide is rising. It's dangerous for her to go on like this. She must be stopped.

Then a horrible thought strikes him. Is she trying to drown herself? Impossible. The Mannat he has known would never give up on life. Then he remembers that he has progressively lost Mannat over the last few years. This woman walking far out into sea . . . she is probably a stranger to him now.

Unable to bear the very idea, he abandons his hiding place and rushes towards her. Mannat does not hear him wade his way through the water and come to a stop behind her. A mild breeze blows her hair about her face. Her skirt, wet and translucent now, clings to her body. He wants to reach out and touch her, but something about the way she is standing stops him. When she finally turns around, there is an other-worldly glaze over her eyes. She does not even notice him.

"M-Mannat," he gasps.

Her eyes widen in shock. She blinks frantically, as if to make sure her eyes are not deceiving her. She takes a step forward and reaches out to touch him, sure that since it's a phantom she sees, her hand will pass right through him. But it hits him square on his forehead. He reels back, grabbing her hand for support. They both nearly fall, but he manages to steady himself at the last minute. She is in his arms again. He can't believe it. Nothing has changed. Not him. Not her. And nothing between them. His heart soars. Without thinking, he kisses her. She does not struggle or push him away, but neither does she respond. She lies passive in his arms as he brands her fervently with his thwarted passion. She is maddeningly soft and pliant, so much so that he fears he will crush her. Her skin is so warm, he wonders if she has a fever. He can smell his own sweat and alcohol on her.

All of a sudden, though, she goes stiff. He releases her, trying to scan her face. But it's only paler than before.

"Are you happy with him?" he blurts out the question which has been tormenting him for so long now.

She looks at him then, as if she was seeing him for the first time. A slow smile spreads over her face and she nods.

"You are lying," he hisses.

"No." Her voice sounds as if it has been soaked overnight in sea water. "I am not lying, Arpit Singh. You are deceiving yourself. And drunk, are you?" Her words slice through his heart.

"It's my customary state these days."

"If you think this will win my sympathy, you are wrong." She looks down as if to watch the waves lapping at their feet. He looks down too, and finding her attention diverted, he pulls her back into his arms. She closes her eyes while he kisses her lips—first tenderly, then with increasing ferocity. A sharp intake of breath is all he hears as he presses his body against hers.

He reaches for her hand—he wants her to put her arms around him—but he finds it holding something. A mobile phone. She snatches her hand away and holds up the phone to his face just as it starts vibrating silently. It is an incoming call. 'Sunny' it says. He lunges again for it, but it's too late; she has picked up the call and is holding the phone to her ear.

"Sunny, would you mind rushing here, please? I think I'm being followed. No, don't panic, but please get here quickly. You know where to find me, right? Yes . . . our very own spot."

She disconnects the call and turns into a block of ice. "My husband will be here in five minutes. I don't want him to see us like this. Please leave."

He snarls. "Let him."

"Do you really want him to? Are you prepared for what he might do to you?"

"This couldn't be you!" Sheer disbelief prickles his nerves. He increases the pressure of his hands on her wrists, but she continues to stand there

impassively. He hates the hint of a triumphant smirk on her face. "Ah," he says, trying to cover up his hurt with sarcasm, "I should've known. You always wanted to move up in life. Well, you certainly have done well for yourself. After all, what could have been better than marrying a British citizen?"

In one slashing move, she pushes him off her. Throwing him one last look of inexpressible disgust, she starts running back towards the resort.

Anger and pain drum inside his head. His vision starts blurring. "Mannat!" he calls out.

Perhaps it's not someone calling out her name as much as his scalded voice that makes her stop for a moment. The clouds have parted and the moon casts a soft light on the beach. She turns around. He can see her expression clearly. She looks weary and forlorn, almost like a lake sucked dry. If anyone touches her now, she will crumple and wither. He is paralysed. And even as she continues looking at him, she sinks to the ground. From the way she doubles over, he knows she is in pain. But he also knows now that he has no power to alleviate her suffering.

Someone else is striding towards her now, a tall, well-built man. Sunny. Arpit retreats into the shadows of the coconut palms.

"Mandy! Are you okay?" Sunny demands, pulling her into his arms. "I was so worried!"

She clings to him, murmuring words he cannot hear.

"Where is that bastard who was stalking you?"

He watches her shake her head. "He isn't here anymore."

Sunny's voice is clear, though, "Wait, I will contact the beach patrol. He won't get away with this!! I think you need a doctor, Mandy. Let's go back to the resort."

Sunny helps her to her feet and they walk away from him. She does not even look back at him once. He feels himself dissolving now, like salt grains in water. The sea seems to be pulling him back in like a submissive tide.

Arpit awakens with a shock, the taste of weed and water and anguish still in his mouth.

Unlike Arpit, Nishi emerged slowly and gently from the dream. Her composure further enraged him. "What the bloody hell was that?" he demanded. "It all happened exactly as it had happened before! Nothing changed! Not *one* damned thing!"

She continued to look at him in mute sympathy.

"This is all a sham, Nishimaya Gaur . . ."

"Don't mix these two names, Arpit." Her voice rang with warning.

"Like I care! You are a fraud. You *promised* that you will help me turn back each switch. But—"

"No, Arpit. I promised only to guide you to the switch. And I did that, didn't I? I watched the entire scene unfold. I willed you to do what you should have. But that was all I could lawfully do. You, and only you, had the power to bring the change."

"Then why couldn't I?"

"Perhaps because the past has struck deeper roots than you have calculated. It is not enough to just be there and let your wishes translate spontaneously into action. You have to make a *conscious* effort to turn the course of events. Conscious . . . and uphill. You have to go against the grain. It is anything but easy."

"What do I do now, then?" he groaned.

"Go to the sixth switch. We must keep trying till we have reached the end. And it's going to get harder and harder as we go further in."

CHAPTER 11

Arpit locked himself up in his room and drank. When he couldn't drink anymore, he tottered to the bathroom and threw up, not even bothering to wipe his mouth clean afterwards. Sweat and vomit caked his clothes and permeated into his pores, and as the days passed, a morbid exultation stole over him—*he was dying at last. Perhaps she was dying too. Perhaps this was the way they were meant to unite finally. No Nishimaya could help him. Only death could.*

There was no one to disturb him now. Nishi had left after the first redreaming session, and he had thrown away his phone somewhere after she left. But the dreams . . . the dreams were not leaving him alone. Like a jammed record, the scene of the seventh switch kept playing over and over again inside his head, till he could feel the entire sea pressing down upon him. Nothing silenced the echo of the words from that night. And the look on Mannat's face haunted him. But after three days, when he could bear it no longer, he forced himself to take a bath, change his clothes, swallow two slices of dry toast, and step out. Mindlessly, he drove to one of the new swanky malls in Panchkula, wanting to lose himself in the crowd. He had no clue what to do and where to go. Walking unsteadily and drawing wary glances from the people around, he went to one of the coffee shops and pulled a chair without bothering to check whether the table was empty or not. And then he saw her sitting opposite him.

From the way she was dressed and from the coquettish glances she was throwing at him, it did not take him long to understand who she was. The realisation did not repel him. He didn't get up and leave, instead, he ordered the first coffee he saw on the menu and then proceeded to stare shamelessly at her. She responded with a smile and an intentional brush of her leg against his.

Later, he did not bother to hold the door of his car open for her as she got in authoritatively, adjusting the rear-view mirror to check her makeup. Without a word he drove off. His first intention had been to take her to a seedy hotel, but he did not know any seedy hotels. Perhaps a secluded spot near the railway line would be a better idea. They had a car—nothing else was needed.

But as he drove past the railway track which led to Kalka, he felt his nerves scrunch into an unbearable tightness and his vision became blurred. What was he doing?! The next moment, he swerved the car towards the edge of the road, turned it around, and started to drive back towards Chandigarh, his foot pressed hard on the accelerator.

"What's the matter?" she demanded in her accented voice.

He said nothing until he reached the Mani Majra crossing, a busy intersection. Stopping the car there, he mumbled, "Get out."

"What? What the fuck!"

"Out!" He dived into his pockets for all the money he could find. Throwing it at her, he waited only till she had scrambled out—hurling the choicest of abuses at him even as she picked up all the money he had thrown at her—before he rolled up his windows till not even a whiff of fresh air could enter, and shot himself away as fast as he could.

"What was I going to do, Mannat? What are you making me do?"

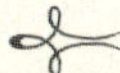

Nishi was waiting at the gate for him when he got back. Her look was reproachful. Without a word, he brushed past her into the house, not waiting to see whether she followed him or not. At that moment, he couldn't have cared less whether she stayed or left. When she walked in behind him, he muttered, "Go make yourself comfortable."

Nishi decided that she owed it to herself to take a bath and eat something before confronting Arpit about his behaviour over the last few days. She had been worried about him. After the first redreaming session, she had been forced to leave him alone in Chandigarh and go back to Delhi for some work. Not only had he never called her back, but he had not picked up her calls either. And she had called a million times. She had understood and expected him to shut himself up after that first session. But his emotional instability and his volatile behaviour had scared her. There was no knowing what he was capable of when left alone.

She looked at him now—sitting on the sofa, tense and edgy, with a wild look in his eyes. She felt as if someone had made a hole in her neck, jabbed a straw in, and sucked out all her powers. What a huge mistake she had made in taking on this thankless nutcase!

But what she wasn't willing to admit just yet was the fact that her motives had not been purely altruistic, for at the back of her mind lurked the wild hope that by saving Arpit and thereby salvaging Meharsar, she might just find the key to reverse the evil spell cast on Gumgyaat twenty-six years ago.

They busied themselves in the restoration project. Arpit wanted the house to be ready by January so that they could open the tour to coincide with the Patiala Heritage Festival. It was a demanding deadline to meet, but Nishi plunged herself into the work.

When more than a month had passed since the last redreaming session, she suggested that they should go back to Chandigarh for the next one.

Back in his house in Chandigarh, just before they were about to start the redreaming, Arpit, edgier than before, looked at Nishi anxiously and said, "I hope it will work this time . . ."

"It better," thought Nishi, anxious too, but outwardly brisk and dismissive of his fears. She kept a bowl of water near Arpit and drew her father's symbol on the floor next to his feet. With one last encouraging look at Arpit, she closed her eyes and slipped into another world almost instantly.

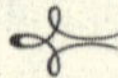

He wakes up inside a sweltering, suffocating room. There are windows in the room, but they are closed shut with wooden shutters. When he tries to open them for a breath of air, they resist stubbornly. He tugs harder and harder till one shutter flies open, sending him staggering backward. Beyond the shutter there are horizontal iron bars through which he can see a dusty, deserted courtyard. There is nothing in the room except a battered charpoy. The floor is dusty, with stray twigs littering it. The room has been closed for so long that the air hangs heavy and still inside it.

He knows he has been here before, perhaps just once, but he can't place it. Frustration gnaws at him as he realises how important it is to retrieve this bit of information. He needs to be prepared not just for what is to come, but also to change it.

There is a nervous tapping on the door. He opens it to find Harjeet, Mannat's youngest brother, standing in the doorway with a scared, pinched look on his face. Now Arpit knows where he is—the abandoned one-room shack on the road connecting Meharsar to the highway. It used to be the post office till the new building was constructed. It is rarely used now, except occasionally by the village lads for a secret game of cards. It was Harjeet who had decided—after giving in to Arpit's agonised pleas—that the room would be the perfect place for him to bring Mannat to meet Arpit.

"Is she with you?" Arpit asks feverishly.

"Yes." Harjeet's voice is heavy with guilt already. He has taken a huge risk in bringing Mannat here with just a day left for the marriage. She is not supposed to leave the house unattended. Right now they should actually be in the beauty salon, with Mannat getting ready for the sangeet. Everyone in the family had insisted that she must be sent to a proper beauty salon before the function. After all, this was the first time anyone from their village was getting married to an NRI. The usual wedding preparations would not do. Everything had to be bigger, grander. The wedding itself would be in Jalandhar, where most of the Shergills' extended family in India was. Despite the expense, Harpal had booked a high-end salon in the city for Mannat's big day. But for today, a modest one in Amritsar would do.

By lying and saying that the salon appointment has been rescheduled, Harjeet has managed to bring Mannat out of the house an hour earlier than she was supposed to. This gives Arpit and Mannat a fighting chance, or so Arpit thinks. He has lulled himself into believing that if Mannat has agreed to this desperate meeting, it means she is ready to be convinced by him. But when she enters the room with noncommittal grimness on her face, showing neither fear nor eagerness, this confidence lurches slightly.

"Praaji, not more than fifteen minutes," pleads Harjeet. "We simply must be in Amritsar by four. If anyone gets wind of this . . ."

"Don't worry, Harjeet. We" —Mannat darts him a sharp glance—

"know how precious every moment is. But where will you go?"

"I will find a place where I can't be seen from the road. If anyone catches sight of me here, there will be a thousand questions to face. And Praaji, for heaven's sake close that window. No one should suspect there is anyone inside this room."

With that, Harjeet tiptoes out of the room and leaves the two of them alone. He is the only one Arpit trusted enough to ask such a favour of. Years ago, when Harjeet had badly torn his brand new school shoes while climbing trees with the other village lads and had been trembling at the thought of what his father would say—it was tough enough for Harpal to put three children through school without having to bear any extra expense—Arpit had given him all the money he had saved from his generous pocket money to buy another pair. Harjeet had never forgotten that.

Mannat bolts the door behind Harjeet and turns around to face Arpit. Her face is no longer stone cold. Her eyes are smouldering with dark anger, her chest is heaving slightly, and she is biting her lower lip. With her face scrubbed clean like a blank canvas for the stylist to paint on later, she looks like a fragile rosebud. Albeit a rosebud with hidden thorns, Arpit thinks.

He comes forward and though she resists, he takes her hands in his own. "Let's not waste time, Mannat," he whispers without a preamble. "It will be too late by tomorrow. Come with me now."

Her gaze scalds him like hot coal tar. "Where?"

"Anywhere," he fumbles. ". . . to Delhi perhaps? Yes, Delhi would be the best. We could stay there for a while. Dad would never find out. And I would . . ." he falters, realising how pathetic he sounds.

"And why should I come with you, Arpit Singh?"

"Because . . . because I love you, Mannat!" Even as he speaks, the words sound lame and childish.

She takes a step towards him and slaps him—one by one on both cheeks. He reels, more from the sight of the solitaire glinting on her left hand than from the slaps.

"Why?" Her voice is like a whiplash, cold with repressed rage. "Why now?"

He grabs her shoulders miserably. "I know I should have said this a long time ago. B-b-but I never imagined that you—" He breaks off suddenly and then looks at her imploringly. "Oh Mannat! Why did you ever agree to marry him? Why?!"

"I don't have time to waste. And I certainly don't want anyone to find me here. So—"

"No, Mannat, listen, my car is ready. We can just hop into it and drive off. Harjeet will tell everyone that you are at the salon. No one will miss you till evening!"

"And then? Then what? What will happen after that, huh? Oh wait, you didn't think of that, did you? Of course not. Why should you care what happens to the reputation of an entire village?"

"Of course I care, but . . ."

"No! You are lying," her voice drops back into its ice tomb. "You never cared. If you did, you would have answered my letters. You would have come when I called you. And even now you would have . . . but never mind. I gave up on you long ago."

"Don't say that!" His voice quavers with despair.

"I must leave now."

Has he simply imagined the muddy moisture seeping into her words? Without waiting for him to reply, she unbolts the door and steps out. Finding himself powerless even to gaze after her, Arpit sinks to the floor.

The scene started to flicker like a movie with a bad print. Nishi could feel herself shivering and trembling, almost as if she would disintegrate any moment now. She knew Mannat must be stopped, but Arpit seemed to be just as helpless now as he had been during the last session. And much as she wanted to, there was simply nothing she could do to help him. She was like a spectator strapped to her seat in a movie theatre.

All of a sudden, the scene snapped back into clarity again. Arpit had gotten up from the floor and he was about to—

Before Mannat can step over the threshold, Arpit summons all his courage and calls out, "Mannat! Wait!"

There is an edge of resolution in his voice which makes her stop and come back inside the room, albeit a little hesitantly. The mask has slipped a bit now—she no longer looks stern and dismissive.

He swallows before saying, "You are right. I didn't think of the consequences of us eloping. I'm sorry. Let me come home with you and talk to Chayaji. I know it's a huge thing to call off a wedding, especially with just one day left, but at least it's better than marrying the wrong person and being miserable for the rest of your life. I know Harpal Chayaji will understand, and if he won't, Chayiji certainly will. If they both refuse, I will talk to Veerji . . ."

"It's no use, Arpit." She shakes her head despairingly. "There will be a scandal either way. And it's the last thing I want for my family. They have seen enough trouble already."

"But your happiness? Our happiness?"

"You have been happy without me for years. I'm sure you will manage. As for me, what makes you think I won't be happy with Sunny? There is absolutely nothing wrong with him."

"You know the answer, Mannat."

"I don't know any answer," she retorts irritably. "But I do know what your Dad's reaction will be. And I don't want him to insult my family any further."

"Any further?" he asks blankly.

"Oh, don't pretend that you don't know," she shoots back waspishly. "And if you really don't, if your father did not tell you what he said to us the last time he was here, then you are a bigger fool than I thought."

"This can't be you speaking."

"Hah! That's exactly what Veerji said to your Dad three months ago,

when he turned down Baoji's proposal for our marriage."

"What?!"

"Your Dad came to Meharsar to claim his share of the ancestral property," Mannat says listlessly. A stunned Arpit fails to notice she is not saying 'Baldev Chayaji' anymore. "Beeji, as you know, had made over the lake-side plot to Veerji. Veerji had been thinking of buying your Dad's land at a good price—he didn't suppose your father would have any interest in the land now, given that he had settled abroad—and merging it with the plot Beeji had left for him. We had a bumper wheat crop last year and some of the village youngsters wanted to set up a bakery to supply bread and biscuits and other confectionary items to all the villages around here. Your Dad's and Beeji's plots put together would have added up to about four hectares of land, all of which Veerji planned to donate for the project. There would be enough land not only for the bakery, but for an entire complex of shops selling other locally-made items as well. Veerji thought that it would help the village youth to stand on their own feet and not be dependent on that factory for jobs. But your Dad ruined everything. His lawyer said he will not sell the land to anyone but lease it out for an important project."

"P-project?"

"You would know better than I do what that is."

"Mannat," he gropes frantically for words now, "how is this possible? Dad never told me anything!"

This time she stares at him not with fury or disappointment, but with a tired flatness. "That's between you and your Dad."

"And . . . and the marriage proposal?"

"Veerji had wanted it since we were children. When Baoji suggested the same thing to him, he . . . never mind that now. But when my father humbly put this suggestion before your Dad, his answer was, 'Manjot is a nice girl by Meharsar standards, Harpal. But surely you are harbouring unrealistic expectations'—your father always knew how to coil words like a noose around a person's neck—'if you think my Stanford-educated son could marry her. They would just not be compatible with each other! I suggest that

you marry her off to some nice village lad before it is too late.' I will never forget the look on Baoji's face to my dying day."

He is paralysed with horror now. His tongue feels thick. He can say nothing more . . . not even to plead his obliviousness to what she has just told him. So his Dad had been coming to India without telling him? Wait, hadn't Nishi suggested the same thing?

Nishi? Who is Nishi?

The next moment he feels wisps of himself flying off, as if he is being clumsily removed from his husk. Mannat and the room waver like ripples in a pond. Now he is acutely conscious of the fact that he is redreaming. He knows that in another instant, he will find himself back in his room, having lost Mannat even harder than he had before . . .

But just before he thuds back to reality, Mannat hisses, "I don't care how rude this sounds, but I hate your father with a hatred I had never thought possible." With that, she walks towards the door and unbolts it. She steps out and is about to leave, when she turns to look at him one last time. "Like father, like son." And she disappears into thin air.

Reality jolted Arpit awake. He grabbed Nishi's shoulder and started sobbing like a child.

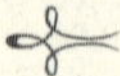

"Are you in your senses?" demanded Nishimaya.

Arpit nodded with calm despair. "I was a fool in the first place to want something like this. Don't waste any more of your time and energy on me, Nishi. Let's call this off."

Stupefied, Nishi stared at him. "You can't give up so soon. You've just managed to turn a switch at last!"

"And what happened after that? What I found out won't let me sleep now. Mannat hates me. She *hates* me! I would've rather died or continued living like before than found out about this!"

"It's not you she hates, Arpit . . ."

"Are you losing your hearing with age, Nishi?" Arpit snapped. "Didn't you hear her say distinctly: 'Like father, like son'?"

Nishi threw up her hands in exasperation. "That was just her . . . her thwarted love speaking, Arpit. You know what your father did to Meharsar. And to top it all, he prevented your marriage to Mannat. He is the real target of her anger. Since he wasn't around, she vented it all on you."

"Done with the psychology?" Arpit asked, bitingly sarcastic. "You do explain everything so well. No wonder you can convince people that you can read their fortunes."

"What's wrong with you?! Wait, you haven't taken anything again, have you?"

"Shouldn't your notable intuition tell you that?"

"No, it doesn't," Nishi snapped. "You and your stupid petulance are draining my intuition, and my patience into the bargain. But you cannot drain my sense of purpose! You're the one who got me into all of this. You can't leave now. It has become as important for me as it is for you."

"Important for you?"

"Yes! I can't make you understand it. I can't even make myself understand it. But what I do know for sure is that we are doing the right thing!"

"I don't deserve her, Nishi," Arpit said sorrowfully. "It will be an unpardonable crime if I try to change my destiny."

"Wait, who told you destiny is static? Haven't I been trying to make you understand that it's all a matter of the choices we make? And right now, you are going to make a disastrous choice if you back out of redreaming. Don't blame it later on destiny."

Belligerence had given way to pensiveness. "If my father had not sent me away at thirteen; if I had been a carefree village boy, tearing my clothes while climbing trees, playing in the heat and dust and coming home all tanned; if I had herded buffaloes and bathed in the village pond; if I knew what it was to farm the land and eat under the shade of a tree; if on hot afternoons, Mannat had brought me rotis and onions and cold *lassi*; if I had snatched the glass and kissed her, and poured out my feelings behind a haystack, safe from prying eyes; if we had sneaked out at night to meet on a lonely rooftop . . . I would have won her. Wouldn't I, Nishi?"

Nishi's eyes shone with rare mischief at his romantic musings. "I think the mosquitoes would have been a bit of a deterrent to your romantic nocturnal rendezvous. Grow up, Arpit. You would have cribbed about a thousand things had you stayed on. I'm glad both you and Mannat got a decent education. Feebler minds would have snapped under the weight of this love which refuses to let either of you live, or die, in peace. But you have changed your mind about dying, haven't you? Don't squander this one hope. We have a lot of work to do."

CHAPTER 12

When he got home, Sunny was pleasantly surprised to see Mannat sitting cross-legged on the bed, cutting something from an old newspaper. In the early days of their marriage, he had made it known that he disliked this manner of sitting. It seemed uncouth to him. Mannat had not protested even once before dropping the habit completely. This time, though, the sight of Mannat sitting like that was a relief; it was a sign that she was recovering her old self. Let her be as uncouth and provincial as she wanted, he would not stop her. It would be worth anything to see her okay.

She started on seeing him, and raising her head, smiled her most genuine smile in months. He sat down next to her on the bed and hugged her.

"Careful, the scissors!" she warned. "At least let me put them down first . . ." He tried to take the scissors from her hand, but she pulled them away. "That's not the way! If you do that, it will cut our relationship. Never take a knife, a pair of scissors or anything which cuts, from another's hand directly. Tell them to put it down first,"she explained, setting down her scissors on the bed, "and pick it up from there."

"Meharsar wisdom?"

She nodded, a watery sunrise breaking upon her face, "Indeed!"

"By the way, what were you doing?"

"Just cutting an old newspaper article so that I can scan it for an email attachment. It was written years ago when I was in college, so it doesn't have an online edition."

"An email? To whom are you sending this stuff?"

"To Sunburst Inc., USA," she replied, her face snapping shut again.

"Sunburst? Did you find a hairball in one of their burgers? Come to think of it, I don't recall ever taking you out to one of their restaurants. How about going out tonight, darling? It's been ages. You really need a change. We both do."

Mannat looked at Sunny. He was obviously unaware of Sunburst Inc.'s proposed venture into the Indian market and she didn't want to say anything just yet. "Not tonight. I made *rajma* for you!

"What? What were you doing in the kitchen?! I told you not to cook, didn't I? Mannat, why don't you ever listen to me?" Sunny tried to hide his delight under a mask of exasperation.

"Sunny, please! I am bored of being a part of the bedclothes! I am fine, really. Come now, let me get dinner ready. Okay?"

Sunny mumbled something and let her pass.

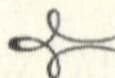

"We need a break," said Sunny. He was sitting at the dining table and watching Mannat bring out the dinner.

"All right, but sample this first," she admonished with mock-sternness, pushing the dish of *rajma* towards him. "I tried not to overdo the gravy. I know you don't like it."

Sunny kissed her hand in reply. She bent down and kissed his cheek. Sighing silently with relief, Sunny continued with his idea, "To think that you have been here nearly a year and you've still not seen London! I feel positively embarrassed. So, I am going to take the whole of next week off, and we will drive around a bit. And haven't you always wanted to see Oxford?"

Mannat's eyes brightened with enthusiasm, but she merely said, "Hmmm . . . and I suppose all of this will be in your accustomed style?"

"Meaning?"

"Meaning we will travel in first-class taxis and stay at the best hotels?" Her mouth twitched just a wee bit.

He shrugged. "What else do you expect? My wife deserves the best."

All of a sudden she put her arms on his shoulder and said softly, "I already have the best."

"Ah, flattery won't make me change my mind, Manjot Shergill. I know you prefer slumming it out, but no hitch hiking or homestay for us. You aren't fit enough yet for such adventure, anyway."

"I am fine now."

"No, you aren't. I will be quaking in my shoes worrying about your health. Besides, you aren't the robust Punjabi girl you used to be, no offence meant. I blame it on the weather, like half my countrymen do for every other thing that goes wrong in their lives. But I can't take any risks. You aren't like that ruddy Kelly who backpacks around the world like it's just another walk in the park. If she weren't so darned good a store accountant, I would never grant her so much leave without a fight. This time she is off to India, to explore her 'roots' apparently."

"India?"

Mandy's hands on his shoulder had suddenly turned into ice. Sunny kicked himself for having mentioned India. Getting up, he turned to face her. "No more of this fascination, Mandy. It will take me a long time to forget what India took away from us.

Let's keep away from this topic."

Her eyes brimmed with tears. "It's my land, Sunny. My home. How can you expect me not to think about it?"

"It may be your land, and I suppose mine too, but *this* is your home, isn't it?" Sunny pleaded, almost pitiably.

She looked down. "I want it to be."

"Do you? Sometimes I think you have left half your heart behind in India. You and your beloved Meharsar . . . how can I ever hope to compete with that?"

Just before they left for their holiday, Mannat finally received a reply from the PR Department of Sunburst Inc. Informing her that they 'were committed to delivering a quality food-experience across the globe', the email insisted that 'Sunburst Inc. takes its responsibility towards the environment very seriously'. They had gone through the articles she had sent, they said, and in a very noncommittal language, they assured her that they were 'taking utmost care in our international franchises to ensure that we give much more than we take from the Earth. We thoroughly check the credentials of every company and individual we associate with' and 'take pride in our outlets' integration with the local community.' The email went on to list the environment-friendly projects that the company was sponsoring, such as tree plantation drives and garbage recycling initiatives. There was no direct mention of Baldev's company, or of any action which they were willing to take against it.

The parting shot was an invitation to 'visit our brand new outlets coming up in a number of small towns and villages, and savour a revolutionary eating experience at the world's fastest-growing chain of restaurants.' Attached was a list of Sunburst restaurants in the Leeds area.

Indignant, Mannat deleted the email reflexively and pushed the laptop away from herself, only to pounce on it the next moment and retrieve the email from the trash folder—there was wisdom, after all, in preserving records. Her lips were pressed tightly together. She had read enough about Sunburst's environmental violations across the world to know that this was just the beginning of Meharsar's ruin. From inhuman and primitive methods of slaughtering cattle and poultry and encouraging supplier monopolies and crop monoculture, to phenomenal amounts of waste being generated by its outlets every day and the irresponsible and dangerous patterns of waste disposal it indulged in, Sunburst Inc. abused every single privilege that it had.

"What a fool I was to appeal to them!" She mentally slapped herself.

And Sunny, who came in at this moment, saw her grim, determined face and muttered to himself, "There she goes again! Are we to have no peace at all?!"

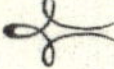

Navneet Sodhi's staff snickered on seeing Veerji approach. Sodhi wasn't too pleased to see him either, but the look he gave to his staff immediately quelled them. He had been sitting peacefully in his verandah, savouring the charm of a departing monsoon on a rain-washed evening, when Veerji barged into his reverie. Some instinct prodded him to ask that they be left alone. His security guards were happy to oblige—they needed a cigarette break, besides, what harm could an eccentric old man do?

Veerji had barely sat down, when Sodhi began, with a touch

of exasperation, to talk. "Veerji, what you plan to do will be of no use. Do you still think we are living in the times of the British? All this fasting and *satyagraha* business will not move anyone. These people are coming here to do business; let them do their work, and you carry on with yours."

Veerji smiled slightly. "Navneetji, I am not a small child who can be pacified. You ask me to stick to my own work—well, my work is farming the land. The day your big company opens its shop in the middle of our fields, this work will be in permanent danger. I have an inkling of what they have done in that, that big country near America . . . what was it now? Ah, yes, Brazil, isn't it? My grandchildren are very intelligent. They keep track of everything that is happening in the world and tell me. They are the ones who said that this Sunburst company . . ." And he launched into a detailed attack on Sunburst's economic and environmental transgressions. "I hope you know that the plot on which they are going to build their burger shop is just about a kilometre-and-a-half from our Holy Lake. Navneetji" —Veerji sounded old and worn now— "you are no stranger to Meharsar. You know what the cola plant has done to our lake. We can't possibly allow another thunderstorm now. And as for the fertility of our land . . ."

Navneet Sodhi was a trifle embarrassed at having underestimated Veerji. The old man had clearly done his research well. Well, it was certainly a shame. While Baldev Singh had a right to decide what to do with his land, the EIA report Sodhi had been instrumental in preparing had clearly warned against any large-scale commercial use of the rich agricultural land of Meharsar and its neighbours. Besides the pollution, there was the threat of a rapid change in land-use patterns once the surrounding areas got converted into residential colonies to accommodate the growing workforce.

And how many of the locals would find work in these new industrial units? Sodhi had data from the last fifteen years of Verva's operations in that area to confirm that while they had been hiring villagers as production-line and front-desk staff, the middle and top management had always been 'imported' from Delhi and other big cities. And even this lower-rung force had precious little job security. Verva Cola was notorious for its hire-and-fire policy which saved it lakhs of rupees every year by doing away with pay raises that it would have had to pay had its staff reached senior positions. And from what Sodhi had heard, Sunburst was even worse.

There was another thing Sodhi knew, but he chose not to tell Veerji about it—the location of the proposed Sunburst project was so ecologically fragile that someone less powerful than Baldev Singh would not have managed to get the environmental clearances so easily. Oh, the man had connections all right, even more than he himself had managed to build after years in politics. He had even opposed the project in the Assembly, citing the EIA report, but to no avail.

Sodhi could have redeemed his respect in Veerji's eyes by telling him of this little fact, but no one in Meharsar was a stranger to the strained relationship between Veerji and his once-upon-a-time-favourite Baldev Singh. Telling him about this would have touched a raw nerve, and for some strange reason he did not want to wound Veerji's feelings any more than could be helped.

The meeting ended in a stalemate. Veerji was adamant. The fast-unto-death would start if the franchise plan was not scrapped. Sodhi knew by now that it was pointless arguing with him. Therefore he privately resolved to at least press for having the restaurant shifted a few kilometres away from the lake so that it would not be an immediate threat to it. And though he knew

Veerji would continue his agitation regardless, at least this might dissuade him from putting his life on the line.

But it wouldn't be easy to achieve even this little. Sodhi's party bosses weren't too happy with his sneaking support to Veerji. He would have to tread carefully so that no one could guess he was behind this. He needed to find someone to be the face of his decision.

Mandy had been more than a little absent-minded throughout their trip. She'd seemed to be recovering so well lately, and now . . . Sunny sighed in exasperation. Did it have something to do with his inadvertent mention of India the other day? No, his friends and family brought it up in their conversations scores of times. The email, then? What had been in that email which had agitated her so much? Sunny was seized by a momentary desire to hack into his wife's email account and read the email for himself. The next instant however, he felt ashamed.

"Sunny! Sunny!"

He looked up to see Mandy calling him and waving excitedly to catch his attention. They had been walking around London and she had just spotted the Big Ben. She was smiling from ear to ear. "Do you know," she informed him gleefully, "that a newspaper once ran a report—on April Fools' day—saying that the Big Ben was to turn digital? The poor Brits nearly choked with indignation."

He laughed, more out of relief than out of actual mirth. He, of course, had already known this fact. Impulsively, he pulled her into his arms and kissed her, right in the middle of the road, amidst a continuous stream of indifferent commuters. But Mannat froze, just for a fraction of a second—it was the first time after the miscarriage that he had touched her like this—before she nestled against his chest. She did make a feeble murmur of protest, though, "Sunny! People are staring!"

"Let them. This is nobody's business but ours."

Mannat looked up and stared at him, her eyes opening wide with shocked surprise. "What did you just say?"

"I said, it is nobody's business but ours. And you jolly well know it isn't. This isn't your—Why, what's the matter, Mandy?"

"*Nobody's business*. Yes, that was it! *Chak de phatte!* Thank you, thank you, thank you! I must write this down before I forget it again." Before Sunny could register what she was saying, she had fished out her cell phone and was typing frantically.

He had no idea what was happening, but he felt sure it had nothing to do with him . . . once again. He hunched his shoulders with dissatisfaction and hailed a taxi. It wasn't any use sightseeing now.

CHAPTER 13

Arpit was busy taking a group of about thirty tourists around Delhi. They were a mixed bunch—three Norwegian teenagers who were roaming around the world before settling down to the college grind, an elderly but energetic Canadian couple celebrating their golden wedding anniversary, five French musicians of whom three were of Indian origin, a couple of professionals from different parts of the United Kingdom, a pretty Danish exchange student, and a sprinkling of Indians who wanted a change from their usual family holidays and business trips. Arpit was enjoying his guests. He was about to finish the Delhi circuit of the tour and take his 'flock' to a lesser-known archaeological site in Haryana when Nishi called him up.

"Hello, Arpit, I am in Delhi and am free tomorrow. Do you mind if I tag along with your group?"

"Would love it, but you do understand that this comes out of your pay, right?" He grinned into the receiver.

"Whenever you happen to give it, that is," she retorted immediately. "But thanks, I'll see you tomorrow."

They were all in the bus, on their way to the last stop in Delhi when it happened.

Arpit was sitting next to Kelly—her real name was Kulwant—Chaddha, the spunky petite girl who had short-cropped hair, much to the horror of her devout Sikh parents, she gleefully told Arpit, and wore a faded red tee-shirt and flared pyjamas in a lurid print today. Kelly spoke fluent Punjabi, interspersing it colourfully with British cuss-words. Arpit had found himself rapidly warming to her throughout the tour. Apparently Kelly had 'romped around' most of the habitable globe at 'dirt-cheap rates.' She had dozens of funny anecdotes up her sleeve, and she preferred to relate those in Punjabi.

"Why?" Arpit asked, peering over Kelly's shoulder at his other British guest—a middle-aged stock broker who looked like Delhi's humidity was not agreeing with him. "It would be nice if you stuck to English, your countryman is feeling a bit left out."

"My jokes are the embodiment of reverse racism," she shot back. "The poor *firang* will not know what has hit him."

"You are rather unconventional, aren't you?"

"That's exactly what my long-suffering parents say, albeit in more censorious tones. What's the point in being normal and boring, I always ask. My boss, now, well, he is a sweetheart, letting me fly off with a week's notice with nothing but a few growls . . . but he hasn't a particle of imagination. You won't catch *him* taking a ride like this. Still, I do love working there."

"Hmm . . . and what exactly do you do?"

"I supervise the accounts for this dear little departmental store in Leeds. There are two of us in charge, but I am the better accountant, of course."

Nishi had been sitting right across the aisle from Arpit. She swivelled around the minute she heard Kelly say Leeds and asked, "What's the name of the store?" And though Kelly's answer did not ring any bells, Nishi's stomach lurched with a queer, salty premonition. She could not stop Kelly from going on matter-of-factly.

"It belongs to an Indian, actually. My parents consider it to be the one wise decision I took—working under an Indian boss, and a Punjabi to boot. They would much rather have a Shergill than a Sheffield. But he avoids even the mention of India like the plague ever since his wife suffered a miscarriage there. Who would have thought it . . . that too on an idyllic holiday in Goa, of all places, poor chap!"

Nishi couldn't bear to look at Arpit. Her eyes were closed as she desperately pleaded with higher powers. The bus slammed to a halt.

"Check that your shoelaces are tied, folks!" Arpit's assistant called out cheerfully. "From here we start our excursion into the quaint bylanes of Old Delhi."

Arpit didn't move as his guests got down. Even after the bus had emptied and the whole entourage stood waiting below for his briefing, Arpit did not move. Nishi smiled at his assistant with great effort and gestured to him to take over. She placed a hand on Arpit's arm. His eyes looked red, as if all the blood in his body had rushed into them.

"Go home," she whispered frantically. "You won't be able to keep your composure here. Don't worry about the tour, the others will handle it well. And I will help out as much as I can."

"No, Nishi, don't stay here. Come with me, please." His voice struck her as the last cry of a dying mountain.

"All right. I will just tell everyone that you aren't feeling too well. They'll have to manage without you. Come, I'll take you home."

He was running a temperature by the time they reached her house. Chivvying him into bed, she admonished him to try and sleep. But he was too restless to keep still for more than a few seconds.

"What have I done?! What have I done to her, Nishi?" he cried over and over again as he tossed and turned on the bed.

Nishi watched him with growing anxiety. Should she have told him the truth when she had guessed it? How could she have been so stupid as to think that he could somehow be shielded from it? Poor Kelly, she had no idea of the destruction she had wrought with a few innocent sentences.

Arpit was now muttering indistinctly, cursing and abusing his own self. If this went on any longer, Nishi knew he would become delirious. Determined to not let that happen, she got up and left Arpit's side for a minute. Rummaging in a long-locked drawer, she fished out a tiny corked bottle filled with a livid red liquid. Carefully measuring out two drops of the liquid into a spoon, she held it to Arpit's mouth and commanded, "Take this."

He squirmed like a peevish child, but she would not let him escape. "It's been years since I administered this to anyone. If I'm doing it now, it's only because you need it desperately. Please, Arpit, drink it. I don't want anything to happen to you!"

Perhaps more than her words, it was the raw note of actual fear in her voice which jolted him into submission. He swallowed the liquid, bitter and fiery even in that tiny dose.

"My father's concoction," Nishi said quietly.

In a few minutes he seemed quieter, though he was far from being calm.

"Now, Arpit, will you listen to me?"

He nodded dully.

"I can guess what you are thinking," she went on. "But in Goa, you did not know that she was pregnant. If you had, you would have acted differently. And Mannat could have told you had she wanted to."

"She was afraid to tell me . . . afraid that I would lose my mind completely and do something unpardonable."

"I don't think she was afraid. In fact, I think that for a few moments, she had become that long-lost girl from Meharsar. Perhaps, she had even forgotten the truth for that little while."

"How is that possible?"

"It's possible with Mannat and her love for you. It was so powerful that the plain facts of her having married and moved to another country weren't enough to stem the pain of separating from you. That's why she has divided herself up. Mannat has tried to discard her old self for a new and painless one—a self you would have no power to hurt. But when you confronted her that night, that old Mannat overpowered her all over again."

"I know, I know! And I came back and revived her pain!"

"No, you just *reminded* her of the unresolved pain which had been festering inside her all along."

"But the baby might have healed her, Nishi! She *was* trying to heal. She told me she was happy with Sunny, but I did not believe her. Because I did not *want* to believe her! I could not imagine her happy. I could not imagine her agony being even a degree lesser than mine. But she was telling the truth. She had a ray of hope in her life, Nishi. And I blocked it forever. I prevented her from being happy with him."

"Do you regret it?" Nishi asked quietly, and in the loaded stillness that followed her question, Arpit's head sank dejectedly to his chest until he was so still and quiet that Nishi had to lean forward to check if he was conscious.

"Arpit?" She shook him slightly.

"I don't . . . really . . . regret coming between her and Sunny," Arpit spoke in a broken whisper, continuing from before as if there had been no pause, no momentary break in his speech at all. "I am still jealous . . . but it kills me . . . that I gave her another reason to hate me." Dragging the words from the darkest depths of his heart, he spoke half to himself and half to Nishi, unmindful of what she would think of him after he confessed.

"Arpit, please, listen to me. It's impossible for Mannat to hate you. But if you believe me, the only way to do it is to continue with what we have started. Go back and reverse all the wrongs you have ever done. And then—"

"But I can't reverse this one," Arpit broke in.

"There won't be any need for it if you reverse the previous ones; the chain of events which led to this transgression will snap automatically."

"Only in your dream-world, Nishi. You yourself seem to have forgotten what you told me in the beginning—that it is impossible to actually change the past."

"I also told you that redreaming will bring about *corresponding changes in your present.* Why don't you remember that? When you turned the sixth switch, you came to know a vital fact, that not only did your father throw a spanner in your relationship with Mannat, but he also has some malevolent plans regarding Meharsar. This is your chance, Arpit. What you took away from Mannat was unintentional, but what your father plans to take away from Meharsar is clearly a cold-blooded strategic move. If you really want to make it up to Mannat, you must find out what these plans are and stop them from coming to pass."

Arpit shook his head. "He will never tell me. Certainly not now when we aren't exactly on the best of terms. But Mannat had said something about the size of the plot . . . umm, my father's share would be about two hectares, I guess. That might give us a clue about the nature of the project. Hang on." Suddenly animated, Arpit lunged for his laptop. Turning it on, he started typing furiously. A minute later, he uttered an exclamation of dismay. "How could I have missed this? It has been all over the business news these ten days! Damn, this couldn't get any worse!" He turned the laptop around towards Nishi so that she could read what he had been reading.

Nishi saw several news items about an Indian company becoming the franchisee of international fast-food giant Sunburst Inc., but how this piece of news was related to Arpit was not evident to her. She glanced at him in perplexity.

"This," he jabbed at the screen indignantly, "is my father's company! He plans to open Sunburst outlets all over our villages!"

"Oh, no!" Nishi exclaimed. "This will be the death of Meharsar, Arpit! There must be some way of stopping this! You have to do something!"

"Damn it!" Arpit banged the table in frustration. "How do I stop them? This is big business we are talking about here, Nishi. I thought this was my private battle I was fighting here—with you for my charioteer. How did it turn into a war against such forces?"

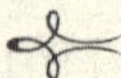

"Arpit, Chandigarh tomorrow?" Nishi burst into Arpit's room without so much as a knock on the door.

"Tomorrow? Impossible. My guests catch their return flights tomorrow. I have to be present to clear their all-important bills and see them off. But what's the matter?"

Nishi had sat down heavily on his bed, looking agitated. "I have been talking to people—scientists, journalists, lawyers, NGO workers. There is a very strong case against Sunburst Inc. starting its operations at all in India. Even in America, there have been citizens' groups which have agitated against Sunburst and won. Look," she threw a sheet of paper on the bed, "this is the list of all the controversies they have been involved in, right from putting smaller eateries out of business to filling their workforce with illegal immigrants. And this is just in America. A lot of what they have done in Asia and South America isn't even documented."

"Then why the hell is our government even allowing them to set up operations here?"

"Because too many vested interests stand to profit from allowing them entry, and, I'm afraid, your dad is one of them."

"You don't need to tell me that," Arpit replied bitterly. "What can we do, then? Dad is ruthless when it comes to profits. And he is powerful. I don't even know the extent of his reach . . ."

"You are overestimating him, Arpit. He has reached where he is by using the system to his advantage. Anyone who does that, eventually becomes a victim of the system. I have seen that happen with Soundarya's father. Do you know how he died? He promised to get some influential builder a prime piece of land in South Delhi using his 'friendship' with some politicians. Those politicians, however, turned out to be hand-in-glove with a rival builder and had Rajendra Bisht quietly disposed of. Apparently he was thrown into the Yamuna while he was *still alive*. His body was never found. His wife eloped with one of his partners a year later," Nishi ended with a shudder.

"Poetic justice," Arpit muttered. "The man who killed a river was killed by a river."

"Hmm . . . but it doesn't always happen with such dramatic finality, although karma does catch up in the end."

"But I can't sit around and wait for my dad's karma to catch up with him. What about *our* karma? What do we do now?"

"Now we are talking! Well, since you are busy tomorrow,

I will leave for Chandigarh early tomorrow morning. A friend who teaches in JNU is a consultant for an NGO in Ropar. They were the first to highlight Verva Cola's excesses in Punjab. They have a very active media wing and I can bet that they've been in touch with Veerji over this issue. I'm sure they can help us. Give me your house keys."

"Huh?"

"I will go there first, freshen up, and head straight for Ropar. You finish your work here and hurry to Chandigarh. By the time you arrive, I will be back with all the facts."

"That is fast! What would I do without you, Nishi?"

She smiled and gave him a sudden hug. "And what would I do without the opportunity you have given me—of obliterating a twenty-six-year old wrong?" Slipping back into her calm professionalism, she reminded him, "Don't forget to bring all the maps, and a bottle of mustard oil. We need to do a lot more while we are there."

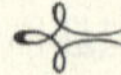

The two-room office looked unpromising from the outside. But when Nishi stepped in she found it a veritable greenhouse. To her surprise, the first room had a mud floor, with grass growing in its crevices. Except for a narrow pathway in the centre, every inch of space in the room was covered with potted plants. There was even a wall entirely covered with creepers. The handsome young man who burst out through the connecting door, chuckled loudly on seeing her expression.

"You see, Ma'am, no one can accuse us of not being close to our roots. Come on in." He ushered her into an inner room which had a desk and chair and a paved floor, but whose brick walls were exposed and covered with countless crudely-framed documents. Before Nishi could move to take a closer look at them, the young man warned, "Don't mistake them for letters of appreciation. These are defamation notices. We haven't been winning many popularity contests lately. It's not for nothing that we are Nobody's Business!"

"Nobody's Business?" Nishi asked, intrigued.

"That's our name. We are Nobody's Business, NB, in short," Vishwas said and grinned.

"But NB stands for Navuday Bharat, right?" asked Nishi.

"Only in the official records," Vishwas replied, grimacing. "The rules require us to have some sanctimonious self-congratulatory name, so we came up with this at the last moment. Actually, our Founder-Director wanted Nobody's Business . . ."

"Why did—"

"Nishi*ji*, in India, if you are poor and disadvantaged, you are a 'nobody'. The upwardly-mobile middle class doesn't have time to care about this nobody's business. They are too busy buying their three-bedroom flats and their diesel cars and putting their children through elite schools with air-conditioned classrooms. We take up the issues that no one else gives a shit about. I'm a bit rusty in the Art of False Modesty. So I don't mind telling you frankly that had it not been for us, that incredibly courageous Nobody Singh Meharsar would not have managed to get Verva Cola to clear up the toxic waste they were blissfully littering up the countryside with!"

Half an hour later, Nishi was thoroughly convinced that she had indeed come to the right place.

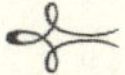

When Arpit reached Chandigarh later that night, he was

greeted by a visibly excited Nishi. "The good news or the bad news first?" she demanded.

"The bad, I am more used to it," he replied wryly.

"Well, we are up against formidable forces. Verva Cola not only choked up your Meharsar lake, it is also involved in a few other rackets. It has 'manufactured' the careers of quite a few celebrities and sponsored large-scale construction projects involving dubious land acquisitions. To cap it all, some of the directors of Verva have opened charities in their relatives' names. So, whenever some incriminating bit of news comes up against them, they wave their CSR flag by making enormous donations to these charities. Of course, a part of these generous contributions trickle back into their pockets. But who's to say anything about that?! Oh, what a tangled web, Arpit . . ."

"I know, Nishi. I know. But I was rather prepared for all this. I knew it was not going to be a simple picture. Anyway, what is the good news?"

"The good news is," she paused dramatically, "that NB, the NGO I visited today, is more than ready to take up cudgels for our cause. In fact Vishwas, the PR guy, said that they had been keeping an eye on the activities of Sunburst Inc. for a while and are in the process of compiling a fact-sheet. He will email it to me in a few days."

Arpit's face lit up with the first smile she had seen since the day of Kelly's unintended avalanche. "How do we celebrate?" he squirmed boyishly.

Nishi sternly pulled back the truant corners of her mouth, "By moving on to the fifth switch. Redreaming tonight."

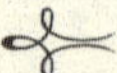

This time, there is no terror, no suffocation. He descends smoothly into

a great white peace and wakes up to the benevolent clamour of a city he recognises in an instant—Amritsar.

He is standing in front of Harmandir Sahib. And Mannat is with him.

He has just adjusted her green and yellow leheriya chunni—he would never let go of any excuse to touch her.

"I wanted to say this to you before the gaze of God . . ." she whispers.

He looks deeply into her eyes. He is not going to wait for her words; he knows exactly what she is going to say. This time, he is not afraid. He stills her hands where they were fiddling agitatedly with the corners of her chunni and says, "Wait, Mannat. Let me say it first." And before she can say anything to him or plead with him to stop, he tells her, "I love you, Mannat. I love you with all my heart and I have loved you ever since I can remember."

Nishi nearly whooped with delighted disbelief. But she composed herself immediately. The session was far from over and her excitement could land Arpit in the grave danger of either breaking the trance, or worse still, of muddying it with elements from her own subconscious. How can you be so irresponsible, Nishimaya? She chided herself.

Arpit takes Mannat's hands in his own and raises them to his heart. She glances around nervously—who knows when an old acquaintance might collide with them, gazing thus at each other? Then again, what if someone does? She does not fear her family finding out about their love. Veerji and everybody else loves Arpit. They will never object to their love. And if they do, she is sure now that Arpit will convince them otherwise.

Nishi nearly jumped as the realization dawned on her that she had just read Mannat's thoughts! Why should this happen when she was watching the scene through Arpit's eyes? Was she losing her invaluable detachment again?! She forced herself to snap out of it immediately, but it was not to be so.

Arpit and Mannat's faces are so close that Nishi can feel the heat rising in her own cheeks. Arpit takes Mannat's hand and they walk through the city lanes, wordlessly remembering their childhood days, until they come to the shops selling phulwadiyan and phulkari. "Anything you want to buy?" he asks.

"No, Arpit. I did not bring you to Amritsar to go shopping."

"Then why did you bring me here, my . . . Mannat?" he leans flirtatiously towards her.

Her blush lasts only a moment. Looking up at him, her eyes dark and serious, she says, "I knew you would never have come this far if I had told you the truth . . ." She hesitates now, afraid he will get annoyed and leave. A faint flicker of hope, however, makes her rush forward. "Arpit, my . . . umm . . . my real purpose was to take you to Meharsar to meet Veerji and everyone else. Come on, Arpit, please. You haven't visited us since Beeji's death. Everyone misses you, Arpit. Especially Veerji." She waits a few moments. Finding his expression inscrutable, she pleads, "Please? You can go back today itself. I won't ask you to stay the night."

He goes still. So does Nishi's heart, waiting in agonised expectation for him to do something. He should not step back this time. Instinctively, Nishi reaches for his hand. But this is against the rules of redreaming. Suddenly, everything starts dissolving into infinite hues. She realises what is happening and wants to scream out in frustration at what she has done, but she controls herself just in time, knowing that her momentary rashness can destroy Arpit.

For the first time since she started her psychic practices, Nishi is scared. Just then, to her utter astonishment, the colours start settling back into their places as if an expert painter has pushed the bleeding streams back into their outlines.

Nishi looks at Arpit in alarm. His face is taut, his unflinching gaze the thread which had pulled the scene back together. In the next moment, Nishi can see everything snap back to clarity. Arpit is clearly in charge of the redreaming now.

"No, not Meharsar," Arpit shakes his head.

"Why not? They all miss you!" Mannat pleads.

Arpit is silent again as he struggles with his feelings. How can he possibly tell Mannat, without breaking this precious, precious moment, that he isn't charmed with the idea of renewing his rustic ties; that he has grown beyond Meharsar; that a new world awaits him, a world into which he wants to spirit her . . . He thinks of a day in the near future when they both will walk through the busy streets of New York City with the same familiarity with which they navigated through these old, dusty lanes of Amritsar. She would be a woman-of-the-world—smart and primping and preening like those freshly-minted beauties he has seen sashaying out of salons. He would have transformed her. Arpit laughs at his own fantasies. Is he a man of the world, yet?

Mannat is puzzled by his laughter and a trifle offended too. She starts telling him about the groundwater problem in Meharsar and how it is all due to the Verva Cola plant, as if this might fuel him into driving to Meharsar this instant. But when she sees him nodding indifferently with a smile tugging at the corners of his mouth, she pulls her hand out of his grasp.

"I think I will take the bus to Meharsar. You can go back to Chandigarh," she declares.

Arpit is flabbergasted. "What? Why? You aren't going anywhere alone. We were going to spend the day here, and so we will."

Mannat's voice is frozen. "Our concerns no longer match."

"Mannat, do you really care so much for Meharsar?"

There is a catch in her voice as she answers. "Do you doubt it?"

"Hmmm." Though they have just eaten at the langar in the gurdwara, he leads her now to one of their favourite dhabas for lassi. "We need to talk, Mannat." And he tells her about his Dad's big plans for him—the advanced MBA from Stanford, him joining his business, the possibility of settling down abroad, everything. "Mannat, when we were kids, we could not imagine a life beyond Meharsar and Amritsar. You know what childhood is like . . . an hour passes like a week and a glint in the grass

means a diamond. We overrated everything, and we thought this was our world. But, Mannat, my world has expanded! And it's freaking HUGE*! Don't you . . . don't you want to see it with me?"*

She places her hand over his and says, "I certainly do, but not before I have done my duty towards Meharsar."

He is exasperated now. "What duty? You have lived there and followed its customs for one-fourth of your life. That's enough."

She is calmly resolute. "No. It's not enough. I owe it to them to at least try and get that factory moved away from there. It's ruining the soil, poisoning the ground water, and the smaller farmers are being driven to quit the land."

"Good for them. They will move to the cities and get into better-paying jobs and services."

"And are there enough jobs for so many people? And if everyone quits agriculture, where will the food come from?"

He doesn't know what to say anymore and squints distastefully at his tumbler, noticing for the first time that it's not been washed properly.

Mannat is staring at him disappointedly. The next moment, she throws him a challenge. "If you think the problem isn't that serious, why don't you come with me to Meharsar and find out for yourself?"

"What the! Mannat, I just told you—"

"That you love me," she interrupts him with a whisper. "So, shouldn't my family know about this? Don't you want them to see us together in the future?"

He stares at her in confusion. He needs to decide how deeply he has got himself into this confession. He loves her, yes. But does he love her with the baggage she carries—her stubborn loyalties to the past? Is he in danger of being sucked back into that past, too? Is his love strong enough to crack his brand-new shell of ambition? And is . . . wait a minute, she still hasn't told him whether she loves him or not.

He raises his eyebrows and is about to ask her, but she interrupts him yet again.

"I know what you want to ask," she says. "But I will give you my answer only in my village. The choice is yours."

They abruptly snapped back into reality. Nishi's face was lined with guilt. "I nearly blew it! I don't understand how that happened. I should have stayed in control."

"For a few seconds I thought everything was over," Arpit admitted. "But when I saw her slipping away from me, I just couldn't bear it. I had to do something to make her stop. So I just fixed my eyes on her retreating face and begged, *Come back, come back!* I can't describe the agony I went through before things finally started snapping back into focus."

"But this time you've really channelled the stream down a different path. You've really made it work. Who knows what it would have led to had it continued . . ."

Arpit slid off the bed and began to pace the room, too excited to sit in one place and assimilate the meaning of the redreaming. "I did, didn't I?" he asked, almost to himself. Then, abruptly stopping next to Nishi, he demanded, "Does this mean she now knows?"

"Knows what?"

"That I love her?!"

Nishi burst out laughing. "Do you really think she doesn't know it already? Hadn't you told her that you love her a day before her marriage?"

"My telling was of no use when she didn't believe me," Arpit muttered.

"I think the trouble was that she believed you completely," Nishi replied softly. "Though I agree that your timing was a bit off, but some change will certainly happen now, I feel it in my bones."

"Nishi, what do you think would have happened afterwards

had the dream continued a little longer? Would I have gone to Meharsar with her?" He tapped his fingers impatiently against the sideboard, frustrated with the abrupt snapping of the redreaming session. "To think I was *this* close to finding out how she felt . . . *this* close."

"She loved you, Arpit," Nishi spoke steadily.

"Really?" He parried, a trifle jealously. "Do you claim to know her better than I do? I, who have known her since childhood?"

"You are forgetting I have some, erm, special powers. And you might be surprised to know how closely I have been acquainted with Mannat's feelings for a while now."

Suddenly he knelt by her chair and placed his hand imploringly on her knee. "I pray that you are right, Nishi. It's my own strength of character, not Mannat's heart, which has always been under doubt. But this time I felt like I had overcome a major hurdle, and I did it for Mannat and because of Mannat. You are bang on, Nishi. There is some big change heading our way, and I can't wait for it to hit."

CHAPTER 14

Within a few minutes of reaching home, Mannat was sitting at her computer, her fingers trembling slightly as she googled Nobody's Business. It was lucky that Sunny should have inadvertently dropped a cue! She had been wondering about the name of the NGO that had helped Veerji in his battle against Verva Cola, but the name had been eluding her memory. But she had it now. Nobody's Business!

When she finally found the link to the NB website, she saw that it contained all the studies they had undertaken since their foundation in 2004.

Their Founder-Director, FoDi as the site fondly nicknamed her, was a woman, a girl in fact, her own age. Mannat was suitably impressed. She must have started the NGO right after college. She should have done the same thing, instead of cavorting with Arpit in an idyllic mountain fantasy.

Her fingers felt clammy. *Arpit, Arpit, Arpit!* screamed her brain. *Isn't it high time you exorcised him?*

Shaking her head to clear her vision, Mannat read the FoDi's name and instantly found it a bit familiar. But she had never met anyone by the name of Binita Baruah. Then why?

Dismissing the thought from her mind, Mannat quickly wrote an email to NB and sent it hurriedly, lest any misgivings stop her. She knew the email would sound rather feeble when it was read. All she had managed to write, with Sunny peering disapprovingly over her shoulder, was that she was someone who belonged to Meharsar and therefore, was very concerned about Sunburst's expansion plans there. She had debated about whether or not to mention her relationship with Veerji, but had decided against it. At the moment it might be better to let them think of her as a public-spirited NRI who was worried about the environmental violations taking place in her native village.

The FoDi's name continued to prod her. There were hardly any details about her on the website except her schooling—from an elite Darjeeling boarding-school—and her graduation from a Delhi University college. For a moment she wondered if it was the same . . . no, it had not been Arpit's college. She was sure about that, at least.

It was only when a brusque, blunt, approving reply shot into her email inbox from the FoDi herself, did it prompt Mannat to ransack her memory one more time for her name. Finally the associations snapped into place. It helped that she had searched the Internet for Binita's college and found that it was located right opposite the one Arpit went to. Binita Baruah had been Arpit's reluctant girlfriend in Delhi.

For some reason, she found the idea hugely amusing.

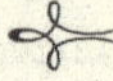

Vishwas was better than his word. Within a week he had emailed the fact-sheet about Sunburst Inc. to Nishimaya, and because she was extremely busy with the restoration of the Patiala homestead, she forwarded it to Arpit. Arpit read the fact-sheet with a mixture of dismay and determination—things were not good; something had to be done, and it had to be done fast.

He called Vishwas immediately and began to bombard him with questions.

"We have a solid following on Facebook and Twitter, and about thirty percent of them are actually involved. Whatever we say will spread like wildfire," Vishwas assured him, before continuing, "The point is not what we say, but what we do. Will you join us if we take to the streets?"

"What? Is that the only way left?" Arpit exclaimed.

"I know. What a pity the streets aren't air-conditioned yet." Vishwas' tone bristled with sarcasm.

"I didn't mean it that way, dude! But surely there are some legal measures?"

"Of course there are." Vishwas cooled down a little. "We will file a PIL, but the court has started treating us as a bit of a nuisance lately. And since Sunburst has been bombarding the middle-class with images of the instant hedonism awaiting them, we won't be winning too many hearts. That's why I am in favour of raising a ruckus. It buys us time, stalls projects, and makes the more faint-hearted stakeholders think twice. And there are always those political parties who, for their own interest, give us a temporary show of support. You don't happen to know any celebrities, do you? They would be useful in grabbing a few eyeballs for us—though don't tell FoDi I said this. Binita will skin me alive!"

"Binita?"

"Our FoDi, I mean, Founder-Director. She started NB when she was just twenty one. Some woman! Admirable, but, well, whoever said that the pen is mightier than the sword was never at the cutting edge of Binita Baruah's tongue. Wait . . . are you *laughing*?!"

"Unbelievable!" Arpit interspersed gasps with chuckles. "Life is unbelievable!"

“I guess I underestimated that girl,” Arpit mused. He had just finished telling Nishi about Binita and how he had once known her. “I used to think of her as a pseudo-intellectual nutcase. She was thoroughly annoying, what with all her opinions about everything and everybody under the sun. I was pretty sure that she would go on studying till her teeth fell off, and then settle down with some grumpy, constipated professor of History.”

“That’s a mean thing to say about your ex-girlfriend,” Nishi scolded him, mockingly. “Who knows, this might be a quirk of destiny? Maybe life is giving you a second chance to get back together . . .” Nishi laughed when she saw Arpit’s look of abject horror.

“For heaven’s sake, Nishi, there was never any romance between us! You know that.” His voice dropped an octave. “It was Mannat. Always Mannat.”

She smiled sympathetically at him. “I was only teasing you. Okay, now back to work. My drawings are complete, and thankfully, we seem to have seen the last of the monsoons as well. We must get solid work done now if the house has to be finished by February. But why are you looking so uncomfortable?”

Arpit paused for a few seconds before replying cautiously. “I wonder how Binita will react when she comes to know that I am from Meharsar.”

“She doesn’t know? Didn’t you tell her while you two were in college?”

“No. I let her have a vague idea that I was from Chandigarh. It was embarrassing to admit to my village ties . . . no, don’t give me that look, Nishi. You know I am thoroughly ashamed of it now.”

"Hmmm . . . we will have to tell her," Nishi returned firmly. "She needs to know the extent of your emotional involvement in this business. Besides, your relationship with Veerji will be a tremendous boost to your credibility."

He sighed deeply. "You are right. I guess it will be a relief to tell her the truth. But there is one thing I will never remind her of, Nishi: the fact that I am Baldev Singh's son. Let's just pray that she has forgotten it in these eight years."

She nodded pensively. "I suppose so. If she finds out about it now, she might suspect your integrity. One day, though, she will find out. What will you do then?"

"Pray that our goal is accomplished before that," Arpit replied, anxiety lacing his voice. Wanting to change the subject now, he asked, "Nishi, remember you had once mentioned how you spent an entire night near the Witches' Lake in your village? I want to hear that story."

"I may as well; this is the perfect setting after all," Nishi quipped. They were in the Patiala homestead, having decided to stay the night there instead of driving all the way back to Chandigarh. "I hope you won't get scared, though."

And so, in that crumbling building haunted by past tragedies and future hopes, Nishi began telling Arpit about how, at the age of ten, on hearing that the witches of the land used to emerge from their hiding places and gather around Pret Tal, a shallow lake down in the valley, every new moon to dance and carry out secret rituals to keep themselves immortal, she had decided to investigate. She told no one, for no one would've let her go if they had the slightest inkling of her intentions. Rumour had it that the few foolhardy ones who had tried to spy on the witches' dance had gone insane and met their deaths falling off the steep mountainside. But her Baba had suspected, yet he had made no attempts to stop her.

"Why?" asked Arpit.

"Wait for the rest of the story."

She had been determined to witness the macabre sight, if macabre it really was, for she was inclined to believe that the witches were probably nice women who wouldn't harm children at least. The thought had given her courage. All those who had gone mad after watching the witches' dance had been adult men. What if those men had been punished for intruding upon the private rituals of these feminine forces?

So she went into the forest and hid behind a well-known and revered grove of deodar trees near Pret Tal when it was still dusk. It was a dangerous thing to do, notwithstanding the witches, because of the jackals and leopards that roamed the forest. But she did not understand such dangers, for she had never ventured into the forest without her Baba until then. She would've been missed had there not been a wedding in Gumgyaat that evening. In the clamour and confusion of the entire village gathering and celebrating, her mother had not missed her. Neither had she noticed that her husband was nowhere to be seen as well.

By the time it was well and truly dark, she found her eyelids starting to droop. With no way of telling the time and with no sign of the witches' making an appearance anytime soon, she decided to climb up one of the deodars and settle down to sleep in its branches.

It seemed like only a few minutes had passed when she was awakened by a queer rasping sound. At first she squinted at the ground, wondering if there was a jackal lurking near the base of her tree. Had it smelled her? But it was too dark for her to see anything. Then she looked up in the direction of the lake and nearly jumped out of her skin. There was an eerie yellowish light emanating from Pret Tal, and surrounding the lake were a few indistinct figures, dimly outlined against that ghostly light, with their faces turned towards the lake. She was thankful she couldn't see them properly—she wasn't prepared to see their disfigured countenances at all. From where she sat, all she could see was their matted hair descending down their backs. One of them was standing up, while the others stooped, almost leaning into the lake. She counted how many witches there were—one, two, three, four. Only four? Legends had put the number at anything between seven and twelve. She felt slightly relieved now—there weren't so many of them; it would be easier to flee if they happened to see her.

She waited for them to start their infamous rituals, but the witches seemed to be in no hurry. They continued squatting by the Tal and muttering to each other, indistinct sounds which she could make no sense of. Slowly, though, one sound emerged from them—a strangely choked, mutilated, ravaged sound which gradually rose to a shrill, piercing wail. She wanted to close her eyes but could not. They were fixed helplessly on the terrifying scene before her.

Suddenly, one of them threw back her head and howled. The sound cut right through her bone marrow, making her shake like a leaf. The next moment, she lost her grip on the branch and fell. And as she fell through the air, the last coherent thought that ran through her mind was that she shouldn't have slipped away from home without telling anyone. She squeezed her eyes shut, expecting to hit hard ground the next moment. But she never did. She fell, not on rocky thorny ground but straight into a pair of flesh-and-blood arms. They had caught her! For the first time in her life, she knew what utter, unspeakable terror was. She opened her mouth to scream, but no sound came out.

"Shhh!" someone whispered.

The voice sounded familiar and warm, as did the arms that held her. She opened her eyes tentatively. It was her father who had caught her! She immediately buried her head into his chest, sobbing out her relief. He murmured comfortingly in her ear, asking her softly to quieten.

But someone had heard them. The howling of the witches had stopped abruptly. An angry, ragged hiss shot towards them from the ghostly lake shore. The witches had seen them!

Paralysed with fear, she held onto her father even more tightly than before, expecting him to run for safety. But he did something shocking. He raised his head towards the lake and uttered a clear, reassuring call. Immediately, the angry hissing and spluttering coming from the witches' direction stopped and low wails, which now seemed more and more like aggrieved moans, filled the air. She shivered. Her father looked down at her and whispered, "Let's go back."

On their way back to the village, he told her that he had seen her slipping away, but instead of stopping her, he followed her to make sure she would be safe. He had been hiding near the tree where she had stowed herself away, keeping an eye on her.

It was Arpit's turn to shiver now. He looked warily around the decrepit room. It was full of cobwebs and shadows which now seemed mysterious and sinister. He shuddered, and turning to Nishi, he said, "Nishi, as indelicate as this may seem, I am going to spend the night in this room with you around to protect me. I don't even have the guts to go to the bathroom now!"

Nishi suppressed her chuckle with some difficulty. "Don't you want to hear the rest of the story?"

"Sure, why not?" Arpit muttered, but his voice sounded hollow.

She was bursting with questions when they reached home, firing them at her father, left right and centre. Why did he not stop her from slipping away? Was *he* not scared of the witches? *Why* was he not scared? And this most importantly, what power did he have which had subdued the witches in a moment?

Sympathy, he said. It was sympathy which had saved them. When she continued to look at him with confusion, he tenderly stroked her hair and told her the truth about the 'witches'.

Years ago, when he had been just a boy, a nomadic tribe had travelled from the upper reaches of the Himalayas to seek temporary shelter around Gumgyaat. All they had wanted was to camp on the slopes around the village and live off the herbs and fruits that grew abundantly in the forests around. They were vegetarians following an ancient Hindu sect, or so they claimed. Some of the high-caste villagers, however, took their claims as a personal offence. How could these lowly nomads claim to belong to the same religion which they, devout Brahmins and Kshatriyas, had been following for generations? Still, this would have remained a minor irritant if the livestock from nearby villages had not started disappearing after a few days of the tribe's arrival. Assuming them to be the culprits, angry panchayat representatives accosted the tribal leaders and warned them to get packing within two days.

The outsiders protested innocence. "We told you we are vegetarians," they insisted, "and we only need a place to stay till the summer arrives and we can return to the higher slopes of the Himalayas. Please do not send us away." Their pleadings earned them an uneasy temporary reprieve. And they retreated back to the shores of the lake where they had set camp.

A few days later, however, all hell broke loose. A village lad disappeared, leaving no traces behind. His body was found a week later on the lower slopes—mutilated, half-eaten, and rotting. With bloodshot eyes, inhabitants of the surrounding villages descended on the nomads with their sickles and spears, hungry for immediate revenge. Only one village did not side with them. Gumgyaat village listened to their voice of reason—

their Panditji, Mahaveer Prasad Gaur, Nishi's grandfather—and stayed back.

Hopelessly outnumbered, the nomads were slaughtered mercilessly, about thirty of them, women and children included. The angry mob showed no mercy, and when they were finished, there was not a single living soul in the camp. They glared at the massacred bodies, feeling strangely vindicated. But unknown to them, there were four survivors: four women who had been out gathering firewood when it all happened. They had nearly walked right into the scene, but they hid in the shadows of the forest along the lake and watched as their tribe got hacked and speared to death. The fear which took away their voices in those horrifying moments and made them turn back into the forest and hide, was the fear which also saved their lives.

They came back, late at night, after the villagers, their faces and clothes splattered with blood, had left. They walked through their camp, numb with shock until they came upon the small, dead bodies of their children with their heads smashed with rocks. They ran then. They ran to the upper slopes of the mountain in spite of the cold wind and the darkness, and then they started wailing. In long, blood-curdling howls they let out their fury and their anguish. And the still forest listened, as did the animals. And in the villages down below, the murderers heard them too, cowering inside their houses, scared witless, still not comprehending the enormity of what they had done.

The next afternoon, some forest officials arrived in Gumgyaat and called a meeting of all the villages around to warn them about a man-eating leopard which had been spotted thereabouts. They asked if it had attacked any of the villagers. But the latter could not answer the forest officials. The burden of their crime had struck them speechless.

Some of those who had led the slaughtering party lost their

nerve and confessed. They were led away while those who had aided and abetted them were left to atone for what they had done. As shock wore off and crushing guilt took its place, priests were summoned and rituals were conducted.

"Baba was very young at that time," Nishi went on. "But the incident left an indelible impression on him. That night, he told me about the two lessons he had learned from the tragedy: first, to weigh all the available evidence in the balance of reason and intuition before taking a decision, and second, a Pandit was a spiritual counsellor for those around him, and not a mere conductor of rituals. It was because of my grandfather that the people of Gumgyaat were saved from committing a heinous crime that day. Baba made up his mind to follow in his footsteps."

"And you are following in his," put in Arpit.

Nishi's face lit up with rare radiance. "It's the pinnacle of my aspirations."

"Nishi, do you remember I once told you I envied you because your father was the inspiration mine could never be? But today, I almost pity you, to have lost someone so invaluable. I can't even imagine the extent of your loss."

"What makes you think I have lost him?" Nishi asked, her voice laden with the tears she refused to shed.

When Arpit didn't say anything, Nishi continued with the rest of her story. "The women never came near our villages, but soon after the massacre, they were seen by some men who had ventured into the deeper parts of the forest while looking for firewood. The women ran and hid themselves when they saw the men, but it was evident to the villagers that they were survivors of the massacre. But such was their horror and guilt over what they had done, that the villagers chose to ignore the fact of the women's presence and eventually they just assumed that the women had either died or moved away. Baba however, instinctively knew that they still lived in the forest. On his long rambles along the lower slopes, he had occasionally come across the remains of a fire. And one day, he saw them, gathering berries in a clearing. He was aghast to see their appearance—torn clothes, matted hair, bloated faces, eyes still haunted by the horror of that night. When they looked up at him, he ran away, unable to bear looking at the blank despair on their faces. A few days later, he came back with my grandmother's discarded saris and a few *chappatis*. He placed them in the same clearing where he had seen the women and went back. When he came back two days later, the saris and the food were gone. He was not sure whether the women had taken them or some animal, but from that day onwards he kept bringing something or the other at regular intervals."

"But why did those women not go away from the place which had taken everything from them?"

"Attachment to the dead. They had buried the bodies in the lake itself. When winter came, the lake froze over, and the decomposing bodies stayed thus till summer came and the ice melted. Those who saw the thawing corpses at the bottom of the lake nearly went mad. People stopped visiting the lake after that, and started calling it Pret Tal . . ."

"So the 'witches' were actually the victims of a mindless massacre?"

"Yes. The tragedy had taken place on a new moon night, so they came to the lake every such night to mourn their dead. The eerie light I had seen emanating from the lake had actually been the fire they had lit at its shore to perform some rites for the departed souls. They probably continued living there till they died. With such a heavy cross upon their hearts, I doubt they could have survived much longer."

"Sometimes God gives us long lives to draw out our suffering," remarked Arpit.

"Man's suffering is the result of his own folly," Nishi retorted.

"What about the legends surrounding the lake, the one about the people who had gone mad?"

"Chiefly rumours. I think you better sleep now. Just to comfort you, it is believed that all spirits and ghosts retire to their heavenly homes after 4 a.m. You can make a trip to the bathroom after that if you don't feel up to it now."

As he drifted off to sleep a little later, Arpit caught hold of a thought. Or had he carried it back from some dream-destination? "Perhaps the river's death was the punishment ordained for those villages, then?"

Long after Arpit carried his musings into sleep, Nishi tossed and turned on her makeshift bed. One sentence had lodged itself like a thorn in her heart: "I almost pity you." She looked accusingly at the sleeping Arpit. She had spoken bravely in front of him. She had always assured herself that her Baba was always with her in spirit. And with that assurance, she had tried transforming herself from the disillusioned Himani to the inscrutable Nishimaya. But despite her best efforts, the mantle of resilience fell away sometimes, and tonight was one such night.

When she was sure Arpit was in deep sleep, she slipped away to the courtyard below. For some inexplicable reason, the mango tree that stood alone at one end of the courtyard seemed to call out to her. She walked up to the decrepit tree and ran her hands along its bark. It felt dry and warm at the same time.

When she pulled her hands back, they were streaked with

chalk. She peered closely at the tree. Not seeing any chalk marks that could have rubbed off onto her hands, she walked around the tree. And then she saw it. A star with lotus-petal rays, enclosed within a circle, drawn with chalk, its perfection unmarred by the rough canvas.

Nishi looked around wildly, but there was no one there. She rushed to the gate and ran down the lane, looking for the person who must have drawn the star, but the lane was entirely empty. There was not a single soul in sight. Not willing to give up so easily, Nishi continued running down the lane, but after ten minutes she was forced to accept that whoever had drawn the symbol had left long ago. Could it have been a tramp? Impossible. No tramp would ever be able to replicate the symbol with such perfection. She ran back to the tree and stared at the lotus star. Touching it reverently, she knew. *It had been him* . . . it had to be her father.

CHAPTER 15

"Let me go first, please," begged Arpit. "It would be a treat to see her huffy face after all these years."

"Arpit! Be serious now," Nishi reprimanded. "This is no joking matter. We must have Binita on our side. Though Vishwas has more-or-less committed that NB will be with us, we can't count upon it until we're sure that Binita likes us and is willing to help us."

"Why on earth wouldn't she like us?"

"Because this 'us' includes you, and Binita doesn't know it yet," returned Nishi drily.

They were on their way to Ropar to meet Binita. Arpit had been unable to reconcile himself with this incredulous reappearance of Binita Baruah in his life. And to think that she held his future, rather their future, in her hands! Arpit shuddered. There was no knowing what Binita would do when she found out about him. But Nishi was right, as always. He had to win Binita over if she was to help them save Meharsar.

When Vishwas greeted them cheerfully and ushered them into Binita's office where she was waiting for them, Arpit took a deep breath and braced himself for the encounter. The next moment, they were standing in front of Binita, Vishwas was introducing them, and Binita was getting up from her chair and extending her hand in greeting. But there was not even a flicker of recognition on her face. Not when she saw him. Not when Vishwas said, "And this is Arpit Singh." Nothing. Not even a blink.

Was this apparent amnesia on Binita's part, a good thing or a bad thing? Arpit found himself in a quandary. He stared at her. She had hardly changed, not unless one counted the substitution of bright cotton kurtis and churidars with a crisply starched, wide-bordered cotton sari, as a major shift in personality. Everything else about her was the same—the stylish black-framed glasses, the long silver earrings, the excessive kohl in her eyes, the restless drumming of her fingers, and the cold, demanding voice in which she was asking, "Have you ever heard of the word *slactivism*?"

"Huh?" Arpit snapped out of his thoughts.

"These days, drawing room intellectuals have shed their upholstered-sofa skins to become keyboard activists, the ones who think clicking on a Facebook 'like' for a Third World cause will expunge all their sins from this world and throw open the gates of the next one for them. Are you sure this is not a passing fad with you two? You both look bourgeois enough to do this for the photo coverage."

Arpit began to splutter with indignation, but a sideways glance at Nishi's face made him simmer down. She was still smiling politely at Binita. From where had this woman mined such an inexhaustible stock of patience? Well, he gritted his teeth, if she could keep her cool, so could he.

His resolve lasted only for the next few minutes, until Binita's bitingly sarcastic tone became too much to bear. Pushing back his chair, he stood up. Placing his hands on Binita's table, he glared down at her and said, "Ms Binita Baruah, I may be a 'slactivist' as you put it, but at least I'm not a tight-ass pseudo-reformer who uses social work as an excuse to fart off her frustration on anyone within range."

Binita did not even bat an eyelid. She stared back at him for an entire minute before speaking, her voice cool, collected, and clear. "Sit down, Arpit. You haven't changed much in the last eight years. Evolution seems to have passed right by you. Anyway, you might be surprised to know that I no longer bristle at childish insults, especially not like the one you pitched rather feebly at me just now. I suggest you shut that mouth of yours. There are flies around here."

Arpit stuttered. Was there a note of triumphant mirth in Binita's voice? He couldn't decide. He turned towards Nishi for some backing, but saw her doubled over with helpless laughter.

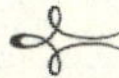

"You painted such a prejudiced picture of her. She's a nice girl, very intelligent, and pretty too. What a pity you didn't see it all those years ago," Nishi teased Arpit on their way back. "Well, she isn't married yet. Maybe this was what Fate had in store for you, hmm?"

"Stop it, Nishi!" groaned Arpit. "You're the last person from whom I would have expected—" He stopped suddenly to look at her, a new thought dawning upon him. "Nishi?"

She turned inquiringly towards him. "Yes?"

He felt awkward asking her the question, but curiosity made him press on. "How come *you* never got married?"

He regretted his words immediately. Nishi had gone white. Arpit slammed on the brakes and pulled the car over. "Never mind. You don't need to answer that."

"He lived in the same village as I did," Nishi spoke softly, almost as if she hadn't heard Arpit. "We used to attend school together. Remember that special weekly school I told you about?"

Arpit nodded silently. "We used to travel together on that pony procession. He was a bright student, and very ambitious. He wanted to join the Army, but his parents were dead against it. They were terrified with the idea of him facing enemy bullets at the border. But he did die. In a rock fall at the dam site, just a few kilometres away from his home. He had hated the idea of working there, but his family needed the money, and he did not want to leave the village like most of the other young men had. Their little farm had not been doing so well ever since the diversion of the river. So he had no option but to accept the job Rajendra Bisht was offering him."

Arpit stared silently at the steering wheel. Long moments later, he finally managed to ask, "How old was he when . . . when it . . ."

"Eighteen." Nishi's voice suddenly sounded as dead as a dried up river. "We had left the village by then, but we came to know about it from our old neighbours."

"A good thing you were spared the sight," he said sympathetically.

"I don't know." For the first time, Arpit detected a hint of bitterness in Nishimaya's voice. "Perhaps if I had been there . . . or if Baba had been there . . ." She sighed heavily. "That was the only time in my life when I felt angry with Baba for having left us. He was the only one who could have prevented it."

"Perhaps he knew he couldn't, and that's why he left?"

Nishi turned and stared at him. "You might be right." After a pause she went on, "Well, after Prashant, there could be no one else. Of course my mother tried to get me married, but I knew it was not the path I was meant to walk in this lifetime. It was then that I started taking my intuitive flashes seriously. I thought maybe this is how my powers are meant to be channelised, powers which the responsibilities of a household would have sapped. So this is how you have come to know me as Nishimaya," she tried to smile.

"I wish I had known this earlier. I would have avoided all those rude outbursts."

"I'm glad you did not know this earlier. Our focus was, and should remain, on *your* story."

Impulsively, Arpit reached out and took Nishi's hands in his and looked directly at her. "Nishi," he asked her earnestly, "do you think Prashant loved you just as much as you loved him?"

Nishi closed her eyes, shivering slightly. She tried linking herself to the girl she once had been, pushing through the barriers her subconscious had constructed over the years, to answer Arpit's question. "Yes, he did."

"Then," Arpit replied, "I *know* you will meet him again someday . . . someplace. I don't know how, but you will." His voice held a rare note of conviction.

Before Nishi could answer him, Arpit made a surprising request. "Nishi, I want to see Prashant's photograph . . . and you are the only one who can reproduce it."

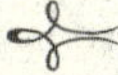

Though Nishi refused point-blank to comply with his unexpected request, Arpit was hopeful that she could be persuaded in time. Ever since the last redreaming session, Nishi had been moving around with an aura of absentmindedness around her. At first he attributed it to the hidden gash in her psyche being reopened with his questions about Prashant. But somehow, he couldn't bring himself to accept full responsibility for Nishi's state. And as the days went by and she continued to be listless and vague, he felt sure that there was something else bothering her.

The change in Nishi became apparent at their next attempt at redreaming. As much as he tried, Arpit found himself unable to slip into a trance. He thought he wasn't concentrating hard enough, but when he finally gave up in exasperation and opened his eyes, he saw that Nishi's eyelids were still shut tightly, almost as if she was trying to rein in some thought too powerful for her.

The session was a total failure. Arpit, keen on making greater headway than the last time, was clearly disappointed. Nishi however, did not even apologise for it. But the next day she made a surprising announcement.

"Let's turn the fourth switch in Patiala. I have a hunch we will get better results there." She offered no further explanations, either of her behaviour over the last couple of days, of the failure of the last redreaming session, or of her strange suggestion now.

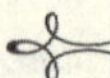

"There are two ways of beating the system," Vishwas explained. "One is to meet it head-on and take to the streets, organise protests marches and rallies, go to court. Basically, the 'bulldozer' way. And then there is the 'termite' way."

"What is that?" enquired Arpit, amused.

"Stay in the system and eat away at it from the inside. First you pretend to be on their side, and then you launch a quiet rebellion. At NB we use a two-pronged approach."

"So far, I have seen only the bulldozer-ing. Not surprising, really," Arpit couldn't resist adding, "considering who your FoDi is!"

Vishwas grinned. "Don't get me fired! Anyway, I am trying to rope in someone who looks deceptively pro-establishment, but who will really be working for us. Meanwhile, watch out for the first pieces of newspaper propaganda starting tomorrow. My journalist friends have more-or-less torn Sunburst to shreds. The only problem however, is that the editors are not our friends. Out of the five articles we managed to put together, only two have a real chance of making it to newsprint. Still, something is always better than nothing."

"Hmmm," Arpit got up to leave. Just as he reached the door, Vishwas called out to Arpit and said very casually, "By the way, FoDi says hi."

"Huh? To me?" Arpit looked at Vishwas blankly.

"No, to that cow across the road! Of course to you, dude! You two were college buddies, right?" Despite his air of nonchalance, Vishwas could not hide his curiosity.

"Not exactly buddies," admitted Arpit wryly. "But nice of her to say so. Give her my regards."

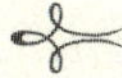

The mountains are almost sinister in their pristine beauty. He looks down from where he is standing at the precipice and sees the old valley stretch out in front of him in swathes of green and shadow blues, until it disappears into mist and clouds. The cold mountain air is cutting in its austerity. He is about to turn around and start walking back when something pulls him towards the edge, and then he is falling. He is falling off the mountain and the ground is rushing up to meet him, to swallow him up in one big gulp. The valley has disappeared and in its place is a chasm, opening itself further and further still, to take him in. Panic seizes him. He opens his mouth to scream but no sound comes out. Instead, the taste of melted chocolate and home-made butter fills his mouth, confusing his senses. He feels the softness of shy, but eager lips pressing against his own. And then, Mannat is in his arms and they are on the Mall Road in Kasauli, away from the crowds and lost in a kiss he will never forget. They come out from the kiss, gasping for breath. There had been something potent about the moment, and he is not

willing to let go of Mannat's arms. He does not want the moment to end. If only it could be pulled through till eternity . . .

Out of nowhere then, a thought whacks him on his head—it's been barely a month since he split from his 'girlfriend' Binita, and here he was, kissing Mannat with abandon!

Why did Binita have to pop into his mind at the wrong moment? Typical of her! Or wait, was it him, carrying fragments of his waking life into redreaming?

Focussing on Mannat again, he is successful in brushing all thoughts of Binita aside, but the magic is lost now. The moment has been corrupted, for another thought is now running amok inside his brain: Mannat's consciousness is crystal clear. His is not. There are too many splatters of copycat ambitions and borrowed dreams marring his consciousness, and his misadventures with love have scratched it in several places. His consciousness is pock-marked with his failure. They are no longer equals, not in the lives they lead and not in the purity of their hearts. He has to make himself worthy of her. Again.

The moment of truth passes, and taking her hand, he pulls her along and starts walking down the road. He can sense her eyes boring holes into his back, but he doesn't turn around and say anything to her; he does not answer the questions she has not asked. Instead, he presses her fingers tighter between his and hurries his pace, until she gives a slight start of pain. He stops, let's go of her hand, and turns around to look at her. She is rubbing her fingers and grimacing at him. She is unbearably beautiful! He pulls her into his embrace once again and kisses her. He pours his entire self into the kiss with such passion that she gets frightened and starts squirming to get out of his grasp. But he is merciless.

When he finally lets her go, she steps back, looks piercingly at him, and slaps him. Hard. It stings, but he laughs. She slaps him again. He laughs again, and he goes on laughing until she starts laughing too. When they stop, it's because they have to catch their breaths.

He takes her hand once again and they walk back to the city centre, mingling with the crowd. She tells him she wants to shop, but nothing catches her fancy. Nothing, except a display of charcoal and ink drawings, hung up on a bit of twine by the roadside. She pauses to inspect them closely and looks around for the artist, but he is nowhere to be found. Does he not care about the drawings being stolen? Perhaps he thinks they are worthless.

One charcoal sketch catches Mannat's attention particularly. It's an enormous wheel with snakes entwined around its spokes. Flames rising from the bottom of the picture lap ominously at the wheel, threatening to destroy it. There are no other elements in the picture, except for the chief figures of interest—an unlucky man and woman who are falling off the wheel into sure doom. Their unclothed bodies have been sketched in broad, careless strokes, with no care to distinguish physical features. The artist has not even bothered to depict the agony on their faces: their expressions are crudely complacent. Yet Mannat is so riveted that he feels a rush of irritation. He isn't impressed. The absence of colour takes away from the entire effect, he feels.

She doesn't protest when he takes her arm possessively and hisses, "Come on, now, let's get going. And since when did you become an art connoisseur?"

"An art what?"

"Never mind." He suppresses a smile and drags her away.

As they walk further down the road, they meet an old man—stooping with age, his skin wrinkled and dry like parchment paper—painstakingly carving obscure symbols on wooden beads with which he makes necklaces and embellishes steel rings. His 'shop' is nothing more than a low wooden table by the roadside. He fascinates Mannat, and she stops to watch him work. Half-squatting, half-sitting on a broken old stool, the old man continues with his work until he becomes aware of them standing and staring at him. He raises his head, nods towards them in greeting, and asks hopefully if they want something.

Arpit shakes his head in answer and tugs at Mannat's arm. "Come on, Mannat," he says, clucking impatiently, "surely you want something better than such cheap childish trinkets?!"

"But they are beautiful!" She exclaims, more to the eager old man than to him. And before he can protest, she has bought two bracelets, one with beads forming an 'A' and the other with an 'M'. He wants to admonish her, but he finds himself smiling at her simplicity instead.

As he offers the old man money for the bracelets, his eyes fall upon a ring which the man has just set aside after completing it. Curious, he picks it up. It is just like the others—a carved wooden bead studded on a steel hoop, but he likes the design for some reason so he buys it.

It's Mannat's turn to protest now. "Not that one! Can't you see it's too small for you?"

He ignores her and pockets his purchase. As they are walking away, she demands, "Did you really like the ring or were you trying to give the poor old man another sale?"

Poor old man? Suddenly, he turns back to look at the old man again. He is still there, sitting on the broken stool and bending over his work, oblivious to the swarm of tourists around him. But the moment his eyes fall on him, the old man raises his head and flashes a knowing smile at him. He is taken aback with the familiarity in the man's smile. He grabs Mannat's elbow—she has not turned back to see this mysterious, momentary exchange—and marches her back hurriedly to his motorbike. "We should be getting back home," he mutters tersely. Mannat, not having seen what just happened, cannot understand his sudden curtness. She opens her mouth to question him, but the aloof look on his face silences her effectively.

Once they are back home, they are so engulfed in familial jollity that it's only late at night before he can go back to his room. The first thing he does is to take out the ring from his pocket. Throwing away the newspaper scrap it had been wrapped in, he peers at the ring closely. It's a curious design. A star with seven rays, all of them shaped like lotus petals, carved in white on an inky blue bead. The old man's face, with its secretive smile, flashes before his eyes.

Clutching the ring tightly in his fist, he opens the door of his room and walks across the passage towards Mannat's room. The rest of the house has retreated into sleep and deep silence. Mannat's door is slightly ajar, and he enters it without warning.

Clad in an old cotton salwar, her chunni thrown carelessly over the foot of the bed, she is combing her long hair, smoothening out the tangles from the day spent in Kausali. She gives a little scream on seeing him.

He scrambles hurriedly across the room and puts his hand on her mouth, silencing her. "Shut up!" he hisses. "Do you want everyone to wake up?"

She pushes his hand away angrily. "What do you think you are doing here?! And that too at this time of the night?"

"I . . ." he fumbles, "I just wanted to talk."

"And haven't we been doing that all day?" she demands, trying her best to be sarcastic, but melting visibly at his unabashed proximity.

"Were we . . . erm, talking?" He asks, his eyes glinting devilishly.

Blushing beetroot-red, Mannat tries to back away from him, but he seizes her hand. This time there is real anxiety in her eyes. "No, Arpit!" she whispers frantically.

Guilt assails him again as he sees the apprehension in Mannat's eyes. He staggers back. What was he about to do? He steps back, away from her, and takes a long deep breath. The next instant his head clears and he is fully in control again.

Opening his hand now, he shows her what he has brought. Puzzled, she stares at the ring.

"You were right," he says. "It is several sizes too small for me. But," he pauses meaningfully, "I didn't buy it for myself."

She raises her downcast eyes to him now. A question rises and dies on her lips. Taking her left hand, he slips the ring onto her third finger, and bringing her hand to his lips, he kisses it softly.

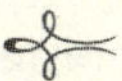

For several minutes after resurfacing from the trance, Arpit's mind was a blank white sheet. He felt calm and secure, as if a soft white quilt was covering him and blanking out all the harsh realities of his life. The fourth switch had been triumphantly turned, at least in *one* realm of reality—yes, reality, for he was now starting to believe all that Nishi had told him about transforming worlds.

"Nishi, I did it this time, didn't I?" he asked eagerly, not opening his eyes in an attempt to stay longer in the world of his dreams.

When there was no answer, he got up to peer at Nishi in the straggling light of dawn. They had started the session at night, right after dinner. He had been more than a little apprehensive about the redreaming session, more so since they were doing it in the Patiala homestead and Nishi's story about the witches of Pret Tal had left him feeling spooked and unsettled. However, contrary to his misgivings, he had slipped easily into the trance. The dream had been long and extremely detailed, but had it really lasted the entire night?

Arpit looked at Nishi. She was sitting still, like she was lost in another dimension where he was denied entry. He hated to disturb her, but really, he could not wait another moment to know what she thought about this session. Eagerly then, he tapped her shoulder. It gave a sharp, reflexive twitch, but Nishi did not wake up.

It was then that he noticed that her lips were moving. She was mumbling something feverishly under her breath, but the words made no sense to him. Was she delirious? Anxiety seized him. What was he going to do if Nishi did not come out of this stupor? He thought of the tiny bottle filled with that vivid red liquid which Nishi had administered to him the night he had found out about Mannat's miscarriage. *No!* His mind screamed.

It would do no good to think about that right now. He had to focus on Nishi. He had to make her snap out of this trance.

Arpit looked around the room, hoping for some inspiration. Suddenly, his attention was pulled to the queer pattern which Nishi had drawn with chalk on the wall behind him. It was the same pattern which she always drew at the foot of his bed in Chandigarh, every time they conducted a redreaming session. It was to protect him, she had said. But wait a minute, wasn't it the same—?? His head spun dizzily as he realised that the queer symbol on the wall was the same as the design on the ring he had slipped on Mannat's finger in his redreaming!

Fighting down his rising panic and confusion, Arpit shook Nishi hard to wake her up, but she just kept mumbling incoherently. Looking around, he saw a bottle of water on the windowsill next to him. Without a moment's hesitation, he picked it up, and opening it, splashed its entire contents on Nishi's face.

Jumping awake, Nishi gasped, "Baba!"

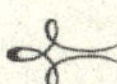

"It was him!" Nishi cried hoarsely. "That old man who sold you the ring was my Baba! He was in Kasauli when you went there with Mannat. You were on the verge of meeting him!"

"This is beyond me, Nishi," Arpit shifted helplessly. "Perhaps you have been missing your father so much that he reared up in your imagination during the redreaming and seeping through my consciousness, lent his face to the old craftsman?" He had been afraid to suggest it, but Nishi had been acting so strange lately that he could not shake off his uneasy conviction that she was no longer in complete control of the process.

But Nishi refused to agree with him. "No, how could that be? I never allow my mind to play such games, especially not during a redreaming session." But her voice shook slightly as she said it, as if she was not so sure anymore.

And Arpit did not dispute her word. He was too busy trying to shake off the frightening possibility that he had never turned any switches at all, that all they had seen so far had been a figment of his and Nishi's collective imaginations.

CHAPTER 16

Binita Baruah was not in the habit of mincing her words, even if she was talking to a member of Punjab's Legislative Assembly.

"Mr Sodhi, this is scandalous, and what's more, this is happening in your own constituency. But are you doing anything besides clucking your tongue in fake sympathy?" She tossed a file of newspaper clippings in his direction.

Vishwas swallowed and glanced nervously at Binita. Really, the FoDi better tone down her aggression a little; after all, it was an MLA she was talking to! There was not a crack of expression, however, on Navneet Sodhi's face. "Ms Baruah, you do know, I hope, that I was the one who undertook the preparation of the EIA report, from my very own MLA fund no less, which I then duly submitted in the Vidhan Sabha a day after it was handed to me?" he asked with scrupulous politeness.

"I don't bother to document events which have had no lasting effect," Binita shot back, just as coolly. "The report wasn't even discussed properly in the Assembly. It has been gathering dust for two years now. Or more perhaps, but I don't waste my time over such details. I believe in action. Now, Mr Sodhi, what I want is your help."

"Ahh! You do? Well, then I am grateful for such an honour. So tell me, how can this humble servant be of use to you?"

"For starters, Mr Sodhi, can you throw a shoe at the Leader of the Opposition in the Assembly tomorrow morning?" Binita, unmindful of Sodhi's obvious sarcasm, asked coolly.

"*What*??"

"Oh come on, Mr Sodhi. Don't tell me that you haven't felt like doing it at least once in all your time in the Assembly. He is . . . well, never mind my opinion about him. Anyway, if you feel squeamish, maybe one of your younger, more hot-blooded party men can do it? It would be a catharsis for you, not to say a Godsend for the news channels. And for us, it will create much-needed chaos. The House will be adjourned and your parties will be baying for each other's blood."

"Do you want to start a riot in this state??"

"Please, Mr Sodhi, you know as well as I do that there would be no riots in this country if those in power did not wish it to be so. There were no riots in ancient and medieval India even with all the immigrants and invaders pouring in. But let's not get into all that at the moment. While tempers fly high inside the House, we will be taking to the streets in your area to protest against your party's pro-Sunburst stand. Normally, such a protest finds only a thin crowd of about forty to fifty supporters. People don't give a damn about pollution when they are struggling with inflation and unemployment. But we have plans to make this protest a big one. First, we will reveal some damning evidence which will call Sunburst's bluff about its vegetarian menu. That always strikes a raw nerve. Second, the Opposition party's disgruntled workers will join us because we are staging an anti-your party demonstration. That will ensure a huge turnout, and extensive media coverage. And by the time the tempers will have cooled enough for your party and the Opposition to make peace over a cup of tea, we will be in the news for all the right reasons."

"So, you want to paint my party as the villain, and the

Opposition goons as heroes to get your work done?" Sodhi spoke slowly. Despite his apparent indignation, there was a tinge of horrified admiration in his voice.

"We can't rope in your party anyway, they are the ones supporting our enemy. And you can't openly go against your party diktat. However, if you follow the plan, once the House is back in order, you can loudly condemn the demonstration and try to slam us down, only verbally of course. This will effectively remove any doubts in your bosses' minds about where your loyalties lie."

"No no no! It's an outrageous suggestion. It may even create a law and order situation with your protest march going out of hand!" Sodhi protested a bit weakly. The last thing he wanted was for this young upstart to find out how impressed he was by her audacity.

"I will say this one last time, Mr Sodhi. Nothing will happen if you don't wish it to happen. The protest march and the demonstration will happen in your constituency so you can easily make sure the police keep things under control. We don't want violence either. Your supervision of the situation will ensure that nothing goes out of control. Plus, you will have direct access to me to keep you updated about the ground situation. You hardly have anything to worry about! Later, you can tell your party that you did not let those filthy Opposition opportunists go out of hand and wreak permanent damage."

"But what purpose will all this rabble-rousing serve? You can't count on those people to support your protest indefinitely; the next day things will go back to normal and your supporters will drop to fifty again. Then what will you do?"

Binita smiled one of her rare smiles. "So who told you that we will be counting on them? All we want is to tell the complacent Indian middle class that there is *something* lurking behind all these pretty pictures and catchy slogans. And it takes a Big Noise to tell them that and wake them up from their slumber. Our aim, to quote Bhagat Singh, 'is to throw a bomb to make the deaf hear!'"

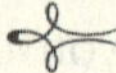

A gaping hole had opened in the floor of Arpit's universe. Perhaps he had placed too much faith in Nishi's powers. Had she been simply projecting her own memories and ideas into his subconscious all this while, where they mingled with his frustrated dreams to produce the scenes he had been experiencing? Had she been merely hypnotising him, filling his mind with suggestions of a changed past? No, no, it had all been too vivid for a mere projection. He had felt it all. He had been *in* the dream . . . in the redreaming.

And why 'redreaming'? He had never asked her about it. He had been re-living the past in his trance sessions and trying to change it; this was the basic process as he knew it. Why had Nishi been calling it redreaming, then? Didn't it imply that he would be merely dreaming what he had already dreamed before? Had the past been just a dream, then? And if so, what was real and what was a figment of imagination? Were the present and the future also just dreams?

Unable to trust his heart for the time being, Arpit turned to hard logic and began meticulously combing through everything that had happened like a lawyer running over the evidence in a case.

When he had tried to turn the seventh switch, nothing had happened. Nishi had said it was because he had become too involved in the scene to remember his objective in redreaming it. But couldn't there be a simpler and more cynically logical explanation?

What if, because it had been the beginning of the process, Nishi had still not gained enough control over his subconscious to hypnotise him into thinking that he was making the changes himself? Naturally, nothing would happen which had not happened before. By the sixth switch however, she was better attuned to him, and was, probably without realising it herself, making him *imagine* that he was rewriting his past.

But how could this explain what Mannat had told him during his redreaming, about his father's opposition to their marriage?

The next moment, Arpit gasped, his skin prickling as cold apprehension gripped him. Nishi had deeply empathised with his story. She had even suggested that Baldev might've visited Meharsar without his knowing and that he might have taunted and insulted Mannat's family. She must've conjectured it all and it must've taken such strong root in her subconscious that she started believing it as a fact, and ended up passing it on to him during his trance as something which would occur within the scope of his redreaming.

The miscarriage! The miscarriage which he had caused! Arpit groped around frantically for some coherence now. It couldn't be mere coincidence, could it, that he had come to know about it right after turning the sixth switch? Surely that was true. Nishi couldn't have manipulated things inside his head and *outside*!

If it wasn't true, it relieved him of the enormous burden of guilt he had been carrying ever since then. But it also took away the means of reversing other wrongs.

Another thing struck Arpit. Each switch was supposed to be located at a point in his life where he had made a critically wrong choice. The fourth switch, therefore, should've taken him not to Kasauli where he had made no mistake in demonstrating his passion, but to Bangalore where he had first started ignoring Mannat's letters. What he had seen, instead, was an engrossing but false tale conjured up by his inflated fancies along with Nishi's nostalgia for her father. The redreaming was nothing but the extension of their convoluted imaginations coming together. And that was the harsh reality he had to accept.

There was, of course, no doubt about Nishi's intuitive powers. The purity of her motives too, was beyond question. She was a truth-seeker and a genuine friend, and her essential nobleness was not something acquired or assumed. Despite all this, however, redreaming was as much an experiment for her as for him, and anything could go wrong. Perhaps it already had!

Nishi had told him that for every switch he successfully turned, there would be a corresponding change in his present life. He had turned four switches by now—if at all there had been any switches, that is—and three of these attempts had been successful. There should be three changes staring him in the face, in that case . . .

The first had been his coming to know about Mannat's miscarriage.

The second was his meeting Binita and at last finding some hope to help Meharsar.

And the third . . . the third change should be on its way now. Three days had passed since the last session. It was now or never. If a significant development took place now, he would set his doubt and disbelief aside and continue with the redreaming. And if it didn't, well, he did not know what he would do then. If only he could somehow prove that the redreaming was actually working, that it wasn't all just conjecture on Nishi's part. He needed something to prove the veracity of Nishi's claims . . . just one thing.

The photographic projection of Prashant's face! That would be his proof!

"I have no answers to give you," Nishi said quietly.

"No answers, no redreaming," shot back an extremely agitated Arpit. "I want solid proof that there is an actual dream-place to which I have been travelling to all this while and not merely being hypnotised into believing so."

"Your own experience is the best proof of things."

"My experience? I have only experienced what you suggested in my subconscious state! You were controlling my mind, Nishi!"

Nishi sighed tiredly. After the last redreaming session, she had shut herself in her house for three days and meditated, if that was indeed the right word for the single-minded frenzy with which she sought answers. Was her own experience, her own intuition betraying her? Had her own mind become her enemy? Or was *she* turning into its enemy by her disbelief? Had it really been her Baba in Kasauli and outside the homestead in Patiala? Was she so lost without him that she had started imagining him everywhere—even in *Arpit's* dreams, which she had no right to meddle with in the first place? And what was she doing to Arpit's mind with her redreaming? Was she, in any way, misusing the faith he had placed in her?

She had tortured herself with these questions during those three days until she could bear it no more. And just when she'd thought that it could get no worse, her mind crumbled under a question which nearly swept her off her feet. 'I will always be with you, even when you don't know it . . .' her father had promised her before he left. So was the presence which had been hovering around her since the last few days, her father's ghost? Did this mean . . . *her father was dead?*

Bringing her wandering mind back to Arpit, Nishi stared at him for one long minute before replying, "No, Arpit, I was never controlling your mind. I was only taking you to the site of that experience; everything else was your own. I had nothing to do with any of it. But if you don't wish to believe, then there is nothing I or anyone else can do to make you believe it. It's like believing in God. There are a thousand miracles which prove his existence daily, but the sceptic can always find a rational explanation for all of them. If you don't have faith, nothing will work."

"Do *you* have faith, Nishi?" Arpit threw the question at her unexpectedly.

Nishi hesitated for just a moment before answering him in a steady voice, "I have faith in the powers which control the process. I have faith that they will never let me misuse my own inferior abilities. Arpit, after the last session even I had started wondering whether my mind was capable enough to guide you safely through this. But I found my answer last night. Even if I make a blunder, Arpit, your own karma will protect you. You have entered this process with the noble intention of reversing your mistakes. These intentions are your armour."

"I have some questions, Nishi. In the last redreaming, I travelled back to one of the best moments of my life, and there was absolutely nothing to mend in it. Why was I taken there?"

"Possibly because redreaming takes you to that point in your life, where you *need* to be taken, not where you *expect* to be taken. You must have missed something the last time, which needed to be shown to you this time . . ."

"What was it? The ring? Or the old craftsman?"

"Maybe both." Nishi sighed again and started to say something, but she stopped herself. Instead she said, "Well, it turned out all right, didn't it? By slipping that ring on Mannat's finger, you promised yourself to her. The fourth switch did serve its purpose after all."

"No, Nishi," Arpit spoke slowly. "Its purpose will not be served till I see what change it brings in the real world. I am sorry. I can't shake off these doubts which have entered my head. But there is one way in which you can convince me."

"How?"

"Generate Prashant's image from your memories, Nishi. Prove that you really can cut through layers of mind and matter."

"Aren't all these pictures on the wall proof enough?"

"I did not see them emerging on paper."

"So you are saying that I am lying?"

"No. But I think you might be entertaining certain delusions." Arpit looked at Nishi defiantly.

Nishi stared at him for a long time. When she finally spoke, her voice was as hard as granite. "Oh, I see. You think all my mysticism has turned me a little soft in the head. I don't need to convince you, Arpit Singh. You were the one who pleaded that we do this. I agreed because I thought you sincerely wanted to break free of the mental conditioning which was behind your past blunders. But I was wrong. You are still caught in the old shackles of scepticism. You are letting your manufactured present defeat your intended past. In this state, I can't help you, and I certainly will not share any one of my life's sacred secrets just to convince you about my abilities."

As he walked away angrily, Nishi stood at the door and watched after him for a few moments. Before moving away, she traced the Lotus Star symbol in the air with her forefinger behind his retreating back. Going back inside, Nish made herself a cup of tea and sat down with the day's newspaper. Her thoughts however, soon began drifting towards her father.

The ring that was to have betrothed Arpit and Mannat, it had the Lotus Star symbol etched on it. And the old craftsman had looked exactly like her father. No, it was her father really. He had crafted the ring. Her father had been in Kasauli all those years ago, and he had been in Patiala too. He could not be a ghost. Ghosts do not leave telltale circles in the dust to show they were there. They don't draw symbols on trees with chalk. Her father was alive. Not dead as she had feared. He was alive and he was somewhere nearby.

Filled with a renewed sense of purpose, Nishi shut herself in her room. Switching off all the lights, she began meditating. In the darkness, she started preparing herself to do what she had never done before—summon from her memory, the face of a person instead of a landscape, and project it on paper. But it was not going to be the face Arpit had demanded.

Long hours later, when she came out of her trance, Nishi smiled as she looked at the photograph which had finally appeared after her concentrated efforts. She would save it for Arpit to see whenever, and if, he would choose to come back.

CHAPTER 17

"Why did you come alone?" demanded Binita. "I can't stand you without that charming lady by your side."

"Meharsar is my village and my problem," snapped Arpit. "Nishimaya is busy, so you will have to deal with me alone. If it helps, I'm not so thrilled about dealing with you either. Where is Vishwas?"

"Seducing an ex-girlfriend. The knowledge that she is a reporter for a prominent news channel has suddenly renewed her worth and attraction in his eyes."

"I can only guess who is behind this. Is this what your idealism has come to, Binita?"

"The end justifies the means," Binita retorted.

"And when did you ditch Marx for Machiavelli?"

"When you ditched me after college. No, don't struggle to look so triumphantly regretful. I didn't break my heart over you. I knew from the very beginning that it was some sort of a joke between you and your friends. I played along simply because it was nice to have someone intelligent to talk to. But getting your religion wrong was an embarrassing mistake. I realised I had been reading too much and observing too little. A careful look at that bangle on your right wrist should've told me everything. But I guess I had always been keyed up about proving myself as an intellectual. That day, however, I decided to stop thinking and start acting. I started NB right after college and it was the best decision of my life."

". . . and you owe it to me!" Arpit could not resist grinning.

"Some people do love to deceive themselves. I turned a moment of truth into a springboard for real action. I could have chosen to continue with my intellectual gymnastics; they are my family's favourite sport after all. I might have gone on studying, presenting pompous papers, and debating till doomsday, but I broke that mental conditioning of twenty years. How many people can do that?"

"Not too many," Arpit answered softly, jolted by a memory—*'You are still caught in the old shackles of scepticism. You are letting your manufactured present defeat your intended past.'*

And for the first time, Arpit looked at Binita with genuine admiration.

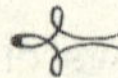

After two nights of battling with himself, Arpit dialled the number with trembling fingers. Amrik Singh, his father's youngest brother, was the only one in the family who was still living in Meharsar and swore by Veerji. He was also the only one who had dared berate Baldev for breaking Beeji's heart, not that his admonitions had had any affect whatsoever on Baldev, but still . . .

A gruff voice with a thick Punjabi accent answered the phone. It was him. Arpit's heart started beating a discordant rhythm. He took a deep, steadying breath and spoke.

"Sat Sri Akal, Chayaji."

"Who is . . . Arpit, is this Arpit?" There was disbelief in the voice on the other end, but not the contempt Arpit had been afraid of.

"Yes, Chayaji, it's me." Impulsively he added, "I am sorry."

After half an hour of teary-eyed conversation, Arpit was wiser by several facts: Veerji was adamant about starting his fast unto death if the twin menace of Verva Cola and Sunburst Inc. was not exorcised from Meharsar and the surrounding villages—"He doesn't listen to anyone, not even to Harpal Praaji. Only one person can perhaps convince him, and that's Manjot. But they are refusing to tell her, lest her married life gets disrupted." Baldev had not phoned his brother even once over the past year, but his lawyer had come to the village several times, bringing a surveyor with him to look over the land. Everyone else in the family had left Meharsar, anticipating that the coming years would see their crops dwindle to what would be barely enough to support them. His children, Arpit's cousins, were all working in city offices now. But he had stayed back. He would die with his village, and Veerji, if need be.

Arpit listened to his uncle talk over the static in the telephone line. For a minute after he was finished, they were both silent. Arpit knew Amrik Chayaji was the only one who could help him with the truth. He might even know if there had ever been any talk about his marrying Mannat, but he couldn't bring himself to ask him about it. But he could ask him for Harjeet's number. And Harjeet was the only one who could tell him if there was any truth to the revelations of that dreadful day.

"Chayaji, do you have Harjeet's telephone number?" Arpit almost choked out his request.

"Harjeet? You mean Harpal Praaji's youngest son? I don't have his number, puttar. But I know he is in Pune for his studies."

"Pune?!"

"I know, none of us have any acquaintances there and it is two days away by train. They were almost on the brink of not sending him to Pune, but Manjot called Harpal several times from England to persuade him. And now, Harjeet is very happy where he is and doing quite well. Manjot's settling abroad has given a new confidence to her and her family. Arpit puttar, the line is getting worse and I can't even hear myself speak. I am going to put the phone down now, but please puttar, do call me again . . . it was good to hear your voice."

The sharp beep which abruptly ended the call seemed to mock him. *Go seek your answers with Nishi and no one else . . . No one else in the world can answer you, except the one person who is your answer,* it seemed to say. He knew he could not avoid Nishi indefinitely. After all, she was not just the conductor of his redreaming sessions, but she was also his architect and they were slated to meet in Patiala the following week for some discussion regarding the homestead project.

To distract himself from the tiring circle of thoughts and questions he had been trapping himself in, Arpit took up the newspaper and began flipping through it. Of late, he had fallen into the habit of going straight to the business section of the newspaper and checking for any updates on the activities of Sunburst Inc., before quickly scanning through the rest of the paper for any information about other environmental movements which might give them some ideas.

Arpit worked his way through the entire newspaper listlessly, nothing catching his attention, until he kept the main newspaper down and picked up the supplement. And then his head reeled.

It was a medium-sized photograph on the right-hand side of the front page, running along an article with screaming headlines:

Indian artist faces plagiarism charges.

Celebrity painter Sandeep Sengupta, whose lifestyle, as one art critic scoffs, is more colourful than his canvas, is in serious trouble this time. For several years now, there have been whispers about his art being inspired by other sources, but thanks to his patrons from the Capital's glitterati, these allegations have never seriously affected his sales. But now, an association representing new and folk artists has accused him of buying their work at throwaway prices and then selling them under his own name.

Joining the aggrieved artists are art experts and critics who point out inconsistencies in the style and technique of Sengupta's collection of works. "There is no way the same person could have painted all of these. There are simply too many variations and too much of eclecticism in Sengupta's work for all of it to have been his own. The only thing perhaps, that is truly his in all these paintings, is his flamboyant signature!" claims Vani Subramaniam, editor of Aesthetica.

Upcoming artist Urvashi Dutta, who exhibits her work at Kala Ghoda, Mumbai, this February, claims that she was shocked to find three of her pencil sketches in the catalogue of Sengupta's Kolkata exhibition last year.

The Association of Folk Artists of Kurmanchal (AFAKA), Almora, has also accused Sengupta of spending almost every summer posing as a tourist holidaying in the hills, getting acquainted with local painters, and buying their Pahari-style paintings, ostensibly for his own personal collection. In some cases, these local artists, having no idea about the real value of their work, have sold paintings and sketches to Sengupta for as low as two hundred rupees for an entire lot. Sengupta, signing across these works of art, then sells them as his own for lakhs of rupees at auctions. The latest example of such alleged thievery is a charcoal sketch titled 'Karma' (inset) which was sold in May this year for a whopping Rs 3.6 lakhs.

Unfortunately, even if the charges are proven true, it will be next to impossible to trace all the real artists who might still be leading lives of anonymity and near penury.

Taking the allegations seriously, two of the country's most famous art galleries—which have previously exhibited Sengupta's work—have served legal notices to the painter. When contacted, Sengupta was unavailable for comment, but his spokesperson rubbished all the charges as being baseless.

It was the same charcoal sketch that he had seen in the last redreaming session—a man and a woman falling off a giant wheel which had serpents coiled about its spokes, hissing threateningly, with flames licking hungrily at the edges of the image as if they would devour everything within a moment. And then he realised that he had also seen the painting at the exhibition in Delhi where he had bumped into Soundarya Sidhwani. She had been right in thinking that it was not Sandeep Sengupta's work at all! Which meant that somewhere in the bylanes of Kasauli, there lived a humble painter who had sold his masterpiece for a pittance. But was it any use looking for this painter after eight long years? Would this man have any answers for him if he found him at all?

All Arpit knew at the moment was that the drawing he had seen during redreaming was not a figment of his imagination. But that did not necessarily mean that the scene in his dream itself was real. He had seen the sketch at the exhibition and it had cast a morbid spell on him. The drawing was a part of his latent memories and it had reappeared during his dream state, mixing itself cleverly with his memories of Kasauli.

Then again, how could all of this be mere coincidence? Hadn't Sandeep been accused of posing as a tourist and picking up local artwork from the hills? Maybe it was from Kasauli that he had bought this particular sketch, from the same roadside display which Mannat had been so entranced with in his redreaming? He could ask Sandeep Sengupta to tell him about the real source of the drawing. But that would be futile, for that would be tantamount to Sengupta admitting to all the accusations of plagiarism. Besides, Arpit didn't even know him personally.

That left only one option now: drive to Kasauli and try to find out whether such a painting had ever been hung in a roadside display along the lower Mall Road. Eight years or not, Arpit would unearth that painter who held the key to his confusion.

They had important guests coming over and everything had to be perfect. Mannat, feeling vaguely guilty about having neglected Sunny over the last few days, what with the Sunburst issue clouding her vision, plunged herself into bringing her house into apple-pie order. Sunny admonished her periodically to not over-strain herself, though he was secretly pleased to see her take so much interest in things.

Patricia Beech, the woman coming over along with her husband to see them, was the great-grandniece of Mrs Samuel Spencer who had been on long, intimate terms with Sunny's grandparents in Jalandhar. After the British Raj had packed up and left, Mrs Spencer had refused to move back to England, choosing instead, to live on in her adopted country. She moved up to the hills where she built herself a cosy cottage. Though her children and grandchildren had moved to England, they visited India every two years, maintaining a part-sentimental part-fashionable tie with India. Mrs Spencer, unable to visit Sunny's grandparents as frequently as she would have liked to, wrote to them every month, and the friendship between her and the Shergills had continued to flourish through the years until her death a few months ago. The reading of her will revealed that she had bequeathed some of her prized paintings and curios to Sunny's grandparents. But despite their affection and respect for the old lady, his grandparents were rather nonplussed. What were they going to do with such a present? Their home was already overflowing with knick-knacks, and there were no art enthusiasts amongst their children.

Sunny had no interest in art either, but when he happened to mention this little incident to Mannat, her eyes glowed with eagerness. "Can't they send the paintings to us?" she asked hesitantly, as if afraid of her own question.

"I suppose they can, since no one wants them, but . . . why, Mandy? Since when have *you* become an art expert?"

"A connoisseur," she corrected him, hiding a secret smile.

Seeing her so keen, Sunny had asked his grandparents to send the paintings through Patricia Beech who had gone to India to attend her great-aunt's funeral. Sunny had thought it only polite to invite Patricia and her husband to dinner as thanks for all the trouble they had taken in bringing the paintings back with them to England.

After dinner, Mrs Beech suggested that Mannat unpack the paintings before them.

"We were all so busy with the funeral and then we had to rush back immediately; I didn't get any time to take a look at the paintings before they were packed," she explained. "I would like to see them now . . ."

The paintings were a mixed bag. Some of them had probably been picked up from exhibitions where debuting artists struggled to find buyers for their work, while most others had presumably been picked up from roadside displays. Some were brutal reproductions of everyday squalor, and some an outburst of macabre fantasy. There were oil paintings, charcoal and pencil sketches, and ink drawings. Altogether, there were about a dozen.

While everyone cooed with dutiful appreciation, it was clear that they did not share Mannat's delight in these pictures. One of the sketches was particularly riveting, and despite Sunny's protests—"But it's so depressing, darling! All those greys will throw me into Monday morning blues even on holidays!"—she had decided to hang it up on the wall facing her bed. It was a charcoal sketch of a man and a woman falling off a gigantic wheel, the spokes of which were covered with serpents. Below it, in a vivid red that was incongruent with the obvious dullness of the rest of the piece, was an indistinguishable scrawl bearing the artist's signature.

A couple of days later, Sunny burst excitedly into their bedroom, carrying his laptop in his arms. "Sit down, Mandy," he gasped. "I have some astounding news."

For a moment, Mannat's heart thudded irrationally. Had Sunburst decided . . .? But no, that was a naïve hope . . .

"Read through this article, my dear wife," Sunny said excitedly, "and you will understand." He put down the laptop in front of Mannat and pointed towards the screen.

Mannat skimmed through the article hurriedly before looking up blankly at him.

Sunny nodded and grinned, "Yes, Mandy, this charcoal sketch hanging on our wall is worth Rs 3.6 lakhs! How much would that be in pounds? Wait, let me access the converter. I'm just too excited for mental mathematics."

"So Mrs Spencer left your family a masterpiece, and no one guessed it," Mannat mumbled, a little dazed.

"Exactly! And that's the astonishing part. Why did she not leave the painting for one of her own descendants? I hope there won't be any legal trouble over this. For all we know, now that the news is public, the Beeches or someone else from their family might stake a claim to the painting. What do you suggest we do in that case, darling? I don't want any controversy, but now that I know what it's worth, I would hate to give it up so easily . . ."

"I don't know. I am still dazed. Maybe they will not want it back? Oh, but Sunny, that poor, poor painter!"

"Huh? Are you actually feeling sorry for that inglorious copycat?"

"Not him! I was thinking of the original artist. Perhaps he continues to display his work before indifferent tourists along some hill station's Mall Road . . . you don't suppose we can track down the artist, do you?"

"And why should we be bothered about that? Just sit and rejoice over the fact that you now have a valuable, genuine artwork in your house, and pray, for you believe in prayers, that none of Mrs Spencer's relatives come to know about the real value of this sketch. Meanwhile, I will have to discreetly look around for an expert who can evaluate the rest of the paintings. I don't think they are worth much, but well, you never know!"

Long after Sunny had bounced out of the room, Mannat continued to stare pensively at the sketch hanging on the wall in front of her. No matter how hard she tried, she could not think of it in terms of its monetary worth. It continued to weave the same surreal spell on her which it had since the very first time she had seen it. But the longer she looked at it, the more she felt that she had seen it somewhere before, that she had known the painting for years.

This was his first visit to Kasauli since he had come here with Mannat. In the eight years in between, the place had changed little, except in an increase in the clamour and bustle of people and cars. But for him, every spot became a phantom-spot, as if what he saw wasn't real, and the only Kasauli that was actually real was the one in which he had kissed Mannat. But what if it was the other way round? What if everything he saw was tangibly rooted in physical reality and he was the only unreal one? The phantom?

Arpit shook his head to clear it of such brooding thoughts and decided to concentrate on the task he had set for himself. He was carrying the newspaper clipping with the photograph of the charcoal sketch. He'd figured that it might just help him find the artist. He also had a picture of Sandeep Sengupta which he had downloaded from the Internet, just in case.

The spot he had seen in his redreaming was quite easy to locate. It was a side road, just off the place where he had parked his motorcycle eight years ago. He remembered now how Mannat had wanted to explore this road that day, but being in a hurry to get back and also quite embarrassed by his outburst of passion a while ago, he had rudely hustled her back to Chandigarh.

He turned into the side road and drove as far as the car could go down the narrow, winding road. Eventually though, he had to stop and park. Trudging down the path on foot now, Arpit looked around for some sign of an art display anywhere. But there was nothing. Perhaps he had arrived too early, he reasoned. The mountainfolk would still be winding up their morning chores before setting out to open shop for the day.

He walked further down the narrow road before stopping abruptly. Surely . . . surely this was the spot where Mannat had stopped to look at the charcoal sketch? Yes, this had been the place where the artist had haphazardly hung up his fancies on a clothesline for all to see and for an unscrupulous, would-be artist to take away for a measly price. So the place, at least, was real. But wait, there was no artwork to be seen anywhere!

The only shop open around there was a small dhaba which appeared to serve tea and snacks. Arpit walked over to the dhaba. Being the lone city man walking down that road at so early an hour, he had already attracted the attention of the proprietor. Perhaps the man could help him with his quest; he looked old enough to have been around for quite some time. Nodding to the man now, Arpit ordered a cup of tea and sat down on one of the benches laid out in the clearing in front of the dhaba. With the sun trickling in through the pines and warming his back,

Arpit wished Mannat was there with him to enjoy this too brief a moment of tranquil silence. But that was not to be . . .

Arpit lost himself to the sounds of his tea being made and the dhaba preparing itself for yet another day. He jumped when the boy tapped him on his shoulder and held out a plate of brown, soggy-looking biscuits, and his cup of tea. Refusing the plate of biscuits, Arpit took the tea and decided that it was time to see what the proprietor knew about the sketch and its artist. But the man appeared mostly clueless—Yes, a few artists did display their paintings here once in a while. No, they didn't do it every day. No, he wasn't sure if it was the same person every time. It could be different artists, he never paid much attention anyway.

Arpit didn't think it was any use showing him the news clipping or Sandeep's photo, but he still did. There was no trace of interest, much less of recognition, in the man. Giving up, Arpit paid him for the tea and started walking back along the road. By now a few other shops had started opening their shutters. But inquiring at them proved just as fruitless. Some of the shopkeepers were able to name the artists who came often to display their work, but identifying a particular sample of their work was out of the question for them.

"Can't you tell me where these chaps live?" Arpit pleaded to the owner of the last shop. "I really want to talk to them."

The man looked at him with undisguised surprise. "Is there a famous painter among them? Are you also a painter, *sa'ab*?"

Desperate, Arpit lied. "No, but I'm a reporter who wants to expose a famous painter. Do you know that this man" —he held up Sandeep's photograph— "has been buying the works of these poor local artists and selling them under his own name? I want to find out which paintings he has bought from here and who the original artists are, and see if I can help them."

There was a flicker of indignation on the man's face. "That's what all these big people do, rob us poor men. I wish I could help you, *sa'ab*, but I have never seen this man before. To tell you the truth, I hardly pay attention to the faces of tourists. I just look at how they are dressed. It helps me to decide how to talk to them."

"Is there an artists' *basti* nearby?"

"None that I know of. Would you like some fresh pomegranate juice, *sa'ab*? My shop is the most hygienic in Kasauli. But if you prefer the packaged variety, I stock that too."

"No, thanks," Arpit muttered dejectedly and began walking back to his car. Had this been a foolish quest then? After all, who would remember a stupid charcoal sketch after so many years? Would even the artist himself remember? He sat down on a makeshift stone bench and lit another cigarette. An elderly woman passing by with bags stashed full of groceries in both her hands, glanced at him with faint disapproval. He stared back at her, taking long rebellious drags and cursing under his breath. But the next moment he felt ashamed. Stubbing the cigarette, he threw it away and, on an impulse, strode briskly after the lady. "I'm sorry," he said when he caught up with her.

She turned around and looked at him, astonishment writ large on her face. "Do I know you, young man? And what are you apologising for?!"

"I thought you didn't like seeing me smoke."

The woman threw back her head and burst out laughing. "Have I really started looking like a holier-than-thou old maid then? You were mistaken, my dear. I was lost in thought. I've been scowling all the way back from the baker's. The bread . . . oh, it's nothing that will interest you. But since you are here, I *would* appreciate someone carrying this bag for me. I live just a little way down the road."

Arpit took the heaviest parcel from the old woman's hand and began walking beside her in awkward silence. Part of him was already regretting his hasty apology and the offer to help. He had to politely excuse himself somehow. He only had one day before meeting Nishi in Patiala and he couldn't bear the idea of facing her without having his doubts sorted.

But he continued walking, hoping that they were nearing the lady's house. Suddenly, she turned her grey-blue eyes on him and winked. "I am pretty fond of the pipe myself. However, I don't fancy cigarettes at this time of the day. Would you care to join me for tea? I'm sure you must be hungry."

"No . . . Actually . . . I . . ."

"Stuff and nonsense! I can see you are ravenous, young man. Here is my house. Come inside."

Having no choice but to obey her, Arpit waited for her to fish out the keys from her handbag and unlock the door. It was a delightfully old-fashioned house, with ivy growing over the facade and a huge brass knocker sitting proudly on the polished wooden door. A small garden, slumbering in the early morning sunlight, lay to his right, and on the old rocker that stood right beside the main door of the house, sat an old tabby staring at him with imperious curiosity. Following her inside, the first thing Arpit saw was a huge portrait of a Rajput chieftain, in full ceremonial attire, hanging from the wall in front of him. When she caught him staring at it, the old woman sighed and said, "That was my great-grandfather, one of the most celebrated commanding officers of the army of the erstwhile kingdom of Mewar. I won't go into details; young people like you tend to get bored easily. I invited you in for a cup of tea, so a cup of tea is what you will get. Oh and yes! Something to eat as well. What would you like? I have a bit of chocolate cake and . . . but, oh my goodness, we still haven't introduced ourselves!"

She was Sindoora Jaisingh-Kunjru. Her hyphenated surname, she clarified, bore no trace of reluctant matrimony. "I am a spinster by choice. I took on both my parents' family names since I couldn't decide which one had a more illustrious legacy. But most people labour under the delusion that I am a rich widow, and that is a little inconvenient since it keeps the old bachelors away!" She trilled, reminding Arpit of a little girl giggling at her own joke.

Buttered bread and chocolate cake accompanied the very English tea that Ms Jaisingh-Kunjru, who insisted that Arpit call her Dora, "like my friends used to," served up. "I used to get such excellent bread from that baker down the lane, whatshisname . . . Roshan! Yes, Roshan. He would deliver the freshly-baked loaf, still warm in its brown paper wrapping and smelling like good pastry which goes to heaven. But then the food authorities have been after him for some time now to print the calorific value and the brand name and all that nonsense on his packages. If he doesn't, he loses business. The poor boy can hardly read, so he's figured that it's easier to simply stock the more commercially manufactured bread, you know the ones that circulate in all the local markets everywhere? The other day he said that his business still does well, but it's not fun anymore. Isn't it a shame? I don't need any food value rubbish on my bread. I know it's good because Roshan bakes it. But I am forced to buy this brand now" —she waved dismissively at the bread on the table— "and goodness knows what kind of flour they use or whether it is really baked well or just coloured brown. On top of everything else, I still have to pay two rupees more for it than what I used to pay for Roshan's bread."

Arpit had been nodding along seriously to Dora's narration of her bread tragedy, when he suddenly remembered the reason he had come to Kasuali. "Dora," he interrupted, "I need a bit of help from you. I am looking for a local artist whose work was stolen by a rather famous artist and sold under his own name from a gallery in Delhi. I want you to tell me if you've seen this sketch anywhere, or if you know who the real artist is."

Arpit pulled out the newspaper clipping from his pocket and passed it to Dora. Looking questioningly at him, Dora took the newspaper and began reading the article with interest. "3.6 lakhs! That's robbery!" She adjusted her reading glasses and peered closely at the picture of the charcoal sketch and exclaimed, "Dear God! I can swear that I have seen this very piece somewhere in this town!"

Arpit's hands went cold in spite of the hot cup of tea he was holding.

"Now where did I . . ." Dora was mulling, ". . . where did I see it? You know, that's the only problem with being single—there is no old man around to remind you about things which you are likely to forget. It wasn't too long ago either when I saw . . . Oh! Grace!"

Arpit stared expectantly at Dora. She smiled rather wistfully though her eyes shone with definite excitement.

"My best friend Grace, Mrs Grace Samuel Spencer, died a couple of months back. She was a dyed-in-the-wool art lover. I'm surprised she didn't ask for her art collection to be buried with her. Anyhow, she left it all instead, to some friends of hers in Jalandhar. I could have had it if I had asked for it, but I am not an art fanatic. And this particular sketch, yes, now I remember it. It used to hang in her guestroom, to scare off uninvited guests, I presume."

Arpit sat staring at her, trying to search for his voice in the bewildering dark wilderness that seemed to be descending on his brain. "So . . . so Mrs Spencer bought this painting from Sandeep Sengupta's exhibition in New Delhi?"

"For that amount of money? Impossible! Grace was rich, but she was not a rich fool to throw her money away like this. She bought the sketch from a roadside painter right here in Kasauli, and that too for a couple of thousand rupees. She knew what the drawing was worth, and she wanted to encourage the painter. She was sentimental about things like that. Anyway, what she paid was definitely more than what any tourist would have ever paid for that piece of artwork."

"But then, how did it turn up in Sandeep's collection?"

"My dear boy, the locals aren't as gullible as people believe them to be. They know how to mass-produce a thing which sells. You see, I often walk down that road where I met you, to get groceries. On at least four different occasions, I have seen copies of this same sketch being sold to four different buyers. Your celebrity painter was probably one of them. So, the sketch which he sold to some poor fool for Rs 3.6 lakhs has at least four more copies floating around, and none of them is worth more than a few hundred rupees!"

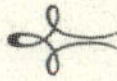

"Ninety-four percent in my four primary subjects!" He exults, holding up his marksheet proudly and casting a sly glance at Mannat to check whether she is suitably impressed or not. "I am ready for any cut-off list now!"

"But my family thinks Home Science is a waste of time," Mannat says gloomily. "They don't understand the concept of a nutritionist at all."

"Well, there is one thing even I can't understand. Why can't you come to Delhi with me? I will look after you. You won't have to worry about a thing!"

She can't hold back her amused smile. "And a fine caretaker I will have too! You do know that all college hostels have rules about local guardians, right? And it can't be someone my own age!"

"Dad will be your LG. I will make him be your LG . . ."

"Arpit, stop it. You know you can't 'make' him be my LG."

Her words sting him, and he gets up and starts walking away. She doesn't stop him. He keeps walking till he finds himself in a bustling, steaming, chaotic place—a college canteen. A bespectacled figure is sitting at a table in the far end of the canteen, absorbed in a book. He walks up and takes the empty seat opposite her.

A thought slices through his consciousness (or subconsciousness?): How did he arrive from Meharsar to Delhi University in an instant, even if this is a dream? Isn't he supposed to be turning a switch rather than wasting his time grappling with Binita and time-travelling across distance?

A distant, familiar voice answers, "You had missed something which needs to be shown now." He does not argue with it.

"If history repeats itself, why do you need to study it again, year after year?" he quips.

Binita gives him a withering look. "To help uncaring machines like you to recognise history when it reoccurs . . . to help you from falling for the old agendas of oppression which have taken on a new, smiling packaging within the ugly contours of our present society."

"All this is going over my head. What do you mean by 'agenda'? Do you mean that all the wrongs that took place in history were planned? Premeditated?"

"Well, the motive to exploit certainly was."

"No, Binny—"

"Binita!" she snaps, interrupting him.

"All right, MISS Binita Baruah, I will take Partition as an example. It could've been avoided. But once we started fighting amongst ourselves over religion, the British had no choice but to divide the country. There was no 'agenda' involved here. It was our own foolishness that led to that catastrophe."

"Ah, the product of an Anglophile school!" Binita says, her voice

dripping with sarcasm. "So that's what they have fed you? That Partition was the result of communal strife fanned by religious fanatics? And of course, the poor, well-meaning Brits had no other way to save us, the illiterate backward barbarians, from killing each other than to divide us, right?"

"I am not a fan of the British rule," he answers sulkily, cowed by her scathing attack. "But it was our fault that we landed up as two countries instead of one. We accepted their divide-and-rule policy. Had we been united and strong enough, they would never have been able to establish their empire here in the first place."

"That's easy to say. But did the common people really have a choice? Who sold us, Arpit? Your ordinary farmer or tradesman or artisan? No! We were ransomed out by the nawabs, the maharajas, and the zamindars who wanted to align themselves with the powerful, the nation be damned." She goes on passionately, "Throughout history, the rich and the powerful have been the least loyal to their soil, and the victim has always been the common man. It happened then and it is happening now . . . and will continue to happen till doomsday consumes us all unless we rise up and revolt!"

He shoots up from his chair. "Revolution, revolution! Down with the rich! Inquilab Zindabad!"

People at the neighbouring tables burst into appreciative laugher. Glaring at them with unspeakable contempt, Binita hustles Arpit outside. "This is all a joke for you, isn't it? Neo-urbanites like you who live in a bubble of prosperity won't know—"

"Hold it there, Binita," he warns, irritated at last. "I am from a village. I know something about what the farmers go through. Don't preach to me all right? I am not your dumb neo-urbanite."

Even as he utters the words, he feels a twinge of guilt. Does he really know what the farmers in his village are going through? Has he even bothered to find out about their plight in the last few years? Then he catches himself thinking: "Had we continued this conversation the last time? Or had I let Binita assume I am a city boy, too embarrassed to acknowledge my rural roots?"

Now her tone is taut with challenge. "You probably don't know about what I am going to tell you. It was never made public for the truth would've been very inconvenient to certain influential people. Anyway, since you are from Punjab, you might have heard of the Meharsar Lake . . ."

He stares at her in surprise and then starts to shifts uncomfortably before admitting, "Yes, I know something about it."

She goes on as if he hasn't spoken, "It has fascinated limnologists for a while now. Once, it used to be a seasonal lake, barely larger than a pool, but then it suddenly swelled and overflowed its banks and became the major water body for Meharsar and its surrounding villages. There is also some religious yarn attached to it, but that's beside the point. Have I told you about Janaki?"

"Several times," he replies wryly, rolling his eyes. Janaki is the pride of the Baruah clan—the over-achieving cousin who gives Binita a huge inferiority complex, though she would die before admitting it. He has been told countless times that Janaki is a junior scientist in one of the top-notch geographical research institutions in the country.

"Well, Janaki got this bit of information straight from some of her seniors. In the early nineties, some limnologists and environmental scientists drafted a proposal to convert the land adjoining the Meharsar lake into a Wetland Conservation Reserve. In their assessment report, the waters of the Meharsar lake were high quality and almost free of impurities. It would've been suitable for breeding certain threatened species of aquatic plants. Furthermore, they wanted to convert the barren land along the eastern shores of the lake into a green belt through active reforestation. The native community would be involved in the project, and it would have really increased job opportunities for the villagers. The proposal was sent to the powers-that-be, and was on the verge of being passed when . . ."

"When? When what?" he asks impatiently, a strange sense of foreboding making him afraid of the rest of Binita's story.

"When there came another proposal, this one from a far bigger lobby. Verva Cola wanted to set up their plant in Meharsar. They wanted land

and cheap labour, and if the Wetland Reserve project came through, they would get neither. So they sent one of their smoothest brokers, their oiliest agent—a man called Baldev Singh—who knew which string to pull where and which palms to oil. Thanks to him, the Wetland project was soon buried under a mountain pile of official files and the Verva Cola proposal got the go-ahead."

Someone has put a long stick into his head and is churning his insides violently. "Enough!" cries a voice inside him. Let this dream break, let him go deaf, let him be flung far away from Binita Baruah's accusing words . . .

But there is no escape. She continues, "Now, you see, this Baldev Singh had loads of money and connections. Nobody knows much about him, but it was clear even then that he wasn't a farmer. He obviously didnt care two hoots about what this Verva Cola project would mean for the villages in the long run. This was my point all along, wasn't it—the people worst affected by such decisions are the ones who've had no say in taking them. Therefore, history repeats itself . . ." she winds up triumphantly.

Arpit woke up with a jolt. Rubbing his eyes, he looked around him. From the window facing his bed, moonlight streamed into his room, playing a morose game of shadows on the wall. He looked to the left of his bed. Where was Nishi? His eyes scanned the room apprehensively before he realised that she was nowhere around.

Had he, then, descended into redreaming on his own? But how was that even possible?!

CHAPTER 18

Mannat tried to sympathise with her husband, but she just couldn't.

Even before Sunny could get hold of an expert to assess the value of Mrs Spencer's paintings, news from India had crushed all his hopes. The sketch 'Karma' that they possessed, the one Mannat had fallen in love with, was apparently not an original. What was more, there were at least three more copies of the same sketch floating around. The one actually bearing Sandeep Sengupta's signature had been sold to a Soundarya Sidhwani, a Delhi socialite. It was clear that painting was not an original piece of work. Sandeep Sengupta had either stolen it from an unassuming artist somewhere, or he had copied the design in entirety. Soundarya Sidhwani, understandably furious about having paid a whooping 3.6 lakhs for a plagiarised work, had said in her statement to the media that she was planning to sue Sandeep Sengupta.

"Three more copies! Can you believe that?! Apparently all of them were bought from some roadside display in some hill town. This means that our copy is practically worthless!" Sunny thundered.

"What? Which hill town was that?" Mannat enquired, suddenly interested. For her part, she had been quite relieved when news broke out that their copy of the painting was worthless. Nobody would pay any attention to it anymore. The painting was hers in entirety now, and she was the only one who would value it.

"I don't know. But if you are so curious, why don't you find out about it yourself?" Sunny snapped and walked out of the room, but not before casting a glance of cold fury at the painting hanging on the wall.

Mannat was left behind to mull over the developments. All the copies of the sketch had been bought from a hill town. Mrs Spencer used to live in a hill town. It was natural to assume she had bought it from her local mart. Mannat definitely had never seen the picture before. But she couldn't easily shrug off the delicate cloak of connection with it. She was seized with curiosity to find out which town it was. Could it possibly be . . .?

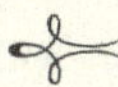

"Yessss . . .?" A sleepy voice drawled dangerously.

"Binita, this is Arpit. I need to talk to you . . ."

"Arpit Singh?! At 4 a.m. *you* want to talk to *me*? You know, *you* might be preparing for bed after a night of wild debauchery, but I am enjoying a well-earned sleep and I did not intend to be woken before six. And you, definitely, will not have anything as earth-shattering as to justify your spoiling my sleep at this unearthly hour. Anyway, since you have aroused my curiosity now and have killed all hopes of my being able to fall asleep again, you might as well go ahead and spill the beans."

"Sorry! Sorry! What I wanted to ask you was this: Do you remember a conversation we once had about Partition? It was a long time back obviously, we were sitting in your college canteen."

"Hmm . . . We might have. I vaguely remember something

of the kind. But please tell me that this is not why you disturbed my slumber?"

"Well, if we had continued . . . Erm . . . forget it. Where is your cousin Janaki these days?"

"Somewhere in the Maldives, researching coral reefs. Why? You know, this is getting curioser and curioser. If you go on like this for another minute, my hypothesis that you've been heading towards insanity for a long time will be proven true."

"Please, Binita, listen to me." The note of urgency in his voice silenced Binita. "I really need to know this. Did Janaki ever tell you about a Wetland Conservation Reserve project in Meharsar?"

There was silence at the other end—a silence spanning infinite distances.

Finally, puzzled and perplexed, Binita spoke up, "I don't think so. If she had told me something of that kind, surely it would have come back to me when I was gathering all that information about the Sunburst issue, right? Something like that would definitely be valuable to us. Where did you hear of it, anyway?"

"Forget about it." Arpit disconnected the phone before Binita could say anything. The last thing he needed was for her to question him about this whole Wetland Conservation thing. He was too disappointed to deal with her right now.

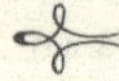

"You had a redream by yourself?" There was awe in her voice, and a tremor too. Arpit looked at her for reassurance, but Nishi was too lost in the implications of what he had just told her.

"I am not sure it was a redream," he replied listlessly. "It might just have been a subconscious mish-mash. I was physically and mentally exhausted after Kasauli and I just—"

"You went to Kasauli?" Nishi interrupted, her eyebrows arching in mild surprise.

Arpit mutely nodded his head. When she didn't say anything, he looked at her sheepishly and told her everything.

Nishi would have loved to say 'Well, now you know I wasn't hypnotising you,' but Arpit's abashed expression clearly told her that he had taken care of his doubts and that his faith was back, stronger than before.

"I won't doubt the process again, Nishi, nor your powers, for that matter. But I don't understand what happened last night. How could I have had a dream on my own?!"

"Honestly, even I don't know. I mean, I can't explain. It wasn't something I was expecting. But I'm sure it's a good sign. It shows that your mind is getting finely attuned to that dream-pool which we were thinking only I could lead you to. It's a good thing, Arpit, it's a good thing . . ."

Arpit sighed rather pessimistically. "I hope so, Nishi. But I don't think I turned a switch."

"You might have," said Nishi slowly. "You did have that conversation with Binita years ago, but it never reached the point where she could tell you about the Wetland project. But something in your dream-conversation this time took you down a different course from the past, and gave you a piece of information which might turn out to be important. So even if it doesn't look like you turned a switch, you might just have hit on something crucial."

"But Binita never knew of such a project. I called her last night and asked her. She said Janaki had never spoken of a Conservation project in Meharsar. So even if we had continued talking when the conversation was actually happening all those years ago, she could not have told me about it."

"Arpit, this is a dream different from your other redreams," Nishi mulled. "It might be a mined revelation."

"A what?! What do you mean?"

Nishi leaned towards him, her face suddenly looking years younger and her eyes alight with excitement. "Arpit, maybe your dream was trying to tell you something? To give you a message that might just prove important to your present-day struggle? I don't know how and why this should happen, but we can verify if this conjecture is true. We must find out if such a proposal was ever drafted."

"But how, Nishi? If at all it existed, its records would've been buried years ago. Binita knows nothing about it. So where do you propose we even begin to seek a verification for the existence of such a proposal? It's an impossible thing, Nishi."

"Janaki! That's where we need to start! Arpit, you have to ask Binita to talk to Janaki."

"And how will I convince her to do it? If I tell her I dreamt about all of this, she will laugh her head off and write me off as loony. She has been dying to do that for years. And anyway, even if she buys my rather incredulous story, she won't do it for me. She detests me."

"If you can't persuade her, I will step in. But I am sure it won't come to that," Nishi said and smiled. "She wouldn't have spent so many hours arguing with you if she didn't like you."

"Yeah yeah. You don't know Binita Barauh, Nishi," Arpit grumbled as he picked up the phone to call Binita and fix up an appointment.

True to his predictions, Binita flatly refused to talk to Janaki, with whom—she was finally forced to admit—she had not been on talking terms for years ever since a bitter family feud had caused a rift between the two cousins.

"Besides," she parried, peering suspiciously at Arpit, "you still haven't told me where you got this outlandish idea from. Or wait, is it from a spam email? Like that Taj Mahal one, maybe?"

Arpit groaned; Binita would never let things go. But he needed her right now, so he redoubled his efforts. Eventually, Binita seemed to be convinced of his desperation if not of the validity of his quest. "Arpit, it's not all in my power. Please understand that. Even if I could bring myself to talk to her, *she* won't answer me. Then what do I do? To whom do I . . . wait!" Binita stopped mid-sentence, a glimmer of hope beginning to break across her face. "I think there is someone who might help us!"

But before he could even think of asking her to explain who she had in mind, Binita shooed him away and firmly shut the door on his face. The minute Arpit was out of the door Binita fished out her cell phone and put a call through to Navneet Sodhi. In her regular bulldozer-ish manner, she didn't spend too long in cajoling and coercing the MLA into helping her. But once she disconnected the phone, she couldn't help wondering about a tiny detail which had been niggling inside her head since the whole Meharsar thing had begun. It wasn't the Wetland Conservation Reserve which intrigued her at the moment, though if it were to be true it would be a great boost to their campaign. It was a name. A name she had been hearing on and off ever since NB had taken up the cudgels for Meharsar—Baldev Singh, aka Dave of India Mantra Ltd., the Indian franchisee of Sunburst.

Somehow she could not shake off the feeling that she had heard this name before, and that she had heard it in an entirely different context.

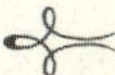

It was dawn by the time Joginder Singh Meharsar had bathed and gotten ready. He had wanted to see the sun rise over his beloved lake and tint its waters a piercing gold, before embarking on the most important day of his life.

He knelt in the small village gurdwara now, praying for strength of body and mind to carry this task through. All his life, he had longed to do something worthwhile for the country, or for his village and his people. And that day had finally arrived.

Meanwhile, Harpal and Sukhmani had quietly roused the other members of the household. Their neighbours—Amrik Singh's family amongst them—gradually joined them. No one had been able to dissuade Veerji from going on the hunger strike. So they were doing the next best thing—supporting him wholeheartedly. All of them would be fasting with him on the first day. Harpal was hoping that it would be the only day of fasting for any one of them, and that the NB people from Ropar would be able to fix everything in a day. He had his fingers crossed.

Step One of their campaign against Sunburst Inc. was a smashing success. As planned, Navneet Sodhi threw a slipper at the Leader of the Opposition in the Vidhan Sabha which caused instant pandemonium in the House, causing it to be adjourned within half an hour.

Meanwhile, NB activists and their supporters—a mixed bag of environmental scientists, citizens' groups, and students—took to the streets. First, they demonstrated outside the Verva Cola plant, calling it a product of the 'rebirth of *videshi* imperialism' ("Such rhetoric always works," Binita whispered to an excited Vishwas). And then they began marching towards their real destination—Meharsar. As they walked, actively sloganeering and protesting, a huge crowd of workers and supporters from the opposition party, furious with the insult of their leader, began joining them and swelled their ranks.

By the time they reached Meharsar and staged the last leg of their protest in front of the controversial plot of land, a short distance away from the threatened lake, the protestors numbered nearly a thousand. The regional media was torn between covering them and the Honourable Members of the Legislature who were vying with each other to grab media space and throw vitriolic quotes at their opponents. The ruling party had already come out with a statement dismissing the NB agitation as the work of 'vested interests', while the opposition welcomed it as an 'uprising of the common man against the *sarkar*'s neglect of the farmer's plight', and had pledged its unequivocal support to the agitation.

`Am enjoying myself tremendously. Wish you were here to see this...`

Binita texted Arpit from Meharsar. Arpit chuckled when he read her message. He'd been on tenterhooks since dawn, wondering how things would fare out. Though her message allayed his fears a little, he wished he were there to witness it all firsthand. But he also knew that as much as he wanted to confront and defeat the consequences of his father's greed and his own immobility, he did not have the courage to face Veerji, yet.

`Keep me posted.`

He wrote back to Binita, not knowing what else to write to her. Within a minute, his phone beeped with her reply.

`Switch on the TV...`

Veerji's face filled up the screen the minute Arpit switched on the television. Age had not left any visible marks on Veerji, neither had it slowed him down. The strength and the calmness

Veerji exuded was still there, but the indefatigable glint in his eyes was just a bit jaded now. Perhaps repeated disappointments and betrayals had dimmed it.

Arpit felt his eyes begin to water. He knew the image on the screen in front of him was incomplete. While Harpal Chayaji and Sukhmani Chayiji sat next to Veerji, giving him all the support they could muster, Arpit knew he was the missing element in the picture. He should've been the one taking Veerji's hand in his own and gently leading him to face the crowd which cheered madly when they saw the old man. And Mannat should have been there too, right with him. They would've been at the forefront then, facing the enemy without a flicker of fear. But he could only watch from the sidelines for now.

Halfway across the globe, Baldev Singh watched the NB protest reach Meharsar on his TV screen and spluttered viciously over his morning coffee.

And in Leeds, Mannat watched with rising apprehension as a thousand strangers marched to her village to stage a protest against what was happening there and as Veerji, her own Veerji, started his fast unto death.

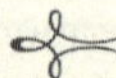

Things started rolling almost immediately. Within two days, the Union government set up a hurriedly-constituted expert committee to look into the charges against Sunburst Inc., and to assess the environmental damage the passage of the proposal would cause. NB, on the other side, was bang in the eye of a storm—Binita, Vishwas, and others who had participated in the protest had started receiving threatening calls.

"Nonchalance comes with experience," Binita grinned, waving away Nishi and Arpit's worries about her safety. "This is not the first time it's happening. These days I tell myself that the guardian angel who was sweet enough to send me the only, token boyfriend I ever had" —she winked saucily at Arpit, who shifted uneasily in his chair— "will be solicitous enough to guard my life as well!"

"You are incorrigible, Binita!" Nishi smiled slightly and admonished her.

Arpit smiled too. Nishi's growing fondness for Binita was apparent, but Binita herself had mellowed down. Actually she was borderline likeable now.

In a moment, though, Binita was back to attacking him.

"Next time, Nishiji, tell Chicken Little here to tag along."

"I am not afraid; I have personal reasons for staying away from Meharsar," Arpit replied.

"And what might these 'personal' reasons be?" Binita demanded, leaning forward rather aggressively.

Nishi stepped in, coming to Arpit's rescue. "Binita, Arpit has an equation with Meharsar that only he understands. I don't think either of us has a right to intrude upon that. But I am certain that his reluctant feet will carry him back to Meharsar one day."

Binita got the message. "Pshaw to all intrusions! Now, I need to tell you about phase two of Operation Meharsar."

After she had finished, there was an astounded silence in her office for a full minute. It was Arpit who broke it by gasping out loud, "You can't be serious!"

Binita adjusted her glasses and peered at him in triumphant amusement. "Brilliance often gets such a reaction from mediocrity."

"Cut the crap," Arpit retorted. "You're crazy if you think

you can make Veerji do this. I've known him since I was born. He will never agree to your preposterous suggestion."

"If he is committed enough to put his life on the line, he can surely be convinced to carry out this little drama."

"But posing as the reincarnation of the Sufi mystic after whom Meharsar is named?! Ridiculous!"

"Oh no, not a reincarnation! That is chronologically impossible. Veerji must've been a little boy in 1947 when, according to the legend, that Mehar Baba camped by the lake. So he cannot be a reincarnation. We will pitch him instead, as the fakir himself who had disappeared after bestowing his blessings upon the village. Tell me this, how does this yarn sound—'*Bhagat Mehar Baba had accomplished his last task on Earth. He meant to retire peacefully to the heavens, but something told him that his work was not over yet; something told him that he would be needed in this village many years thence. He needed to stay on Earth a little while more. He had already discarded his human body by then, so he sought the body of a pure-minded child who was fated to leave the earth that very day. He found one who was named Joginder Singh Meharsar and took over his body. Since that day, the holy man has been living with the villagers as one of them. And now it is time for him to carry out the final challenge which God has entrusted him with—saving the hallowed culture of Meharsar and Punjab from that American monster called Sunburst Inc.*'"

Binita finished her tale with a flourish and smiled brightly at them, expecting them to applaud her genius, but all Arpit could manage rather weakly was, "You can't be serious!"

But Binita shook her head and said, almost gloatingly, "All those anti-dam protests in Uttaranchal gave me this idea. It's easier to rouse public sentiment when the place under threat has some sort of a religious significance. There are a couple of *sadhus* in Hardwar right now, fasting to save the Ganga from massive hydroelectric projects which will change the entire course of the river. And trust me, they are gathering more media publicity and support than any stunt that you and I pull off ever could. I've just blatantly ripped off their idea, except that I manufactured my own holy man, of course. That's really all that there is to this . . .

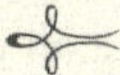

Mannat put the phone down with trembling fingers. Patricia Beech had answered all her questions. Her instincts had been correct. It was Kasauli! Mrs Spencer had lived in Kasauli and she had bought that sketch, along with a few others, from a roadside display in Kasauli! It was the same Kasauli where she and Arpit had first opened the sluices of passion. But what could it have to do with them now? Was it mere coincidence that a sketch drawn in that town had made its way to her across two continents of separation and an ocean of regret? And a coincidence, too, that every time she looked at the picture, she felt that they had left something behind when they had left Kasauli hurriedly, and that finally it was trying to come back to her?

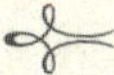

"Are you all right?" Arpit asked Nishi a little after they had started on their way back from Ropar to Patiala. Sceptical about Binita's proposition, he had turned away from her and had looked at Nishi for some help to convince Binita otherwise, when he saw how pale she looked and how transfixed her gaze on Binita was. It was then that in a moment of flash realisation, he figured that the talk of Uttaranchal and the dam had hit Nishi hard, bringing back bitter memories for her.

"Hmm . . ." Nishi replied wanly. "I sometimes wonder, Arpit—" Abruptly, she fell silent.

"It would help you to tell me."

When Nishi didn't answer and continued to gaze at the distant hills as if seeking answers from them, he ventured, "I think I know what the matter is. Binita doesn't know where you are from or all that you have faced. I . . . I am sure it must've hurt you terribly to be reminded of all that."

Nishi turned and managed to smile at Arpit. He had gotten to know her better, that much she had to accept. Answering him, she said, "It does hurt, yes. But I can't shut my ears every time a dam is mentioned. I can't let the dam damn my rationality now, can I?"

Arpit did not chuckle at her valiant quip, but continued driving silently.

"Nishi!" Arpit exclaimed suddenly. "Is it possible that . . . I mean, do you want to go to Hardwar to check whether . . .?"

"Check whether one of those sadhus campaigning for the Ganga is my father?" Nishi asked, finishing Arpit's unspoken question. She smiled softly at him. "I don't need to, Arpit. The media has covered them intensively; I have seen their faces a hundred times now, and I know he isn't among them. Besides . . ." she added softly, "I have a hunch he isn't in Uttaranchal at all, but he's much—"

"But much what?"

"Nothing. Nothing at all," Nishi replied hurriedly. Arpit had a dozen questions to ask, but she changed the subject and said, "I have brought something for you."

"For me? Now, what can this be?" he asked, surprised and curious when she fished out a brown envelope from her bag. "Let me guess: it's a painting bought from a roadside display in Kasauli, right? Perhaps this is yet another copy of the disputed Sandeep Sengupta sketch . . . Is it?"

"That picture has caused enough confusion already. However,

I still think the sketch is going to prove itself significant in your life. Anyway, this is not that sketch. This is not a sketch at all. It is a photograph, rather it's a projection resembling a photograph."

"You produced Prashant's photograph from your memory?" Arpit asked incredulously. "But you had refused! Nishi . . . I am sorry! I didn't mean to force you . . ."

"This is not Prashant's picture," Nishi answered quietly. "It took me a long time to soften the edges of my pain, Arpit. Even for you, and for the sake of your belief, I would not be willing to reopen that wound and sharpen its pinch. But pull over and take a look at the photograph."

Arpit nodded and pulled the car over. Taking the envelope from Nishi, he slid the glossy print out and turned it towards himself. When he saw whose picture it was, he could not take his eyes off it, and he sat there, dumbly, looking at her even as tears blurred his vision.

"You did not keep any photographs of her save that one where she was still a child . . ." Nishi murmured tenderly. "But when I saw her during redreaming, she was more beautiful than even you could've ever described. It was a face I could not resist reproducing. And somehow, Arpit, though I know something of the agony which you are going through now looking at her photograph, I felt certain that you would be happier to have it."

"Thank you, Nishi . . ." Arpit replied, his voice choked with tears that couldn't fall. If only the photograph could suck him in and freeze him forever with Mannat. If only he could sit like this, and stare at her picture for all of time . . . But there was still a long battle ahead of him. Brushing away his tears, Arpit started the car and began driving back to Patiala again.

CHAPTER 19

In Meharsar, it was the fifth day of Veerji's fast, but the expert committee appointed by the government was proceeding with its investigation at a typically '*sarkari*' pace. "Which means it will submit its report in the next fifty years . . . hopefully," as Binita put it.

In Leeds, Mannat followed the news with a fearful heart. She'd been spending hours every day at the community's gurdwara, praying for Veerji's well-being. As for Sunny, neither did he stop her, nor did he ask her about Veerji even once.

In Chandigarh, Nishi tried to console an increasingly-frantic Arpit. "He will be fine," she reassured him, trying to muster all the conviction she could. "Binita sounds cynical about the report, but you know that that's just the way she is. If they try to delay the report or hush it down, rest assured that she will make sure they hustle."

"Nishi . . ." Arpit put his hand on her arm pleadingly, "you can see people's futures. Can't you take a peep into Veerji's future and tell me whether he will be okay or not?"

"What makes you think I haven't tried it already?" she smiled a little tiredly. "But Veerji is different from the other people I have done predictions for. His concerns are not so banal or materialistic. Whenever I have tried to look at what's in store for him, I get this warm, serene feeling that all will be well."

"Really?" he interrupted eagerly.

"Yes. But Arpit, what *Veerji* construes as 'all well' is not necessarily what an 'all well' means for you and me. For him, it could mean one of two things—one, that he succeeds in his mission and gets the Sunburst Inc. project scrapped."

"And the second thing?"

"That he will die trying and attain that state of bliss which comes to all martyrs at death."

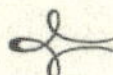

Her eyes are like two miniature lakes—deep and full, tears held back with desperate control. "Arpit, can you not convince Baldev Chayaji to come and meet Veerji?" He listens with only half a heart. What he wants is to plunge into these golden-blue depths. And the next moment he has. He has dived in and the lake begins to pull him to its bottom, but he does not feel the slightest suffocation. It's like being bathed in divinity. Very soon, too soon, however, he has shot back to the surface again and is clambering to the shore. He heaves himself to the ground and then gazes back wistfully. If only he could have stayed in those soothing depths for a little while longer. He bends down and cups the water in his hand and raises it to watch the morning sun glint upon it.

He looks at his hands then. They are knobby and wrinkled, with thick veins standing out against his dry skin. He pushes back the sleeve of the crisp white kurta that he is wearing and sees that the rest of his arm is just as wrinkled and withered as his hands. He looks down and sees a white beard reaching down from his chin to his chest. His feet look the same too—wrinkled, dried, and withered. When he reaches up to touch his head, he finds a turban wrapped around his head, but its weight does not disturb him. In fact, strangely enough, he accepts this transformation of his body without a murmur of protest. He has aged, but there is nothing but contentment inside his mind.

He brings his cupped hands, with the water from the lake still in them, close to his face, wanting to draw some strength from the holy waters, but his nostrils are assailed by a strange smell—the metallic-diesel-sooty-sweaty smell of a third-class train compartment. He blinks in confusion, for he is hurtling through strange lands in a train now. He looks around him, at the people travelling with him, but they all appear to be wrapped up in their own little worlds. He finds the stub of a ticket in his hand. It says Delhi, in black, clean alphabets. So he is going to Delhi to meet Baldev, who is as dear to him as his own son. He knows this is all a misunderstanding. Baldev would never work against his own village and his own people. All that is needed now is to get Baldev himself to come back with him to Meharsar and give his explanation to the people. Baldev, he knew, would set everything right again.

The train jolts to a standstill. People begin to stream in and out with a studied urgency. No one stops to look at him, or even acknowledge his presence. Suddenly, he feels cool air brush against his face. The metallic stench in the air has also been replaced by a soft subtle fragrance that he does not quite recognise. The noise of the train has also receded somewhere, to be replaced now with soft whispers and the occasional ring of a telephone. He becomes aware now that he is standing in the plush reception area of some corporate office. This must be Baldev's office! Happy with Baldev's success, he also feels a little intimidated with all the grandeur of the place. Mustering up his confidence, he walks to the desk behind which there is a rather jaded-looking girl working on a computer. "Uncleji, I just told you that he is extremely busy and won't be available for the next two hours. Please wait there. Have a seat, all right? Would you like some water?" she asks with thinly-disguised impatience.

He stares at her before shaking his head in refusal. Walking towards a long couch at the end of the reception area, he sinks into it tiredly. Sleep must have overpowered him, for when his eyes snap open, he sees someone towering over him. "Veerji!" There is surprise but no pleasure in the tone. "I wasn't expecting you here, of all places."

It's Baldev. He gets up slowly and embraces Baldev. When he pushes him away to look at him properly, he realises sorrowfully that the face before him is cold, hard, and inscrutable. The bored receptionist and the plush office and the cool air, everything has receded into some dark background. There are only the two men now. Two men and the sharp stinging wind of betrayal whistling maliciously between them . . .

"I never thought you would do this deliberately." He shakes his head in disbelief. One look at Baldev's face had been enough to tell him that the truth was not what he had imagined it to be all this while. ". . . all this while I kept telling myself it was some big mistake."

There is a flash of resentment in Baldev's eyes. "And why shouldn't I?" he spits out. "Have I done anything wrong in bringing prosperity to Meharsar? These little side-effects that you are foolishly fussing over? These are the inevitable price of development. Veerji, you are living in a dark well and you want to drag everyone with you into that well. If you had your way, you would not let any of us venture beyond Amritsar."

Only his ears are alive, burning with the words he is hearing. The rest of him has atrophied and fallen off in shock. Baldev continues with mounting bitterness, "Had we been living in some halfway-decent place, had Loveleen not been so irrationally attached to that lake, we would've had the best doctors to treat her. She would've been saved. I said nothing when she died. I absorbed that blow and went on struggling for a better life. My son, at least, should have the best I could give him. That was the sole purpose of my life. But he turned out to be just like you all. You people" —he stabs the words with vicious emphasis now— "hijacked Arpit. Your mollycoddling, your emotional blackmail, your harping on about loyalty to the village and all those sentimental traps turned him into a blubbering fool. I knew I would have trouble extracting him from your clutches and putting him into that school I had so carefully chosen. But thankfully, he listened to me for once. And look at him now! He is on his way to becoming the man I always wanted him to be. You don't own him anymore! I've gotten my son back . . ."

He finds himself staring like an old fool at the stranger in front of him. Finally, when he manages to find his voice, he answers simply, steadily. "Loving is not owning, puttar. I wish I could've made you understand this. It is probably my own fault that I couldn't. "

"You were never responsible for me," Baldev retorts with a sneer on his face. "So please, don't over-stretch your solicitousness for my principles. I can take care of myself. And of my son."

He closes his eyes for a brief moment before turning to leave, but then he pauses. Looking at Baldev, he speaks without any trace of anger, "You may be able to look after yourself. So can your son. If you feel we were dragging you backwards, don't let the same thing happen to Arpit. But puttar, don't put the fetters of your ambitions on him, that is all I ask. You know best, of course, but still . . . May God look after you." He starts walking out of the office. He opens the glass door and walks past an indifferent guard, straight into an endless darkness that seemed to have been just waiting to swallow him up. A few moments later, he steps into water and continues walking deeper and deeper into it, till the water first reaches his mouth and then his nose. He can smell and taste the metallic poison that has killed the water of his beloved lake. He stops and stands still now, for there is nowhere he can go now. And as he waits for the end to come, the water rushes vindictively into him and he is torn apart.

"VEERJI!" Arpit screamed and woke up violently from the nightmare, his hand reaching out into empty space in an attempt to bring Veerji back, but only upsetting the glass of water kept on his bedside table. He threw off the bedclothes and jumped out of bed. What was happening to him? Was this one of the risks Nishi had talked about before starting the process? For the second time now, a redream had crept upon him unbidden. He had just dreamed of Veerji; he had, in fact, dreamed that he *was* Veerji. He had seen the past through his eyes. But what was the meaning of his having taken on Veerji's self in the dream? Did it not mean that . . . that Veerji's spirit had been guiding Arpit's mind while he slept? That Veerji was no longer . . .??

NO! He screamed at himself. Nothing like that had happened. He would call Amrik Chayaji this very moment and find out. But just as he reached for his phone, the doorbell started ringing insistently. Who could it be at five a.m.? He knew Nishi was flying to Bombay in another hour or so for an assignment and would be back only after two days. Then who?

The bell continued to ring furiously even as someone started banging on the door. Who the hell was trying to break into his house? Arpit ran downstairs and flung the door open. Binita and Vishwas barged into the room.

"What on earth!" he began, but the icy look in Binita's eyes stopped him. Fear gripped his heart. "Is everything all right? Is . . . is Veerji all right?"

"I hate to disappoint you, Arpit, but Veerji is still in good health and holding strong," Binita hissed like a wounded snake.

"How can you even say that?" Arpit exclaimed and turned incredulously from her to Vishwas, but he also wore the same accusing expression.

"Enough of this hypocrisy, Arpit Singh, son of Baldev Singh, better known as Dave, the Chairman of India Mantra Ltd., son of the man responsible for the battle of Meharsar!"

Everything around him began to spin dizzily. Was this a part of the dream as well? But no, Binita and Vishwas stood before him in avenging concreteness. He sank limply into the nearest chair and said, "Yes, he is my father. Baldev Singh is my father. How did you come to know?"

Binita shook a file in his face. "Do you know what this is? It's the entire report of the government proceedings on the proposed Wetland Reserve project! Oh no, not so fast!" she exclaimed, handing the file quickly back to Vishwas as Arpit reached for it eagerly. "If you think I will hand it to you on a platter, you are mistaken. The cat is out of the bag, Arpit Singh. *Now* I see how you knew about a project which had been buried so many years ago. *Your father* was the one who converted a potential lake sanctuary into a toxic dump. And you wanted to make sure that nobody ever found out about it. So you asked *me* to dig up the report, probably thinking that you would dispose it before it reached anyone else. Perhaps I would have unsuspectingly handed it to you too, had the name of your father not rung an unfortunate bell. Mr Sodhi, who incidentally helped to retrieve this report, told me that Baldev Singh was a native of Meharsar. He gave me as detailed a biography of your father as I could wish for. Of course, there was nothing about his son in it, but then, I remembered how, during college, we had once argued about the succession of sons to their father's business empires and you had rather pompously emphasised how your father was a self-made man and how he had risen from his humble origins. Click! Suddenly I also recalled an application form you were filling out once, which you happened to leave in one of my books. And that was where I had come across your father's name. Double click!"

Pausing for just a moment to catch her breath, Binita went on, "You have fooled me, fooled all of us magnificently. Now I understand why you didn't join the protest in Meharsar. This show of support was only to throw us off-guard and know our plans, right? All that drama about emotional ties to Meharsar and a unique relationship with Veerji which we could never understand? Bullshit. Colossal bullshit!"

"It was NOT drama!" Arpit managed to cry out at last. "I was never fooling you! Vishwas," he turned impatiently to the young man, "I hope I can make *you* understand, at least. I'm on Veerji's side . . . always will be. But I can't openly show my support for him."

"Of course you can't!" Binita interrupted sarcastically. "It will never do to antagonise dear Daddy and have him cut off sonny boy's allowance of a few paltry crores now, would it?"

"Stop it! You don't know anything about what I feel for Meharsar, or where I stand with Dad, or his relationship with Veerji. You don't know anything."

How could he tell them about what he had witnessed in his redreaming a few minutes ago? How could he tell them about the blighted affection of a father for a son who continually disappointed him by responding to another, more simply and naturally offered love? A love that the man himself had never been able to internalise? All these years he had wondered uneasily why his Dad harboured such a strong dislike for Meharsar, and especially for Veerji.

Tonight's dream had given him the answer—*"You people hijacked Arpit."* His Dad had always hovered sulkily at the borders of the world that Meharsar was. Those within were his rivals for Arpit's affection. He never understood that they were neither winning nor owning, they were just sharing love.

He did not know whether he had turned a switch or not, but he had certainly unravelled the most perplexing riddle of his life. The knowledge did not make him any happier, but it gave him greater clarity.

Turning back to Binita, Arpit softly tried to explain his situation, "If my Dad comes to know I am with Veerji and am associated with what's going on in Meharsar, it will only make him angrier. In his wrath, he will pull out all the stops to have his way. That will be a huge risk for you, for Veerji, and for everyone connected with this movement."

"Do you really expect us to believe that?" Vishwas retorted.

"You will have to. I am telling the truth."

"We are not 'some of those people' you can fool all the time,"

Binita put in icily. "NB won't be your pawn in this game any longer. We are withdrawing our support from this movement."

Stunned, Arpit shot up from his chair. "You can't! Binita, you can't! It will kill Veerji!"

"He has enough supporters to carry on his struggle by himself. He can do without us. Incidentally, if you are so concerned, how about joining him in his fast?"

"I told you the reason just now! Oh, to hell with that! You guys are pulling the political and legal strings. If you back out, so will the media. And do you know what that means?" Arpit nearly screamed at her. "It means that Veerji will be left to starve to death! You know he is too resolute to give up even if he is the last man standing. Don't punish him because of me, Binita. I am imploring you. Stay on at least till something happens to make him withdraw this fast unto death, even temporarily. Can't you understand what I'm saying? Please!" he grabbed Binita's arm in desperation.

Giving him one last look of contempt, Binita pushed Arpit back and rapidly made her way to the door with Vishwas following her. Arpit stood staring at their retreating backs in shocked disbelief for a moment, before he followed them, stumbling over the furniture and calling out brokenly to them to stop and listen to him.

Before getting into her car, Binita turned and looked at Arpit and said, with uncharacteristic wistfulness, ". . . and I thought you were finally growing into a worthwhile creature!"

She started the car and they sped off, kicking smoke and dust into his face.

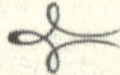

"You couldn't have been serious back there!" Vishwas

exclaimed as they drove back to their office. "We can't do that to Veerji! His life depends on our support. We can't just abandon him!"

"I didn't mean it," confessed Binita, massaging at her worry lines with restless fingers. "I was so beside myself with fury that I spat out the first thing I could think of. I suppose I was hoping to see how Arpit would react, whether he would give himself away or not."

"Hmm . . . to do him justice," ventured Vishwas, "he seemed frantic at the very idea. What if he is telling the truth?"

"Maybe he is, but I can't risk that right now," she sighed. "Things are only going to go uphill from here, Vishwas. Here, take a look at this. I received them within a span of twenty-four hours." She handed him her phone to show him her text message inbox. Vishwas scrolled through the inbox and saw that it was filled with abusive, menacing text messages sent from several different numbers.

"What the hell! FoDi, you could have at least told me about this!"

"I have already done what I could. I contacted my service provider and told them to fish out the names under which these SIM cards were purchased. Then, later last night, I also filed an FIR, but I don't know how seriously they took it. Actually, Vishwas, I'm too anxious about Veerji to think straight, and now this Arpit turns out to be that Baldev's son. I am completely flummoxed." She waved her hands distractedly in the air.

"I will handle this text message business. Don't you worry about it," Vishwas soothed her. "But I can understand what this means for the people of Meharsar. Our opponents certainly mean business, and Veerji is a soft target."

"Exactly! That's why I want Dave and Co. to get the impression that we are pulling out. At this moment, Arpit might be ringing up Daddy dearest and congratulating him. I want these people to let down their guard. However, we will not issue an official statement. It will dampen Veerji's credibility. Besides, we are the ones keeping the media spotlight there. The moment it withdraws, the struggle is derailed."

"The media's presence also ensures no one attacks Veerji . . ." put in Vishwas.

"Absolutely. So to convey the impression that NB isn't interested in Meharsar anymore, and to do it without losing eyeballs, we send out mixed signals. It always works. I am leaving this to you, Vishwas. By tonight I want all of India to be buzzing with rumours of a rift between NB and Veerji. Keep them guessing, play politician, give contradictory statements. I know you are good at it."

Vishwas grinned. "You bet!"

"But this also means that now we can't go ahead with our plan of painting Veerji as Mehar Baba, not that he would have agreed, anyway," Binita rued. "Like a lamb I handed over my glorious idea to that double-crosser. He would've already spilled the beans on that one!"

"And Nishimaya? Is she Arpit's partner in crime or is he merely using her? What do you think?" Vishwas asked.

"I . . . don't . . . know," Binita mulled uneasily. "Somehow, I can't believe that Nishiji can be so twisted."

"Neither can I. There must be a mistake somewhere. Anyway, we are on high alert now. Trust to be strictly rationed. FoDi, do you remember the woman from UK whose email I forwarded to you?"

"Who was it now? Wait, Manjot Shergill? I remember answering her. Quite an enthusiastic young lady."

"Yeah! She emails everyday to ask how the movement is getting on. Could she possibly be Dave's spy? She claims to be from Meharsar, but do you think that is reason enough to be so hung up on the old lake?"

"Give nothing away," warned Binita. "Don't answer her emails at all. It's only a matter of two more days now. This Wetland report is our trump card, Vishwas. Mr Sodhi is going to rake up such a scandal against Baldev Singh that no one will give him any business for the next five years at least."

"Sorry FoDi, but I'm afraid of such optimism. That guy can pull a million strings in this country without so much as stirring out of his Manhattan office. At the most, we can set his plans back by a few months. But I don't think we can stop him altogether."

"And that is enough to call off Veerji's fast," Binita snapped. "For heaven's sake, don't rattle me any more than I already am. Is there anything else I can possibly do to better this messed up situation?"

"Yes, you can," Vishwas replied calmly. "You can stop the car and exchange seats. Your driving is making my blood run cold."

With trembling fingers, Arpit tried to call Nishi. Twice, he dialled the wrong number, and when he finally did manage to stab at the right buttons, he listened with a sinking heart as a mechanical voice spoke, "The number you are trying to call is currently switched off. Please try again, later." Of course, Nishi would be in the flight right now.

Finally, with no other alternative left, he typed her a message, asking her to call him back urgently. After that, he could do nothing but wait.

He switched on the television for news about Veerji. But

all the channels were busy covering some high-profile minister's arrest, and the meagre snippets he could glean about Meharsar from here and there only repeated news from the day before.

He could not tell when he fell asleep, but when his eyes flew open, it was late in the afternoon and the TV was still on. He had not eaten a thing since morning. Half-heartedly, he dragged himself to the kitchen to get a bite. Heaping some leftover food onto a plate, he was about to put it inside the microwave when a news anchor's voice drifted in from the living room, proclaiming as dramatically as he could: "IS NAVUDAY BHARAT HAVING SECOND THOUGHTS ABOUT MEHARSAR? P.R.O. SAYS NO COMMENTS. CRUSADER'S FATE NOW HANGS IN BALANCE."

Dropping his plate, Arpit swerved wildly around and ran into the living room. No, Binita. NO! YOU CAN'T DO THIS! His mind screamed. The news report that followed did nothing to assuage his alarm. He sat and watched as Vishwas appeared briefly on the television screen and gave roundabout statements which the news anchor read volumes of meaning into. Though Vishwas said nothing final, it was clear that NB was no longer pledging unequivocal support to Veerji's crusade. He gave no reasons, no explanations. The rest of the story saw people venturing forth with guesses as to why such a development had taken place and what it would mean for the people of Meharsar.

When Arpit finally switched off the television, he realised that Nishi had been right, as always. It was time for his reluctant feet to carry him back to Meharsar where Veerji needed him.

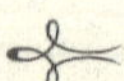

"You look preoccupied. What's the matter?" Sunny enquired with a touch of impatience.

"Nothing much, just that an email I was expecting hasn't arrived," Mannat replied hurriedly, hoping Sunny would leave it at that. Increasingly now, Sunny had started to look with disapproval at everything that she did.

"I didn't know that people who sit at home all day also have urgent business to transact through emails," Sunny retorted before leaving the room. The jibe was unmistakable. Mannat stared after him for a moment before sighing and picking up the TV remote. Of course the NB people were up to their neck in work. Where would they get the time to answer emails? Still, it would have put her anxiety to rest if she got even a line from them. Her frantic phone calls home had not given her satisfactory answers. It was clear that her parents, relatives, and neighbours had got their orders from Veerji to not tell her the alarming details. Just this morning, when she had talked to Sukhmani, her mother had cooed rather exaggeratedly, "There is nothing to worry about, *puttar*. You know Veerji. He has been experimenting with fasting for years now."

"But for *this* long, Ma? And at his age?"

Her father snatched the phone at this moment. "Oye, Manjot, we will win this battle very soon. These NGO people are helping us at every step. Veerji is fine. *You* don't worry. You just look after yourself and your husband." And he had disconnected before she got a chance to ask anything else.

Perhaps the news would give her some information about Veerji. She hurriedly surfed through the Indian channels before finally arriving at one covering the developments at Meharsar. What she saw had her head reeling in disbelief. NB was thinking of withdrawing its support? *Didn't they know what this would mean for Veerji?*

Over the next few hours, Mannat waged a losing battle against her own mind. There had to be a mistake somewhere.

The NB people had not confirmed that they were pulling out. Perhaps the Sunburst supporters were spreading these rumours? But then why was the PRO of NB issuing one vague statement after another? Where was that idealistic Binita Baruah who had roared like a tigress and declared, "We won't let Meharsar go to the pigs!"?

Mannat kept trying the numbers of her family, calls which no one answered, confirming her numbing conviction that something had gone horribly, horribly wrong. She gave up when Sunny got home from work. But later, long after her husband had gone to sleep with his face turned away from her, Mannat opened her laptop and softly typed out an email to Binita—

Dear Ms Baruah,

I had been following the movement against Sunburst's entry in Meharsar eagerly. I had tremendous faith in you and your NGO because I thought that some people, at least, are honest and dedicated to their cause. But I was wrong. Seeing the news today, I have realised one thing—you can't expect support from anyone other than your own people. Only someone from Meharsar can feel the pain of Meharsar.

I don't know why you are doing all this. Maybe you have a good reason, but it will never be good enough for me. Anyway, thank you for reminding me of my duty towards my village. I would have stayed here, just watching things unravel one after the other, if you had not let us down. Now Veerji will not be alone. I will go back to Meharsar to stand by him, even if everyone else leaves him.

Thank you for all that you have done till now.

Wishing you all the luck for your future endeavours.
Manjot Kaur Meharsar
(granddaughter of Joginder Singh Meharsar)

CHAPTER 20

The next day at noon, Navneet Sodhi, MLA from Meharsar, took his life and his political career in his hands to address an urgently-summoned press conference in Chandigarh. The entire Wetland Conservation Reserve project report was made public, along with darker details about how it had lain buried under a hundred other government files because of motivated apathy for almost two decades. There was an instant uproar—in newsrooms, in drawing-rooms, in the State Legislature, and in the Centre.

Meanwhile, Veerji's fast had lasted nearly a week. All that an anxious Harpal could think of was pulse and breathing, and he repeatedly kept questioning the doctor who was now on round-the-clock attendance about his father's vital signs. One ear, however, was strained towards the outside world, waiting for news that the tide had turned in their favour at last.

Vishwas had already discreetly informed him and the rest of the immediate family about their real plan so that they wouldn't panic when rumours of NB withdrawing its support from the movement started floating around. While Harpal had full faith in NB, he had less faith in Veerji's pliability. Would his father refuse to break his fast even after the government ordered an inquiry into the Wetland report? Would he insist on continuing till there was a complete ban on Sunburst? Harpal knew that such a ban could take days, weeks, even months in being passed. And death would not have the patience to wait that long. Somehow, they would have to persuade Veerji to settle for this interim victory.

Suddenly, feeling extremely hopeless and vulnerable, he wished Mannat was around. If there was one person in the world who could convince Veerji to break his fast, it was her. He had lied to her on the phone that Veerji had already broken it, but he knew he was a bad liar and his daughter a bad believer of bad lies. Harpal wouldn't have been surprised to see her standing before his eyes the very next moment.

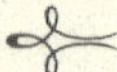

When Nishi finally managed to call Arpit back, he rapidly updated her on all the events that had taken place after her departure. He also told her that he was headed to Meharsar. Nishi had smiled knowingly on hearing this, a smile Arpit couldn't see over the phone. As fervently as she wanted to accompany him on his homecoming, a voice inside her head told her that it was best for him to go alone. But she promised him that the moment she got back from Bombay, she would join him. Before that, however—and this she did not tell Arpit—she would confront Binita. Navneet Sodhi might be one of that rare breed of truly public-spirited politicians, but Nishi knew who was really behind the press conference which had tilted the entire battle in their favour. She also had a fair idea why Binita did not want anyone to know about her involvement. It was time to clear her misunderstandings about Arpit.

All Nishi had to decide now was how much about Mannat she could avoid mentioning while telling Binita about the Arpit she had never known . . .

In the pandemonium following the press conference, Sodhi's position in the party staggered dangerously. He received an immediate summon from the High Command, asking him to provide an explanation as to how he had dared to make such an announcement without consulting them. Explanations and negotiations lasted well into the night, but, to his own surprise, he was finally let off with nothing more than a stern warning. After all, their party had not been in power when the Wetland file had been buried. It was easy to publicly claim ignorance about the whole affair and embarrass the rival party which *had* been ruling at the time.

As civil activists, intellectuals, scientists, and the media buzzed angrily with the findings, the Centre could not avoid confronting the issue. One of its key allies had threatened to withdraw support if the Prime Minister did not immediately order an inquiry into the charges against Baldev Singh. And so, India Mantra Ltd. was issued a notice, with Baldev Singh being ordered to come back to the country and face the charges.

The Punjab government, not to be outdone by the Centre, put an immediate ban on all further construction of Sunburst outlets in the state. Following its lead, other Indian states placed similar bans on Sunburst activities in their respective states and began to set up committees and boards for assessment of environmental damage.

In Meharsar, even as Harpal sank thankfully to the earth on hearing the news, Veerji, now dangerously weak, cast his tired eyes around his beloved fields and sent a silent prayer of thanks to the gods above. "Wahe Guru, Wahe Guru," he muttered weakly, before beckoning to Sukhmani to bring him the glass of juice she had been pleading him to drink for such a long time now.

But just as Sukhmani brought the glass and held it to his lips, as if prompted by some intuition, he raised his eyes and looked towards the lake.

"Drink, Veerji," Sukhmani implored softly. When he appeared to have not even heard her, Sukhmani looked up to see what had so caught his attention. What she saw made her hands tremble, but she steadied herself, not wanting to drop the glass. "Veerji?" she said softly, as if waiting for him to say something.

Veerji tried to raise his hand, but it rose and fell limply in his lap. Turning slowly to Sukhmani, he smiled and whispered, "Tell Arpit to stop standing there and come hold this glass. I will drink from his hands. He will break my fast."

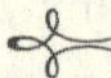

"Manjot Kaur Meharsar?" Binita looked even more perplexed than she had been on the morning of the confrontation with Arpit. "Didn't she say she was Manjot Shergill or something?"

Vishwas nodded impatiently. "Maiden name, of course."

"But did she actually write back saying she is Veerji's granddaughter?"

"Well, she signed herself as such. And she says she is coming to India to be with him."

Binita played rather agitatedly with one end of the stylish scarf draped with deliberate carelessness around her shoulder. The media would be waiting for them in Chandigarh. She had to look every inch the part of a vindicated crusader. "How do we know whether she is telling the truth or not?"

"Well, she *sounded* genuine enough to me."

"You can't tell how a person 'sounds' from an email," Binita retorted. "Damn. I guess we will just have to wait and watch. And if she does come to Meharsar . . ." she trailed off.

"If she does come to Meharsar and if she is indeed Veerji's granddaughter, it would explain why she was so emotionally involved in this whole business, right? But what I don't understand is why the hell didn't she tell us before about this? I don't get it—we have two people who claim to be extremely concerned about Meharsar, but both of them are secretive about their family roots. I still can't figure out why that Arpit didn't tell us the truth about his father. But surely, he must have guessed by now that our retreat was only a sham."

"It doesn't matter now. We have won the battle, Vishwas, though mind you, the war is not yet won. We still have to rout India Mantra horse, foot, and artillery and get that Verva Cola factory removed from Meharsar. Long walk to freedom . . ." Binita sighed.

"I hope they have managed to convince Veerji to break his fast. I've been surfing the net feverishly, but there is not a single live video of Meharsar!" Vishwas grunted. Because Binita was the one driving them both from their Ropar office to Chandigarh, much to his trepidation, he had the liberty to constantly keep a check on the latest updates on Meharsar through his laptop. But he clicked his tongue in exasperation. "Look at this! Another stupid celebrity goes and gets engaged and eats up all the bandwidth! And what the heck is that Ashwin doing? I *told* him to report every fifteen minutes from the site. It's been over half an hour now! I hope Veerji is fine . . ."

Almost as if in answer, his phone buzzed impatiently. Binita and Vishwas looked at each other, the same dreadful thought flashing through their minds, and though he had not asked her to, Binita swung the car to a halt even as Vishwas took a deep breath and answered the call. "Ashwin! What the hell man! I was waiting, dude . . . what . . . is Veerji . . . Oh! Are you serious?? Him? And they let him??! Oh—"

"Did he break the fast? Did he?" Binita pounded Vishwas with her question even as he tried to fend her off with his free hand.

When he finally disconnected, relief and triumph were writ clearly on his face. "My dear FoDi," he began (much later he would wonder what had possessed him to address her like that, though she didn't even notice), "we were *not* backing the wrong horse all along. Arpit is in Meharsar this very minute, feeding Veerji juice with his own hands!"

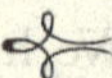

"Why India?" Sunny demanded with a controlled fury that she had never witnessed in him before. "And why now?"

"My village needs me, Sunny. Veerji needs me."

"And so do I! Does our life here mean nothing to you, Manjot?" He had not called her Mandy for many days now. It was a clear sign of his growing displeasure.

She flushed guiltily. He was right. In their one-and-a-half years of marriage, how much had she really bothered about *his* needs? True, she had tried to be a good wife, at least before that mishap, but with most of her heart still left behind in Meharsar, it had made for a poor performance.

"I have always had the greatest respect for your family, Manjot," he continued, "and I have never interfered in your relationship with them. But I had no idea that the umbilical cord would threaten to strangle us one day. And you know I have a dread of India ever since that disaster happened. In spite of all this, you still want to go? To me, that proves that you don't care. First, you go around moping to the extent that nothing I do can cheer you up, then you spoil our holiday with your constant and obsessive checking and sending of emails, and then you demand that those paintings be brought to our house all the way from India—"

"The paintings?" Mannat cut in. "Where do the paintings come in, in all this?" she demanded, stung. "I asked for them because I wanted some beauty in our house. I never thought you would start seeing them in terms of their price or where they came from! Disappointed, aren't you, that they all turned out to have no monetary value? I never thought you were like this, Arpit! I never thought you would change so much . . ."

"What did you just say?" Sunny asked, stopping her short in the middle of her tirade.

She gasped. No, she couldn't, *couldn't* have let *that* slip. She glanced at Sunny's face, but it was inscrutable.

The next moment, he asked coldly, "Were you saying that *I* am the one who has changed?"

Mannat heaved a sigh of relief despite Sunny's accusing tones. "No. The problem is not that I have changed, but that I haven't changed enough. I did try, Sunny, to be the woman who could fit neatly into your life here. I am still trying. But there is some unfinished business which needs to be wrapped up before we can truly move forward. I guess," she surrendered to the inevitable, "It's time I tell you everything . . ."

And she told him all that she could without mentioning Arpit—about Baldev, about his love-hate relationship with Veerji, and the series of disappointments that marked the end of their relationship. She told him about the Verva Cola plant and the inexplicable hostility of a man towards the place of his birth.

But as she finished, Sunny looked hard at her and then asked slowly, "And where does 'Arpit' come into all this?"

Her gaze flickered from him to the wall opposite, where the sketch still hung, to her own fingers clamped apprehensively around each other, back to her husband's eyes of ice. He repeated his question, still in that tone of seething, incredulous distaste. "Who and what is Arpit in all this business . . . in your life . . . in our life?"

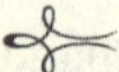

"The way you went on about your 'estrangement' with Meharsar, I thought it would be a billion trans-galactic years before they would even consider letting you near Veerji again," Vishwas spoke with suspicious casualness.

Arpit smiled. "I am the prodigal son who has been, mercifully, forgiven. These are my large-hearted people, Vishwas. *They* don't leave something or someone in the lurch over a misunderstanding."

"Being sarcastic is *FoDi's* trademark, dude. And only someone as slow as you could have failed to perceive the simple fact that this entire business could not have been wrapped up so beautifully without NB working overtime behind the scenes. Anyway, I am big enough to admit that I misjudged you. You were on our side after all."

"It was *my* side all along. You people were just playing supporting roles. But I am big enough, too. I forgive you," Arpit replied with a twinkle in his eye.

Vishwas decided against retorting to Arpit's last jibe. There was a lot of ground left to cover, and Binita had given him instructions to 'pump' Arpit for more information. "So are you reinstalled in their circle of confidence? Can we all work together now and save all the time we have been wasting in harbouring doubts and seeking clarifications?"

"I am hoping so . . . although Harpal Chayaji hasn't forgiven me," he added wistfully. "He has all the right to be angry though . . ."

"But why now? The matter has been sorted out. Of course, we still have to keep fanning the fire till the real culprits are punished. Are you aware, by the way, of the rumours floating around in corporate circles? Sunburst Inc., USA, is considering terminating its franchise agreement with India Mantra . . ."

Arpit shot up instantly. ". . . which means . . ."

". . . no Sunburst in India, at least not until they find a new franchisee. And with the entire hullabaloo created over this issue, that won't be easy," completed Vishwas, watching Arpit's face carefully to gauge his reaction.

Arpit gripped Vishwas's shoulders in exultation. "So this is victory for us, isn't it? Their packaging tie-up with Verva will also go for a toss."

"Won't your father be very upset when he comes to know that you are behind all this? After all, it was you who tipped FoDi off about that Wetland report," Vishwas persisted.

"With suspect motives, or so Binita thinks," Arpit retorted dryly. His eyes flashed for a moment, but he did not say a word more.

Vishwas understood that he wouldn't get any further details from Arpit about Baldev, or about what had made father and son range themselves on opposite sides of a war in which their relationship would inevitably make up the collateral damage.

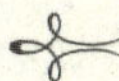

"So, I finally did manage to run you to earth!" Nishi smiled warmly. "Quite the woman of the moment, aren't you? Congratulations . . . and thank you, for all that you have done."

"You are welcome," Binita replied rather guardedly, motioning Nishi towards a seat at their table in a posh restaurant in Chandigarh.

"Why aren't you in Meharsar right now, Binita? Is it because you still suspect Arpit's intentions? But I thought his going back to Veerji would've convinced you."

"Vishwas keeps harping about the same thing," admitted Binita. "But Nishiji, I never mistrusted *you*. Logically, I should've thought of you as his accomplice, but it just did not feel right. I'm so glad we can still be friends."

Nishi tenderly placed her hand on Binita's and said, "I would have remained your friend even if you had doubted me. I don't blame you for reacting the way you did. Everything was stacked up against us. But I have learned from experience, Binita, that the evidence of the heart is greater than the evidence of the senses. Besides, it's high time now that you learned to trust Arpit."

"I . . . don't know about that, Nishiji," Bintia replied indecisively, her words hinting loudly enough at the grudge she held against Arpit. "One would think that having known him from before, I would be better acquainted with his character. But I realised the other day that I had never really known this person . . . had never bothered to acquaint myself with either his personality or his history, in fact. To think that after having done History Honours, I had no clue about the *history* of my only friend in college!"

Binita was interrupted for a minute when the waiter came to take their order. When he left, Nishi leaned forward and said, "You are right, Binita. You never really knew Arpit, and that is why I am here today. I want you to know who Arpit is, and what his life has been like all this while. But I am not telling you all this to satisfy your curiosity. I want you to understand that there is a lot more to Meharsar than just the story of Big Men's Greed versus Little Men's Resistance."

"Oh, I knew even back then that he was pretending to be something he was not. That wannabe, cool dude air did not deceive me. Of course, I was faking it too, but in a wholly different way!" Binita admitted wryly. "Thank goodness we both grew out of it. When I realised that I would never be able to match up to my cousin, Janaki, I decided that I better do what I believed in rather than spending my life trying to be one up on her all the time. But guess what, Nishiji, after that Wetland report went public, I got an indignant call from somewhere in the Maldives demanding how I had managed to ferret out a document whose existence was known only to the top-notch scientists of the country. Even though Mr Sodhi did the honours, Janaki knows how to put two and two together. Apparently, she has been following my work closely, and a trifle enviously. She wanted to know exactly what was going on, to the extent that she brushed aside all her old grudges and took my phone number from my brother and called me. Ah, I managed to upstage her this one time! And we made up that silly family quarrel into the bargain!"

". . . All thanks to Arpit," Nishi put in.

"Rub it in if you want to. But there is still one thing I don't understand. Vishwas tells me that a few in the Meharsar clan are still not welcoming Arpit back into their fold. Why? It's his father who is to blame, not him."

Nishi braced herself. This was the moment she had been trying to side-step. Arpit would never want her to tell anyone else about Mannat, and she could not betray his confidence, but she wanted Binita to understand who Arpit was as well. Therefore, keeping her answer as brief as possible, Nishi replied, "Arpit did not use the little power he had over his father to stop him from doing what he did and wreaking havoc in Meharsar. That's one reason why he is not being forgiven in entirety. The other reason, well, that is more personal. I can't tell you the details—Arpit won't like me to—but there are members of that family who were deeply injured by his actions and his inaction . . .

and Harpalji isn't as forgiving as Veerji. Dont ask me to explain things any further though, because I won't be able to do that . . ."

Binita gave her a piercing look before proceeding, "I won't, despite your words tempting me more than ever to ask. Speaking of family members, there was something I wanted to double-check with you. There is this lady in the UK who claims that she is Veerji's granddaughter and says she is coming back to Meharsar, but I just wanted to ask . . . Nishiji? Did I say something wrong? What happened? Why do you look so pale?!"

Nishi, her face pale and pallid, stared at Binita.

"What is it, Nishiji? Are you all right?!" Binita asked, concern lining her face and making her reach across the table to touch Nishi's arm.

"What . . . what did she say her name was?" Nishi croaked.

"Who? Oh, the lady from UK? Manjot Kaur Meharsar." Closing her eyes, Nishi struggled to focus her inner compass on what Binita had just told her. "When is she expected to arrive in India?" she asked.

"I don't exactly know," Bintia replied, a little perplexed with Nishi's reaction. "We received her email two days ago, saying she would be coming to India. When, she didn't say. Maybe now that Veerji has broken his fast, she might not see the need to come at all, unless she is already on a plane. I hope she is coming and we can meet her. She can be valuable to us."

"Oh, you have no idea just how valuable she is!" Nishi thought to herself. Surely Mannat would come, even if Veerji had already broken his fast, and more so if she had seen who had held the glass of juice to Veerji's lips. Or would that be a deterrent to her coming?

And then the most crucial question of all stalked into her consciousness, impetuously silencing all other questions and musings: *What should she tell Arpit . . . and when?*

CHAPTER 21

The scent of mustard oil still lingered about in the old house. Things had not changed much, or perhaps he was looking at everything through the rose-screen of memory . . .

Harpal Chayaji was still resolutely ignoring him and Chayiji was hovering around him in ambiguous circles. Several of his childhood companions were missing, having scattered on the winds of distant ambitions. Amrik Chayaji, was perhaps the only one, apart from Veerji, who had been overjoyed to see him return. He had hugged him long and hard, as if to make up for all the years lost in between, and it was their old family house that he was staying in right now. He had wanted to sleep next to Veerji, but clearly that house was still making up its mind about him. Regaining their faith would be a slow process. But he was ready. Veerji's unquestioning welcome had given him the courage to face it all. Suddenly, everything seemed possible.

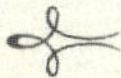

A thick, glossy brochure with alluring photographs of expansive playing fields, state-of-the-art classrooms, a computer lab equipped with the latest machines, and smiling schoolboys in spanking new uniforms . . . He wants all of these. But then he also wants his home. How can one have both?

He knows he can reconcile himself to the loss of his home if only she accompanies him on his new adventure. But will that happen? Surely his Dad will be willing to settle the little difficulties which stand in the way of her coming to Shimla along with him? Harpal Chayaji will convince him. Of course he will.

A mocking smile, a grim nod, some cruel words, and a crack of disillusionment later, he has suddenly become aware of the strange currents that run underground in the world of adults. He does not want to see anymore. Slipping out of the house, he makes his way to the lake and sits down by its shore. Like always, he looks for his mother's reflection in the water. For a moment, he even fancies her staring back at him. Then he realises that it is Mannat who has followed him from the house. As she settles herself wordlessly next to him, he does not turn to look at her or say a word. They continue staring at the lake, searching for elusive shadows.

What is she trying to see, he wonders. The next moment she sighs and answers his question.

"You know, Arpit," she says, hunching her shoulders as if suppressing a sudden thrill, "when I look closely at these strange shapes that flicker and glimmer in the water, they seem like blue mountains with the sun dancing just behind them. I know it's just a trick of the light falling on water, but sometimes . . ."

"Sometimes?"

"Sometimes I wonder what would happen if I jumped into the lake and kept going down and down and down until I reach the end . . . Maybe I will find an underwater town at the bottom with hills running around it! Do you think it is possible?"

"No, it's not. Don't be so dumb, Mannat. If you stayed so long underwater you would drown."

She pouts and concedes to his logic before continuing, "Someday, I would love to go to Kashmir . . ."

"Silly you. Kashmir is full of terrorists."

"But they will be driven out someday or the other. And by then I would

be an adult earning loads of money. I will take a month-long vacation there. You can come along if you want to . . ." she offers, making him smile at her magnanimity, and then trails off.

They both fall silent for a few minutes. Then he breaks the silence and says, "I would prefer Switzerland. It's more beautiful than Kashmir."

"It isn't. Kashmir is the most beautiful place on earth."

"Really? And how do you know that? Have you been there?" he mocks, glad to grab this opportunity to shake off his gloom.

They keep up this light banter till she abruptly plunges her hands into the lake and splashes a generous amount of water on his face. He reciprocates, laughing. But a few minutes later, when she starts shivering from the cold, he grows concerned and chides her.

"As if you aren't wetter than me!" she shoots back. "Anyway, if I have to travel to the mountains, I must learn to bear the cold. Lucky you! You will be going to Shimla! Give my love to the snow."

"It doesn't snow there all the time, idiot," he retorts a little too quickly. His heart is sinking now. He has sensed the tiny hope in her heart. She is dreaming of going to Shimla with him, of living in the mountains she has such a fascination for. Even as they talk and argue by the lakeside, her ears are glued in the direction of the house. Any moment now, she expects her father to come running and tell her what she so desperately wants to hear. But he knows better—or worse. He knows there will be no Shimla for Mannat. A sickening feeling begins to grip his heart. He looks at the lake, searching for his mother's face in the ripples, but she is nowhere to be seen.

He turns back to Mannat, but her face is moving further and further away, getting fainter and hazier. The smoke and the soot of the train station envelopes him now. He looks at all of them through the bars of the window. They have come to see him and his father off—Amrik Chayaji, Harpal Chayaji, Sukhmani Chayiji, Harjeet, and Mannat. Harpal Chayaji had stiffly embraced his father and wished him luck, their relation marred forever now. But he had not let his behaviour towards Arpit reflect any of the bitterness he felt towards his father. He had hugged him and run his hands through his hair before telling him to study hard and do them all proud. Chayiji, blinking a little more than usual, had hurriedly handed him a packet wrapped in newspaper—aloo-puri, his meal for the long journey—at which Baldev had shot a glance of distaste. Harjeet had handed him a comic book that he bought with his pocket money for him, a farewell gift. And Mannat . . . she stood holding her Baoji's hand, her face serene and trusting. When he looks at her standing right outside his window at the crowded Kalka station, he knows she holds no rancour towards him or his father for thwarting her chances. But there is a wistfulness in her eyes that is unfamiliar to him. What he does not know is that this wistfulness will never really leave her in the years to come.

The train now starts chugging out of the station. There are hurried goodbyes and frantic handwaves. He feels a sudden rush of panic. He wants to jump out of the train, but his father sits right next to him, grim and forbidding, muttering under his breath, "Four hours or less by taxi, but this boy had to insist on going by train. So we waste five hours coming to Kalka, and another six winding slowly up the hill on this baby locomotive." Stop! He wants his father to stop being angry like this. Frantically, he now turns back towards the window, but the station has flashed past already and the ones he loves are now gone.

As the train winds through the mountains, Arpit cannot help but get thrilled with the journey. His mother had often described this train route from Kalka to Shimla, having spent many a childhood holidays in Shimla. What he remembers most now is how she described herself shivering in delight as they crossed one dark length of a tunnel after another along the route. He looks forward now to those dank, damp intervals where he can disappear temporarily from his father's unsettling scrutiny. His excitement, however, is diluted with the sour aftertaste of disappointment and betrayal. Had his father willed, Mannat would've been with him on this journey. He opens the tiffin Sukhmani Chayiji had packed for him. The smell of puris and pickle drifts into the train compartment, filling him with nostalgia once again. Morosely he starts eating, knowing better than to offer the food to his father.

Suddenly, the train starts losing speed. When it grinds to a halt next to a nondescript-looking settlement of a few cottages, his father clucks in impatience and says, "Stay here. I am going to check what's wrong. In this country they can't even run a train properly!" He gets up from his seat and begins to walk down the aisle, but comes back. "On second thoughts," he says a little awkwardly, "perhaps it will do you good to stretch your legs. Come along then."

Much as he would love to step off the train and explore the picturesque little station, he is afraid of watching his father interrogate the train's staff in that condescending manner of his. So he shakes his head and mumbles, "I am okay here." His father shrugs and walks off.

He glances around now at the other passengers, half-fearful of their sympathetic glances, but no one is interested. There is a honeymooning couple who are too engrossed in each other to notice him, and a family of three riotous children and their harried parents, who seem even more embarrassed than him.

He knows that his father would've gone straight up to the driver and demanded an explanation as to why they had stopped like this. Their coach is the farthest from the engine, so his father would take a bit of time to go and come back. For the time being therefore, he can relax. He decides to step out and walk around a bit. Fresh, sharp mountain air greets him the minute he steps off the train. Primal exultation rushes in. The village lad in him grins and stretches himself. He knows he cannot go back to the train now. Its confinement is something he just cannot bear for another instant. Casting a quick glance towards the engine to see if his father is coming back, he scuttles off in the opposite direction . . . away from the train, away from his father's law, away from everything. He is free!

Taking the first trail he can find, he starts clambering down the hillside into a small clearing with scattered signs of habitation—a peasant's hut, a ramshackle cottage, and even a camper's tent—but there are no people to be seen. Good. He will be spared unnecessary questions.

Leaving the clearing behind, he walks on, the vegetation growing thicker around him. A strange heavy silence descends upon the place. Even the merry chirping of the birds that had brought a smile to his face a while back has now stopped. There is no sound, save his footfall on the forest floor. The sunlight that is streaming in through gaps in the forest also looks eerie and weighed down. He wants to leave this place behind now. He turns around to start retracing his steps back to the train, but the forest has closed in around him and the trail has disappeared into dense undergrowth. Just as his spirit starts wavering and the slightest hint of panic starts setting in, he becomes aware of a gurgling sound coming from somewhere to his right. He stands perfectly still and listens. Gradually, he is able to separate the sound from the whisper of the pines towering all around him. It's the giggle and tumble of a brook.

Turning, he carefully pushes away the pine needles brushing his face and walks towards the sound. When he reaches the brook a few minutes later, he is thankful for the water, for he is thirsty and he has left his water bottle and his lunch behind in the train.

Just as he bends down to scoop some water into his palm, he becomes aware of a man sitting a few metres away from him.

He stiffens. His panic-stricken twelve-year-old brain has already conjured up images of a ghost, a kidnapper, a murderer, and even a terrorist on the run. The man could be anybody! All the adventure comics he has ever read, dance through his head threateningly. He wants to run, but it appears that his body has suddenly become paralysed. Has the man cast a spell on him?! He shudders.

The man now raises his head and looks at him. His eyes are deep and black, and the intensity of his gaze is more than a little unnerving. He smiles now, his eyes crinkling. "Lost, little boy?" he asks, his voice tinged with a quaint accent.

Fear gives way to indignation. "I am going to join the seventh standard," Arpit answers, his voice bristling with adolescent dignity.

The man laughs, revealing a set of fine, even teeth. He relaxes slightly now. According to him, a monster's first characteristic is a mouth full of rotting, slimy teeth. This man clearly does not fit the prototype.

"That's not very old compared to the age of the Universe. I am quite a young man myself."

Now that's being unnecessarily mysterious and cryptic, he thinks. Surely this stranger is older than his father! In fact, peering at him closely, he can see that the man is only a little younger than Veerji.

And suddenly, Veerji, Meharsar, Beeji, Mannat, everybody assault him in a great wave of remembrance, and all he wants is to go back home to be with them.

Almost as if he could read his thoughts, the old man speaks up again, "You won't get any closer to home by running away, boy."

"Huh??"

"This brook did not cut a path for itself through the rocks and the bushes . . . it flowed along whatever terrain came its way. It did not play truant and meander away on another course, nor did it collect itself into a shallow pool somewhere because it was too lazy to keep moving . . . You are resisting too much, little boy."

"I don't understand," he complains a bit sulkily. "I came here to drink water, that's all. Now I must go."

"You won't reach your village like this . . ." comes the grave reply. "Your path has already been carved, and it's best that you follow it. Listen to the ground . . . it will tell you where to go next. You can't decide where it will lead you to . . . You can roar into the arms of a mighty river or trickle into insignificance, but you cannot decide where it will take you. All that you can decide is to choose what can flow along with you, and till where. That's all . . ."

He is silent for a full minute before asking, piecing together his words carefully, "But what if I lose something along the way? Can I not turn back for it?"

The man shakes his head sympathetically. "It's not possible for a brook or a river to wind back on its course. But whatever it is that you lose will get unstuck one day and then it will find its way downstream to you. That is, if you do not clog the way with sediment. Oh, the waters are wise, Arpit. They know exactly what to do with themselves—the lakes stay still and wait, the rivers run purposefully, and the streams and the brooks gurgle and sing and savour the beauty around them."

"How do you know . . ." he gasps, but the forest begins closing in upon the mysterious man. Green leaf and green twilight . . . the man is fading away. But before he vanishes completely, Arpit manages to yell out one last question, "Which water are you, then?"

He does not know whether he actually hears a distant voice answer his question or whether he just imagines it, but words fall softly through the approaching twilight, "Ever heard of underground rivers, Arpit?"

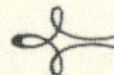

Although it was still dark outside, his phone revealed that it was well past five a.m. already. Arpit sat up in his bed, trying to collect his thoughts, but his brain just refused to work. He would go to the lake and try to figure things out, he decided.

Getting up quietly, he pulled on his light jacket and slipped out of the house. The fields lay silent and peaceful in the yawning dawn, as if they had nothing to fear now. He breathed in the fresh air and hurried his pace. When he reached the lake, he immediately bent and stared hard into its waters. A few moments later however, he gave up and stared into the horizon, a trifle disappointed. What had he been expecting? The answer to his questions blazoned in bold Gurumukhi right across the water? Or was it his mother's image that he was looking for?

A face suddenly flitted over the water. Arpit froze. It wasn't . . . it wasn't *her*. It couldn't be her! He turned around wildly only to find Nishi smiling at him.

"I am sure I am not either one of the two people you are looking for," she said, reading his mind. "But I hope you are glad to see me."

"Oh, I am!" he gasped, his gladness shimmering in the morning rays. "But how come you are here at this hour?"

"Drove down with a friend. Your friend actually . . . Can you guess who she is?" Nishi replied, a playful smile breaking across her tired face.

"Ahhhh shucks, I can! The peace of the countryside is all set to be shattered by Binita Baruah's unfailing flow of opinions."

"You forgot who was the one who saved it in the first place," retorted an unmistakable voice whose owner suddenly appeared from behind Nishi. Binita certainly did not seem fatigued after her night journey.

"Veerji saved the countryside, not you."

"Speaking of Veerji, why aren't you where you claimed to be before all the news channels—by his side, you chosen favourite of his?"

Arpit's voice dropped in defeat. "He is still quite weak, so there is a doctor sleeping on the bed next to him. Distractions and visitors are strictly restricted. And according to Harpal Chayaji, I am a mere visitor, even if Veerji believes otherwise."

"Hmm . . ." Binita mulled. "Tell me this, why do you address Harpalji, as Chayaji?"

"Because he has been like a part of my own family, just like Veerji has been like a grandfather to me as well."

"Hey! That reminds me . . . if you are so close to the family then you would surely know about Veerji's—" The morning was still not bright enough for Binita to notice the apprehension on Nishi's face, nor her relief a second later when Binita's buzzing phone abruptly ended the conversation.

While Binita walked away to take the call, Arpit turned towards Nishi and said gravely, "There is a lot I have to tell you."

"I have a lot to tell you, too, Arpit. But it's morning already and I've had a long night. Why don't you take me to the house where you are staying? I will freshen up and eat something and then we can find somewhere quiet to talk, all right?

Arpit nodded his head and they waited for Binita to finish her call before they all started walking back towards his house.

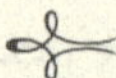

The rest of the day was spent in a flurry of activities that left Nishi and Arpit with no time to sit down and talk. It was much later in the evening, after everyone had had an early dinner and retired for the day, that they found themselves alone and free enough to talk. Throughout the day, Nishi had tried hard to align her mental energies with the holy vibes that surrounded Meharsar, but she was too restless to do it effectively. Her mind was abuzz with questions she just couldn't settle with definite answers: Should she tell Arpit about Mannat's impending arrival, raising what might be nothing but false hopes? Binita could be right, now that Veerji had broken his fast, Mannat might not come after all. And even if she came, would the purpose for which they had gone through redreaming be answered? Would she have forgiven Arpit? Could there be any possibility of . . .

As much as she tried, she had been unable to see into the nebulous pulsating mass that Arpit's future was. It was almost as if the Universe was withholding information from her which it could not trust her with. And she knew where she had transgressed . . . she had let go of her objectivity and become dangerously involved. From a detached spectator, she had become an emotional participant. Would Arpit be penalised for her errors? "Let me not be a treacherous guide . . ." she prayed.

They had reached the summit of their journey. From here, there would either be a sheer drop into fiendish valleys or an irrevocable step into long-sought cloud country.

❦

"Let's walk to the lake," Arpit suggested. Dinner had been a simple, but fulfilling affair. After the running around of the day, they should've been dropping dead, but he could see that Nishi, like him, was not sleepy at all.

"All right, but let me go and get a shawl. There's the slightest touch of cold in the air, and I don't want to fall sick . . ." Nishi replied, before walking back to her room and fetching a thin shawl.

They walked in silence as they made their way across the dark fields to the lake, Arpit's torch cutting a path of light for them. When they reached the lake, they saw it glistening darkly under a pale moon. In the absolute stillness of the place, it was only their heavy breathing that broke the spell that the lake seemed to cast on them.

"Nishi," Arpit said, finally breaking the silence, "we are very close to our goal. I turned the final switch this morning."

"Alone? Again?" So the redreaming was complete. She could not put off telling him the truth any longer. Mannat . . . Mannat might set foot in Meharsar any time now.

"Hmm . . . remember how you had told me long back that redreaming would work best in Meharsar? Well, you were right. Perhaps it is a good thing that I did it on my own. Now my logic-obsessed fool of a brain can't suspect that you hypnotised me into seeing what I saw."

As Arpit began describing in minute detail what he saw, Nishi found her mind straying back again and again to the one question she could not bring herself to ask . . . not just yet. When she forcefully turned her attention back to Arpit, he was saying, "I did not recognise him while I was dreaming, but I remembered him as soon as I woke up. The old man I met by the brook was the same one I had seen in Kasauli while turning the fourth switch. Your father, Nishi! He was your father. And this time, I know it was no subconscious mirage. I was supposed to have met him eighteen years ago."

"No, Arpit!" She was finally speaking, uttering the words as if plucking them off the sacred forces swirling around her. "You were not supposed to have met him eighteen years ago. You were supposed to have met him *now.* Have you still not understood the message my father was trying to give you in your dream?"

"But Nishi, he told me to follow the path already carved for me! And that was exactly what I didn't do. At every step, I took the wrong bend. All that I cared for was left behind, stuck somewhere along the way between rocks."

"No, Arpit, you have missed the most important part of what he said—*Whatever you lose will flow downstream eventually, if you do not block its way.* And you have unclogged the way, Arpit. Your repentance and the redreaming have cleared all the sediment that was blocking your life from taking its natural course. You can see it happening already, can't you? You have been reunited with those you left behind in Meharsar . . ."

But Arpit shook his head dejectedly. "It's not the same anymore. Your father also told me that it is impossible to turn back. And I can understand that now. I have tried to bend the laws of Time, foolishly believing that I could succeed. Redreaming has made me wiser, Nishi, but it has not made me richer. If Mannat were to meet me today, the most I could hope for would be her forgiveness. But nothing can bring back the purity of what could have been, right? I can't bring her back into my life. Not now. Not ever. I can't put off facing reality any longer."

"If the whole world is illusory, Arpit, how is one 'reality' greater than another?"

"What do you mean?"

"Arpit, have you ever wondered about the meaning of my name?"

"Nishimaya? Umm . . . you kept it so that you wouldn't need to add a surname, isn't that it?"

"No, Arpit, that was the purpose of my name, not the *meaning* of it. Tell me, what does Nishimaya mean in Hindi?"

"Hmmm . . . Nishi is night, and Maya is illusion," he ruminated, still perplexed. "So, it means what? Night illusions? Night of illusions?"

"Consider this—the Illusion of Night," Nishi smiled, her eyes crinkling just like those of the man by the mountain brook in Arpit's redream. "Wake up, Arpit. It's time you wake up and realise that you have left all your dark dreams behind. Mannat is coming to Meharsar."

CHAPTER 22

Mannat arrived with the next day's dawn. She had not informed anyone about her arrival. Binita and her NB team, the only ones expecting her, were fast asleep at that hour. Nishi was awake, but seemed to have dived into some underground stream of her own. Arpit did not spend time looking for her. He knew she would be fine. Ever since he had told her about his final redream, she had transformed into a Nishimaya different from the one he had known these past few months. Oddly, though, this change had not rendered her a stranger in his eyes; rather she seemed vaguely familiar, as if some long-lost loved one of his was walking evanescently through her.

His entire being was consumed with a restlessness he had never known before. He oscillated throughout the night between dread and hesitant delight. Nishi and her father were made of other-worldly stuff. They could disbelieve in the reality of loss, but he needed a tangible Mannat for that.

Sleep having eluded him completely, he got up before even the sun had opened one eye, and slipped away to the lake. By its shore, he tried to assume the contemplative posture he had seen Nishi's father in by the side of the brook in his redream. If he stayed long enough like this, perhaps he would get to absorb some of that wisdom and philosophy which he badly needed to face Mannat. He wished she would arrive with selective memory, remembering only what could not make her rebuff him.

But he was no Pandit Devishankar Gaur—he could not concentrate. A gentle breeze blew from the lake, bringing with it an unmistakable scent. The scent percolated his bones, entranced his brain, and made his skin shiver with anticipation.

She was here. He could not doubt it a moment longer. Jumping to his feet, he sped off towards Veerji's house.

When he arrived there, all the lights were on. He stood in the shadows and waited.

⁂

The wooden door of the cottage seemed ready to fall off its hinges under the persistent banging. "Who is it, now?" groaned a sleepy Binita.

"FoDi, open the door ASAP!" Vishwas called urgently from outside.

"Do you want the firecracker first or the bomb?" he demanded the minute Binita opened the door.

"People who save the environment don't use such terminology," chided Binita. "All right, the firecracker first. I need something to wake me up before I can digest another shock."

"The granddaughter is here. She landed here early this morning!" Vishwas announced.

"Wonderful. Not that we need her that badly now, but it's good to know that she was authentic. What is the other news, now?"

"Mehar Baba has reappeared, that too on the very spot where he used to camp sixty-five years ago—"

"What! What the!" Binita exclaimed, interrupting Vishwas. "If that Arpit Singh has dared to plagiarise my idea, I will sue him! But how did he manage to rope in Veerji for this hare-brained scheme?"

"For heaven's sake," cut in Vishwas impatiently, "let me finish first! This man is *not* Veerji. In fact, the family was the first to discover his presence. It's the doctor who called me and gave me all the details and *he* wouldn't exaggerate, right? Apparently, after the initial shock of seeing Manjot appear unexpectedly at their doorsteps had worn off, Manjot's mother insisted that they all go to the gurdwara. Veerji insisted on coming along, though it seems they had to nearly carry him there. Anyway, when they reach the gurdwara, what do you think they see? The fakir, Mehar Baba, sitting on the gurdwara steps, deep in prayer!"

"Impossible! Some practical joker is posing as the fakir for cheap publicity."

"Not according to Veerji. He says that the fakir is real. It seems that when the fakir had appeared in the village for the first time, Veerji had been a kid of about four or five. He claims that he distinctly remembers the man's face, which, apparently, has aged remarkably little."

"Poor Veerji. That's age and failing memory talking."

"Try telling the villagers that. They are all flocking to the spot even as we speak. In fact, the entire district seems to be making a beeline for him. We need to rush if we want a closer look at this fakir!"

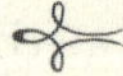

Vishwas had surmised correctly. It was nearly impossible for him and Binita to cut through the crowd and cross the few metres that lay between them and the proclaimed Bhagat Mehar Baba. When they finally saw him, even the sceptical, cynical Binita was overwhelmed by a searing moment of faith.

He sat on the front steps of the village gurdwara, clad in faded saffron, with deep black eyes peeking out from crinkly half-open eyelids. There was an indecipherable expression in those eyes. It could have been as much a glaze coming from pure divine ecstasy, as much as a twinkle of amusement. His face, though slightly wrinkled, shone smoothly with what could only be reasoned as an inner brilliance, and nothing about it gave his age away. He had long grey hair which flowed in loose waves down his shoulders. His sat upright in a cross-legged posture, seemingly oblivious of the silent crowd gathering around him.

Veerji sat to his right, a couple of steps lower, leaning on a young woman for support. That must be Manjot, Binita surmised. To the fakir's left sat Nishimaya, not a step lower but on level with him, her head leaning against his shoulder, lost to the rest of the world. The fakir did not seem to mind this familiarity in the least. And just a step below Nishi, sat Arpit, his hand gently holding Nishi's hand in comfort and strength and his gaze sweeping from Mehar Baba to Manjot.

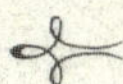

Neither Mehar Baba nor Nishi were to be found the next morning. The villagers were unperturbed. They were convinced this was not the last they had seen of miracles.

When the doubtful NB volunteers asked them how they could be so sure, they just pointed towards the lake, as if it would explain everything. Some could see several rainbows dancing off its surface—one, two, three . . . seven? Were there seven rainbows? But some saw no rainbows at all.

Much later, after the crowds had dispersed, Arpit walked to the lake. Awe still gripped him. An image floated in and out of his consciousness—the image of Bhagat Mehar Baba, who had materialised on the gurdwara steps yesterday. It was not the first time he had seen that face. Clearly, neither had Nishimaya. And he wasn't at all surprised about the disappearance of both.

He might have stayed up all night, calculating births and rebirths and disappearances and reappearances, had there not been another thing to occupy him. He smiled now. Peering into the lake, he saw not a rainbow, but a star with seven rays, rays the shape of lotus petals. A gust of chilly wind swooped down from the mountains. But he did not flinch. Someone placed a tender hand on his shoulder. This time he shivered, but it was not from the cold.

The lotus-rayed star in the lake had metamorphosed into another image. A face. A face redreamed . . .

FiNGERPRINT! DIARIES

Author	Anjali Bhatia
Date of Birth	7th November
Sun sign	Scorpio

The Author

Anjali Bhatia was born in Siliguri, West Bengal, and grew up in Dehradun, Uttarakhand, where she lives with her family. Holding a Doctorate in Psychology, she believes that her academic grounding helps her to visualise her characters better. Her articles and short stories have been published in various literary magazines and newspapers. *Twice Upon A Time* is her first full-fledged novel. She is passionate about nature and individual freedom. Metaphors and symbolism fascinate her, and she would love to continue writing about other-worldly realities. In a perfect world, she would remain a college student all her life.

Favourites:

Movie: *Jo Jeeta Wohi Sikander* and *Inception.*

Author(s): I have to start with my childhood favourite, Enid Blyton, whose books gave me the inspiration to write in the first place. Then, Jane Austen (I have read everything she wrote, including the *Juvenilia* and her unfinished works), Daphne Du Maurier, Vikram Seth, Chitra Banerjee Divakaruni, and Ruskin Bond, who, when I met him at a book signing and told him I'm a struggling writer, quipped, "So am I!"

In Conversation

What was the first book you ever read?
I am pretty sure it was a Chacha Chaudhary comic.

What are you reading right now?
Earth Democracy by Vandana Shiva.

Is there a book which you wish you had written?
The Golden Gate by Vikram Seth. How did he manage to write such an exquisite novel in such fiendishly difficult verse?

You are an avid reader, if you had a book club as well, what would it be reading?
Girlish fan fiction. Seriously!

Have you ever read or seen yourself as character in a book or a movie?
Hehehe, yes. Hermoine from the Harry Potter books.

Book(s):	*Emma, An Equal Music,* and *Sister of My Heart.*
Drink:	Chai-pani . . . no, no, it's not what you are thinking! Tea and water recharge me like no other beverage.
Cuisine:	Italian and Indian street food . . . and erm, what category does ghar ka khana fall into?
Quote:	"Ye shall know the Truth, and the Truth shall make you free . . ." from the Bible. What could be sweeter?

Is there a book that instantly put you to sleep?

How does one give a politically correct answer to this one? Ok, so, at the risk of sounding like a newbie desperately vying for publicity by pulling down an acclaimed work, it's *The Inheritance of Loss*. I tried to read it, but a few chapters into it, and I was still waiting for the story to take off.

But, wait, you didn't specify that it has to be a novel! So I do get to give a politically-correct answer! My Experimental Psychology textbook which I would recommend as a sure-fire remedy for insomnia.

Do you have a dog? Has your dog ever eaten up your manuscript?

No, not anymore. I have grown fond of cats, though. They come home and purr amiably while they are planning to adopt us. Dogs like to be around people; cats like to have people around.

Favourites:

Fictional character: Frank Churchill and Jane Fairfax, for being such idiots in love.

TV shows: *The Mahabharata*. Right, I know what you are thinking. Since when did it become a TV show? Well, it has been made into a few, hasn't it? It beats the *saas-bahu* intrigues hollow!! It is also the most complex drama in the world, with everything from action to romance to morality to politics.

Are the names of the characters in your book important to you?
Absolutely! The story doesn't feel right until I have hit on the most suitable names for my characters and places. I spend more time thinking up names than planning the story.

Do you ever wish that you had an entirely uncreative, mundane job like data entry or working in a factory?
I am a teacher by profession, so I get to do a lot of mundane work alongside the far more rewarding part of working with young people. But yeah, if you asked me to become an accountant or an engineer, I would use Redreaming to permanently delete you from my memory.

Movie adaptations of books: Hmm . . . quite rare isn't it, to find good movie adaptations of books? But to answer the question, for me, there are three movies that are great adaptations—*The Sound of Music, Guide,* and *3 Idiots.*

Cartoon character: Captain Haddock!

Are there any occupational hazards of being a writer?

There must be, but I am not writer-ish enough at this moment. A few books down the line, I am sure there will be fanatics and propagandists sending me hate mail.

What is the most blatant lie you have ever told?

This may sound like my biggest lie, but I don't lie. Period.

What's the oddest place where inspiration has struck you?

It's not a place exactly, but a situation. Sometimes when I am watching a really bad movie or a TV show, I start thinking about how I would have handled the scene differently, how I would have used each character to its full potential and so on. And I have spent the better part of the last few years shuttling between Dehradun and Delhi on the Jan Shatabdi Express, so there was plenty of time to think about all sorts of impossible plots. Or maybe their tomato soup had something to do with it . . .

Who introduced you to books?

Everyone in my family. We had books strewn all over the house. That said, I think it's my brother who deserves the real credit because I used to read whatever he read, as long as I didn't lend out anything from his precious collection of Tintins.

How did you come up with the idea of writing this book?

As a child, a time machine was one of the things I wanted most ardently. Then I grew up (much against my will) and found even more and more reasons to want one. I started wondering how things might have been had I taken a different decision at such-and-such juncture of my life. And that was how the idea of this novel was born.

Your favourite part of the book?

When Nishimaya recognises the old man in Kasauli in Arpit's dream. Oh wait, and all the parts where Binita is outlining her audacious plans.

What was the most challenging part in this book for you as a writer?

Explaining the metaphysical concepts without making them sound like mumbo-jumbo mysticism.

And the mundane details of your routine while writing this book?

I used to think that writing was all about pouring one's heart out, pounding away at the keyboard when the inspiration hit you, but when writing this book, I realised the importance of being methodical. I set myself a deadline and managed to finish the text in just a little over that time period. I planned out chapters, timelines, and character sketches. If this sounds clinical, let me assure you that it wasn't. I enjoyed it more this way. It ensures that the novel is complex, without crowding it with too many ideas. My early works (not fit to be read) were scribbled on notebooks with a cloggy ballpoint pen. The fact that I deleted and then rewrote more than half of what I had managed to put on paper, didn't help either. So MS Word was a blessing for me. Getting disciplined was a tough call, but one of my dear friends pushed me into setting a daily goal. After that, I chugged out a thousand words a day on my old desktop which, mind you, used to hang every time I was at an interesting point in a story.

Who is your favourite character in the book? Is he/she based on someone real? Someone you know, perhaps?

Arpit, unheroic as he is, is my favourite. And yes, a lot of his personality is based on people I have observed in real life.

Any favourite lines from the book?

"Memories are dreams of what once was, and dreams are but memories of what is to be."

What is next up your sleeve?

A love story against a dystopian backdrop. Actually, I have already thought out the titles of my next few novels. Whether I will ever get around to actually writing them is another thing altogether . . .

What advice would you give to your younger self?

Be silly and foolish more often.

Which famous person, living or dead would you like to meet and why?
Jinnah, so that I could tell him, "No point dividing the country, dude. You won't be around long enough to rule over the one you created."

What are books for?
To compensate for all the weird people you will meet in life.

What would the last line of your autobiography be?
"See you all soon . . ."

One thing you would want to say to the Prime Minister of India?
"Speak up, for heaven's sake!"

If you were shipwrecked on a deserted island, what are the three things you would want to keep with you?
My doll collection (yes, I am childish enough for it!), plenty of food (being a vegetarian, I am not taken by the idea of eating raw fish caught with my bare hands), and of course, BOOKS!

ACKNOWLEDGEMENTS

The universe allowed me to pluck one of its tales, and then, these people helped me fashion it into a novel:

My publishers, Fingerprint!, who showed faith in a debut novelist. Arcopol, Shikha, and Gayatri, who took me through the baby steps of editing, designing, promoting, and everything else!

My teachers at Cambrian Hall and MKP, for letting me believe that I had a gift for writing, and for sticking up for me when I chose Literature and History over Science.

Rupali, who told me I wouldn't get anywhere by just sighing and wishing, for pushing me to set a daily writing schedule, and for telling me my work was good when I had given up all hope of it ever being so.

Nupur, who did the same without the kid gloves, but with every bit as much concern.

Riya, aka Shreya, who counted me amongst her favourite writers even before I got published.

Alok Sir, for living a life of inspiration instead of aspiration.

Shalini, for showing me how to value a dream for the dream itself; Reshma, for dreaming with me, and Prachi, for making a dream come true.

Nitu, Meghna, and Vidushi, for giving me the thinking reader's perspective.

Bharti Ma'am, Namrata, Simran, Aarti, Padmini, Mansi, Ela, and Sunayna, for not letting my excitement flag.

My long list of didis and kiddos—Anjali didi, Anju didi, Bindi didi, Madhu didi, Meena didi, Neelam didi, Sangeeta didi, Vimla didi, Aabha, Ananya, Meghna, Lubi, Poonam, Shanti, Tani, Titli, and Tina—whose generous praise for my silly little stories stirred me to seek a bigger goal.

My family, for teaching me that what most call 'idealism' is really the truth.

And above all, well beyond my ability to thank them, are my Gurus who are the real writers of everything . . .